Everything Is Nice

Jane Bowles: Collected Stories, Sketches and Plays

Everything Is Nice

Collected Stories, Sketches and Plays

Jane Bowles

With a Biographical Note and Introduction by

Paul Bowles

Thanks to: Kenneth Lisenbee, who runs the excellent Paul and Jane Bowles website (www.paulbowles.org); Julie de Chazal at the Wylie Agency; and Nikky Twyman for proofreading.

Photo credits
Page 11 Jane Bowles with a parrot © Emilio Sanz de Soto (courtesy Archivo de la Residencia de Estudiantes, Madrid).
Page 14: Jane Bowles with Paul Bowles and Truman Capote © The Estate of Paul Bowles.
Page 196: Jane Bowles in Mexico, 1941, at the time of writing *Two Serious Ladies*; and page 370: Jane Bowles at a party in Tangier, 1949 © The Estate of Paul Bowles.
Page 404: Jane Bowles, Tangier 1956 © Terrence Spencer/Getty Images.

This edition first published in 2012 by
Sort Of Books, PO Box 18678, London NW3 2FL.

Typeset in Goudy and Gill Sans to a design by Henry Iles.
Printed in Italy by Legoprint.

416pp.

A catalogue record for this book is available
from the British Library
ISBN 978-1908745156

Also by Jane Bowles
published by Sort Of Books

Two Serious Ladies
(a novel)

A note on the texts

In her brief writing life, Jane Bowles published just one novel (*Two Serious Ladies*, 1943), a play (*In the Summer House*, 1953), and six stories. The latter, published in various anthologies and magazines, were collected by Jane's husband, the novelist Paul Bowles, with (as he put it) her 'ambivalent' agreement as *Plain Pleasures* in the UK and in the US as her *Collected Works* (1966).

This book includes the stories from *Plain Pleasures* and the full text of *In the Summer House*, and gathers together the fragments of two unfinished novels, *Out in the World* and *Going to Massachusetts*, and other stories from Jane's notebooks, which Paul Bowles published after her death as *Feminine Wiles* (Black Sparrow Press, 1976) and in Virago's *Everything Is Nice: Collected Stories* (1989). Paul Bowles wrote the biographical note and introduction following for these two collections.

Together with her novel *Two Serious Ladies*, this book represents the collected fiction of Jane Bowles.

Contents

Sketches

In the Summer House

Six Letters

About Jane Bowles

Paul Bowles

Jane Sidney Auer was born in New York City on February 22, 1917. Her childhood was spent in Woodmere, Long Island, where she attended public school. Her secondary education was continued at Stoneleigh. A fall from a horse there put an end to this period of her life. The following year she entered a hospital at Leysin, Switzerland, where she remained in traction for two years. During this time she was tutored intensively by a French professor who introduced her to the works of Gide. She began a novel in French (*Le Phaéton Hypocrite*) which she completed in New York in 1935. It was never published, and the typescript has disappeared.

In 1937 she met Paul Bowles and went to Mexico with him, along with the Dutch painter Tonny and his wife. The next year she and Bowles were married. They spent several months in Central America, and continued to Paris, finally taking a house on the Côte d'Azur. At this point Jane had already begun to work on a novel which was finished in

Mexico in 1941 as *Two Serious Ladies*. Knopf accepted the book in 1942, and it was published in the Spring of 1943.

In New York, at the suggestion of Oliver Smith, she began to write a play. The writing of *In the Summer House* occupied her from 1944 until the end of the road tour of the Playwright's Company production at the close of 1953. (Prior to this there had been two trial productions, the first at the Hedgerow Theatre in Philadelphia, and one at Ann Arbor, Michigan, starring Miriam Hopkins.)

She saw Tangier first in 1947, and always preferred it to the other Moroccan cities, in spite of the fact that she wrote very little there beyond the fragments appearing in the present volume. In the *Collected Works*, only 'Everything is Nice' was written in Tangier. 'Camp Cataract' dates from Fez in 1948, and 'A Stick of Green Candy' from the Sahara in 1949.

She began to have difficulty writing in the 'fifties, mainly because she had become hypercritical of her work. In 1957 she suffered a cerebral haemorrhage which destroyed half her field of vision. Reading and writing became almost impossible for her. From then on, her health declined slowly, and she was in and out of hospital over a period of sixteen years. She died on May 4, 1973, in Málaga, Spain.

Biographical note for the book Feminine Wiles, *a collection of Jane Bowles's 'Stories and Sketches' (Black Sparrow Press, 1976).*

Jane Bowles in Tangier, 1949
photo by Emilio Sanz de Soto

Ambivalence was her natural element

Paul Bowles

Ambivalence was her natural element; to be obliged to make a decision filled her with anguish. The possibilities for a sudden *volte-face* had to be kept open. If something were about to be published, she decided it should not be published: the work was not good enough, and it would be 'humiliating' (one of her favourite words) to see it in print. In 1944, a year after the appearance of *Two Serious Ladies*, she was asked for a contribution to a hard-cover anthology being prepared in New York. When she mentioned it to me, she remarked that she was not bothering to reply since she had nothing to submit. I thought then of the long discarded section of the novel. (Originally there had been three serious ladies; then, as the novel took shape, the number was reduced to two, and the entire part dealing with Señorita Córdoba was scrapped.) It seemed to me that there was material here which could be removed from its context and used without a word of rewriting. Jane disagreed. Excerpts cut from anything, particularly from abandoned material, could not be considered finished work. I went ahead nevertheless, excised a passage of 'Señorita Córdoba' which I thought made a complete story, and showed it to Jane. She shrugged, fixed me with a mistrustful stare, and said: "You seem to be very interested in having it published."

"I am. Aren't you?"

"It's just a lot of debris. It has no interest."

"Well, I love it," I said. With that, I carried the typescript myself to the offices of Fischer and gave it to the editor with the title 'A Guatemalan Idyll'. It was published in 1944. The following year the same editor asked for a further piece for a second anthology, and I removed 'A Day in the Open' from the same mass of rejected narrative. Twenty years later, when the time came to publish *Plain Pleasures* as a collection in book form, I was thankful that I had gone against her wishes with regard to these two pieces, because the original manuscript had long since disappeared, and had they not been published there would have remained no trace of them.

This constitutional indecisiveness on Jane's part had been reinforced by the critical reception accorded *Two Serious Ladies* when it first appeared. Save for a handful of 'sophisticated' critics, the American reviews had qualified the novel as inept and chaotic, a meaningless absurdity. The publisher's blurb on the front flap of the dust-jacket began with the unfortunate sentence: "Here is a startlingly unusual novel that will shock you to attention." Responding to this, one critic wrote: "The only shocking thing about this novel is that it ever managed to find its way into print."

While Jane pretended to take all reviews lightly, favourable or otherwise, she was nevertheless very much aware that even though Knopf had made a second printing, the book had not achieved the success she had envisaged for it. It was easy to lay the blame on bad timing: 1943 was a poor year for a literary debut in any country, but she waved away explanations. The novel had been ill-fated, and a failure. From bitter references she made later, in the 'fifties and 'sixties, to these early reviews I realized that she had taken them very seriously indeed, even to the point of being persuaded that they had been justified. When we discussed sections of her novel-in-progress *Out in the World*, she said: "I certainly have no intention of repeating myself, if that's what you mean. *Two Serious Ladies* was no good. Bah! Everybody hated it. This has got to be something completely different."

I think it was this insistence upon arriving at the "completely different" mode of expression which made it impossible for her to develop any idea at length without scrutinizing it, analysing it, and thus killing it. If she read me a few pages of her manuscript and I was enthusiastic, she would smile and say: "I know. You like it because it reminds you of *Two Serious Ladies*. I can't leave it this way." My pleas that she refrain from changing it in any way were brushed aside. "You don't really understand what I'm trying to say, that's the trouble. *I* know how I want it to sound." When the possibility of a British edition of *Two Serious Ladies* was broached, she rejected the idea straightaway: she did not want to be a laughing-stock in London as well as New York. After the customary arguments she agreed to let me send one of the two precious copies we possessed to London.

The book was published, and received perceptive and laudatory notices, but Jane was troubled by a suspicion that all this had been arranged by friends, and more out of sympathy for her because of the state of her health than out of enthusiasm for her work. The following year, when her London publisher suggested a volume of short stories, she informed me triumphantly that she hadn't

Jane Bowles with Truman Capote (left) and Paul Bowles, Tangier, 1949

wanted to tell me before, but all copies of them were lost – they had been in a suitcase that had been left behind several years earlier at a hospital in England. This presented no insurmountable problem: all the material had been published, and I had tear-sheets of everything at hand, including a travel article she had written for *Mademoiselle*. I saw that in ten minutes it could be transformed into a story. As I expected, she refused to consider it. So I did it myself, called it 'Everything Is Nice', and included it with the manuscripts to be sent to London. When I showed her the result, she said angrily: "Do whatever you like."

The publication of her *Collected Works* in New York the same year gave her no apparent satisfaction. When a friend asked her to inscribe his copy, she wrote on the flyleaf: 'The Collected Works of Dead Jane Bowles'.

In all probability she would have objected strenuously to seeing the last nine pieces included in the present volume.* If she were alive and we could discuss it together, I think she would maintain that there was an obvious unfairness in representing a writer by bits and pieces, and I think that for once I should be in agreement. But those of us who have survived her are justified, I believe, in presenting these small scenes as valid examples of her work.

Paul Bowles, Tangier, 1981. Introduction to Jane Bowles's Everything is Nice: The Collected Stories *(Virago, 1981).*

* The nine stories Paul Bowles refers to are: 'Andrew', 'Emmy Moore's Journal', 'Going to Massachusetts', 'The Iron Table', 'Lila and Frank', 'Friday', 'Looking for Lane', 'Señorita Córdoba' and 'Laura and Sally'.

Plain Pleasures

These four stories and a play were collected by Paul Bowles as Plain Pleasures *(Peter Owen, UK, 1966) and in* The Collected Works of Jane Bowles *which appeared the same year in the US. These collections also included 'A Guatemalan Idyll' and 'A Day in the Open', which appear in the following section of this book.*

Plain Pleasures

ALVA PERRY WAS A DIGNIFIED and reserved woman of Scotch and Spanish descent, in her early forties. She was still handsome, although her cheeks were too thin. Her eyes particularly were of an extraordinary clarity and beauty. She lived in her uncle's house, which had been converted into apartments, or tenements, as they were still called in her section of the country. The house stood on the side of a steep, wooded hill overlooking the main highway. A long cement staircase climbed halfway up the hill and stopped some distance below the house. It had originally led to a power station, which had since been destroyed. Mrs Perry had lived alone in her tenement since the death of her husband eleven years ago; however, she found small things to do all day long and she had somehow remained as industrious in her solitude as a woman who lives in the service of her family.

John Drake, an equally reserved person, occupied the tenement below hers. He owned a truck and engaged in free-lance work for lumber companies, as well as in the collection and delivery of milk cans for a dairy.

Mr Drake and Mrs Perry had never exchanged more than the simplest greeting in all the years that they had lived here in the hillside house.

One night Mr Drake, who was standing in the hall, heard Mrs Perry's heavy footsteps, which he had unconsciously learned to recognize. He looked up and saw her coming downstairs. She was dressed in a brown overcoat that had belonged to her dead husband, and she was hugging a paper bag to her bosom. Mr Drake offered to help her with the bag and she faltered, undecided, on the landing.

"They are only potatoes," she said to him, "but thank you very much. I am going to bake them out in the back yard. I have been meaning to for a long time."

Mr Drake took the potatoes and walked with a stiff-jointed gait through the back door and down the hill to a short stretch of level land in back of the house which served as a yard. Here he put the paper bag on the ground. There was a big new incinerator smoking near the back stoop and in the center of the yard Mrs Perry's uncle had built a roofed-in pigpen faced in vivid artificial brick. Mrs Perry followed.

She thanked Mr Drake and began to gather twigs, scuttling rapidly between the edge of the woods and the pigpen, near which she was laying her fire. Mr Drake, without any further conversation, helped her to gather the twigs, so that when the fire was laid, she quite naturally invited him to wait and share the potatoes with her. He accepted and they sat in front of the fire on an overturned box.

Mr Drake kept his face averted from the fire and turned in the direction of the woods, hoping in this way to conceal somewhat his flaming-red cheeks from Mrs Perry. He was a very shy person and though his skin was naturally red all the time it turned to such deep crimson when he was in the presence of a strange woman that the change was distinctly noticeable. Mrs Perry wondered why he kept looking behind him, but she did not feel she knew him well enough to question him. She waited in vain for him to speak and then, realizing that he was not going to, she searched her own mind for something to say.

"Do you like plain ordinary pleasures?" she finally asked him gravely.

Mr Drake felt very much relieved that she had spoken and his color subsided. "You had better first give me a clearer notion of what you mean by ordinary pleasures, and then I'll tell you how I feel about them," he answered soberly, halting after every few words, for he was as conscientious as he was shy.

Mrs Perry hesitated. "Plain pleasures," she began, "like the ones that come without crowds or fancy food." She searched her brain for more examples. "Plain pleasures like this potato bake instead of dancing and whisky and bands ... Like a picnic but not the kind with a thousand extra things that get thrown out in a ditch because they don't get eaten up. I've seen grown people throw cakes away because they were too lazy to wrap them up and take them back home. Have you seen that go on?"

"No, I don't think so," said Mr Drake.

"They waste a lot," she remarked.

"Well, I do like plain pleasures," put in Mr Drake, anxious that she should not lose the thread of the conversation.

"Don't you think that plain pleasures are closer to the heart of God?" she asked him.

He was a little embarrassed at her mentioning anything so solemn and so intimate on such short acquaintance, and he could not bring himself to answer her. Mrs Perry, who was ordinarily shut-mouthed, felt a stream of words swelling in her throat.

"My sister, Dorothy Alvarez," she began without further introduction, "goes to all gala affairs downtown. She has invited me to go and raise the dickens with her, but I won't go. She's the merriest one in her group and separated from her husband. They take her all the places with them. She can eat dinner in a restaurant every night if she wants to. She's crazy about fried fish and all kinds of things. I don't pay much mind to what I eat unless it's a potato bake like this. We each have only one single life which is our real life, starting at the cradle and ending at the grave. I warn Dorothy every time I see her that if she doesn't watch out her life is going to be left aching and starving on the side of the road and she's going to get to her grave without it. The farther a man follows the rainbow, the harder it is for him to get back to the life which he left starving like an old dog. Sometimes when a man gets older he has a revelation and wants awfully bad to get back to the place where he left his life, but he can't get to that place – not often. It's always better to stay alongside of your life. I told Dorothy that life was not a tree with a million different blossoms on it." She reflected upon this for a moment in silence and then continued. "She has a box that she puts pennies and nickels in when she thinks she's running around too much and she uses the money in the box to buy candles with for church. But that's all she'll do for her spirit, which is not enough for a grown woman."

Mr Drake's face was strained because he was trying terribly hard to follow closely what she was saying, but he was so fearful lest she reveal some intimate secret of her sister's and later regret it that his mind was almost completely closed to everything else. He was fully prepared to stop her if she went too far.

The potatoes were done and Mrs Perry offered him two of them.

"Have some potatoes?" she said to him. The wind was colder now than when they had first sat down, and it blew around the pigpen.

"How do you feel about these cold howling nights that we have? Do you mind them?" Mrs Perry asked.

"I surely do," said John Drake.

She looked intently at his face. "He is as red as a cherry," she said to herself.

"I might have preferred to live in a warm climate maybe," Mr Drake was saying very slowly with a dreamy look in his eye, "if I happened to believe in a lot of unnecessary changing around. A lot of going forth and back, I mean." He blushed because he was approaching a subject that was close to his heart.

"Yes, yes, yes," said Mrs Perry. "A lot of switching around is no good."

"When I was a younger man I had a chance to go way down south to Florida," he continued. "I had an offer to join forces with an alligator-farm project, but there was no security in the alligators. It might not have been a successful farm; it was not the risk that I minded so much, because I have always yearned to see palm trees and coconuts and the like. But I also believed that a man has to have a pretty good reason for moving around. I think that is what finally stopped me from going down to Florida and raising alligators. It was not the money, because I was not raised to give money first place. It was just that I felt then the way I do now, that if a man leaves home he must leave for some very good reason – like the boys who went to construct the Panama Canal or for any other decent reason. Otherwise I think he ought to stay in his own home town, so that nobody can say about him, 'What does he think he can do here that we can't?' At least that is what I think people in a strange town would say about a man like myself if I landed there with some doutbful venture as my only excuse for leaving home. My brother don't feel that way. He never stays in one place more than three months." He ate his potato with a woeful look in his eye, shaking his head from side to side.

Mrs Perry's mind was wandering, so that she was very much startled when he suddenly stood up and extended his hand to her.

"I'll leave now," he said, "but in return for the potatoes, will you come and have supper with me at a restaurant tomorrow night?"

She had not received an invitation of this kind in many years, having deliberately withdrawn from life in town, and she did not know how to answer him. "Do you think I should do that?" she asked.

Mr Drake assured her that she should do it and she accepted his invitation. On the following afternoon, Mrs Perry waited for the bus at the foot of the short cement bridge below the house. She needed help and advice from her sister about a lavender dress which no longer fitted her. She herself had never been able to sew well and she knew little about altering women's garments. She intended to wear her dress to the restaurant where she was to meet John Drake, and she was carrying it tucked under her arm.

Dorothy Alvarez lived on a side street in one half of a two-family house. She was seated in her parlor entertaining a man when Mrs Perry rang the bell. The parlor was immaculate but difficult to rest in because of the many bright and complicated patterns of the window curtains and the furniture covers, not the least disquieting of which was an enormous orange and black flowerpot design repeated a dozen times on the linoleum floor covering.

Dorothy pulled the curtain aside and peeked out to see who was ringing her bell. She was a curly-headed little person, with thick, unequal cheeks that were painted bright pink.

She was very much startled when she looked out and saw her sister, as she had not been expecting to see her until the following week.

"Oh!" Dorothy exclaimed.

"Who is it?" her guest asked.

"It's my sister. You better get out of here, because she must have something serious to talk to me about. You better go out the back door. She don't like bumping up against strangers."

The man was vexed, and left without bidding Dorothy goodbye. She ran to the door and let Mrs Perry in.

"Sit down," she said, pulling her into the parlor. "Sit down and tell me what's new." She poured some hard candy from a paper bag into a glass dish.

"I wish you would alter this dress for me or help me do it," said Mrs Perry. "I want it for tonight. I'm meeting Mr Drake, my neighbor, at the restaurant down the street, so I thought I could dress in your house and leave from here. If you did the alteration yourself. I'd pay you for it."

Dorothy's face fell. "Why do you offer to pay me for it when I'm your sister?"

Mrs Perry looked at her in silence. She did not answer, because she did not know why herself. Dorothy tried the dress on her sister and pinned it here and there. "I'm glad you're going out at last," she said. "Don't you want some beads?"

"I'll take some beads if you've got a spare string."

"Well, I hope this is the right guy for you," said Dorothy, with her customary lack of tact. "I would give anything for you to be in love, so you would quit living in that ugly house and come and live on some street nearby. Think how different everything would be for me. You'd be jollier too if you had a husband who was dear to you. Not like the last one ... I suppose I'll never stop dreaming and hoping," she added nervously because she realized, but, as always, a little too late, that her sister hated to discuss such matters. "Don't think," she began weakly, "that I'm so happy here all the time. I'm not so serious and solemn as you, of course ..."

"I don't know what you've been talking about," said Alva Perry, twisting impatiently. "I'm going out to have a dinner."

"I wish you were closer to me," whined Dorothy. "I get blue in this parlor some nights."

"I don't think you get very blue," Mrs Perry remarked briefly.

"Well, as long as you're going out, why don't you pep up?"

"I am pepped up," replied Mrs Perry.

◆ ◆ ◆

Mrs Perry closed the restaurant door behind her and walked the full length of the room, peering into each booth in search of her escort. He had apparently not yet arrived, so she chose an empty booth and seated herself inside on the wooden bench. After fifteen minutes she decided that he was not coming and, repressing the deep hurt that this caused her, she focused her full attention on the menu and succeeded in shutting Mr Drake from her mind. While she was reading the menu, she unhooked her string of beads and tucked them away in her purse. She had called the waitress and was ordering pork when Mr Drake arrived. He greeted her with a timid smile.

"I see that you are ordering your dinner," he said, squeezing into his side of the booth. He looked with admiration at her lavender dress, which exposed her pale chest. He would have preferred that she be bareheaded because he loved women's hair. She had on an ungainly black felt hat which she always wore in every kind of weather. Mr Drake remembered with intense pleasure the potato bake in front of the fire and he was much more excited than he had imagined he would be to see her once again.

Unfortunately she did not seem to have any impulse to communicate with him and his own tongue was silenced in a very short time. They ate the first half of their meal without saying anything at all to each other. Mr Drake had ordered a bottle of sweet wine and after Mrs Perry had finished her second glass she finally spoke. "I think they cheat you in restaurants."

He was pleased she had made any remark at all, even though it was of an ungracious nature.

"Well, it is usually to be among the crowd that we pay large prices for small portions," he said, much to his own surprise, for he had always considered himself a lone wolf, and his behavior had never belied this. He sensed this same quality in Mrs Perry, but he was moved by a strange desire to mingle with her among the flock.

"Well, don't you think what I say is true?" he asked hesitantly. There appeared on his face a curious, dislocated smile and he held his head in an outlandishly erect position which betrayed his state of tension.

Mrs Perry wiped her plate clean with a piece of bread. Since she was not in the habit of drinking more than once every few years, the wine was going very quickly to her head.

"What time does the bus go by the door here?" she asked in a voice that was getting remarkably loud.

"I can find out for you if you really want to know. Is there any reason why you want to know now?"

"I've got to get home some time so I can get up tomorrow morning."

"Well, naturally I will take you home in my truck when you want to go, but I hope you won't go yet." He leaned forward and studied her face anxiously.

"I can get home all right," she answered him glumly, "and it's just as good now as later."

"Well, no, it isn't," he said, deeply touched, because there was no longer any mistaking her distinctly inimical attitude. He felt that he must at any cost keep her with him and enlist her sympathies. The wine was contributing to this sudden aggressiveness, for it was not usually in his nature to make any effort to try to get what he wanted. He now began speaking to her earnestly and quickly.

"I want to share a full evening's entertainment with you, or even a week of entertainment," he said, twisting nervously on his bench. "I know where all the roadside restaurants and dance houses are situated all through the county. I am master of my truck, and no one can stop me from taking a vacation if I want to. It's a long time since I took a vacation – not since I was handed out my yearly summer vacation when I went to school. I never spent any real time in any of these roadside houses, but I know the proprietors, nearly all of them, because I have lived here all of my life. There is one dance hall that is built on a lake. I know the proprietor. If we went there, we could stray off and walk around the water, if that was agreeable to you." His face was a brighter red than ever and he appeared to be temporarily stripped of the reserved and cautious demeanor that had so characterized him the evening before. Some quality in Mrs Perry's nature which he had only dimly perceived at first now sounded like a deep bell within himself because of her anger and he was flung backward into a forgotten and weaker state of being. His yearning for a word of kindness from her increased every minute.

Mrs Perry sat drinking her wine more and more quickly and her resentment mounted with each new glass.

"I know all the proprietors of dance houses in the county also," she said. "My sister Dorothy Alvarez has them up to her house for beer when they take a holiday. I've got no need to meet anybody new or see any new places. I even know this place we are eating in from a long time ago. I had dinner here with my husband a few times." She looked around her. "I remember *him*," she said, pointing a long arm at the proprietor, who had just stepped out of the kitchen.

"How are you after these many years?" she called to him.

Mr Drake was hesitant about what to do. He had not realized that Mrs Perry was getting as drunk as she seemed to be now. Ordinarily he would have felt embarrassed and would have hastened to lead her out of the restaurant, but he thought that she might be more approachable drunk and nothing else mattered to him. "I'll stay with you for as long as you like," he said.

His words spun around in Mrs Perry's mind. "What are you making a bid for, anyway?" she asked him, leaning back heavily against the bench.

"Nothing dishonorable," he said. "On the contrary, something extremely honorable if you will accept." Mr Drake was so distraught that he did not know exactly what he was saying, but Mrs Perry took his words to mean a proposal of marriage, which was unconsciously what he had hoped she would do. Mrs Perry looked at even this exciting offer through the smoke of her resentment.

"I suppose," she said, smiling joylessly, "that you would like a lady to mash your potatoes for you three times a day. But I am not a mashed-potato masher and I never have been. I would prefer," she added, raising her voice, "I would prefer to have *him* mash my potatoes for *me* in a big restaurant kitchen." She nodded in the direction of the proprietor, who had remained standing in front of the kitchen door so that he could watch Mrs Perry. This time he grinned and winked his eye.

Mrs Perry fumbled through the contents of her purse in search of a handkerchief and, coming upon her sister's string of beads, she pulled them out and laid them in her gravy. "I am not a mashed-potato masher," she repeated, and then without warning she clambered out of the booth and lumbered down the aisle. She disappeared up a dark brown staircase at the back of the restaurant. Both Mr Drake and the proprietor assumed that she was going to the ladies' toilet.

Actually Mrs Perry was not specifically in search of the toilet, but rather for any place where she could be alone. She walked down the hall upstairs and jerked open a door on her left, closing it behind her. She stood in total darkness for a minute, and then, feeling a chain brush her forehead, she yanked at it brutally, lighting the room from a naked ceiling bulb, which she almost pulled down together with its fixtures.

She was standing at the foot of a double bed with a high Victorian headboard. She looked around her and, noticing a chair placed underneath a small window, she walked over to it and pushed the window open, securing it with a short stick; then she sat down.

"This is perfection," she said aloud, glaring at the ugly little room. "This is surely a gift from the Lord." She squeezed her hands together until her knuckles were white. "Oh, how I love it here! How I love it! How I love it!"

She flung one arm out over the window sill in a gesture of abandon, but she had not noticed that the rain was teeming down, and it soaked her lavender sleeve in a very short time.

"Mercy me!" she remarked, grinning. "It's raining here. The people at the dinner tables don't get the rain, but I do and I like it!" She smiled benignly at the rain. She sat there half awake and half asleep and then slowly she felt a growing certainty that she could reach her own room from where she was sitting without ever returning to the restaurant. "I have kept the pathway open all my life," she muttered in a thick voice, "so that I could get back."

A few moments later she said, "I am sitting there." An expression of malevolent triumph transformed her face and she made a slight effort to stiffen her back. She remained for a long while in the stronghold of this fantasy, but it gradually faded and in the end dissolved. When she drew her cold shaking arm in out of the rain, the tears were streaming down her cheeks. Without ceasing to cry she crept on to the big double bed and fell asleep, face downward, with her hat on.

Meanwhile the proprietor had come quietly upstairs, hoping that he would bump into her as she came out of the ladies' toilet. He had been flattered by her attention and he judged that in her present drunken state it would be easy to sneak a kiss from her and perhaps even more. When he saw the beam of light shining under his own bedroom door, he stuck his tongue out over his lower lip and smiled. Then he tiptoed down the stairs, plotting on the way what he would tell Mr Drake.

Everyone had left the restaurant, and Mr Drake was walking up and down the aisle when the proprietor reached the bottom of the staircase.

"I am worried about my lady friend," Mr Drake said, hurrying up to him. "I am afraid that she may have passed out in the toilet."

"The truth is," the proprietor answered, "that she has passed out in an empty bedroom upstairs. Don't worry about it. My daughter will take care of her if she wakes up feeling sick. I used to know her husband. You can't do nothing about her now." He put his hands into his pockets and looked solemnly into Mr Drake's eyes.

Mr Drake, not being equal to such a delicate situation, paid his bill and left. Outside he crawled into his freshly painted red truck and sat listening desolately to the rain.

◆ ◆ ◆

The next morning Mrs Perry awakened a little after sunrise. Thanks to her excellent constitution she did not feel very sick, but she lay motionless on the bed looking around her at the walls for a long time. Slowly she remembered that this room she was lying in was above the restaurant, but she did not know how she had gotten there. She remembered the dinner with Mr Drake, but not much of what she had said to him. It did not occur to her to blame him for her present circumstance. She was not hysterical at finding herself in a strange bed because, although she was a very tense and nervous woman, she possessed great depth of emotion and only certain things concerned her personally.

She felt very happy and she thought of her uncle who had passed out at a convention fifteen years ago. He had walked around the town all the morning without knowing where he was. She smiled.

After resting a little while longer, she got out of bed and clothed herself. She went into the hall and found the staircase and she descended with bated breath and a fast-beating heart, because she was so eager to get back down into the restaurant.

It was flooded with sunshine and still smelled of meat and sauce. She walked a little unsteadily down the aisle between the rows of wooden booths and tables. The tables were all bare and scrubbed clean. She looked anxiously from one to the other, hoping to select the booth they had sat in, but she was unable to choose among them. The tables were all identical. In a moment this anonymity served only to heighten her tenderness.

"John Drake," she whispered. "My sweet John Drake."

First published in *Harper's Bazaar* (February 1946).

Everything Is Nice

THE HIGHEST STREET in the blue Moslem town skirted the edge of a cliff. She walked over to the thick protecting wall and looked down. The tide was out, and the flat dirty rocks below were swarming with skinny boys. A Moslem woman came up to the blue wall and stood next to her, grazing her hip with the basket she was carrying. She pretended not to notice her, and kept her eyes fixed on a white dog that had just slipped down the side of a rock and plunged into a crater of sea water. The sound of its bark was earsplitting. Then the woman jabbed the basket firmly into her ribs, and she looked up.

"That one is a porcupine," said the woman, pointing a henna-stained finger into the basket.

This was true. A large dead porcupine lay there, with a pair of new yellow socks folded on top of it.

She looked again at the woman. She was dressed in a haik, and the white cloth covering the lower half of her face was loose, about to fall down.

"I am Zodelia," she announced in a high voice. "And you are Betsoul's friend." The loose cloth slipped below her chin and hung there like a bib. She did not pull it up. "You sit in her house and you sleep in her house and you eat in her house," the woman went on, and she nodded in agreement. "Your name is Jeanie and you live in a hotel with other Nazarenes. How much does the hotel cost you?"

A loaf of bread shaped like a disc flopped on to the ground from inside the folds of the woman's haik, and she did not have to answer her question. With some difficulty the woman picked the loaf up and stuffed it in between the quills of the porcupine and the basket handle. Then she set the basket down on the top of the blue wall and turned to her with bright eyes.

"I am the people in the hotel," she said. "Watch me."

She was pleased because she knew that the woman who called herself Zodelia was about to present her with a little skit. It would be delightful to watch, since all the people of the town spoke and gesticulated as though they had studied at the *Comédie Française*.

"The people in the hotel," Zodelia announced, formally beginning her skit. "I am the people in the hotel."

" 'Good-bye, Jeanie, good-bye. Where are you going?'

"I am going to a Moslem house to visit my Moslem friends, Betsoul and her family. I will sit in a Moslem room and eat Moslem food and sleep on a Moslem bed.'

" 'Jeanie, Jeanie, when will you come back to us in the hotel and sleep in your own room?'

" 'I will come back to you in three days. I will come back and sit in a Nazarene room and eat Nazarene food and sleep on a Nazarene bed. I will spend half the week with Moslem friends and half with Nazarenes.' "

The woman's voice had a triumphant ring as she finished her sentence; then, without announcing the end of the sketch, she walked over to the wall and put one arm around her basket.

Down below, just at the edge of the cliff's shadow, a Moslem woman was seated on a rock, washing her legs in one of the holes filled with sea water. Her haik was piled on her lap and she was huddled over it, examining her feet.

"She is looking at the ocean," said Zodelia.

She was not looking at the ocean; with her head down and the mass of cloth in her lap she could not possibly have seen it; she would have had to straighten up and turn around.

"She is *not* looking at the ocean," she said.

"She is looking at the ocean," Zodelia repeated, as if she had not spoken.

She decided to change the subject. "Why do you have a porcupine with you?" she asked her, although she knew that some of the Moslems, particularly the country people, enjoyed eating them.

"It is a present for my aunt. Do you like it?"

"Yes," she said. "I like porcupines. I like big porcupines and little ones, too."

Zodelia seemed bewildered, and then bored, and she decided she had somehow ruined the conversation by mentioning small porcupines.

"Where is your mother?" Zodelia said at length.

"My mother is in her country in her own house," she said automatically; she had answered the question a hundred times.

"Why don't you write her a letter and tell her to come here? You can take her on a promenade and show her the ocean. After that she can go back to her own country and sit in her house." She picked up her basket and adjusted the strip of cloth over her mouth. "Would you like to go to a wedding?" she asked her.

She said she would love to go to a wedding, and they started off down the crooked blue street, heading into the wind. As they passed a small shop Zodelia stopped. "Stand here," she said. "I want to buy something."

After studying the display for a minute or two Zodelia poked her and pointed to some cakes inside a square box with glass sides. "Nice?" she asked her. "Or not nice?"

The cakes were dusty and coated with a thin, ugly-colored icing. They were called *Galletas Ortiz*.

"They are very nice," she replied, and bought her a dozen of them. Zodelia thanked her briefly and they walked on. Presently they turned off the street into a narrow alley and started downhill. Soon Zodelia stopped at a door on the right, and lifted the heavy brass knocker in the form of a fist.

"The wedding is here?" she said to her.

Zodelia shook her head and looked grave. "There is no wedding here," she said.

A child opened the door and quickly hid behind it, covering her face. She followed Zodelia across the black and white tile floor of the closed patio. The walls were washed in blue, and a cold light shone through the broken panes of glass far above their heads. There was a door on each side of the patio. Outside one of them, barring the threshold, was a row of pointed slippers. Zodelia stepped out of her own shoes and set them down near the others.

She stood behind Zodelia and began to take off her own shoes. It took her a long time because there was a knot in one of her laces. When she was ready, Zodelia took her hand and pulled her along with her into a dimly lit room, where she led her over to a mattress which lay against the wall.

"Sit," she told her, and she obeyed. Then, without further comment she walked off, heading for the far end of the room. Because her eyes had not grown used to the dimness, she had the impression of a figure disappearing down a long corridor. Then she began to see the brass bars of a bed, glowing weakly in the darkness.

Only a few feet away, in the middle of the carpet, sat an old lady in a dress made of green and purple curtain fabric. Through the many rents in the material she could see the printed cotton dress and the tan sweater underneath. Across the room several women sat along another mattress, and further along the mattress three babies were sleeping in a row, each one close against the wall with its head resting on a fancy cushion.

"Is it nice here?" It was Zodelia, who had returned without her haik. Her black crepe European dress hung unbelted down to her ankles, almost grazing her bare feet. The hem was lopsided. "Is it nice here?" she asked again, crouching on her haunches in front of her and pointing at the old woman. "That one is Tetum," she said. The old lady plunged both hands into a bowl of raw chopped meat and began shaping the stuff into little balls.

"Tetum," echoed the ladies on the mattress.

"This Nazarene," said Zodelia, gesturing in her direction, "spends half her time in a Moslem house with Moslem friends and the other half in a Nazarene hotel with other Nazarenes."

"That's nice," said the women opposite. "Half with Moslem friends and half with Nazarenes."

The old lady looked very stern. She noticed that her bony cheeks were tattooed with tiny blue crosses.

"Why?" asked the old lady abruptly in a deep voice. "*Why* does she spend half her time with Moslem friends and half with Nazarenes?" She fixed her eye on Zodelia, never ceasing to shape the meat with her swift fingers. Now she saw that her knuckles were also tattooed with blue crosses.

Zodelia stared back at her stupidly. "I don't know why," she said, shrugging one fat shoulder. It was clear that the picture she had been painting for them had suddenly lost all its charm for her.

"Is she crazy?" the old lady asked.

"No," Zodelia answered listlessly. "She is not crazy." There were shrieks of laughter from the mattress.

The old lady fastened her sharp eyes on the visitor, and she saw that they were heavily outlined in black. "Where is your husband?" she demanded.

"He's traveling in the desert."

"Selling things," Zodelia put in. This was the popular explanation for her husband's trips; she did not try to contradict it.

"Where is your mother?" the old lady asked.

"My mother is in our country in her own house."

"Why don't you go and sit with your mother in her own house?" she scolded. "The hotel costs a lot of money."

"In the city where I was born," she began, "there are many, many automobiles and many, many trucks."

The women on the mattress were smiling pleasantly. "Is that true?" remarked the one in the center in a tone of polite interest.

"I hate trucks," she told the woman with feeling.

The old lady lifted the bowl of meat off her lap and set it down on the carpet. "Trucks are nice," she said severely.

"That's true," the women agreed, after only a moment's hesitation. "Trucks are very nice."

"Do *you* like trucks?" she asked Zodelia, thinking that because of their relatively greater intimacy she might perhaps agree with her.

"Yes," she said. "They are nice. Trucks are very nice." She seemed lost in meditation, but only for an instant. "Everything is nice," she announced, with a look of triumph.

"It's the truth," the women said from their mattress. "Everything is nice."

They all looked happy, but the old lady was still frowning. "Aicha!" she yelled, twisting her neck so that her voice could be heard in the patio. "Bring the tea!"

Several little girls came into the room carrying the tea things and a low round table.

"Pass the cakes to the Nazarene," she told the smallest child, who was carrying a cut-glass dish piled with cakes. She saw that they were the ones she had bought for Zodelia; she did not want any of them. She wanted to go home.

"Eat!" the women called out from their mattress. "Eat the cakes." The child pushed the glass dish forward.

"The dinner at the hotel is ready," she said, standing up.

"Drink tea," said the old woman scornfully. "Later you will sit with the other Nazarenes and eat their food."

"The Nazarenes will be angry if I'm late." She realized that she was lying stupidly, but she could not stop. "They will hit me!" She tried to look wild and frightened.

"Drink tea. They will not hit you," the old woman told her. "Sit down and drink tea."

The child was still offering her the glass dish as she backed away toward the door. Outside she sat down on the black and white tiles to lace her shoes. Only Zodelia followed her into the patio.

"Come back," the others were calling. "Come back into the room."

Then she noticed the porcupine basket standing nearby against the wall. "Is that old lady in the room your aunt? Is she the one you were bringing the porcupine to?" she asked her.

"No. She is not my aunt."

"Where *is* your aunt?"

"My aunt is in her own house."

"When will you take the porcupine to her?" She wanted to keep talking, so that Zodelia would be distracted and forget to fuss about her departure.

"The porcupine sits here," she said firmly. "In my own house."

She decided not to ask her again about the wedding.

When they reached the door Zodelia opened it just enough to let her through. "Good-bye," she said behind her. "I shall see you tomorrow, if Allah wills it."

"When?"

"Four o'clock." It was obvious that she had chosen the first figure that had come into her head. Before closing the door she reached out and pressed two of the dry Spanish cakes into her hand. "Eat them," she said graciously. "Eat them at the hotel with the other Nazarenes."

She started up the steep alley, headed once again for the

walk along the cliff. The houses on either side of her were so close that she could smell the dampness of the walls and feel it on her cheeks like a thicker air.

When she reached the place where she had met Zodelia she went over to the wall and leaned on it. Although the sun had sunk behind the houses, the sky was still luminous and the blue of the wall had deepened. She rubbed her fingers along it: the wash was fresh and a little of the powdery stuff came off. And she remembered how once she had reached out to touch the face of a clown because it had awakened some longing. It had happened at a little circus, but not when she was a child.

'Everything Is Nice' was first published as a piece of non-fiction entitled 'East Side, North Africa' – in which Jane writes of herself as the foreign woman – in *Mademoiselle* (1951). This fictionalised version was revised by Paul Bowles for *Plain Pleasures* (1966).

Camp Cataract

BERYL KNOCKED ON Harriet's cabin door and was given permission to enter. She found her friend seated near the window, an open letter in her hand.

"Good evening, Beryl," said Harriet. "I was just reading a letter from my sister." Her fragile, spinsterish face wore a canny yet slightly hysterical expression.

Beryl, a stocky blond waitress with stubborn eyes, had developed a dogged attachment to Harriet and sat in her cabin whenever she had a moment to spare. She rarely spoke in Harriet's presence, nor was she an attentive listener.

"I'll read you what she says; have a seat." Harriet indicated a straight chair and Beryl dragged it into a dark corner where she sat down. It creaked dangerously under the weight of her husky body.

"Hope I don't bust the chair," said Beryl, and she blushed furiously, digging her hands deep into the pockets of the checked plus-fours she habitually wore when she was not on duty.

" 'Dear Sister,' " Harriet read. " 'You are still at Camp Cataract visiting the falls and enjoying them. I always want you to have a good time. This is your fifth week away. I suppose you go on standing behind the falls with much enjoyment like you told me all the guests did. I think you said only the people who don't stay overnight have to pay to stand behind the waterfall ... you stay ten weeks ... have a nice time, dear. Here everything is exactly the same as when you left. The apartment doesn't change. I have something I want to tell you, but first let me say that if you get nervous, why don't you come home instead of waiting until you are no good for the train trip? Such a thing could happen. I wonder of course how you feel about the apartment once you are by the waterfall. Also, I want to put this to you. Knowing that you have an apartment and a loving family must make Camp Cataract quite a different place than it would be if it were all the home and loving you had. There must be wretches like that up there. If you see them, be sure to give them loving because they are the lost souls of the earth. I fear nomads. I am afraid of them and afraid for them too. I don't know what I would do if any of my dear ones were seized with the wanderlust. We are meant to cherish those who through God's will are given into our hands. First of all come the members of the family, and for this it is better to live as close as possible. Maybe you would say, "Sadie is old-fashioned; she doesn't want people to live on their own." I am not old-fashioned, but I don't want any of us to turn into nomads. You don't grow rich in spirit by widening your circle but by tending your own. When you are gone, I get afraid about you. I think that you might be seized with the wanderlust and that you are not remembering the apartment very much. Particularly this trip ... but then I know this cannot be true and that only my nerves make me think such things.

It's so hot out. This is a record-breaking summer. Remember, the apartment is not just a row of rooms. It is the material proof that our spirits are so wedded that we have but one blessed roof over our heads. There are only three of us in the apartment related by blood, but Bert Hoffer has joined the three through the normal channels of marriage, also sacred. I know that you feel this way too about it and that just nerves makes me think Camp Cataract can change anything. May I remind you also that if this family is a garland, you are the middle flower; for me you are anyway. Maybe Evy's love is now flowing more to Bert Hoffer because he's her husband, which is natural. I wish they didn't think you needed to go to Camp Cataract because of your spells. Haven't I always tended you when you had them? Bert's always taken Evy to the Hoffers and we've stayed together, just the two of us, with the door safely locked so you wouldn't in your excitement run to a neighbor's house at all hours of the morning. Evy liked going to the Hoffers because they always gave her chicken with dumplings or else goose with red cabbage. I hope you haven't got it in your head that just because you are an old maid you have to go somewhere and be by yourself. Remember, I am also an old maid. I must close now, but I am not satisfied with my letter because I have so much more to say. I know you love the apartment and feel the way I feel. You are simply getting a tourist's thrill out of being there in a cabin like all of us do. I count the days until your sweet return. Your loving sister, Sadie.' "

Harriet folded the letter. "Sister Sadie," she said to Beryl, "is a great lover of security."

"She sounds swell," said Beryl, as if Harriet were mentioning her for the first time, which was certainly not the case.

"I have no regard for it whatsoever," Harriet announced in a positive voice. "*None*. In fact, I am a great admirer of the nomad, vagabonds, gypsies, seafaring men. I tip my hat to them; the old prophets roamed the world for that matter too, and most of the visionaries." She folded her hands in her lap with an air of satisfaction. Then, clearing her throat as if for a public address, she continued. "I don't give a tinker's damn about feeling part of a community, I can assure you ... That's not why I stay on at the apartment ... not for a minute, but it's a good reason why she does ... I mean Sadie; she loves a community spirit and she loves us all to be in the apartment because the apartment is in the community. She can get an actual thrill out of knowing that. But of course I can't ... I never could, never in a thousand years."

She tilted her head back and half-closed her eyes. In the true style of a person given to interminable monologues, she was barely conscious of her audience. "Now," she said, "we can come to whether I, on the other hand, get a thrill out of Camp Cataract." She paused for a moment as if to consider this. "Actually, I don't," she pronounced sententiously, "but if you like, I will clarify my statement by calling Camp Cataract my *tree house*. You remember tree houses from your younger days ... You climb into them when you're a child and plan to run away from home once you are safely hidden among the leaves. They're popular with children. Suppose I tell you point blank that I'm an extremely original woman, but also a very shallow one ... in a sense, a *very* shallow one. I am afraid of scandal." Harriet assumed a more erect position. "I despise anything that smacks of a bohemian dash for freedom; I know that this has nothing to do with the more serious things in life ... I'm sure there are hundreds of serious people who kick over their traces and jump into the gutter; but I'm too shallow for anything like that ... I know it and I enjoy knowing it. Sadie on the other hand cooks and cleans all day long and yet takes her life as seriously as she would a religion ... myself and the apartment and the Hoffers. By the Hoffers, I mean my sister Evy and her big pig of a husband Bert." She made a wry face. "I'm the only one with taste in the family but I've never even suggested a lamp for the apartment. I wouldn't lower myself by becoming involved. I do however refuse to make an unseemly dash for freedom. I refuse to be known as `Sadie's wild sister Harriet.' There is something intensively repulsive to me about unmarried women setting out on their own ... also a very shallow attitude. You may wonder how a woman can be shallow and know it at the same time, but then, this is precisely the tragedy of any person, if he allows himself to be griped." She paused for a moment and looked into the darkness with a fierce light in her eyes. "Now let's get back to Camp Cataract," she said with renewed vigor. "The pine groves, the canoes, the sparkling purity of the brook water and cascade ... the cabins ... the marshmallows, the respectable clientele."

"Did you ever think of working in a garage?" Beryl suddenly blurted out, and then she blushed again at the sound of her own voice.

"No," Harriet answered sharply. "Why should I?"

Beryl shifted her position in her chair. "Well," she said, "I think I'd like that kind of work better than waiting on tables. Especially if I could be boss and own my garage. It's hard, though, for a woman."

Harriet stared at her in silence. "Do you think Camp Cataract smacks of the gutter?" she asked a minute later.

"No, sir ..." Beryl shook her head with a woeful air.

"Well then, there you have it. It is, of course, the farthest point from the gutter that one could reach. Any blockhead can see that. My plan is extremely complicated and from my point of view rather brilliant. First I will come here for several years ... I don't know yet exactly how many, but long enough to imitate roots ... I mean to imitate the natural family roots of childhood ... long enough so that I myself will feel: 'Camp Cataract is *habit*, Camp Cataract is life, Camp Cataract is not escape.' Escape is unladylike, habit isn't. As I remove myself gradually from within my family circle and establish myself more and more solidly into Camp Cataract, then from here at some later date I can start making my sallies into the outside world almost unnoticed. None of it will seem to the onlooker like an ugly impetuous escape. I intend to rent the same cabin every year and to stay a little longer each time. Meanwhile I'm learning a great deal about trees and flowers and bushes ... I am interested in nature." She was quiet for a moment. "It's rather lucky too," she added, "that the doctor has approved of my separating from the family for several months out of every year. He's a blockhead and doesn't remotely suspect the extent of my scheme nor how perfectly he fits into it ... in fact, he has even sanctioned my request that no one visit me here at the camp. I'm afraid if Sadie did, and she's the only one who would dream of it, I wouldn't be able to avoid a wrangle and then I might have a fit. The fits are unpleasant; I get much more nervous than I usually am and there's a blank moment or two." Harriet glanced sideways at Beryl to see how she was reacting to this last bit of information, but Beryl's face was impassive.

"So you see my plan," she went on, in a relaxed, offhand manner, "complicated, a bit dotty and completely original ... but then, I *am* original ... not like my sisters ... oddly enough I don't even seem to belong socially to the same class as my sisters do. I am somehow" – she hesitated for a second – "more fashionable."

Harriet glanced out of the window. Night had fallen during the course of her monologue and she could see a light burning in the next cabin. "Do you think I'm a coward?" she asked Beryl.

The waitress was startled out of her torpor. Fortunately her brain registered Harriet's question as well. "No, sir," she answered. "If you were, you wouldn't go out paddling canoes solo, with all the scary shoots you run into up and down these rivers ..."

Harriet twisted her body impatiently. She had a sudden and uncontrollable desire to be alone. "Good-bye," she said rudely. "I'm not coming to supper."

Beryl rose from her chair. "I'll save something for you in case you get hungry after the dining room's closed. I'll be hanging around the lodge like I always am till bedtime." Harriet nodded and the waitress stepped out of the cabin, shutting the door carefully behind her so that it would not make any noise.

◆ ◆ ◆

Harriet's sister Sadie was a dark woman with loose features and sad eyes. She was turning slightly to fat in her middle years, and did not in any way resemble Harriet, who was only a few years her senior. Ever since she had written her last letter to Harriet about Camp Cataract and the nomads Sadie had suffered from a feeling of steadily mounting suspense – the suspense itself a curious mingling of apprehension and thrilling anticipation. Her appetite grew smaller each day and it was becoming increasingly difficult for her to accomplish her domestic tasks.

She was standing in the parlor gazing with blank eyes at her new furniture set – two enormous easy chairs with bulging arms and a sofa in the same style – when she said aloud: "I can talk to her better than I can put it in a letter." Her voice had been automatic and when she heard her own words a rush of unbounded joy flooded her heart. Thus she realized that she was going on a little journey to Camp Cataract. She often made important decisions this way, as if some prearranged plot were being suddenly revealed to her, a plot which had immediately to be concealed from the eyes of others, because for Sadie, if there was any problem implicit in making a decision, it lay, not in the difficulty of choosing, but in the concealment of her choice. To her, secrecy was the real absolution from guilt, so automatically she protected all of her deepest feelings and compulsions from the eyes of Evy, Bert Hoffer and the other members of the family, although she had no interest in understanding or examining these herself.

The floor shook; recognizing Bert Hoffer's footsteps, she made a violent effort to control the flux of her blood so that the power of her emotion would not be reflected in her cheeks. A moment later her brother-in-law walked across the room and settled in one of the easy chairs. He sat frowning at her for quite a little while without uttering a word in greeting, but Sadie had long ago grown accustomed to his unfriendly manner; even in the beginning it had not upset her too much because she was such an obsessive that she was not very concerned with outside details.

"God-damned velours," he said finally. "It's the hottest stuff I ever sat on."

"Next summer we'll get covers," Sadie reassured him, "with a flower pattern if you like. What's your favorite flower?" she asked, just to make conversation and to distract him from looking at her face.

Bert Hoffer stared at her as if she'd quite taken leave of her senses. He was a fat man with a red face and wavy hair. Instead of answering this question, which he considered idiotic, he mopped his brow with his handkerchief.

"I'll fix you a canned pineapple salad for supper," she said to him with glowing eyes. "It will taste better than heavy meat on a night like this."

"If you're going to dish up pineapple salad for supper," Bert Hoffer answered with a dark scowl, "you can telephone some other guy to come and eat it. You'll find me over at Martie's Tavern eating meat and potatoes, if there's any messages to deliver."

"I thought because you were hot," said Sadie.

"I was talking about the velvet, wasn't I? I didn't say anything about the meat."

He was a very trying man indeed, particularly in a small apartment, but Sadie never dwelled upon this fact at all. She was delighted to cook and clean for him and for her sister Evelyn so long as they consented to live under the same roof with her and Harriet.

Just then Evelyn walked briskly into the parlor. Like Sadie she was dark, but here the resemblance ceased, for she had a small and wiry build, with a flat chest, and her hair was as straight as an Indian's. She stared at her husband's shirt sleeves and at Sadie's apron with distaste. She was wearing a crisp summer dress with a very low neckline, an unfortunate selection for one as bony and fierce-looking as she.

"You both look ready for the dump heap, not for the dining room," she said to them. "Why do we bother to have a dining room ... is it just a farce?"

"How was the office today?" Sadie asked her sister.

Evelyn looked at Sadie and narrowed her eyes in closer scrutiny. The muscles in her face tightened. There was a moment of dead silence, and Bert Hoffer, cocking a wary eye in his wife's direction, recognized the dangerous flush on her cheeks. Secretly he was pleased. He loved to look on when Evelyn blew up at Sadie, but he tried to conceal his enjoyment because he did not consider it a very masculine one.

"What's the matter with you?" Evelyn asked finally, drawing closer to Sadie. "There's something wrong besides your dirty apron."

Sadie colored slightly but said nothing.

"You look crazy," Evelyn yelled. "What's the matter with you? You look so crazy I'd be almost afraid to ask you to go to the store for something. Tell me what's happened!" Evelyn was very excitable; nonetheless hers was a strong and sane nature.

"I'm not crazy," Sadie mumbled. "I'll go get the dinner." She pushed slowly past Evelyn and with her heavy step she left the parlor.

The mahogany dining table was much too wide for the small oblong-shaped room, clearing the walls comfortably only at the two ends. When many guests were present some were seated first on one side of the room and were then obliged to draw the table toward themselves, until its edge pressed painfully into their diaphragms, before the remaining guests could slide into their seats on the opposite side.

Sadie served the food, but only Bert Hoffer ate with any appetite. Evelyn jabbed at her meat once or twice, tasted it, and dropped her fork, which fell with a clatter onto her plate.

Had the food been more savory she might not have pursued her attack on Sadie until later, or very likely she would have forgotten it altogether. Unfortunately, however, Sadie, although she insisted on fulfilling the role of housewife, and never allowed the others to acquit themselves of even the smallest domestic task, was a poor cook and a careless cleaner as well. Her lumpy gravies were tasteless, and she had once or twice boiled a good cut of steak out of indifference. She was lavish, too, in spite of being indifferent, and kept her cupboards so loaded with food that a certain quantity spoiled each week and there was often an unpleasant odor about the house. Harriet, in fact, was totally unaware of Sadie's true nature and had fallen into the trap her sister had instinctively prepared for her, because beyond wearing an apron and simulating the airs of other housewives, Sadie did not possess a community spirit at all, as Harriet had stated to Beryl the waitress. Sadie certainly yearned to live in the grown-up world that her parents had established for them when they were children, but in spite of the fact that she had wanted to live in that world with Harriet, and because of Harriet, she did not understand it properly. It remained mysterious to her even though she did all the housekeeping and managed the apartment entirely alone. She couldn't ever admit to herself that she lived in constant fear that Harriet would go away, but she brooded a great deal on outside dangers, and had she tried, she could not have remembered a time when this fear had not been her strongest emotion.

Sometimes an ecstatic and voracious look would come into her eyes, as if she would devour her very existence because she loved it so much. Such passionate moments of appreciation were perhaps her only reward for living a life which she knew in her heart was one of perpetual narrow escape. Although Sadie was neither sly nor tricky, but on the contrary profoundly sincere and ingenuous, she schemed unconsciously to keep the Hoffers in the apartment with them, because she did not want to reveal the true singleness of her interest either to Harriet or to herself. She sensed as well that Harriet would find it more difficult to break away from all three of them (because as a group they suggested a little society, which impressed her sister) than she would to escape from her alone. In spite of her mortal dread that Harriet might strike out on her own, she had never brooded on the possibility of her sister's marrying. Here, too, her instinct was correct: she knew that she was safe and referred often to the "normal channels of marriage," conscious all the while that such an intimate relationship with a man would be as uninteresting to Harriet as it would to herself.

From a financial point of view this communal living worked out more than satisfactorily. Each sister had inherited some real estate which yielded her a small monthly stipend; these stipends, combined with the extra money that the Hoffers contributed out of their salaries, covered their common living expenses. In return for the extra sum the Hoffers gave toward the household expenses, Sadie contributed her work, thus saving them the money they would have spent hiring a servant, had they lived alone. A fourth sister, whose marriage had proved financially more successful than Evy's, contributed generously toward Harriet's support at Camp Cataract, since Harriet's stipend certainly did not yield enough to cover her share of their living expenses at the apartment and pay for a long vacation as well.

Neither Sadie nor Bert Hoffer had looked up when Evy's fork clattered onto her plate. Sadie was truly absorbed in her own thoughts, whereas Bert Hoffer was merely pretending to be, while secretly he rejoiced at the unmistakable signal that his wife was about to blow up.

"When I find out why Sadie looks like that if she isn't going to be crazy, then I'll eat," Evelyn announced flatly, and she folded her arms across her chest.

"I'm not crazy," Sadie said indistinctly, glancing toward Bert Hoffer, not in order to enlist his sympathies, but to avoid her younger sister's sharp scrutiny.

"There's a big danger of your going crazy because of Grandma and Harriet," said Evelyn crossly. "That's why I get so nervous the minute you look a little out of the way, like you do tonight. It's not that you get Harriet's expression ... but then you might be getting a different kind of craziness ... maybe worse. She's all right if she can go away and there's not too much excitement ... it's only in spells anyway. But you – you might get a worse kind. Maybe it would be steadier."

"I'm not going to be crazy," Sadie murmured apologetically.

Evelyn glowered in silence and picked up her fork, but then immediately she let it fall again and turned on her sister with renewed exasperation. "Why don't you ask me why I'm not going to be crazy?" she demanded. "Harriet's my sister and Grandma's my grandma just as much as she is yours, isn't she?"

Sadie's eyes had a faraway look.

"If you were normal," Evelyn pursued, "you'd give me an intelligent argument instead of not paying any attention. Do you agree, Hoffer?"

"Yes, I do," he answered soberly.

Evelyn stiffened her back. "I'm too much like everybody else to be crazy," she announced with pride. "At a picture show, I feel like the norm."

The technical difficulty of disappearing without announcing her plan to Evelyn suddenly occurred to Sadie, who glanced up quite by accident at her sister. She knew, of course, that Harriet was supposed to avoid contact with her family during these vacation months at the doctor's request and even at Harriet's own; but like some herd animal, who though threatened with the stick continues grazing, Sadie pursued her thoughts imperturbably. She did not really believe in Harriet's craziness nor in the necessity of her visits to Camp Cataract, but she was never in conscious opposition to the opinions of her sisters. Her attitude was rather like that of a child who is bored by the tedium of grown-up problems and listens to them with a vacant ear. As usual she was passionately concerned only with successfully dissimulating what she really felt, and had she been forced to admit openly that there existed such a remarkable split between her own opinions and those of her sisters, she would have suffered unbelievable torment. She was able to live among them, listening to their conferences with her dead outside ear (the more affluent sister was also present at these sessions, and her husband as well), and even to contribute a pittance toward Harriet's support at the camp, without questioning the validity either of their decisions or of her own totally divergent attitude. By a self-imposed taboo, awareness of this split was denied her, and she had never reflected upon it.

Harriet had gone to Camp Cataract for the first time a year ago, after a bad attack of nerves combined with a return of her pleurisy. It had been suggested by the doctor himself that she go with his own wife and child instead of traveling with one of her sisters. Harriet had been delighted with the suggestion and Sadie had accepted it without a murmur. It was never her habit to argue, and in fact she had thought nothing of Harriet's leaving at the time. It was only gradually that she had begun writing the letters to Harriet about Camp Cataract, the nomads and the wanderlust – for she had written others similar to her latest one, but never so eloquent or full of conviction. Previous letters had contained a hint or two here and there, but had been for the main part factual reports about her summer life in the apartment. Since writing this last letter she had not been able to forget her own wonderful and solemn words (for she was rarely eloquent), and even now at the dinner table they rose continually in her throat so that she was thrilled over and over again and could not bother her head about announcing her departure to Evelyn. "It will be easier to write a note," she said to herself. "I'll pack my valise and walk out tomorrow afternoon, while they're at business. They can get their own dinners for a few days. Maybe I'll leave a great big meat loaf." Her eyes were shining like stars.

"Take my plate and put it in the warmer, Hoffer," Evelyn was saying. "I won't eat another mouthful until Sadie tells us what we can expect. If she feels she's going off, she can at least warn us about it. I deserve to know how she feels ... I tell every single thing I feel to her and Harriet ... I don't sneak around the house like a thief. In the first place I don't have any time for sneaking, I'm at the office all day! Is this the latest vogue, this sneaking around and hiding everything you can from your sister? Is it?" She stared at Bert Hoffer, widening her eyes in fake astonishment. He shrugged his shoulders.

"I'm no sneak or hypocrite and neither are you, Hoffer, you're no hypocrite. You're just sore at the world, but you don't pretend you love the world, do you?"

Sadie was lightheaded with embarrassment. She had blanched at Evy's allusion to her going, which she mistook naturally for a reference to her intention of leaving for Camp Cataract.

"Only for a few days ..." she mumbled in confusion, "and then I'll be right back here at the table."

Evelyn looked at her in consternation. "What do you mean by announcing calmly how many days it's going to be?" she shouted at her sister. "That's really sacrilegious! Did you ever hear of such a crusty sacrilegious remark in your life before?" She turned to Bert Hoffer, with a horror-stricken expression on her face. "How can I go to the office and look neat and clean and happy when this is what I hear at home ... when my sister sits here and says she'll only go crazy for a few days? How can I go to the office after that? How can I look right?"

"I'm not going to be crazy," Sadie assured her again in a sorrowful tone, because although she felt relieved that Evelyn had not, after all, guessed the truth, hers was not a nature to indulge itself in trivial glee at having put someone off her track.

"You just said you were going to be crazy," Evelyn exclaimed heatedly. "Didn't she, Bert?"

"Yes," he answered, "she did say something like that ..."

The tendons of Evelyn's neck were stretched tight as she darted her eyes from her sister's face to her husband's. "Now, tell me this much," she demanded, "do I go to the office every day looking neat and clean or do I go looking like a bum?"

"You look O.K.," Bert said.

"Then why do my sisters spit in my eye? Why do they hide everything from me if I'm so decent? I'm wide open, I'm frank, there's nothing on my mind besides what I say. Why can't they be like other sisters all over the world? One of them is so crazy that she must live in a cabin for her nerves at my expense, and the other one is planning to go crazy deliberately and behind my back." She commenced to struggle out of her chair, which as usual proved to be a slow and laborious task. Exasperated, she shoved the table vehemently away from her toward the opposite wall. "Why don't we leave the space all on one side when there's no company?" she screamed at both of them, for she was now annoyed with Bert Hoffer as well as with Sadie. Fortunately they were seated at either end of the table and so did not suffer as a result of her violent gesture, but the table jammed into four chairs ranged on the opposite side, pinning three of them backward against the wall and knocking the fourth onto the floor.

"Leave it there," Evelyn shouted dramatically above the racket. "Leave it there till doomsday," and she rushed headlong out of the room.

They listened to her gallop down the hall.

"What about the dessert?" Bert Hoffer asked Sadie with a frown. He was displeased because Evelyn had spoken to him sharply.

"Leftover bread pudding without raisins." She had just gotten up to fetch the pudding when Evelyn summoned them from the parlor.

"Come in here, both of you," she hollered. "I have something to say."

They found Evelyn seated on the couch, her head tilted way back on a cushion, staring fixedly at the ceiling. They settled into easy chairs opposite her.

"I could be normal and light in any other family," she said, "I'm normally a gay light girl ... not a morose one. I like all the material things."

"What do you want to do tonight?" Bert Hoffer interrupted, speaking with authority. "Do you want to be excited or do you want to go to the movies?" He was always bored by these self-appraising monologues which succeeded her explosions.

Evy looked as though she had not heard him, but after a moment or two of sitting with her eyes shut she got up and walked briskly out of the room; her husband followed her.

Neither of them had said good-bye to Sadie, who went over to the window as soon as they'd gone and looked down on the huge unsightly square below her. It was crisscrossed by trolley tracks going in every possible direction. Five pharmacies and seven cigar stores were visible from where she stood. She knew that modern industrial cities were considered ugly, but she liked them. "I'm glad Evy and Bert have gone to a picture show," Sadie remarked to herself after a while. "Evy gets high-strung from being at the office all day."

A little later she turned her back on the window and went to the dining room.

"Looks like the train went through here," she murmured, gazing quietly at the chairs tilted back against the wall and the table's unsightly angle; but the tumult in her breast had not subsided, even though she knew she was leaving for Camp Cataract. Beyond the first rush of joy she had experienced when her plan had revealed itself to her earlier, in the parlor, the feeling of suspense remained identical, a curious admixture of anxiety and anticipation, difficult to bear. Concerning the mechanics of the trip itself she was neither nervous nor foolishly excited. "I'll call up tomorrow," she said to herself, "and find out when the buses go, or maybe I'll take the train. In the morning I'll buy three different meats for the loaf, if I don't forget. It won't go rotten for a few days, and even if it does they can eat at Martie's or else Evy will make bologna and eggs ... she knows how, and so does Bert." She was not really concentrating on these latter projects any more than she usually did on domestic details.

The lamp over the table was suspended on a heavy iron chain. She reached for the beaded string to extinguish the light. When she released it the massive lamp swung from side to side in the darkness.

"Would you like it so much by the waterfall if you didn't know the apartment was here?" she whispered into the dark, and she was thrilled again by the beauty of her own words. "How much more I'll be able to say when I'm sitting right next to her," she murmured almost with reverence. "... And then we'll come back here," she added simply, not in the least startled to discover that the idea of returning with Harriet had been at the root of her plan all along.

Without bothering to clear the plates from the table, she went into the kitchen and extinguished the light there. She was suddenly overcome with fatigue.

◆ ◆ ◆

When Sadie arrived at Camp Cataract it was raining hard.

"This shingled building is the main lodge," the hack driver said to her. "The ceiling in there is three times higher than average, if you like that style. Go up on the porch and just walk in. You'll get a kick out of it."

Sadie reached into her pocketbook for some money.

"My wife and I come here to drink beer when we're in the mood," he continued, getting out his change. "If there's nobody much inside, don't get panicky; the whole camp goes to the movies on Thursday nights. The wagon takes them and brings them back. They'll be along soon."

After thanking him she got out of the cab and climbed the wooden steps onto the porch. Without hesitating she opened the door. The driver had not exaggerated; the room was indeed so enormous that it suggested a gymnasium. Wicker chairs and settees were scattered from one end of the floor to the other and numberless sawed-off tree stumps had been set down to serve as little tables.

Sadie glanced around her and then headed automatically for a giant fireplace, difficult to reach because of the accumulation of chairs and settees that surrounded it. She threaded her way between these and stepped across the hearth into the cold vault of the chimney, high enough to shelter a person of average stature. The andirons, which reached to her waist, had been wrought in the shape of witches. She fingered their pointed iron hats. "Novelties," she murmured to herself without enthusiasm. "They must have been especially made." Then, peering out of the fireplace, she noticed for the first time that she was not alone. Some fifty feet away a fat woman sat reading by the light of an electric bulb.

"She doesn't even know I'm in the fireplace," she said to herself. "Because the rain's so loud, she probably didn't hear me come in." She waited patiently for a while and then, suspecting that the woman might remain oblivious to her presence indefinitely, she called over to her. "Do you have anything to do with managing Camp Cataract?" she asked, speaking loudly so that she could be heard above the rain.

The woman ceased reading and switched her big light off at once, since the strong glare prevented her seeing beyond the radius of the bulb.

"No, I don't," she answered in a booming voice. "Why?"

Sadie, finding no answer to this question, remained silent.

"Do you think I look like a manager?" the woman pursued, and since Sadie had obviously no intention of answering, she continued the conversation by herself.

"I suppose you might think I was manager here, because I'm stout, and stout people have that look; also I'm about the right age for it. But I'm not the manager ... I don't manage anything, anywhere. I have a domineering cranium all right, but I'm more the French type. I'd rather enjoy myself than give orders."

"French ..." Sadie repeated hesitantly.

"Not French," the woman corrected her. "French type, with a little of the actual blood." Her voice was cold and severe.

For a while neither of them spoke, and Sadie hoped the conversation had drawn to a definite close.

"Individuality is my god," the woman announced abruptly, much to Sadie's disappointment. "That's partly why I didn't go to the picture show tonight. I don't like doing what the groups do, and I've seen the film." She dragged her chair forward so as to be heard more clearly. "The steadies here – we call the ones who stay more than a fortnight steadies – are all crazy to get into birds-of-a-feather-flock-together arrangements. If you look around, you can see for yourself how clubby the furniture is fixed. Well, they can go in for it, if they want, but I won't. I keep my chair out in the open here, and when I feel like it I take myself over to one circle or another ... there's about ten or twelve circles. Don't you object to the confinement of a group?"

"We haven't got a group back home," Sadie answered briefly.

"I don't go in for group worship either," the woman continued, "any more than I do for the heavy social mixing. I don't even go in for individual worship, for that matter. Most likely I was born to such a vigorous happy nature I don't feel the need to worry about what's up there over my head. I get the full flavor out of all my days whether anyone's up there or not. The groups don't allow for that kind of zip ... never. You know what rotten apples in a barrel can do to the healthy ones."

Sadie, who had never before met an agnostic, was profoundly shocked by the woman's blasphemous attitude. "I'll bet she slept with a lot of men she wasn't married to when she was younger," she said to herself.

"Most of the humanity you bump into is unhealthy and nervous," the woman concluded, looking at Sadie with a cold eye, and then without further remarks she struggled out of her chair and began to walk toward a side door at the other end of the room. Just as she approached it the door was flung open from the other side by Beryl, whom the woman immediately warned of the new arrival. Beryl, without ceasing to spoon some beans out of a can she was holding, walked over to Sadie and offered to be of some assistance. "I can show you rooms," she suggested. "Unless you'd rather wait till the manager comes back from the movies."

When she realized, however, after a short conversation with Sadie, that she was speaking to Harriet's sister, a malevolent scowl darkened her countenance, and she spooned her beans more slowly.

"Harriet didn't tell me you were coming," she said at length; her tone was unmistakably disagreeable.

Sadie's heart commenced to beat very fast as she in turn realized that this woman in plus-fours was the waitress, Beryl, of whom Harriet had often spoken in her letters and at home.

"It's a surprise," Sadie told her. "I meant to come here before. I've been promising Harriet I'd visit her in camp for a long time now, but I couldn't come until I got a neighbor in to cook for Evy and Bert. They're a husband and wife ... my sister Evy and her husband Bert."

"I know about those two," Beryl remarked sullenly. "Harriet's told me all about them."

"Will you please take me to my sister's cabin?" Sadie asked, picking up her valise and stepping forward.

Beryl continued to stir her beans around without moving.

"I thought you folks had some kind of arrangement," she said. She had recorded in her mind entire passages of Harriet's monologues out of love for her friend, although she felt no curiosity concerning the material she had gathered. "I thought you folks were supposed to stay in the apartment while she was away at camp."

"Bert Hoffer and Evy have never visited Camp Cataract," Sadie answered in a tone that was innocent of any subterfuge.

"You bet they haven't," Beryl pronounced triumphantly. "That's part of the arrangement. They're supposed to stay in the apartment while she's here at camp; the doctor said so."

"They're not coming up," Sadie repeated, and she still wore, not the foxy look that Beryl expected would betray itself at any moment, but the look of a person who is attentive though being addressed in a foreign language. The waitress sensed that all her attempts at starting a scrap had been successfully blocked for the present and she whistled carefully, dragging some chairs into line with a rough hand. "I'll tell you what," she said, ceasing her activities as suddenly as she had begun them. "Instead of taking you down there to the Pine Cones – that's the name of the grove where her cabin is – I'll go myself and tell her to come up here to the lodge. She's got some nifty rain equipment so she won't get wet coming through the groves like you would ... lots of pine trees out there."

Sadie nodded in silence and walked over to a fantasy chair, where she sat down.

"They get a lot of fun out of that chair. When they're drunk," said Beryl pointing to its back, made of a giant straw disc. "Well ... so long ..." She strode away. "Dear Valley ..." Sadie heard her sing as she went out the door.

Sadie lifted the top off the chair's left arm and pulled two books out of its woven hamper. The larger volume was entitled *The Growth and Development of the Texas Oil Companies*, and the smaller, *Stories from Other Climes*. Hastily she replaced them and closed the lid.

◆ ◆ ◆

Harriet opened the door for Beryl and quickly shut it again, but even in that instant the wooden flooring of the threshold was thoroughly soaked with rain. She was wearing a lavender kimono with a deep ruffle at the neckline; above it her face shone pale with dismay at Beryl's late and unexpected visit. She feared that perhaps the waitress was drunk. "I'm certainly not hacking out a free place for myself in this world just in order to cope with drunks," she said to herself with bitter verve. Her loose hair was hanging to her shoulders and Beryl looked at it for a moment in mute admiration before making her announcement.

"Your sister Sadie's up at the lodge," she said, recovering herself; then, feeling embarrassed, she shuffled over to her usual seat in the darkest corner of the room.

"What are you saying?" Harriet questioned her sharply.

"Your sister Sadie's up at the lodge," she repeated, not daring to look at her. "Your sister Sadie who wrote you the letter about the apartment."

"But she can't be!" Harriet screeched. "She can't be! It was all arranged that no one was to visit me here."

"That's what I told her," Beryl put in.

Harriet began pacing up and down the floor. Her pupils were dilated and she looked as if she were about to lose all control of herself. Abruptly she flopped down on the edge of the bed and began gulping in great drafts of air. She was actually practicing a system which she believed had often saved her from complete hysteria, but Beryl, who knew nothing about her method, was horrified and utterly bewildered. "Take it easy," she implored Harriet. "Take it easy!"

"Dash some water in my face," said Harriet in a strange voice, but horror and astonishment anchored Beryl securely to her chair, so that Harriet was forced to stagger over to the basin and manage by herself. After five minutes of steady dousing she wiped her face and chest with a towel and resumed her pacing. At each instant the expression on her face was more indignant and a trifle less distraught. "It's the boorishness of it that I find so appalling," she complained, a suggestion of theatricality in her tone which a moment before had not been present. "If she's determined to wreck my schemes, why doesn't she do it with some style, a little slight bit of cunning? I can't picture anything more boorish than hauling oneself onto a train and simply chugging straight up here. She has no sense of scheming, of intrigue in the grand manner ... none whatever. Anyone meeting only Sadie would think the family raised potatoes for a living. Evy doesn't make a much better impression, I must say. If they met her they'd decide we were all clerks! But at least she goes to business ... She doesn't sit around thinking about how to mess my life up all day. She thinks about Bert Hoffer. Ugh!" She made a wry face.

"When did you and Sadie start fighting?" Beryl asked her.

"I don't fight with Sadie," Harriet answered, lifting her head proudly. "I wouldn't dream of fighting like a common fishwife. Everything that goes on between us goes on undercover. It's always been that way. I've always hidden everything from her ever since I was a little girl. She's perfectly aware that I know she's trying to hold me a prisoner in the apartment out of plain jealousy and she knows too that I'm afraid of being considered a bum, and that makes matters simpler for her. She pretends to be worried that I might forget myself if I left the apartment and commit a folly with some man I wasn't married to, but actually she knows perfectly well that I'm as cold as ice. I haven't the slightest interest in men ... nor in women either for that matter; still if I stormed out of the apartment dramatically the way some do, they might think I was a bum on my way to a man ... and I won't give Sadie that satisfaction, ever. As for marriage, of course I admit I'm peculiar and there's a bit wrong with me, but even so I shouldn't want to marry: I think the whole system of going through life with a partner is repulsive in every way." She paused, but only for a second. "Don't you imagine, however," she added severely, looking directly at Beryl, "don't you imagine that just because I'm a bit peculiar and different from the others, that I'm not fussy about my life. I am fussy about it, and I *hate* a scandal."

"To hell with sisters!" Beryl exclaimed happily. "Give 'em all a good swift kick in the pants." She had regained her own composure watching the color return to Harriet's cheeks and she was just beginning to think with pleasure that perhaps Sadie's arrival would serve to strengthen the bond of intimacy between herself and Harriet, when this latter buried her head in her lap and burst into tears. Beryl's face fell and she blushed at her own frivolousness.

"I can't any more," Harriet sobbed in anguished tones. "I can't ... I'm old ... I'm much too old." Here she collapsed and sobbed so pitifully that Beryl, wringing her hands in grief, sprang to her side, for she was a most tenderhearted person toward those whom she loved. "You are not old ... you are beautiful," she said, blushing again, and in her heart she was thankful that Providence had granted her the occasion to console her friend in a grief-stricken moment, and to compliment her at the same time.

After a bit, Harriet's sobbing subsided, and jumping up from the bed, she grabbed the waitress. "Beryl," she gasped, "you must run back to the lodge right away." There was a beam of cunning in her tear-filled eyes.

"Sure will," Beryl answered.

"Go back to the lodge and see if there's a room left up there, and if there is, take her grip into it so that there will be no question of her staying in my cabin. I can't have her staying in my cabin. It's the only place I have in the whole wide world." The beam of cunning disappeared again and she looked at Beryl with wide, frightened eyes. "... And if there's no room?" she asked.

"Then I'll put her in my place," Beryl reassured her. "I've got a neat little cabin all to myself that she can have and I'll go bunk in with some dopey waitress."

"Well, then," said Harriet, "go, and hurry! Take her grip to a room in the upper lodge annex or to your own cabin before she has a chance to say anything, and then come straight back here for me. I can't get through these pine groves alone ... now ... I know I can't." It did not occur to her to thank Beryl for the kind offer she had made.

"All right," said the waitress, "I'll be back in a jiffy and don't you worry about a thing." A second later she was lumbering through the drenched pine groves with shining eyes.

◆ ◆ ◆

When Beryl came into the lodge and snatched Sadie's grip up without a word of explanation, Sadie did not protest. Opposite her there was an open staircase which led to a narrow gallery hanging halfway between the ceiling and the floor. She watched the waitress climbing the stairs, but once she had passed the landing Sadie did not trouble to look up and follow her progress around the wooden balcony overhead.

A deep chill had settled into her bones, and she was like a person benumbed. Exactly when this present state had succeeded the earlier one Sadie could not tell, nor did she think to ask herself such a question, but a feeling of dread now lay like a stone in her breast where before there had been stirring such powerful sensations of excitement and suspense. "I'm so low," she said to herself. "I feel like I was sitting at my own funeral." She did not say this in the spirit of hyperbolic gloom which some people nurture to work themselves out of a bad mood, but in all seriousness and with her customary attitude of passivity; in fact, she wore the humble look so often visible on the faces of sufferers who are being treated in a free clinic. It did not occur to her that a connection might exist between her present dismal state and the mission she had come to fulfill at Camp Cataract, nor did she take any notice of the fact that the words which were to enchant Harriet and accomplish her return were no longer welling up in her throat as they had done all the past week. She feared that something dreadful might happen, but whatever it was, this disaster was as remotely connected with her as a possible train wreck. "I hope nothing bad happens ..." she thought, but she didn't have much hope in her.

Harriet slammed the front door and Sadie looked up. For the first second or two she did not recognize the woman who stood on the threshold in her dripping rubber coat and hood. Beryl was beside her; puddles were forming around the feet of the two women. Harriet had rouged her cheeks rather more highly than usual in order to hide all traces of her crying spell. Her eyes were bright and she wore a smile that was fixed and hard.

"Not a night fit for man or beast," she shouted across to Sadie, using a voice that she thought sounded hearty and yet fashionable at the same time; she did this, not in order to impress her sister, but to keep her at a safe distance.

Sadie, instead of rushing to the door, stared at her with an air of perplexity. To her Harriet appeared more robust and coarse-featured than she had five weeks ago at the apartment, and yet she knew that such a rapid change of physiognomy was scarcely possible. Recovering, she rose and went to embrace her sister. The embrace failed to reassure her because of Harriet's wet rubber coat, and her feeling of estrangement became more defined. She backed away.

Upon hearing her own voice ring out in such hearty and fashionable tones, Harriet had felt crazily confident that she might, by continuing to affect this manner, hold her sister at bay for the duration of her visit. To increase her chances of success she had determined right then not to ask Sadie why she had come, but to treat the visit in the most casual and natural way possible.

"Have you put on fat?" Sadie asked, at a loss for anything else to say.

"I'll never be fat," Harriet replied quickly. "I'm a fruit lover, not a lover of starches."

"Yes, you love fruit," Sadie said nervously. "Do you want some? I have an apple left from my lunch."

Harriet looked aghast. "Now!" she exclaimed. "Beryl can tell you that I never eat at night; in fact I *never* come up to the lodge at night, never. I stay in my cabin. I've written you all about how early I get up ... I don't know anything about the lodge at night," she added almost angrily, as though her sister had accused her of being festive.

"You don't?" Sadie looked at her stupidly.

"No, I don't. Are you hungry, by the way?"

"If she's hungry," put in Beryl, "we can go into the Grotto Room and I'll bring her the food there. The tables in the main dining room are all set up for tomorrow morning's breakfast."

"I despise the Grotto," said Harriet with surprising bitterness. Her voice was getting quite an edge to it, and although it still sounded fashionable it was no longer hearty.

"I'm not hungry," Sadie assured them both. "I'm sleepy."

"Well, then," Harriet replied quickly, jumping at the opportunity, "we'll sit here for a few minutes and then you must go to bed."

The three of them settled in wicker chairs close to the cold hearth. Sadie was seated opposite the other two, who both remained in their rubber coats.

"I really do despise the Grotto," Harriet went on. "Actually I don't hang around the lodge at all. This is not the part of Camp Cataract that interests me. I'm interested in the pine groves, my cabin, the rocks, the streams, the bridge, and all the surrounding natural beauty ... the sky also."

Although the rain still continued its drumming on the roof above them, to Sadie, Harriet's voice sounded intolerably loud, and she could not rid herself of the impression that her sister's face had grown fatter. "Now," she heard Harriet saying in her loud voice, "tell me about the apartment ... What's new, how are the dinners coming along, how are Evy and Bert?"

Fortunately, while Sadie was struggling to answer these questions, which unaccountably she found it difficult to do, the stout agnostic reappeared, and Harriet was immediately distracted.

"Rover," she called gaily across the room, "come and sit with us. My sister Sadie's here."

The woman joined them, seating herself beside Beryl, so that Sadie was now facing all three.

"It's a surprise to see you up at the lodge at night, Hermit," she remarked to Harriet without a spark of mischief in her voice.

"You see!" Harriet nodded at Sadie with immense satisfaction. "I was not fibbing, was I? How are Evy and Bert?" she asked again, her face twitching a bit. "Is the apartment hot?"

Sadie nodded.

"I don't know how long you plan to stay," Harriet rattled on, feeling increasingly powerful and therefore reckless, "but I'm going on a canoe trip the day after tomorrow for five days. We're going up the river to Pocahontas Falls ... I leave at four in the morning, too, which rather ruins tomorrow as well. I've been looking forward to this trip ever since last spring when I applied for my seat, back at the apartment. The canoes are limited, and the guides ... I'm devoted to canoe trips, as you know, and can fancy myself a red-skin all the way to the Falls and back, easily."

Sadie did not answer.

"There's nothing weird about it," Harriet argued. "It's in keeping with my hatred of industrialization. In any case, you can see what a chopped-up day tomorrow's going to be. I have to make my pack in the morning and I must be in bed by eight-thirty at night, the latest, so that I can get up at four. I'll have only one real meal, at two in the afternoon. I suggest we meet at two behind the souvenir booth; you'll notice it tomorrow." Harriet waited expectantly for Sadie to answer in agreement to this suggestion, but her sister remained silent.

"Speaking of the booth," said Rover, "I'm not taking home a single souvenir this year. They're expensive and they don't last."

"You can buy salt-water taffy at Gerald's Store in town," Beryl told her. "I saw some there last week. It's a little stale but very cheap."

"Why would they sell salt-water taffy in the mountains?" Rover asked irritably.

Sadie was half listening to the conversation; as she sat watching them, all three women were suddenly unrecognizable; it was as if she had flung open the door to some dentist's office and seen three strangers seated there. She sprang to her feet in terror.

Harriet was horrified. "What is it?" she yelled at her sister. "Why do you look like that? Are you mad?"

Sadie was pale and beads of sweat were forming under her felt hat, but the women opposite her had already regained their correct relation to herself and the present moment. Her face relaxed, and although her legs were trembling as a result of her brief but shocking experience, she felt immensely relieved that it was all over.

"Why did you jump up?" Harriet screeched at her. "Is it because you are at Camp Cataract and not at the apartment?"

"It must have been the long train trip and no food ..." Sadie told herself, "only one sandwich."

"Is it because you are at Camp Cataract and not at the apartment?" Harriet insisted. She was really very frightened and wished to establish Sadie's fit as a purposeful one and not as an involuntary seizure similar to one of hers.

"It was a long and dirty train trip," Sadie said in a weary voice. "I had only one sandwich all day long, with no mustard or butter ... just the processed meat. I didn't even eat my fruit."

"Beryl offered to serve you food in the Grotto!" Harriet ranted. "Do you want some now or not? For heaven's sake, speak up!"

"No ... no." Sadie shook her head sorrowfully. "I think I'd best go to bed. Take me to your cabin ... I've got my slippers and my kimono and my nightgown in my satchel," she added, looking around her vaguely, for the fact that Beryl had carried her grip off had never really impressed itself upon her consciousness.

Harriet glanced at Beryl with an air of complicity and managed to give her a quick pinch. "Beryl's got you fixed up in one of the upper lodge annex rooms," she told Sadie in a false, chatterbox voice. "You'll be much more comfortable up here than you would be down in my cabin. We all use oil lamps in the grove and you know how dependent you are on electricity."

Sadie didn't know whether she was dependent on electricity or not since she had never really lived without it, but she was so tired that she said nothing.

"I get up terribly early and my cabin's drafty, besides," Harriet went on. "You'll be much more comfortable here. You'd hate the Boulder Dam wigwams as well. Anyway, the wigwams are really for boys and they're always full. There's a covered bridge leading from this building to the annex on the upper floor, so that's an advantage."

"O.K., folks," Beryl cut in, judging that she could best help Harriet by spurring them on to action. "Let's get going."

"Yes," Harriet agreed, "if we don't get out of the lodge soon the crowd will come back from the movies and we certainly want to avoid them."

They bade good night to Rover and started up the stairs. "This balustrade is made of young birch limbs," Harriet told Sadie as they walked along the narrow gallery overhead. "I think it's very much in keeping with the lodge, don't you?"

"Yes, I do," Sadie answered.

Beryl opened the door leading from the balcony onto a covered bridge and stepped through it, motioning to the others. "Here we go onto the bridge," she said, looking over her shoulder. "You've never visited the annex, have you?" she asked Harriet.

"I've never had any reason to," Harriet answered in a huffy tone. "You know how I feel about my cabin."

They walked along the imperfectly fitted boards in the darkness. Gusts of wind blew about their ankles and they were constantly spattered with rain in spite of the wooden roofing. They reached the door at the other end very quickly, however, where they descended two steps leading into a short, brightly lit hall. Beryl closed the door to the bridge behind them. The smell of fresh plaster and cement thickened the damp air.

"This is the annex," said Beryl. "We put old ladies here mostly, because they can get back and forth to the dining room without going outdoors ... and they've got the toilet right here, too." She flung open the door and showed it to them. "Then also," she added, "we don't like the old ladies dealing with oil lamps and here they've got electricity." She led them into a little room just at their left and switched on the light. "Pretty smart, isn't it?" she remarked, looking around her with evident satisfaction, as if she herself had designed the room; then, sauntering over to a modernistic wardrobe-bureau combination, she polished a corner of it with her pocket handkerchief. This piece was made of shiny brown wood and fitted with a rimless circular mirror. "Strong and good-looking," Beryl said, rapping on the wood with her knuckles. "Every room's got one."

Sadie sank down on the edge of the bed without removing her outer garments. Here, too, the smell of plaster and cement permeated the air, and the wind still blew about their ankles, this time from under the badly constructed doorsill.

"The cabins are much draftier than this," Harriet assured Sadie once again. "You'll be more comfortable here in the annex." She felt confident that establishing her sister in the annex would facilitate her plan, which was still to prevent her from saying whatever she had come to say.

Sadie was terribly tired. Her hat, dampened by the rain, pressed uncomfortably against her temples, but she did not attempt to remove it. "I think I've got to go to sleep," she muttered. "I can't stay awake any more."

"All right," said Harriet, "but don't forget tomorrow at two by the souvenir booth ... you can't miss it. I don't want to see anyone in the morning because I can make my canoe pack better by myself ... it's frightfully complicated ... But if I hurried I could meet you at one-thirty; would you prefer that?"

Sadie nodded.

"Then I'll do my best ... You see, in the morning I always practice imagination for an hour or two. It does me lots of good, but tomorrow I'll cut it short." She kissed Sadie lightly on the crown of her felt hat. "Good night," she said. "Is there anything I forgot to ask you about the apartment?"

"No," Sadie assured her. "You asked everything."

"Well, good night," said Harriet once again, and followed by Beryl, she left the room.

◆ ◆ ◆

When Sadie awakened the next morning a feeling of dread still rested like a leaden weight on her chest. No sooner had she left the room than panic, like a small wing, started to beat under her heart. She was inordinately fearful that if she strayed any distance from the main lodge she would lose her way and so arrive late for her meeting with Harriet. This fear drove her to stand next to the souvenir booth fully an hour ahead of time. Fortunately the booth, situated on a small knoll, commanded an excellent view of the cataract, which spilled down from some high rock ledges above a deep chasm. A fancy bridge spanned this chasm only a few feet below her, so that she was able to watch the people crossing it as they walked back and forth between the camp site and the waterfall. An Indian chief in full war regalia was seated at the bridge entrance on a kitchen chair. His magnificent feather headdress curved gracefully in the breeze as he busied himself collecting the small toll that all the tourists paid on returning from the waterfall; he supplied them with change from a nickel-plated conductor's belt which he wore over his deer-hide jacket, embroidered with minute beads. He was an Irishman employed by the management, which supplied his costume. Lately he had grown careless, and often neglected to stain his freckled hands the deep brick color of his face. He divided his time between the bridge and the souvenir booth, clambering up the knoll whenever he sighted a customer.

A series of wooden arches, Gothic in conception, succeeded each other all the way across the bridge; bright banners fluttered from their rims, each one stamped with the initials of the camp, and some of them edged with a glossy fringe. Only a few feet away lay the dining terrace, a huge flagstone pavilion whose entire length skirted the chasm's edge.

Unfortunately, neither the holiday crowds, nor the festooned bridge, nor even the white waters of the cataract across the way could distract Sadie from her misery. She constantly glanced behind her at the dark pine groves wherein Harriet's cabin was concealed. She dreaded to see Harriet's shape define itself between the trees, but at the same time she feared that if her sister did not arrive shortly some terrible catastrophe would befall them both before she'd had a chance to speak. In truth all desire to convince her sister that she should leave Camp Cataract and return to the apartment had miraculously shriveled away, and with the desire, the words to express it had vanished too. This did not in any way alter her intention of accomplishing her mission; on the contrary, it seemed to her all the more desperately important now that she was almost certain, in her innermost heart, that her trip was already a failure. Her attitude was not an astonishing one, since like many others she conceived of her life as separate from herself; the road was laid out always a little ahead of her by sacred hands, and she walked down it without a question. This road, which was her life, would go on existing after her death, even as her death existed now while she still lived.

There were close to a hundred people dining on the terrace, and the water's roar so falsified the clamor of voices that one minute the guests seemed to be speaking from a great distance and the next right at her elbow. Every now and then she thought she heard someone pronounce her name in a dismal tone, and however much she told herself that this was merely the waterfall playing its tricks on her ears she shuddered each time at the sound of her name. Her very position next to the booth began to embarrass her. She tucked her hands into her coat sleeves so that they would not show, and tried to keep her eyes fixed on the foaming waters across the way, but she had noticed a disapproving look in the eyes of the diners nearest her, and she could not resist glancing back at the terrace every few minutes in the hope that she had been mistaken. Each time, however, she was more convinced that she had read their expressions correctly, and that these people believed, not only that she was standing there for no good reason, but that she was a genuine vagrant who could not afford the price of a dinner. She was therefore immensely relieved when she caught sight of Harriet advancing between the tables from the far end of the dining pavilion. As she drew nearer, Sadie noticed that she was wearing her black winter coat trimmed with red fur, and that her marceled hair remained neatly arranged in spite of the strong wind. Much to her relief Harriet had omitted to rouge her cheeks and her face therefore had regained its natural proportions. She saw Harriet wave at the sight of her and quicken her step. Sadie was pleased that the diners were to witness the impending meeting. "When they see us together," she thought, "they'll realize that I'm no vagrant, but a decent woman visiting her sister." She herself started down the knoll to hasten the meeting. "I thought you'd come out of the pine grove," she called out, as soon as they were within a few feet of one another. "I kept looking that way."

"I would have ordinarily," Harriet answered, reaching her side and kissing her lightly on the cheek, "but I went to the other end of the terrace first, to reserve a table for us from the waiter in charge there. That end is quieter, so it will be more suitable for a long talk."

"Good," thought Sadie as they climbed up the knoll together. "Her night's sleep has done her a world of good." She studied Harriet's face anxiously as they paused next to the souvenir booth, and discovered a sweet light reflected in her eyes. All at once she remembered their childhood together and the great tenderness Harriet had often shown towards her then.

"They have Turkish pilaff on the menu," said Harriet, "so I told the waiter to save some for you. It's such a favorite that it usually runs out at the very beginning. I know how much you love it."

Sadie, realizing that Harriet was actually eager for this dinner, the only one they would eat together at Camp Cataract, to be a success, felt the terrible leaden weight lifted from her heart; it disappeared so suddenly that for a moment or two she was like a balloon without its ballast; she could barely refrain from dancing about in delight. Harriet tugged on her arm.

"I think we'd better go now," she urged Sadie, "then after lunch we can come back here if you want to buy some souvenirs for Evy and Bert ... and maybe for Flo and Carl and Bobby too ..."

Sadie bent down to adjust her cotton stockings, which were wrinkling badly at the ankles, and when she straightened up again her eyes lighted on three men dining very near the edge of the terrace; she had not noticed them before. They were all eating corn on the cob and big round hamburger sandwiches in absolute silence. To protect their clothing from spattering kernels, they had converted their napkins into bibs.

"Bert Hoffer's careful of his clothes too," Sadie reflected, and then she turned to her sister. "Don't you think men look different sitting all by themselves without women?" she asked her. She felt an extraordinary urge to chat – an urge which she could not remember ever having experienced before.

"I think," Harriet replied, as though she had not heard

Sadie's comment, "that we'd better go to our table before the waiter gives it to someone else."

"I don't like men," Sadie announced without venom, and she was about to follow Harriet when her attention was arrested by the eyes of the man nearest her. Slowly lowering his corn cob to his plate, he stared across at her, his mouth twisted into a bitter smile. She stood as if rooted to the ground, and under his steady gaze all her newborn joy rapidly drained away. With desperation she realized that Harriet, darting in and out between the crowded tables, would soon be out of sight. After making what seemed to her a superhuman effort she tore herself away from the spot where she stood and lunged after Harriet shouting her name.

Harriet was at her side again almost instantly, looking up at her with a startled expression. Together they returned to the souvenir booth, where Sadie stopped and assumed a slightly bent position as if she were suffering from an abdominal pain.

"What's the trouble?" she heard Harriet asking with concern. "Are you feeling ill?"

Instead of answering Sadie laid her hand heavily on her sister's arm and stared at her with a hunted expression in her eyes.

"Please try not to look so much like a gorilla," said Harriet in a kind voice, but Sadie, although she recognized the accuracy of this observation (for she could feel very well that she was looking like a gorilla), was powerless to change her expression, at least for a moment or two. "Come with me," she said finally, grabbing Harriet's hand and pulling her along with almost brutal force. "I've got something to tell you."

She headed down a narrow path leading into a thickly planted section of the grove, where she thought they were less likely to be disturbed. Harriet followed with such a quick, light step that Sadie felt no pull behind her at all and her sister's hand, folded in her own thick palm, seemed as delicate as the body of a bird. Finally they entered a small clearing where they stopped. Harriet untied a handkerchief from around her neck and mopped her brow. "Gracious!" she said. "It's frightfully hot in here." She offered the kerchief to Sadie. "I suppose it's because we walked so fast and because the pine trees shut out all the wind ... First I'll sit down and then you must tell me what's wrong." She stepped over to a felled tree whose length blocked the clearing. Its torn roots were shockingly exposed, whereas the upper trunk and branches lay hidden in the surrounding grove. Harriet sat down; Sadie was about to sit next to her when she noticed a dense swarm of flies near the roots. Automatically she stepped toward them. "Why are they here?" she asked herself – then immediately she spotted the cause, an open can of beans some careless person had deposited inside a small hollow at the base of the trunk. She turned away in disgust and looked at Harriet. Her sister was seated on the fallen tree, her back gracefully erect and her head tilted in a listening attitude. The filtered light imparted to her face an incredibly fragile and youthful look, and Sadie gazed at her with tenderness and wonder. No sound reached them in the clearing, and she realized with a pounding heart that she could no longer postpone telling Harriet why she had come. She could not have wished for a moment more favorable to the accomplishment of her purpose. The stillness in the air, their isolation, the expectant and gentle light in Harriet's eye, all these elements should have combined to give her back her faith – faith in her own powers to persuade Harriet to come home with her and live among them once again, winter and summer alike, as she had always done before. She opened her mouth to speak and doubled over, clutching at her stomach as though an animal were devouring her. Sweat beaded her forehead and she planted her feet wide apart on the ground as if this animal would be born. Though her vision was barred with pain, she saw Harriet's tear-filled eyes, searching hers.

"Let's not go back to the apartment," Sadie said, hearing her own words as if they issued not from her mouth but from a pit in the ground. "Let's not go back there ... let's you and me go out in the world ... just the two of us." A second before covering her face to hide her shame Sadie glimpsed Harriet's eyes, impossibly close to her own, their pupils pointed with a hatred such as she had never seen before.

It seemed to Sadie that it was taking an eternity for her sister to leave. "Go away ... go away ... or I'll suffocate." She was moaning the words over and over again, her face buried deep in her hands. "Go away ... please go away ... I'll suffocate ..." She could not tell, however, whether she was thinking these words or speaking them aloud.

At last she heard Harriet's footstep on the dry branches, as she started out of the clearing. Sadie listened, but although one step followed another, the cracking sound of the dry branches did not grow any fainter as Harriet penetrated farther into the grove. Sadie knew then that this agony she was suffering was itself the dreaded voyage into the world – the very voyage she had always feared Harriet would make. That she herself was making it instead of Harriet did not affect her certainty that this was it.

◆ ◆ ◆

Sadie stood at the souvenir booth looking at some birchbark canoes. The wind was blowing colder and stronger than it had a while ago, or perhaps it only seemed this way to her, so recently returned from the airless clearing. She did not recall her trip back through the grove; she was conscious only of her haste to buy some souvenirs and to leave. Some chains of paper tacked to the side of the booth as decoration kept flying into her face. The Indian chief was smiling at her from behind the counter of souvenirs.

"What can I do for you?" he asked.

"I'm leaving," said Sadie, "so I want souvenirs ..."

"Take your choice; you've got birchbark canoes with or without mailing cards attached, Mexican sombrero ashtrays, exhilarating therapeutic pine cushions filled with the regional needles ... and banners for a boy's room."

"There's no boy home," Sadie said, having caught only these last words.

"How about cushions ... or canoes?"

She nodded.

"Which do you want?"

"Both," she answered quickly.

"How many?"

Sadie closed her eyes. Try as she would she could not count up the members of the family. She could not even reach an approximate figure. "Eleven," she blurted out finally, in desperation.

"Eleven of each?" he asked raising his eyebrows.

"Yes ... yes," she answered quickly, batting the paper chains out of her face, "eleven of each."

"You sure don't forget the old folks at home, do you?" he said, beginning to collect the canoes. He made an individual package of each souvenir and then wrapped them all together in coarse brown paper which he bound with thick twine.

Sadie had given him a note and he was punching his money belt for the correct change when her eyes fell on his light, freckled hand. Startled, she shifted her glance from his hand punching the nickel belt to his brick-colored face streaked with purple and vermilion paint. For the first time she noticed his Irish blue eyes. Slowly the hot flush of shame crept along the nape of her neck. It was the same unbearable mortification that she had experienced in the clearing; it spread upward from her neck to the roots of her hair, coloring her face a dark red. That she was ashamed for the Indian this time, and not of her own words, failed to lessen the intensity of her suffering; the boundaries of her pride had never been firmly fixed inside herself. She stared intently at his Irish blue eyes, so oddly light in his brick-colored face. What was it? She was tormented by the sight of an incongruity she couldn't name. All at once she remembered the pavilion and the people dining there; her heart started to pound. "They'll see it," she said to herself in a panic. "They'll see it and they'll know that I've seen it too." Somehow this latter possibility was the most perilous of all.

"They must never know I've seen it," she said, grinding her teeth, and she leaned over the counter, crushing some canoes under her chest. "Quickly," she whispered. "Go out your little door and meet me back of the booth ..."

A second later she found him there. "Listen!" She clutched his hand. "We must hurry ... I didn't mean to see you ... I'm sorry ... I've been trying not to look at you for years ... for years and years and years ..." She gaped at him in horror. "Why are you standing there? We've got to hurry ... They haven't caught me looking at you yet, but we've got to hurry." She headed for the bridge, leading the Indian behind her. He followed quickly without saying a word.

The water's roar increased in volume as they approached the opposite bank of the chasm, and Sadie found relief in the sound. Once off the bridge she ran as fast as she could along the path leading to the waterfall. The Indian followed close on her heels, his hand resting lightly in her own, as Harriet's had earlier when they'd sped together through the grove. Reaching the waterfall, she edged along the wall of rock until she stood directly behind the water's cascade. With a cry of delight she leaned back in the curve of the wall, insensible to its icy dampness, which penetrated even through the thickness of her woolen coat. She listened to the cataract's deafening roar and her heart almost burst for joy, because she had hidden the Indian safely behind the cascade where he could be neither seen nor heard. She turned around and smiled at him kindly. He too smiled, and she no longer saw in his face any trace of the incongruity that had shocked her so before.

The foaming waters were beautiful to see. Sadie stepped forward, holding her hand out to the Indian.

◆ ◆ ◆

When Harriet awakened that morning all traces of her

earlier victorious mood had vanished. She felt certain that disaster would overtake her before she could start out for Pocahontas Falls. Heavyhearted and with fumbling hands, she set about making her pack. Luncheon with Sadie was an impossible cliff which she did not have the necessary strength to scale. When she came to three round cushions that had to be snapped into their rainproof casings she gave up with a groan and rushed headlong out of her cabin in search of Beryl.

Fortunately Beryl waited table on the second shift and so she found her reading a magazine, with one leg flung over the arm of her chair.

"I can't make my pack," Harriet said hysterically, bursting into Beryl's cabin without even knocking at the door.

Beryl swung her leg around and got out of her chair, "I'll make your pack," she said in a calm voice, knocking some tobacco out of her pipe. "I would have come around this morning, but you said last night you wanted to make it alone."

"It's Sadie," Harriet complained. "It's that cursed lunch with Sadie. I can't go through with it. I know I can't. I shouldn't have to in the first place. She's not even supposed to be here ... I'm an ass ..."

"To hell with sisters," said Beryl. "Give 'em all a good swift kick in the pants."

"She's going to stop me from going on my canoe trip ... I know she is ..." Harriet had adopted the whining tone of a little girl.

"No, she isn't," said Beryl, speaking with authority.

"Why not?" Harriet asked. She looked at Beryl almost wistfully.

"She'd better not try anything ..." said Beryl. "Ever hear of jujitsu?" She grunted with satisfaction. "Come on, we'll go make your pack." She was so pleased with Harriet's new state of dependency that she was rapidly overcoming her original shyness. An hour later she had completed the pack, and Harriet was dressed and ready.

"Will you go with me to the souvenir booth?" she begged the waitress. "I don't want to meet her alone." She was in a worse state of nerves than ever.

"I'll go with you," said Beryl, "but let's stop at my cabin on the way so I can change into my uniform. I'm on duty soon."

They were nearly twenty minutes late arriving at the booth, and Harriet was therefore rather surprised not to see Sadie standing there. "Perhaps she's been here and gone back to the lodge for a minute," she said to Beryl. "I'll find out." She walked up to the souvenir counter and questioned the Indian, with whom she was slightly familiar. "Was there a woman waiting here a while ago, Timothy?" she asked.

"A dark middle-aged woman?"

"That's right."

"She was here for an hour or more," he said, "never budged from this stall until about fifteen minutes ago."

"She couldn't have been here an hour!" Harriet argued. "Not my sister ... I told her one-thirty and it's not yet two."

"Then it wasn't your sister. The woman who was here stayed more than an hour, without moving. I noticed her because it was such a queer-looking thing. I noticed her first from my chair at the bridge and then when I came up here she was still standing by the booth. She must have stood here over an hour."

"Then it was a different middle-aged woman."

"That may be," he agreed, "but anyway, this one left about fifteen minutes ago. After standing all that time she turned around all of a sudden and bought a whole bunch of souvenirs from me ... then just when I was punching my belt for the change she said something I couldn't understand – it sounded like Polish – and then she lit out for the bridge before I could give her a penny. That woman's got impulses," he added with a broad grin. "If she's your sister, I'll give you her change, in case she don't stop here on her way back ... But she sounded to me like a Polak."

"Beryl," said Harriet, "run across the bridge and see if Sadie's behind the waterfall. I'm sure this Polish woman wasn't Sadie, but they might both be back there ... If she's not there, we'll look in the lodge."

◆ ◆ ◆

When Beryl returned her face was dead white; she stared at Harriet in silence, and even when Harriet finally grabbed hold of her shoulders and shook her hard, she would not say anything.

First published in *Harper's Bazaar* (September 1949).

A Quarreling Pair

The two puppets are sisters in their early fifties. The puppet stage should have a rod or string dividing it down the middle to indicate two rooms. One puppet is seated on each side of the dividing line. If it is not possible to seat them they will have to stand. HARRIET, *the older puppet, is stronger-looking and wears brighter colors.*

HARRIET *[The stronger puppet]* I hope you are beginning to think about our milk.

RHODA *[After a pause]* Well, I'm not.

HARRIET Now what's the matter with you? You're not going to have a visitation from our dead, are you?

RHODA I don't have visitations this winter because I'm too tired to love even our dead. Anyway, I'm disgusted with the world.

HARRIET Just mind your business. I mind mine and I am thinking about our milk.

RHODA I'm so tired of being sad. I'd like to change.

HARRIET You don't get enough enjoyment out of your room. Why don't you?

RHODA Oh, because the world and its sufferers are always on my mind.

HARRIET That's not normal. You're not smart enough to be of any use to the outside, anyway.

RHODA If I were young I'd succor the sick. I wouldn't care about culture, even, if I were young.

HARRIET You don't have any knack for making a home. There's blessed satisfaction in that, at any rate.

RHODA My heart's too big to make a home.

HARRIET No. It's because you have no self-sufficiency. If I wasn't around, you wouldn't have the leisure to worry. You're a lost soul, when I'm not around. You don't even have the pep to worry about the outside when I'm not around. Not that the outside loses by that! *[She sniffs with scorn.]*

RHODA You're right. But I swear that my heart is big.

HARRIET I've come to believe that what is inside of people is not so very interesting. You can breed considerable discontent around you with a big heart, and considerable harmony with a small one. Compare your living quarters to mine. And my heart is small like Papa's was.

RHODA You chill me to the marrow when you tell me that your heart is small. You do love me, though, don't you?

HARRIET You're my sister, aren't you?

RHODA Sisterly love is one of the few boons in this life.

HARRIET Now, that's enough exaggerating. I could enumerate other things.

RHODA I suppose it's wicked to squeeze love from a small heart. I suppose it's a sin. I suppose God meant for small hearts to be busy with other things.

HARRIET Possibly. Let's have our milk in my room. It's so much more agreeable to sit in here. Partly because I'm a neater woman than you are.

RHODA Even though you have a small heart, I wish there were no one but you and me in the world. Then I would never feel that I had to go among the others.

HARRIET Well, I wish I could hand you my gift for contentment in a box. It would be so lovely if you were like me. Then we could have our milk in either room. One day in your room and the next day in mine.

RHODA I'm sure that's the sort of thing that never happens.

HARRIET It happens in a million homes, seven days a week. I'm the type that's in the majority.

RHODA Never, never, never ...

HARRIET *[Very firmly]* It happens in a million home

RHODA *Never, never, never!*

HARRIET *[Rising]* Are you going to listen to me when I tell you that it happens in a million homes, or must I lose my temper?

RHODA You have already lost it. *[*HARRIET *exits rapidly in a rage. Rhoda goes to the chimes and sings]*

My horse was frozen like a stone
A long, long time ago.
Frozen near the flower bed
In the wintry sun.
Or maybe in the night time
Or maybe not at all.

My horse runs across the fields
On many afternoons.
Black as dirt and filled with blood
I glimpse him fleeing toward the woods
And then not at all.

HARRIET *[Offstage]* I'm coming with your milk, and I hope the excitement is over for today. *[Enters, carrying two small white glasses]* Oh, why do I bring milk to a person who is dead-set on making my life a real hell?

RHODA *[Clasping her hands with feeling]* Yes, Why? Why? Why? Oh what a hideous riddle!

HARRIET You love to pretend that everything is a riddle. You think that's the way to be intellectual. There is no riddle. I am simply keeping up my end of the bargain.

RHODA Oh, bargains, bargains, bargains!

HARRIET Will you let me finish, you excitable thing? I'm trying to explain that I'm behaving the way I was molded to behave. I happen to be appreciative of the mold I was cast in, and neither heaven, nor earth is going to make me damage it. Your high-strung emotions are not going to affect me. Here's your milk.

[She enters RHODA*'s side of the stage and hands her the milk, but* RHODA *punches the bottom of the glass with her closed fist and sends it flying out of* HARRIET*'s hand.* HARRIET *deals Rhoda a terrific blow on the face and scurries back to her own room. There is silence for a moment. Then* HARRIET *buries her face in her hands and weeps.* RHODA *exits and* HARRIET *goes to the chimes and sings.]*

HARRIET *[Singing]*

I dreamed I climbed upon a cliff,
My sister's hand in mine.
Then searched the valley for my house
But only sunny fields could see
And the church spire shining.
I searched until my heart was cold
But only sunny fields could see
And the church spire shining.
A girl ran down the mountainside
With bluebells in her hat.
I asked the valley for her name
But only wind and rain could hear
And the church bell tolling.

I asked until my lips were cold
But wakened not yet knowing
If the name she bore was my sister's name
Or if it was my own.

HARRIET Rhoda?

RHODA What do you want?

HARRIET Go away if you like.

RHODA The moment hasn't come yet, and it won't come today because the day is finished and the evening is here. Thank God!

HARRIET I know I should get some terrible disease and die if I thought I did not live in the right. It would break my heart.

RHODA You do live in the right, sweetie, so don't think about it. *[Pause]* I'll go and get your milk.

HARRIET I'll go too. But let's drink it in here because it really is much pleasanter in here, isn't it? *[They rise]* Oh, I'm so glad the evening has comet! I'm nervously exhausted. *[They exit]*

'A Quarreling Pair' was first performed, as a puppet show, in 1945, with music by Paul Bowles, in a staging sponsored by John Meyers, editor of the surrealist journal *View*. The play was first published in *Mademoiselle* (December 1966).

A Stick of Green Candy

THE CLAY PIT HAD BEEN DUG in the side of a long hill. By leaning back against the lower part of its wall, Mary could see the curved highway above her and the cars speeding past. On the other side of the highway the hill continued rising, but at a steeper angle. If she tilted her head farther back, she could glimpse the square house on the hill's summit, with its flight of stone steps that led from the front door down to the curb, dividing the steep lawn in two.

She had been playing in the pit for a long time. Like many other children, she fancied herself at the head of a regiment; at the same time, she did not join in any neighborhood games, preferring to play all alone in the pit, which lay about a mile beyond the edge of town. She was a scrupulously clean child with a strong, immobile face and long, well-arranged curls. Sometimes when she went home toward evening there were traces of clay on her dark coat, even though she had worked diligently with the brush she carried along every afternoon. She despised untidiness, and she feared that the clay might betray her headquarters, which she suspected the other children of planning to invade.

One afternoon she stumbled and fell on the clay when it was still slippery and wet from a recent rainfall. She never failed to leave the pit before twilight, but this time she decided to wait until it was dark so that her sullied coat would attract less attention. Wisely she refrained from using her brush on the wet clay.

Having always left the pit at an earlier hour, she felt that an explanation was due to her soldiers; to announce simply that she had fallen down was out of the question. She knew that her men trusted her and would therefore accept in good faith any reason she chose to give them for this abrupt change in her day's routine, but convincing herself was a more difficult task. She never told them anything until she really believed what she was going to say. After concentrating a few minutes, she summoned them with a bugle call.

"Men," she began, once they were lined up at attention, "I'm staying an hour longer today than usual, so I can work on the mountain goat maneuvers. I explained mountain-goat fighting last week, but I'll tell you what it is again. It's a special technique used in the mountains around big cliffs. No machine can do mountain-goat fighting. We're going to specialize." She paused. "Even though I'm staying, I want you to go right ahead and have your recreation hour as usual, like you always do the minute I leave. I have total respect for your recreation, and I know you fight as hard as you play."

She dismissed them and walked up to her own headquarters in the deepest part of the pit. At the end of the day the color of the red pit deepened; then, after the sun had sunk behind the hill, the clay lost its color. She began to feel cold and a little uneasy. She was so accustomed to leaving her men each day at the same hour, just before they thronged into the gymnasium, that now lingering on made her feel like an intruder.

It was almost night when she climbed out of the pit. She glanced up at the hilltop house and then started down toward the deserted lower road. When she reached the outskirts of town she chose the darkest streets so that the coat would be less noticeable. She hated the thick pats of clay that were embedded in its wool; moreover she was suffering from a sense of inner untidiness as a result of the unexpected change in her daily routine. She walked along slowly, scuffing her heels, her face wearing the expression of a person surfeited with food. Far underneath her increasingly lethargic mood lurked a feeling of apprehension; she knew she would be reprimanded for returning home after dark, but she never would admit either the possibility of punishment or the fear of it. At this period she was rapidly perfecting a psychological mechanism which enabled her to forget, for long stretches of time, that her parents existed.

She found her father in the vestibule hanging his coat up on a peg. Her heart sank as he turned around to greet her. Without seeming to, he took in the pats of clay at a glance, but his shifting eyes never alighted candidly on any object.

"You've been playing in that pit below the Speed house again," he said to her. "From now on, I want you to play at the Kinsey Memorial Grounds." Since he appeared to have nothing to say, she started away, but immediately he continued. "Some day you may have to live in a town where the administration doesn't make any provision for children at all. Or it may provide you with a small plot of land and a couple of dinky swings. There's a very decent sum goes each year to the grounds here. They provide you with swings, seesaws and chin bars." He glanced furtively at her coat. "Tomorrow," he said, "I drive past that pit on my way out to Sam's. I'll draw up to the edge of the road and look down. See that you're over at the Memorial Grounds with the other children."

Mary never passed the playgrounds without quickening her step. This site, where the screams of several dozen children mingled with the high, grinding sound of the moving swings, she had always automatically hated. It was the antithesis of her clay pit and the well-ordered barracks inside it.

When she went to bed, she was in such a state of wild excitement that she was unable to sleep. It was the first time that her father's observations had not made her feel either humiliated or ill. The following day after school she set out for the pit. As she was climbing the long hill (she always approached her barracks from the lower road), she slackened her pace and stood still. All at once she had had the fear that by looking into her eyes the soldiers might divine her father's existence. To each one of them she was like himself – a man without a family. After a minute she resumed her climb. When she reached the edge of the pit, she put both feet together and jumped inside.

"Men," she said, once she had blown the bugle and made a few routine announcements, "I know you have hard muscles in your legs. But how would you like to have even harder ones?" It was a rhetorical question to which she did not expect an answer. "We're going to have hurdle races and plain running every day now for two hours."

Though in her mind she knew dimly that this intensified track training was preparatory to an imminent battle on the Memorial playgrounds, she did not dare discuss it with her men, or even think about it too precisely herself. She had to avoid coming face to face with an impossibility.

"As we all know," she continued, "we don't like to have teams because we've been through too much on the battlefield all together. Every day I'll divide you up fresh before the racing, so that the ones who are against each other today, for instance, will be running on the same side tomorrow. The men in our outfit are funny about taking sides against each other, even just in play and athletics. The other outfits in this country don't feel the same as we do."

She dug her hands into her pockets and hung her head sheepishly. She was fine now, and certain of victory. She could feel the men's hearts bursting with love for her and with pride in their regiment. She looked up – a car was rounding the bend, and as it came nearer she recognized it as her father's.

"Men," she said in a clear voice, "you can do what you want for thirty minutes while I make out the racing schedule and the team lists." She stared unflinchingly at the dark blue sedan and waited with perfect outward calm for her father to slow down; she was still waiting after the car had curved out of sight. When she realized that he was gone, she held her breath. She expected her heart to leap for joy, but it did not.

◆ ◆ ◆

"Now I'll go to my headquarters," she announced in a flat voice. "I'll be back with the team lists in twenty-five minutes." She glanced up at the highway; she felt oddly disappointed and uneasy. A small figure was descending the stone steps on the other side of the highway. It was a boy. She watched in amazement; she had never seen anyone come down these steps before. Since the highway had replaced the old country road, the family living in the hilltop house came and went through the back door.

Watching the boy, she felt increasingly certain that he was on his way down to the pit. He stepped off the curb after looking prudently for cars in each direction; then he crossed the highway and clambered down the hill. Just as she had expected him to, when he reached the edge of the pit he seated himself on the ground and slid into it, smearing his coat – dark like her own – with clay.

"It's a big clay pit," he said, looking up at her. He was younger than she, but he looked straight into her eyes without a trace of shyness. She knew he was a stranger in town; she had never seen him before. This made him less detestable, nonetheless she had to be rid of him shortly because the men were expecting her back with the team lists.

"Where do you come from?" she asked him.

"From inside that house." He pointed at the hilltop. "Where do you live when you're not visiting?"

"I live inside that house," he repeated, and he sat down on the floor of the pit.

"Sit on the orange crate," she ordered him severely. "You don't pay any attention to your coat."

He shook his head. She was exasperated with him because

he was untidy, and he had lied to her. She knew perfectly well that he was merely a visitor in the hilltop house.

"Why did you come out this door?" she asked, looking at him sharply. "The people in that house go out the back. It's level there and they've got a drive."

"I don't know why," he answered simply.

"Where do you come from?" she asked again.

"That's my house." He pointed to it as if she were asking him for the first time. "The driveway in back's got gravel in it. I've got a whole box of it in my room. I can bring it down."

"No gravel's coming in here that belongs to a liar," she interrupted him. "Tell me where you come from and then you can go get it."

He stood up. "I live in that big house up there," he said calmly. "From my room I can see the river, the road down there and the road up here, and this pit and you."

"It's not your room!" she shouted angrily. "You're a visitor there. I was a visitor last year at my aunt's."

"Good-bye."

He was climbing out of the pit. Once outside he turned around and looked down at her. There was an expression of fulfillment on his face.

"I'll bring the gravel some time soon," he said.

She watched him crossing the highway. Then automatically she climbed out of the pit.

She was mounting the tedious stone steps behind him. Her jaw was clamped shut, and her face had gone white with anger. He had not turned around once to look at her. As they were nearing the top it occurred to her that he would rush into the house and slam the door in her face. Hurriedly she climbed three steps at once so as to be directly behind him. When he opened the door, she pushed across the threshold with him; he did not seem to notice her at all. Inside the dimly lit vestibule the smell of fresh paint was very strong. After a few seconds her eyes became more accustomed to the light, and she saw that the square room was packed solid with furniture. The boy was already pushing his way between two identical bureaus which stood back to back. The space between them was so narrow that she feared she would not be able to follow him. She looked around frantically for a wider artery, but seeing that there was none, she squeezed between the bureaus, pinching her flesh painfully, until she reached a free space at the other end. Here the furniture was less densely packed – in fact, three armchairs had been shoved together around an uncluttered area, wide enough to provide leg room for three people, providing they did not mind a tight squeeze. To her left a door opened on to total darkness. She expected him to rush headlong out of the room into the dark in a final attempt to escape her, but to her astonishment he threaded his way carefully in the opposite direction until he reached the circle of chairs. He entered it and sat down in one of them. After a second's hesitation, she followed his example.

The chair was deeper and softer than any she had ever sat in before. She tickled the thick velvet arms with her fingertips. Here and there, they grazed a stiff area where the nap had worn thin. The paint fumes were making her eyes smart, and she was beginning to feel apprehensive. She had forgotten to consider that grown people would probably be in the house, but now she gazed uneasily into the dark space through the open door opposite her. It was cold in the vestibule, and despite her woolen coat she began to shiver.

"If he would tell me now where he comes from," she said to herself, "then I could go away before anybody else came." Her anger had vanished, but she could not bring herself to speak aloud, or even to turn around and look at him. He sat so still that it was hard for her to believe he was actually beside her in his chair.

Without warning, the dark space opposite her was lighted up. Her heart sank as she stared at a green wall, still shiny with wet paint. It hurt her eyes. A woman stepped into the visible area, her heels sounding on the floorboards. She was wearing a print dress and over it a long brown sweater which obviously belonged to a man.

"Are you there, Franklin?" she called out, and she walked into the vestibule and switched on a second light. She stood still and looked at him.

"I thought I heard you come in," she said. Her voice was flat, and her posture at that moment did not inspire Mary with respect. "Come to visit Franklin?" she asked, as if suddenly aware that her son was not alone. "I think I'll visit for a while." She advanced toward them. When she reached the circle she squeezed in and sat opposite Mary.

"I hoped we'd get a visitor or two while we were here," she said to her. "That's why I arranged this little sitting place. All the rest of the rooms are being painted, or else they're still too smelly for visiting. Last time we were here we didn't see anyone for the whole two weeks. But he was a baby then. I thought maybe this time he'd contact when he went out. He goes out a lot of the day." She glanced at her son. "You've got some dirt on that chair," she remarked in a tone which did not express the slightest disapproval. She turned back to Mary. "I'd rather have a girl than a boy," she said. "There's nothing much I can discuss with a boy. A grown woman isn't interested in the same things a boy is interested in." She scratched a place below her shoulder blades. "My preference is discussing furnishings. Always has been. I like that better than I like discussing styles. I'll discuss styles if the company wants to, but I don't enjoy it nearly so well. The only thing about furnishings that leaves me cold is curtains. I never was interested in curtains, even when I was young. I like lamps about the best. Do you?"

Mary was huddling as far back into her chair as she could, but even so, without drawing her legs up and sitting on her feet, it was impossible to avoid physical contact with the woman, whose knees lightly touched hers every time she shifted a little in her chair. Inwardly, too, Mary shrank from her. She had never before been addressed so intimately by a grown person. She closed her eyes, seeking the dark gulf that always had separated her from the adult world. And she clutched the seat cushion hard, as if she were afraid of being wrenched from the chair.

"We came here six years ago," the woman continued, "when the Speeds had their house painted, and now they're having it painted again, so we're here again. They can't be in the house until it's good and dry because they've both got nose trouble – both the old man and the old lady – but we're not related. Only by marriage. I'm a kind of relative to them, but not enough to be really classed as a relative. Just enough so that they'd rather have me come and look after the house than a stranger. They gave me a present of money last time, but this time it'll be clothes for the boy. There's nothing to boys' clothes really. They don't mean anything."

She sighed and looked around her.

"Well," she said, "we would like them to ask us over here more often than they do. Our town is way smaller than this, way smaller, but you can get all the same stuff there that you can here, if you've got the money to pay. I mean groceries and clothing and appliances. We've got all that. As soon as the walls are dry we go back. Franklin doesn't want to. He don't like his home because he lives in an apartment; it's in the business section. He sits in a lot and don't go out and contact at all."

The light shone through Mary's tightly closed lids. In the chair next to her there was no sound of a body stirring. She opened her eyes and looked down. His ankles were crossed and his feet were absolutely still.

"Franklin," the woman said, "get some candy for me and the girl."

When he had gone she turned to Mary. "He's not a rough boy like the others," she said. "I don't know what I'd do if he was one of the real ones with all the trimmings. He's got some girl in him, thank the Lord. I couldn't handle one of the real ones."

He came out of the freshly painted room carrying a box.

"We keep our candy in tea boxes. We have for years," the woman said. "They're good conservers." She shrugged her shoulders. "What more can you expect? Such is life." She turned to her son. "Open it and pass it to the girl first. Then me."

The orange box was decorated with seated women and temples. Mary recognized it; her mother used the same tea at home. He slipped off the two rubber bands that held the cover on, and offered her the open box. With stiff fingers she took a stick of green candy from the top; she did not raise her eyes.

A few minutes later she was running alone down the stone steps. It was almost night, but the sky was faintly green near the horizon. She crossed the highway and stood on the hill only a few feet away from the pit. Far below her, lights were twinkling in the Polish section. Down there the shacks were stacked one against the other in a narrow strip of land between the lower road and the river.

After gazing down at the sparkling lights for a while, she began to breathe more easily. She had never experienced the need to look at things from a distance before, nor had she felt the relief that it can bring. All at once, the air stirring around her head seemed delightful; she drank in great drafts of it, her eyes fixed on the lights below.

"This isn't the regular air from up here that I'm breathing," she said to herself. "It's the air from down there. It's a trick I can do."

She felt her blood tingle as it always did whenever she scored a victory, and she needed to score several of them in the course of each day. This time she was defeating the older woman.

The following afternoon, even though it was raining hard, her mother could not stop her from going out, but she had promised to keep her hood buttoned and not to sit on the ground.

The stone steps were running with water. She sat down and looked into the enveloping mist, a fierce light in her eyes. Her fingers twitched nervously, deep in the recess of her rubber pockets. It was unbelievable that they should not at any moment encounter something wonderful and new, unbelievable, too, that he should be ignorant of her love for him. Surely he knew that all the while his mother was talking, she in secret had been claiming him for her own. He would come out soon to join her on the steps, and they would go away together.

Hours later, stiff with cold, she stood up. Even had he remained all day at the window he could never have sighted her through the heavy mist. She knew this, but she could never climb the steps to fetch him; that was impossible. She ran headlong down the stone steps and across the highway. When she reached the pit she stopped dead and stood with her feet in the soft clay mud, panting for breath.

"Men," she said after a minute, "men, I told you we were going to specialize." She stopped abruptly, but it was too late. She had, for the first time in her life, spoken to her men before summoning them to order with a bugle call. She was shocked, and her heart beat hard against her ribs, but she went on. "We're going to be the only outfit in the world that can do real mountain-goat fighting." She closed her eyes, seeking the dark gulf again; this time she needed to hear the men's hearts beating, more clearly than her own. A car was sounding its horn on the highway. She looked up.

"We can't climb those stone steps up there." She was shouting and pointing at the house. "No outfit can, no outfit ever will ..." She was desperate. "It's not for outfits. It's a flight of steps that's not for outfits ... because it's ... because ..." The reason was not going to come to her. She had begun to cheat now, and she knew it would never come.

She turned her cold face away from the pit, and without dismissing her men, crept down the hill.

'A Stick of Green Candy', written in 1949, was Jane's last completed story. It was first published in *Vogue* (February 1957).

Texts from

Three Serious Ladies

These three pieces set in Guatemala – 'A Guatemalan Idyll', 'A Day in the Open' and 'Señorita Córdoba' – formed part of the original draft of Jane Bowles' novel, Two Serious Ladies *(1943), or as it was then called,* Three Serious Ladies. *They were excised by Paul Bowles, who edited the novel with Jane, but he persuaded her to revive the first two for the* Plain Pleasures *collection. The third fragment, 'Señorita Córdoba', was edited by Paul Bowles and Jane's biographer, Millicent Dillon, after her death. It was Señorita Córdoba who was the original 'Third Serious Lady', along with Mrs Copperfield and Miss Goering.*

A Guatemalan Idyll

WHEN THE TRAVELER arrived at the pension the wind was blowing hard. Before going in to have the hot soup he had been thinking about, he left his luggage inside the door and walked a few blocks in order to get an idea of the town. He came to a very large arch through which, in the distance, he could see a plain. He thought he could distinguish figures seated around a far-away fire, but he was not certain because the wind made tears in his eyes.

"How dismal," he thought, letting his mouth drop open. "But never mind. Brace up. It's probably a group of boys and girls sitting around an open fire having a fine time together. The world is the world, after all is said and done, and a patch of grass in one place is green the way it is in any other."

He turned back and walked along quickly, skirting the walls of the low stone houses. He was a little worried that he might not be able to recognize a door of his pension.

"There's not supposed to be any variety in the U.S.A.," he said to himself. "But this Spanish architecture beats everything, it's so monotonous." He knocked on one of the doors, and shortly a child with a shaved head appeared. With a strong American accent he said to her: "Is this the Pension Espinoza?"

"*Si!*" The child led him inside to a fountain in the center of a square patio. He looked into the basin and the child did too.

"There are four fish inside here," she said to him in Spanish. "Would you like me to try and catch one of them for you?"

The traveler did not understand her. He stood there uncomfortably, longing to go to his room. The little girl was still trying to get hold of a fish when her mother, who owned the pension, came out and joined them. The woman was quite fat, but her face was small and pointed, and she wore glasses attached by a gold chain to her dress. She shook hands with him and asked him in fairly good English if he had had a pleasant journey.

"He wants to see some of the fish," explained the child.

"Certainly," said Señora Espinoza, moving her hands about in the water with dexterity. "Soon now, soon now," she said, laughing as one of the fish slipped between her fingers.

The traveler nodded. "I would like to go to my room," he said.

◆ ◆ ◆

The American was a little dismayed by his room. There were four brass beds in a row, all of them very old and a little crooked.

"God!" he said to himself. "They'll have to remove some of these beds. They give me the willies."

A cord hung down from the ceiling. On the end of it at the height of his nose was a tiny electric bulb. He turned it on and looked at his hands under the light. They were chapped and dirty. A barefoot servant girl came in with a pitcher and a bowl.

In the dining room, calendars decorated the walls, and there was an elaborate cut-glass carafe on every table. Several people had already begun their meal in silence. One little girl was speaking in a high voice.

"I'm not going to the band concert tonight, mamá," she was saying.

"Why not?" asked her mother with her mouth full. She looked seriously at her daughter.

"Because I don't like to hear music. I hate it!"

"Why?" asked her mother absently, taking another large mouthful of her food. She spoke in a deep voice like a man's. Her head, which was set low between her shoulders, was covered with black curls. Her chin was heavy and her skin was dark and coarse; however, she had very beautiful blue eyes. She sat with her legs apart, with one arm lying flat on the table. The child bore no resemblance to her mother. She was frail, with stiff hair of the peculiar light color that is often found in mulattoes. Her eyes were so pale that they seemed almost white.

As the traveler came in, the child turned to look at him.

"Now there are nine people eating in this pension," she said immediately.

"Nine," said her mother. "Many mouths." She pushed her plate aside wearily and looked up at the calendar beside her on the wall. At last she turned around and saw the stranger. Having already finished her own dinner, she followed the progress of his meal with interest. Once she caught his eye.

"Good appetite," she said, nodding gravely, and then she watched his soup until he had finished it.

"My pills," she said to Lilina, holding her hand out without turning her head. To amuse herself, Lilina emptied the whole bottle into her mother's hand.

"Now you have your pills," she said. When Señora Ramirez realized what had happened, she dealt Lilina a terrible blow in the face, using the hand which held the pills, and thus leaving them sticking to the child's moist skin and in her hair. The traveler turned. He was so bored and at the same time disgusted by what he saw that he decided he had better look for another pension that very night.

"Soon," said the waitress, putting his meat in front of him, "the musician will come. For fifty cents he will play you all the songs you want to hear. One night would not be time enough. *She* will be out of the room by then." She looked over at Lilina, who was squealing like a stuck pig.

"Those pills cost me three *quetzales* a bottle," Señora Ramirez complained. One of the young men at a nearby table came over and examined the empty bottle. He shook his head.

"A barbarous thing," he said.

"What a dreadful child you are, Lilina!" said an English lady who was seated at quite a distance from everybody else. All the diners looked up. Her face and neck were quite red with annoyance. She was speaking to them in English.

"Can't you behave like civilized people?" she demanded.

"You be quiet, you!" The young man had finished examining the empty pill bottle. His companions burst out laughing.

"O.K., girl," he continued in English. "Want a piece of chewing gum?" His companions were quite helpless with laughter at his last remark, and all three of them got up and left the room. Their guffaws could be heard from the patio, where they had grouped around the fountain, fairly doubled up.

"It's a disgrace to the adult mind," said the English lady. Lilina's nose had started to bleed, and she rushed out.

"And tell Consuelo to hurry in and eat her dinner," her mother called after her. Just then the musician arrived. He was a small man and he wore a black suit and a dirty shirt.

"Well," said Lilina's mother. "At last you came."

"I was having dinner with my uncle. Time passes, Señora Ramirez! *Gracias a Dios!*"

"*Gracias a Dios* nothing! It's unheard-of, having to eat dinner without music."

The violinist fell into a chair, and, bent over low, he started to play with all his strength.

"Waltzes!" shouted Señora Ramirez above the music. "Waltzes!" She looked petulant and at the same time as though she were about to cry. As a matter of fact, the stranger was quite sure that he saw a tear roll down her cheek.

"Are you going to the band concert tonight?" she asked him; she spoke English rather well.

"I don't know. Are you?"

"Yes, with my daughter Consuelo. If the unfortunate girl ever gets here to eat her supper. She doesn't like food. Only dancing. She dances like a real butterfly. She has French blood from me. She is of a much better type than the little one, Lilina, who is always hurting; hurting me, hurting her sister, hurting her friends. I hope that God will have pity on her." At this she really did shed a tear or two, which she brushed away with her napkin.

"Well, she's young yet," said the stranger. Señora Ramirez agreed heartily.

"Yes, she is young." She smiled at him sweetly and seemed quite content.

Lilina meanwhile was in her room, standing over the white bowl in which they washed their hands, letting the blood drip into it. She was breathing heavily like someone who is trying to simulate anger.

"Stop that breathing! You sound like an old man," said her sister Consuelo, who was lying on the bed with a hot brick on her stomach. Consuelo was small and dark, with a broad flat face and an unusually narrow skull. She had a surly nature, which is often the case when young girls do little else but dream of a lover. Lilina, who was a bully without any curiosity concerning the grown-up world, hated her sister more than anyone else she knew.

"Mamá says that if you don't come in to eat soon she will hit you."

"Is that how *you* got that bloody nose?"

"No," said Lilina. She walked away from the basin and her eye fell on her mother's corset, which was lying on the bed. Quickly she picked it up and went with it into the patio, where she threw it into the fountain. Consuelo, frightened by the appropriation of the corset, got up hastily and arranged her hair.

"Too much upset for a girl of my age," she said to herself patting her stomach. Crossing the patio she saw Señorita Córdoba walking along, holding her head very high as she slipped some hairpins more firmly into the bun at the back of her neck. Consuelo felt like a frog or a beetle walking behind her. Together they entered the dining room.

"Why don't you wait for midnight to strike?" said Señora Ramirez to Consuelo. Señorita Córdoba, assuming that this taunt had been addressed to her, bridled and stiffened. Her eyes narrowed and she stood still. Señora Ramirez, a gross coward, gave her a strange idiotic smile.

"How is your health, Señorita Córdoba?" she asked softly, and then feeling confused, she pointed to the stranger and asked him if he knew Señorita Córdoba.

"No, no; he does not know me." She held out her hand stiffly to the stranger and he took it. No names were mentioned.

Consuelo sat down beside her mother and ate voraciously, a sad look in her eye. Señorita Córdoba ordered only fruit. She sat looking out into the dark patio, giving the other diners a view of the nape of her neck. Presently she opened a letter and began to read. The others all watched her closely. The three young men who had laughed so heartily before were now smiling like idiots, waiting for another such occasion to present itself.

The musician was playing a waltz at the request of Señora Ramirez, who was trying her best to attract again the attention of the stranger. "Tra-la-la-la," she sang, and in order better to convey the beauty of the waltz she folded her arms in front of her and rocked from side to side.

"Ay, Consuelo! It is for her to waltz," she said to the stranger. "There will be many people in the plaza tonight, and there is so much wind. I think that you must fetch my shawl, Consuelo. It is getting very cold."

While awaiting Consuelo's return she shivered and picked her teeth.

The traveler thought she was crazy and a little disgusting. He had come here as a buyer for a very important textile concern. Having completed all his work, he had for some reason decided to stay on another week, perhaps because he had always heard that a vacation in a foreign country was a desirable thing. Already he regretted his decision, but there was no boat out before the following Monday. By the end of the meal he was in such despair that his face wore a peculiarly young and sensitive look. In order to buoy himself up a bit, he began to think about what he would get to eat three weeks hence, seated at his mother's table on Thanksgiving Day. They would be very glad to hear that he had not enjoyed himself on this trip, because they had always considered it something in the nature of a betrayal when anyone in the family expressed a desire to travel. He thought they led a fine life and was inclined to agree with them.

Consuelo had returned with her mother's shawl. She was dreaming again when her mother pinched her arm.

"Well, Consuelo, are you coming to the band concert or are you going to sit here like a dummy? I daresay the Señor is not coming with us, but *we* like music, so get up, and we will say good night to this gentleman and be on our way."

The traveler had not understood this speech. He was therefore very much surprised when Señora Ramirez tapped him on the shoulder and said to him severely in English: "Good night, Señor Consuelo and I are going to the band concert. We will see you tomorrow at breakfast."

"Oh, but I'm going to the band concert myself," he said, in a panic lest they leave him with a whole evening on his hands.

Señora Ramirez flushed with pleasure. The three walked down the badly lit street together, escorted by a group of skinny yellow dogs.

"These old grilled windows are certainly very beautiful," the traveler said to Señora Ramirez. "Old as the hills themselves, aren't they?"

"You must go to the capital if you want beautiful buildings," said Señora Ramirez. "Very new and clean they are."

"I should think," he said, "that these old buildings were your point of interest here, aside from your Indians and their native costumes."

They walked on for a little while in silence. A small boy came up to them and tried to sell them some lollipops.

"Five centavos," said the little boy.

"Absolutely not," said the traveler. He had been warned that the natives would cheat him, and he was acually enraged every time they approached him with their wares.

"Four *centavos* ... three *centavos* ..."

"No, no, no! Go away!" The little boy ran ahead of them. "I would like a lollipop," said Consuelo to him.

"Well, why didn't you say so, then?" he demanded.

"No," said Consuelo.

"She does not mean no," explained her mother. "She can't learn to speak English. She has clouds in her head."

"I see," said the traveler. Consuelo looked mortified. When they came to the end of the street, Señora Ramirez stood still and lowered her head like a bull.

"Listen," she said to Consuelo. "Listen. You can hear the music from here."

"Yes, mamá. Indeed you can." They stood listening to the faint marimba noise that reached them. The traveler sighed.

"Please, let's get going if we *are* going," he said. "Otherwise there is no point."

The square was already crowded when they arrived. The older people sat on benches under the trees, while the younger ones walked round and round, the girls in one direction and the boys in the other. The musicians played inside a kiosk in the center of the square. Señora Ramirez led both Consuelo and the stranger into the girls' line, and they had not been walking more than a minute before she settled into a comfortable gait, with an expression very much like that of someone relaxing in an armchair.

"We have three hours," she said to Consuelo.

The stranger looked around him. Many of the girls were barefoot and pure Indian. They walked along holding tightly to one another, and were frequently convulsed with laughter.

The musicians were playing a formless but militant-sounding piece which came to many climaxes without ending. The drummer was the man who had just played the violin at Señora Espinoza's pension.

"Look!" said the traveler excitedly. "Isn't that the man who was just playing for us at dinner. He must have run all the way. I'll bet he's sweating some."

"Yes, it is he," said Señora Ramirez. "The nasty little rat. I would like to tear him right off his stand. Remember the one at the Grand Hotel, Consuelo? He stopped at every table, señor, and I have never seen such beautiful teeth in my life. A smile on his face from the moment he came into the room until he went out again. This one looks at his shoes while he is playing, and he would like to kill us all."

Some big boys threw confetti into the traveler's face.

"I wonder," he asked himself. "I wonder what kind of fun they get out of just walking around and around this little park and throwing confetti at each other."

The boys' line was in a constant uproar about something. The broader their smiles became, the more he suspected them of plotting something, probably against him, for apparently he was the only tourist there that evening. Finally he was so upset that he walked along looking up at the stars, or even for short stretches with his eyes shut, because it seemed to him that somehow this rendered him a little less visible. Suddenly he caught sight of Señorita Córdoba. She was across the street buying lollipops from a boy.

"Señorita!" He waved his hand from where he was, and then joyfully bounded out of the line and across the street. He stood panting by her side, while she reddened considerably and did not know what to say to him.

Señora Ramirez and Consuelo came to a standstill and stood like two monuments, staring after him, while the lines brushed past them on either side.

◆ ◆ ◆

Lilina was looking out of her window at some boys who were playing on the corner of the street under the street light. One of them kept pulling a snake out of his pocket; he would then stuff it back in again. Lilina wanted the snake very much. She chose her toys according to the amount of power or responsibility she thought they would give her in the eyes of others. She thought now that if she were able to get the snake, she would perhaps put on a little act called "Lilina and the Viper," and charge admission. She imagined that she would wear a fancy dress and let the snake wriggle under her collar. She left her room and went out of doors. The wind was stronger than it had been, and she could hear the music playing even from where she was. She felt chilly and hurried toward the boys.

"For how much will you sell your snake?" she asked the oldest boy, Ramón.

"You mean Victoria?" said Ramón. His voice was beginning to change and there was a shadow above his upper lip.

"Victoria is too much of a queen for you to have," said one of the smaller boys. "She is a beauty and you are not." They all roared with laughter, including Ramón, who all at once looked very silly. He giggled like a girl. Lilina's heart sank. She was determined to have the snake.

"Are you ever going to stop laughing and begin to bargain with me? If you don't I'll have to go back in, because my mother and sister will be coming home soon, and they wouldn't allow me to be talking here like this with you. I'm from a good family."

This sobered Ramón, and he ordered the boys to be quiet. He took Victoria from his pocket and played with her in silence. Lilina stared at the snake.

"Come to my house," said Ramón. "My mother will want to know how much I'm selling her for."

"All right," said Lilina. "But be quick, and I don't want them with us." She indicated the other boys. Ramón gave them orders to go back to their houses and meet him later at the playground near the cathedral.

"Where do you live?" she asked him.

"Calle de las Delicias number six."

"Does your house belong to you?"

"My house belongs to my Aunt Gudelia."

"Is she richer than your mother?"

"Oh, yes." They said no more to each other.

There were eight rooms opening onto the patio of Ramón's house, but only one was furnished. In this room the family cooked and slept. His mother and his aunt were seated opposite one another on two brightly painted chairs. Both were fat and both were wearing black. The only light came from a charcoal fire which was burning in a brazier on the floor.

They had bought the chairs that very morning and were consequently feeling lighthearted and festive. When the children arrived they were singing a little song together.

"Why don't we buy something to drink?" said Gudelia, when they stopped singing.

"Now you're going to go crazy, I see," said Ramón's mother. "You're very disagreeable when you're drinking."

"No, I'm not," said Gudelia.

"Mother," said Ramón. "This little girl has come to buy Victoria."

"I have never seen you before," said Ramón's mother to Lilina.

"Nor I," said Gudelia. "I am Ramón's aunt, Gudelia. This is my house."

"My name is Lilina Ramirez. I want to bargain for Ramón's Victoria."

"Victoria," they repeated gravely.

"Ramón is very fond of Victoria and so are Gudelia and I," said his mother. "It's a shame that we sold Alfredo the parrot. We sold him for far too little. He sang and danced. We have taken care of Victoria for a long time, and it has been very expensive. She eats much meat." This was an obvious lie. They all looked at Lilina.

"Where do you live, dear?" Gudelia asked Lilina.

"I live in the capital, but I'm staying now at Señora Espinoza's pension."

"I meet her in the market every day of my life," said Gudelia. "María de la Luz Espinoza. She buys a lot. How many people has she staying in her house? Five, six?"

"Nine."

"Nine! Dear God! Does she have many animals?"

"Certainly," said Lilina.

"Come," said Ramón to Lilina. "Let's go outside and bargain."

"He loves that snake," said Ramón's mother, looking fixedly at Lilina.

The aunt sighed. "Victoria ... Victoria."

Lilina and Ramón climbed through a hole in the wall and sat down together in the midst of some foliage.

"Listen," said Ramón. "If you kiss me, I'll give you Victoria for nothing. You have blue eyes. I saw them when we were in the street."

"I can hear what you are saying," his mother called out from the kitchen.

"Shame, shame," said Gudelia. "Giving Victoria away for nothing. Your mother will be without food. I can buy my own food, but what will your mother do?"

Lilina jumped to her feet impatiently. She saw that they were getting nowhere, and unlike most of her countrymen, she was always eager to get things done quickly.

She stamped back into the kitchen, opened her eyes very wide in order to frighten the two ladies, and shouted as loud as she could: "Sell me that snake right now or I will go away and never put my foot in this house again."

The two women were not used to such a display of rage over the mere settlement of a price. They rose from their chairs and started moving about the room to no purpose, picking up things and putting them down again. They were not quite sure what to do. Gudelia was terribly upset. She stepped here and there with her hand below her breast, peering about cautiously. Finally she slipped out into the patio and disappeared.

Ramón took Victoria out of his pocket. They arranged a price and Lilina left, carrying her in a little box.

◆ ◆ ◆

Meanwhile Señora Ramirez and her daughter were on their way home from the band concert. Both of them were in a bad humor. Consuelo was not disposed to talk at all. She looked angrily at the houses they were passing and sighed at everything her mother had to say. "You have no merriment in your heart," said Señora Ramirez. "Just revenge." As Consuelo refused to answer, she continued. "Sometimes I feel that I am walking along with an assassin."

She stopped still in the street and looked up at the sky. "*Jesu María!*" she said. "Don't let me say such things about my own daughter." She clutched at Consuelo's arm.

"Come, come. Let us hurry. My feet ache. What an ugly city this is!"

Consuelo began to whimper. The word "assassin" had affected her painfully. Although she had no very clear idea of an assassin in her mind, she knew it to be a gross insult and contrary to all usage when applied to a young lady of breeding. It so frightened her that her mother had used such a word in connection with her that she actually felt a little sick to her stomach.

"No, mamá, no!" she cried. "Don't say that I am an assassin. Don't!" Her hands were beginning to shake, and already the tears were filling her eyes. Her mother hugged her and they stood for a moment locked in each other's arms.

María, the servant, was standing near the fountain looking into it when Consuelo and her mother arrived at the pension. The traveler and Señorita Córdoba were seated together having a chat.

"Doesn't love interest you?" the traveler was asking her.

"No ... no ..." answered Señorita Córdoba. "City life, business, the theater ..." She sounded somewhat halfhearted about the theater.

"Well, that's funny," said the traveler. "In my country most young girls are interested in love. There are some, of course, who are interested in having a career, either business or the stage. But I've heard tell that even these women deep down in their hearts want a home and everything that goes with it."

"So?" said Señorita Córdoba.

"Well, yes," said the traveler. "Deep down in your heart, don't you always hope the right man will come along some day?"

"No ... no ... no. Do you?" she said absent mindedly.

"Who, me? No."

"No?"

She was the most preoccupied woman he had ever spoken with.

"Look, señoras," said María to Consuelo and her mother. "Look what is floating around in the fountain! What is it?"

Consuelo bent over the basin and fished around a bit. Presently she pulled out her mother's pink corset.

"Why, mamá," she said. "It's your corset."

Señora Ramirez examined the wet corset. It was covered with muck from the bottom of the fountain. She went over to a chair and sat down in it, burying her face in her hands. She rocked back and forth and sobbed very softly. Señora Espinoza came out of her room.

"Lilina, my sister, threw it into the fountain," Consuelo announced to all present.

Señora Espinoza looked at the corset.

"It can be fixed. It can be fixed," she said, walking over to Señora Ramirez and putting her arms around her.

"Look, my friend. My dear little friend, why don't you go to bed and get some sleep? Tomorrow you can think about getting it cleaned."

"How can we stand it? Oh, how can we stand it?" Señora Ramirez asked imploringly, her beautiful eyes filled with sorrow. "Sometimes," she said in a trembling voice, "I have no more strength than a sparrow. I would like to send my children to the four winds and sleep and sleep and sleep."

Consuelo, hearing this, said in a gentle tone: "Why don't you do so, mamá?"

"They are like two daggers in my heart, you see?" continued her mother.

"No, they are not," said Señora Espinoza. "They are flowers that brighten your life." She removed her glasses and polished them on her blouse.

"Daggers in my heart," repeated Señora Ramirez.

"Have some hot soup," urged Señora Espinoza. "María will

make you some – a gift from me – and then you can go to bed and forget all about this."

"No, I think I will just sit here, thank you."

"Mamá is going to have one of her fits," said Consuelo to the servant. "She does sometimes. She gets just like a child instead of getting angry, and she doesn't worry about what she is eating or when she goes to sleep, but she just sits in a chair or goes walking and her face looks very different from the way it looks at other times." The servant nodded, and Consuelo went in to bed.

"I have French blood," Señora Ramirez was saying to Señora Espinoza. "I am very delicate for that reason – too delicate for my husband."

Señora Espinoza seemed worried by the confession of her friend. She had no interest in gossip or in what people had to say about their lives. To Señora Ramirez she was like a man, and she often had dreams about her in which she became a man.

The traveler was highly amused.

"I'll be damned!" he said. "All this because of an old corset. Some people have nothing to think about in this world. It's funny, though, funny as a barrel of monkeys."

To Señorita Córdoba it was not funny. "It's too bad," she said. "Very much too bad that the corset was spoiled. What are you doing here in this country?"

"I'm buying textiles. At least, I was, and now I'm just taking a little vacation here until the next boat leaves for the United States. I kind of miss my family and I'm anxious to get back. I don't see what you're supposed to get out of traveling."

"Oh, yes, yes. Surely you do," said Señorita Córdoba politely. "Now if you will excuse me I am going inside to do a little drawing. I must not forget how in this peasant land."

"What are you, an artist?" he asked.

"I draw dresses." She disappeared.

"Oh, God!" thought the traveler after she had left. "Here I am, left alone, and I'm not sleepy yet. This empty patio is so barren and so uninteresting, and as far as Señorita Córdoba is concerned, she's an iceberg. I like her neck though. She has a neck like a swan, so long and white and slender, the kind of neck you dream about girls having. But she's more like a virgin than a swan." He turned around and noticed that Señora Ramirez was still sitting in her chair. He picked up his own chair and carried it over next to hers.

"Do you mind?" he asked. "I see that you've decided to take a little night air. It isn't a bad idea. I don't feel like going to bed much either."

"No," she said. "I don't want to go to bed. I will sit here. I like to sit out at night, if I am warmly enough dressed, and look up at the stars."

"Yes, it's a great source of peace," the traveler said. "People don't do enough of it these days."

"Would you not like very much to go to Italy?" Señora Ramirez asked him. "The fruit trees and the flowers will be wonderful there at night."

"Well, you've got enough fruit and flowers here, I should say. What do you want to go to Italy for? I'll bet there isn't as much variety in the fruit there as here."

"No? Do you have many flowers in your country?"

The traveler was not able to decide.

"I would like really," continued Señora Ramirez, "to be somewhere else – in your country or in Italy. I would like to be somewhere where the life is beautiful. I care very much whether life is beautiful or ugly. People who live here don't care very much. Because they do not think." She touched her finger to her forehead. "I love beautiful things: beautiful houses, beautiful gardens, beautiful songs. When I was a young girl I was truly wild with happiness – doing and thinking and running in and out. I was so happy that my mother was afraid I would fall and break my leg or have some kind of accident. She was a very religious woman, but when I was a young girl I could not remember to think about such a thing. I was up always every morning before anybody except the Indians, and every morning I would go to market with them to buy food for all the houses. For many years I was doing this. Even when I was very little. It was very easy for me to do anything. I loved to learn English. I had a professor and I used to get on my knees in front of my father that the professor would stay longer with me every day. I was walking in the parks when my sisters were sleeping. My eyes were so big." She made a circle with two fingers. "And shiny like two diamonds, I was so excited all the time." She churned the air with her clenched fist. "Like this," she said. "Like a storm. My sisters called me wild Sofía. At the same time they were calling me wild Sofía, I was in love with my uncle, Aldo Torres. He never came much to the house before, but I heard my mother say that he had no more money and we would feed him. We were very rich and getting richer every year. I felt very sorry for him and was thinking about him all the time. We fell in love with each other and were kissing and hugging each other when nobody was there who could see us. I would have lived with him in a grass hut. He married a woman who had a little money, who also loved him very much. When he was married he got fat and started joking a lot with my father. I was glad for him that he was richer but pretty sad for myself. Then my sister Juanita, the oldest, married a very rich man. We were all very happy about her and there was a very big wedding."

"You must have been brokenhearted, though, about your uncle Aldo Torres going off with someone else, when you had befriended him so much when he was poor."

"Oh, I liked him very much," she said. Her memory seemed suddenly to have failed her and she did not appear to be interested in speaking any longer of the past. The traveler felt disturbed.

"I would love to travel," she continued, "very, very much, and I think it would be very nice to have the life of an actress, without children. You know it is my nature to love men and kissing."

"Well," said the traveler, "nobody gets as much kissing as they would like to get. Most people are frustrated. You'd be surprised at the number of people in my country who are frustrated and good-looking at the same time."

She turned her face toward his. The one little light bulb shed just enough light to enable him to see into her beautiful eyes. The tears were still wet on her lashes and they magnified her eyes to such an extent that they appeared to be almost twice their normal size. While she was looking at him she caught her breath.

"Oh, my darling man," she said to him suddenly. "I don't want to be separated from you. Let's go where I can hold you in my arms." The traveler was feeling excited. She had taken hold of his hand and was crushing it very hard.

"Where do you want to go?" he asked stupidly.

"Into your bed." She closed her eyes and waited for him to answer.

"All right. Are you sure?"

She nodded her head vigorously.

"This," he said to himself, "is undoubtedly one of those things that you don't want to remember next morning. I'll want to shake it off like a dog shaking water off its back. But what can I do? It's too far along now. I'll be going home soon and the whole thing will be just a soap bubble among many other soap bubbles."

He was beginning to feel inspired and he could not understand it, because he had not been drinking.

"A soap bubble among many other soap bubbles," he repeated to himself. His inner life was undefined but well controlled as a rule. Together they went into his room.

"Ah," said Señora Ramirez after he had closed the door behind them, "this makes me happy."

She fell onto the bed sideways, like a beaten person. Her feet stuck out into the air, and her heavy breathing filled the room. He realized that he had never before seen a person behave in this manner unless sodden with alcohol, and he did not know what to do. According to all his standards and the standards of his friends she was not a pleasant thing to lie beside.

She was unfastening her dress at the neck. The brooch with which she pinned her collar together she stuck into the pillow behind her.

"So much fat," she said. "So much fat." She was smiling at him very tenderly. This for some reason excited him, and he took off his own clothing and got into bed beside her. He was as cold as a clam and very bony, but being a truly passionate woman she did not notice any of that.

"Do you really want to go through with this?" he said to her, for he was incapable of finding new words for a situation that was certainly unlike any other he had ever experienced. She fell upon him and felt his face and his neck with feverish excitement.

"Dear God!" she said. "Dear God!" They were in the very act of making love. "I have lived twenty years for this moment and I cannot think that heaven itself could be more wonderful."

The traveler hardly listened to this remark. His face was hidden in the pillow and he was feeling the pangs of guilt in the very midst of his pleasure. When it was all over she said to him: "That is all I want to do ever." She patted his hands and smiled at him.

"Are you happy, too?" she asked him.

"Yes, indeed," he said. He got off the bed and went out into the patio.

"She was certainly in a bad way," he thought. "It was almost like death itself." He didn't want to think any further. He stayed outside near the fountain as long as possible. When he returned she was up in front of the bureau trying to arrange her hair.

"I'm ashamed of the way I look," she said. "I don't look the way I feel." She laughed and he told her that she looked perfectly all right. She drew him down onto the bed again. "Don't send me back to my room," she said. "I love to be here with you, my sweetheart."

The dawn was breaking when the traveler awakened next morning. Señora Ramirez was still beside him, sleeping very soundly. Her arm was flung over the pillow behind her head.

"Lordy," said the traveler to himself. "I'd better get her out of here." He shook her as hard as he could.

"Mrs Ramirez," he said. "Mrs Ramirez, wake up. Wake up!" When she finally did wake up, she looked frightened to death. She turned and stared at him blankly for a little while. Before he noticed any change in her expression, her hand was already moving over his body.

"Mrs Ramirez," he said. "I'm worried that perhaps your daughters will get up and raise a hullabaloo. You know, start whining for you, or something like that. Your place is probably in there."

"What?" she asked him. He had pulled away from her to the other side of the bed.

"I say I think you ought to go into your room now the morning's here."

"Yes, my darling, I will go to my room. You are right." She sidled over to him and put her arms around him.

"I will see you later in the dining room, and look at you and look at you, because I love you so much."

"Don't be crazy," he said. "You don't want anything to show in your face. You don't want people to guess about this. We must be cold with one another."

She put her hand over her heart.

"Ay!" she said. "This cannot be."

"Oh, Mrs Ramirez. Please be sensible. Look, you go to your room and we'll talk about this in the morning ... or, at least, later in the morning."

"Cold I cannot be." To illustrate this, she looked deep into his eyes.

"I know, I know," he said. "You're a very passionate woman. But my God! Here we are in a crazy Spanish country."

He jumped from the bed and she followed him. After she had put on her shoes, he took her to the door.

"Good-bye," he said.

She couched her cheek on her two hands and looked up at him. He shut the door.

She was too happy to go right to bed, and so she went over to the bureau and took from it a little stale sugar Virgin which she broke into three pieces. She went over to Consuelo and shook her very hard. Consuelo opened her eyes, and after some time asked her mother crossly what she wanted. Señora Ramirez stuffed the candy into her daughter's mouth.

"Eat it, darling," she said. "It's the little Virgin from the bureau."

"Ay, mamá!" Consuelo sighed. "Who knows what you will do next? It is already light out and you are still in your clothes. I am sure there is no other mother who is still in her clothes now, in the whole world. Please don't make me eat any more of the Virgin now. Tomorrow I will eat some more. But it is tomorrow, isn't it? What a mix-up. I don't like it." She shut her eyes and tried to sleep. There was a look of deep disgust on her face. Her mother's spell was a little frightening this time.

Señora Ramirez now went over to Lilina's bed and awakened her. Lilina opened her eyes wide and immediately looked very tense, because she thought she was going to be scolded about the corset and also about having gone out alone after dark.

"Here, little one," said her mother. "Eat some of the Virgin."

Lilina was delighted. She ate the stale sugar candy and patted her stomach to show how pleased she was. The snake was asleep in a box near her bed.

"Now tell me," said her mother. "What did you do today?" She had completely forgotten about the corset. Lilina was beside herself with joy. She ran her fingers along her mother's lips and then pushed them into her mouth. Señora Ramirez snapped at the fingers like a dog. Then she laughed uproariously.

"Mamá, please be quiet," pleaded Consuelo. "I want to go to sleep."

"Yes, darling. Everything will be quiet so that you can sleep peacefully."

"I bought a snake, mamá," said Lilina.

"Good!" exclaimed Señora Ramirez. And after musing a little while with her daughter's hand in hers, she went to bed.

◆ ◆ ◆

In her room Señora Ramirez was dressing and talking to her children.

"I want you to put on your fiesta dresses," she said, "because I am going to ask the traveler to have lunch with us."

Consuelo was in love with the traveler by now and very jealous of Señorita Córdoba, who she had decided was his sweetheart. "I daresay he has already asked Señorita Córdoba to lunch," she said. "They have been talking together near the fountain almost since dawn."

"*Santa Catarina!*" cried her mother angrily. "You have the eyes of a madman who sees flowers where there are only cow turds." She covered her face heavily with a powder that was distinctly violet in tint, and pulled a green chiffon scarf around her shoulders, pinning it together with a brooch in the form of a golf club. Then she and the girls, who were dressed in pink satin, went out into the patio and sat together just a little out of the sun. The parrot was swinging back and forth on his perch and singing. Señora Ramirez sang along with him; her own voice was a little lower than the parrot's.

Pastores, pastores, vamos a Belén!'

A ver a María y al niño también.

She conducted the parrot with her hand. The old señora, mother of Señora Espinoza, was walking round and round the patio. She stopped for a moment and played with Señora Ramirez's seashell bracelet.

"Do you want some candy?" she asked Señora Ramirez.

"I can't. My stomach is very bad."

"Do you want some candy?" she repeated. Señora Ramirez smiled and looked up at the sky. The old lady patted her cheek.

"Beautiful," she said. "You are beautiful."

"Mamá!" screamed Señora Espinoza, running out of her room. "Come to bed!"

The old lady clung to the rungs of Señora Ramirez's chair like a tough bird, and her daughter was obliged to pry her hands open before she was able to get her away.

"I'm sorry, Señora Ramirez," she said. "But when you get old, you know how it is."

"Pretty bad," said Señora Ramirez. She was looking at the traveler and Señorita Córdoba. They had their backs turned to her.

"Lilina," she said. "Go and ask him to have lunch with us ... go. No, I will write it down. Get me a pen and paper."

"Dear," she wrote, when Lilina returned. "Will you come to have lunch at my table this afternoon? The girls will be with me, too. All the three of us send you our deep affection. I tell Consuelo to tell the maid to move the plates all to the same table. Very truly yours, Sofía Piega de Ramirez."

The traveler read the note, acquiesced, and shortly they were all seated together at the dining-room table.

"Now this is really stranger than fiction," he said to himself. "Here I am sitting with these people at their table and feeling as though I had been here all my life, and the truth of the matter is that I have only been in this pension about fourteen or fifteen hours altogether – not even one day. Yesterday I felt that I was on a Zulu island, I was so depressed. The human animal is the funniest animal of them all."

Señora Ramirez had arranged to sit close beside the stranger, and she pressed her thigh to his all during the time that she was eating her soup. The traveler's appetite was not very good. He was excited and felt like talking.

After lunch Señora Ramirez decided to go for a walk instead of taking a siesta with her daughters. She put on her gloves and took with her an umbrella to shield her from the sun. After she had walked a little while she came to a long road, completely desolate save for a few ruins and some beautiful tall trees along the way. She looked about her and shook her head at the thought of the terrible earthquake that had thrown to the ground this city, reputed to have been once the most beautiful city in all the Western Hemisphere. She could see ahead of her, way at the road's end, the volcano named Fire. She crossed herself and bit her lips. She had come walking with the intention of dreaming of her lover, but the thought of this volcano which had erupted many centuries ago chased all dreams of love from her mind. She saw in her mind the walls of the houses caving in, and the roofs falling on the heads of the babies ... and the mothers, their skirts covered with mud, running through the streets in despair.

"The innocents," she said to herself. "I am sure that God had a perfect reason for this, but what could it have been? Santa María, but what could it have been! If such a disorder should happen again on this earth, I would turn completely to jelly like a helpless idiot."

She looked again at the volcano ahead of her, and although nothing had changed, to her it seemed that a cloud had passed across the face of the sun.

"You are crazy," she went on, "to think that an earthquake will again shake this city to the earth. You will not be going through such a trial as these other mothers went through, because everything now is different. God doesn't send such big trials any more, like floods over the whole world, and plagues."

She thanked her stars that she was living now and not before. It made her feel quite weak to think of the women who had been forced to live before she was born. The future too, she had heard, was to be very stormy because of wars.

"Ay!" she said to herself. "Precipices on all sides of me!" It had not been such a good idea to take a walk, after all. She thought again of the traveler, shutting her eyes for a moment.

"*Mi amante! Amante querido!*" she whispered; and she remembered the little books with their covers lettered in gold, books about love, which she had read when she was a young girl, and without the burden of a family. These little books had made the ability to read seem like the most worthwhile and delightful talent to her. They had never, of course, touched on the coarser aspects of love, but in later years she did not find it strange that it was for such physical ends that the heroes and heroines had been pining. Never had she found any difficulty in associating nosegays and couplets with the more gross manifestations of love.

She turned off into another road in order to avoid facing the volcano, constantly ahead of her. She thought of the traveler without really thinking of him at all. Her eyes glowed with the pleasure of being in love and she decided that she had been very stupid to think of an earthquake on the very day that God was making a bed of roses for her.

"Thank you, thank you," she whispered to Him, "from the bottom of my heart. Ah!" She smoothed her dress over her bosom. She was suddenly very pleased with everything. Ahead she noticed that there was a very long convent, somewhat ruined, in front of which some boys were playing. There was also a little pavilion standing not far away. It was difficult to understand why it was so situated, where there was no formal park, nor any trees or grass – just some dirt and a few bushes. It had the strange static look of a ship that has been grounded. Señora Ramirez looked at it distastefully; it was a small kiosk anyway and badly in need of a coat of paint. But feeling tired, she was soon climbing up the flimsy steps, red in the face with fear lest she fall through to the ground. Inside the kiosk she spread a newspaper over the bench and sat down. Soon all her dreams of her lover faded from her mind, and she felt hot and fretful. She moved her feet around on the floor impatiently at the thought of having to walk all the way home. The dust rose up into the air and she was obliged to cover her mouth with her handkerchief.

"I wish to heaven," she said to herself, "that he would come and carry me out of this kiosk." She sat idly watching the boys playing in the dirt in front of the convent. One of them was a good deal taller than the others. As she watched their games, her head slumped forward and she fell asleep.

No tourists came, so the smaller boys decided to go over to the main square and meet the buses, to sell their lollipops and picture postcards. The oldest boy announced that he would stay behind.

"You're crazy," they said to him. "Completely crazy."

He looked at them haughtily and did not answer. They ran down the road, screaming that they were going to earn a thousand *quetzales*.

He had remained behind because for some time he had noticed that there was someone in the kiosk. He knew even from where he stood that it was a woman because he could see that her dress was brightly colored like a flower garden. She had been sitting there for a long time and he wondered if she were not dead.

"If she is dead," he thought, "I will carry her body all the way into town." The idea excited him and he approached the pavilion with bated breath. He went inside and stood over Señora Ramirez, but when he saw that she was quite old and fat and obviously the mother of a good rich family he was frightened and all his imagination failed him. He thought he would go away, but then he decided differently, and he shook her foot. There was no change. Her mouth, which had been open, remained so, and she went on sleeping. The boy took a good piece of the flesh on her upper arm between his thumb and forefinger and twisted it very hard. She awakened with a shudder and looked up at the boy, perplexed.

His eyes were soft.

"I awakened you," he said, "because I have to go home to my house, and you are not safe here. Before, there was a man here in the bandstand trying to look under your skirt. When you are asleep, you know, people just go wild. There were some drunks here too, singing an obscene song, standing on the ground, right under you. You would have had red ears if you had heard it. I can tell you that." He shrugged his shoulders and spat on the floor. He looked completely disgusted.

"What is the matter?" Señora Ramirez asked him.

"Bah! This city makes me sick. I want to be a carpenter in the capital, but I can't. My mother gets lonesome. All my brothers and sisters are dead."

"Ay!" said Señora Ramirez. "How sad for you! I have a beautiful house in the capital. Maybe my husband would let you be a carpenter there, if you did not have to stay with your mother."

The boy's eyes were shining.

"I'm coming back with you," he said. "My uncle is with my mother."

"Yes," said Señora Ramirez. "Maybe it will happen."

"My sweetheart is there in the city," he continued. "She was living here before."

Señora Ramirez took the boy's long hand in her own. The word sweetheart had recalled many things to her.

"Sit down, sit down," she said to him. "Sit down here beside me. I too have a sweetheart. He's in his room now."

"Where does he work?"

"In the United States."

"What luck for you! My sweetheart wouldn't love him better than she loves me, though. She wants me or simply death. She says so any time I ask her. She would tell the same thing to you if you asked her about me. It's the truth."

Señora Ramirez pulled him down onto the bench next to her. He was confused and looked out over his shoulder at the road. She tickled the back of his hand and smiled up at him in a coquettish manner. The boy looked at her and his face seemed to weaken.

"You have blue eyes," he said.

Señora Ramirez could not wait another minute. She took his head in her two hands and kissed him several times full on the mouth.

"Oh, God!" she said. The boy was delighted with her fine clothes, her blue eyes, and her womanly ways. He took Se'lora Ramirez in his arms with real tenderness.

"I love you," he said. Tears filled his eyes, and because he was so full of a feeling of gratitude and kindness, he added: "I love my sweetheart and I love you too."

He helped her down the steps of the kiosk, and with his arm around her waist he led her to a sequestered spot belonging to the convent grounds.

◆ ◆ ◆

The traveler was lying on his bed, consumed by a feeling of guilt. He had again spent the night with Señora Ramirez, and he was wondering whether or not his mother would read this in his eyes when he returned. He had never done anything like this before. His behavior until now had never been without precedent, and he felt like a two-headed monster, as though he had somehow slipped from the real world into the other world, the world that he had always imagined as a little boy to be inhabited by assassins and orphans, and children whose mothers went to work. He put his head in his hands and wondered if he could ever forget Señora Ramirez. He remembered having read that the careers of many men had been ruined by women who because they had a certain physical stranglehold over them made it impossible for them to get away. These women, he knew, were always bad, and they were never Americans. Nor, he was certain, did they resemble Señora Ramirez. It was terrible to have done something he was certain none of his friends had ever done before him, nor would do after him. This experience, he knew, would have to remain a secret, and nothing made him feel more ill than having a secret. He liked to imagine that he and the group of men whom he considered to be his friends, discoursed freely on all things that were in their hearts and in their souls. He was beginning to talk to women in this free way, too – he talked to them a good deal, and he urged his friends to do likewise. He realized that he and Señora Ramirez never spoke, and this horrified him. He shuddered and said to himself: "We are like two gorillas."

He had been, it is true, with one or two prostitutes, but he had never taken them to his own bed, nor had he stayed with them longer than an hour. Also, they had been curly-headed blonde American girls recommended to him by his friends.

"Well," he told himself, "there is no use making myself into a nervous wreck. What is done is done, and anyway, I think I might be excused on the grounds that: one, I am in a foreign country, which has sort of put me off my balance; two, I have been eating strange foods that I am not used to, and living at an unusually high altitude for me; and, three, I haven't had my own kind to talk to for three solid weeks."

He felt quite a good deal happier after having enumerated these extenuating conditions, and he added: "When I get onto my boat I shall wave good-bye to the dock, and say good riddance to bad rubbish, and if the boss ever tries to send me out of the country, I'll tell him: 'not for a million dollars!' " He wished that it were possible to change pensions, but he had already paid for the remainder of the week. He was very thrifty, as, indeed, it was necessary for him to be. Now he lay down again on his bed, quite satisfied with himself, but soon he began to feel guilty again, and like an old truck horse, laboriously he went once more through the entire process of reassuring himself.

◆ ◆ ◆

Lilina had put Victoria into a box and was walking in the town with her. Not far from the central square there was a dry-goods shop owned by a Jewish woman. Lilina had been there several times with her mother to buy wool. She knew the son of the proprietress, with whom she often stopped to talk. He was very quiet, but Lilina liked him. She decided to drop in at the shop now with Victoria.

When she arrived, the boy's mother was behind the counter stamping some old bolts of material with purple ink. She saw Lilina and smiled brightly.

"Enrique is in the patio. How nice of you to come and see him. Why don't you come more often?" She was very eager to please Lilina, because she knew the extent of Señora Ramirez's wealth and was proud to have her as a customer.

Lilina went over to the little door that led into the patio behind the shop, and opened it. Enrique was crouching in the dirt beside the washtubs. She was surprised to see that his head was wrapped in bandages. From a distance the dirty bandages gave the effect of a white turban.

She went a little nearer, and saw that he was arranging some marbles in a row.

"Good morning, Enrique," she said to him.

Enrique recognized her voice, and without turning his head, he started slowly to pick up the marbles one at a time and put them into his pocket.

His mother had followed Lilina into the patio. When she saw that Enrique, instead of rising to his feet and greeting Lilina, remained absorbed in his marbles, she walked over to him and gave his arm a sharp twist.

"Leave those damned marbles alone and speak to Lilina," she said to him. Enrique got up and went over to Lilina, while his mother, bending over with difficulty, finished picking up the marbles he had left behind on the ground.

Lilina looked at the big, dark red stain on Enrique's bandage. They both walked back into the store. Enrique did not enjoy being with Lilina. In fact, he was a little afraid of her. Whenever she came to the shop he could hardly wait for her to leave.

He went over now to a bolt of printed material which he started to unwind. When he had unwound a few yards, he began to follow the convolutions of the pattern with his index finger. Lilina, not realizing that his gesture was a carefully disguised insult to her, watched him with a certain amount of interest.

"I have something with me inside this box," she said after a while.

Enrique, hearing his mother's footsteps approaching, turned and smiled at her sadly.

"Please show it to me," he said.

She lifted the lid from the snake's box and took it over to Enrique.

"This is Victoria," she said.

Enrique thought she was beautiful. He lifted her from her box and held her just below the head very firmly. Then he raised his arm until the snake's eyes were on a level with his own.

"Good morning, Victoria," he said to her. "Do you like it here in the store?"

This remark annoyed his mother. She had slipped down to the other end of the counter because she was terrified of the snake.

"You speak as though you were drunk," she said to Enrique. "That snake can't understand a word you're saying."

"She's really beautiful," said Enrique.

"Let's put her back in the box and take her to the square," said Lilina. But Enrique did not hear her, he was so enchanted with the sensation of holding Victoria.

His mother again spoke up. "Do you hear Lilina talking to you?" she shouted. "Or is that bandage covering your ears as well as your head?"

She had meant this remark to be stinging and witty, but she realized herself that there had been no point to it.

"Well, go with the little girl," she added.

Lilina and Enrique set off toward the square together. Lilina had put Victoria back into her box.

"Why are we going to the square?" Enrique asked Lilina.

"Because we are going there with Victoria."

Six or seven buses had converged in one of the streets that skirted the square. They had come from the capital and from other smaller cities in the region. The passengers who were not going any farther had already got out and were standing in a bunch talking together and buying food from the vendors. One lady had brought with her a cardboard fan intended as an advertisement for beer. She was fanning not only herself, but anyone who happened to come near her.

The bus drivers were racing their motors, and some were trying to move into positions more advantageous for departing. Lilina was excited by the noise and the crowd. Enrique, however, had sought a quiet spot, and was now standing underneath a tree. After a while she ran over to him and told him that she was going to let Victoria out of her box.

"Then we'll see what happens," she said.

"No, no!" insisted Enrique. "She'll only crawl under the buses and be squashed to death. Snakes live in the woods or in the rocks."

Lilina paid little attention to him. Soon she was crouching on the edge of the curbstone, busily unfastening the string around Victoria's box.

Enrique's head had begun to pain him and he felt a little ill. He wondered if he could leave the square, but he decided he did not have the courage. Although the wind had risen, the sun was very hot, and the tree afforded him little shade. He watched Lilina for a little while, but soon he looked away from her, and began to think instead about his own death. He was certain that his head hurt more today than usual. This caused him to sink into the blackest gloom, as he did whenever he remembered the day he had fallen and pierced his skull on a rusty nail. His life had always been precious to him, as far back as he could recall, and it seemed perhaps even more so now that he realized it could be violently interrupted. He disliked Lilina; probably because he suspected intuitively that she was a person who could fall over and over again into the same pile of broken glass and scream just as loudly the last time as the first.

By now Victoria had wriggled under the buses and been crushed flat. The buses cleared away, and Enrique was able to see what had happened. Only the snake's head, which had been severed from its body, remained intact.

Enrique came up and stood beside Lilina. "Now are you going home?" he asked her, biting his lip.

"Look how small her head is. She must have been a very small snake," said Lilina.

"Are you going home to your house?" he asked her again.

"No. I'm going over by the cathedral and play on the swings. Do you want to come? I'm going to run there."

"I can't run," said Enrique, touching his fingers to the bandages. "And I'm not sure that I want to go over to the playground."

"Well," said Lilina. "I'll run ahead of you and I'll be there if you decide to come."

Enrique was very tired and a little dizzy, but he decided to follow her to the playground in order to ask her why she had allowed Victoria to escape under the buses.

When he arrived, Lilina was already swinging back and forth. He sat on a bench near the swings and looked up at her. Each time her feet grazed the ground, he tried to ask her about Victoria, but the question stuck in his throat. At last he stood up, thrust his hands into his pockets, and shouted at her.

"Are you going to get another snake?" he asked. It was not what he had intended to say. Lilina did not answer, but she did stare at him from the swing. It was impossible for him to tell whether or not she had heard his question.

At last she dug her heel into the ground and brought the swing to a standstill. "I must go home," she said, "or my mother will be angry with me."

"No," said Enrique, catching hold of her dress. "Come with me and let me buy you an ice."

"I will," said Lilina. "I love them."

They sat together in a little store, and Enrique bought two ices.

"I'd like to have a swing hanging from the roof of my house," said Lilina. "And I'd have my dinner and my breakfast served while I was swinging." This idea amused her and she began to laugh so hard that her ice ran out of her mouth and over her chin.

"Breakfast, lunch, and dinner and take a bath in the swing," she continued. "And make *pipi* on Consuelo's head from the swing."

Enrique was growing more and more nervous because it was getting late, and still they were not talking about Victoria.

"Could I swing with you in your house?" he asked Lilina.

"Yes. We'll have two swings and you can make *pipi* on Consuelo's head, too."

"I'd love to," he said.

His question seemed more and more difficult to present. By now it seemed to him that it resembled more a declaration of love than a simple question.

Finally he tried again. "Are you going to buy another snake?" But he still could not ask her why she had been so careless.

"No," said Lilina. "I'm going to buy a rabbit."

"A rabbit?" he said. "But rabbits aren't as intelligent or as beautiful as snakes. You had better buy another snake like Victoria."

"Rabbits have lots of children," said Lilina. "Why don't we buy a rabbit together?"

Enrique thought about this for a while. He began to feel almost lighthearted, and even a little wicked.

"All right," he said. "Let's buy two rabbits, a man and a woman." They finished their ices and talked together more and more excitedly about the rabbits.

On the way home, Lilina squeezed Enrique's hand and kissed him all over his cheeks. He was red with pleasure.

At the square they parted, after promising to meet again that afternoon.

◆ ◆ ◆

It was a cloudy day, rather colder than usual, and Señora Ramirez decided to dress in her mourning clothes, which she always carried with her. She hung several strands of black beads around her neck and powdered her face heavily. She and Consuelo began to walk slowly around the patio.

Consuelo blew her nose. "Ay, mamá," she said. "Isn't it true that there is a greater amount of sadness in the world than happiness?"

"I don't know why you are thinking about this," said her mother.

"Because I have been counting my happy days and my sad days. There are many more sad days, and I am living now at the best age for a girl. There is nothing but fighting, even at balls. I would not believe any man if he told me he liked dancing better than fighting."

"This is true," said her mother. "But not all men are really like this. There are some men who are as gentle as little lambs. But not so many."

"I feel like an old lady. I think that maybe I will feel better when I'm married." They walked slowly past the traveler's door.

"I'm going inside," said Consuelo suddenly.

"Aren't you going to sit in the patio?" her mother asked her.

"No, with all those children screaming and the chickens and the parrot talking and the white dog. And it's such a terrible day. Why?"

Señora Ramirez could not think of any reason why Consuelo should stay in the patio. In any case she preferred to be there alone if the stranger should decide to talk to her.

"What white dog?" she said.

"Señora Espinoza has bought a little white dog for the children."

The wind was blowing and the children were chasing each other around the back patio. Señora Ramirez sat down on one of the little straight-backed chairs with her hands folded in her lap. The thought came into her mind that most days were likely to be cold and windy rather than otherwise, and that there would be many days to come exactly like this one. Unconsciously she had always felt that these were the days preferred by God, although they had never been much to her own liking.

The traveler was packing with the vivacity of one who is in the habit of making little excursions away from the charmed fold to return almost immediately.

"Wow!" he said joyfully to himself. "I sure have been giddy in this place, but the bad dream is over now." It was nearly bus time. He carried his bags out to the patio, and was confused to find Señora Ramirez sitting there. He prompted himself to be pleasant.

"Señora," he said, walking over to her. "It's good-bye now till we meet again."

"What do you say?" she asked.

"I'm taking the twelve o'clock bus. I'm going home."

"Ah! You must be very happy to go home." She did not think of looking away from his face. "Do you take a boat?" she asked, staring harder.

"Yes. Five days on the boat."

"How wonderful that must be. Or maybe it makes you sick." She put her hand over her stomach.

"I have never been seasick in my life."

She said nothing to this.

He backed against the parrot swinging on its perch, and stepped forward again quickly as it leaned to bite him.

"Is there anyone you would like me to look up in the United States?"

"No. You will be coming back in not such a long time?"

"No. I don't think I will come back here again. Well ..." He put out his hand and she stood up. She was fairly impressive in her black clothes. He looked at the beads that covered her chest.

"Well, good-bye, señora. I was very happy to have met you."

"*Adios*, señor, and may God protect you on your trip. You will be coming back maybe. You don't know."

He shook his head and walked over to the Indian boy standing by his luggage. They went out into the street and the heavy door closed with a bang. Señora Ramirez looked around the patio. She saw Señorita Córdoba move away from the half-open bedroom door where she had been standing.

'A Guatemalan Idyll' was the original beginning of *Three Serious Ladies*. It was first published as a stand-alone story in *Cross Section 1944: A Collection of New American Writing* (1944). Jane later turned the story into a play, entitled 'Once by Fire', though this was never staged.

A Day in the Open

IN THE OUTSKIRTS OF THE CAPITAL there was a low white house, very much like the other houses around it. The street on which it stood was not paved, as this was a poor section of the city. The door of this particular house, very new and studded with nails, was bolted inside and out. A large room, furnished with some modern chromium chairs, a bar, and an electric record machine, opened onto the empty patio. A fat little Indian boy was seated in one of the chairs, listening to the tune 'Good Night, Sweetheart', which he had just chosen. It was playing at full volume and the little boy was staring very seriously ahead of him at the machine. This was one of the houses owned and run by Señor Kurten, who was half Spanish and half German.

It was a gray afternoon. In one of the bedrooms Julia and Inez had just awakened. Julia was small and monkey-like. She was appealing only because of her extraordinarily large and luminous eyes. Inez was tall and high-breasted. Her head was a bit too small for her body and her eyes were too close together. She wore her hair in stiff waves.

Julia was moaning on her bed.

"My stomach is worse today," she said to Inez. "Come over and feel it. The lump on the right side is bigger." She twisted her head on the pillow and sighed. Inez was staring sternly into space.

"No," she said to Julia. "I cannot bear to feel that lump. *Santa María!* With something like that inside me I should go wild." She made a wry face and shuddered.

"You must not feel it if you do not want to," said Julia drowsily. Inez poured herself some *guaro*. She was a heavy drinker but her vitality remained unimpaired, although her skin often broke out in pimples. She ate violet lozenges to cover the smell of liquor on her breath and often popped six or seven of them into her mouth at once. Being full of enterprise she often made more money outside the whorehouse than she did at her regular job.

Julia was Mexican and a great favorite with the men, who enjoyed feeling that they were endangering her very life by going to bed with her.

"Well," said Inez, "I think that this afternoon I will go to the movies, if you will lend me a pair of your stockings. You had better lie here in your bed. I would sit here with you but it makes me feel very strange now to stay in this room. It is peculiar because, you know, I am a very calm woman and have suffered a great deal since I was born. You should go to a doctor," she added.

"I cannot bear to be out in the street," said Julia. "The sun is too hot and the wind is too cold. The smell of the market makes me feel sick, although I have known it all my life. No sooner have I walked a few blocks than I must find some park to sit in, I am so tired. Then somebody comes and tries to sell me orchids and I buy them. I have been out three times this week and each time I have bought some flowers. Now you know I can't afford to do this, but I am so weak and ill that I am becoming more like my grandmother every day. She had a feeling that she was not wanted here on this earth, either by God or by other people, so she never felt that she could refuse anyone anything."

"Well, if you are going to become like your grandmother," said Inez, "it will be a sad mistake. I should forget this sort of thing. You'll get to the doctor. Meanwhile, sit in the sun more. I don't want to be unkind ..."

"No, no. You are not unkind," Julia protested.

"You sit in this dark room all day long even when there is sun and you do not feel so sick."

Julia was feeling more desperately lonely than she had ever felt before in her life. She patted her heart. Suddenly the door pushed open and Señor Kurten came into the room. He was a slight man with a low forehead and a long nose.

"Julia and Inez," he said. "Señor Ramirez just telephoned that he is coming over this afternoon with a friend. He is going to take you both out to the country on a picnic and you are to hurry up and be ready. Try to bring them back to the bar in the evening."

"Hans," said Julia. "I am sick. I can't see Señor Ramirez or anyone else."

"Well, you know I can't do anything if he wants to see you. If he was angry he could make too much trouble. I am sorry." Señor Kurten left the room, closing the door slowly behind him.

"He is so important," said Inez, rubbing some eau de cologne over Julia's forehead. "So important, poor child. You must go." Her hand was hard and dry.

"Inez—" Julia clutched at Inez's kimono just as she was walking away. She struggled out of bed and threw herself into the arms of her friend. Inez was obliged to brace herself against the foot of the bed to keep from being knocked over.

"Don't make yourself crazy," said Inez to Julia, but then Inez began to cry; the sound was high like the squeal of a pig.

"Inez," said Julia. "Get dressed and don't cry. I feel better, my little baby."

They went into the bar and sat down to await the arrival of Señor Ramirez and his friend. Julia's arm was flung over the side of the chair, and her purse was swinging from her hand on an unusually long strap. She had put a little red dot in the corner of each eye, and rouged her cheeks very highly.

"You don't look very good," said Inez. "I'm afraid in my heart for you."

Julia opened her eyes wide and stared fixedly ahead of her at the wall. The Indian boy was polishing a very large alarm clock with care.

Soon Señor Ramirez stuck his head through the doorway. He had a German face but there was something very Spanish in the angle of his slouched fedora hat. His mustaches were blond and abundant. He had just shaved, and the talcum powder was visible on his chin and on his cheeks. He wore a pink shirt and a light tweed jacket, and on the fourth finger of each hand a heavy gold ring studded with a jewel.

"Come on, daughters," he said. "The car is waiting outside, with my friend. Move along."

Señor Ramirez drove very quickly. Julia and Inez sat uncomfortably on the edge of the back seat, hanging onto the straps at the side.

"We are going on a picnic," shouted Señor Ramirez. "I've brought with me five bottles of champagne. They are in the back of the car and they were all packed in ice by my cook. There is no reason why we should not have everything we want with us. They are inside a basket in the back. She wrapped the ice in a towel. That way it doesn't melt so quickly, but still we have to get there in a pretty short time. I drink nothing but American whiskey, so I brought along a quart of it for myself. What do you think of that?"

"Oh, how nice," said Julia.

"I think we shall have a wonderful time," said Inez.

Señor Ramirez's friend Alfredo looked ill and disgruntled. He did not say anything himself, nor did the angle of his head indicate that he was listening to a word that anyone else was saying. It was a cold day and the parasols under which the policemen stood were flapping in the wind. They passed a new yellow brick building, high at the top of six or seven flights of yellow brick steps.

"That is going to be a new museum," said Señor Ramirez. "When it opens we are all going to have a big dinner there together. Everyone there will be an old friend of mine. That's nothing. I can have dinner with fifty people every night of my life."

"A life of fiesta," put in Inez.

"Even more than that. They are more than just fiestas," he said, without quite knowing what he meant himself.

The sun was shining into Julia's lap. She felt lightheaded and feverish. Señor Ramirez turned the radio on as loud as he could. They were broadcasting *Madame Butterfly* as the car reached the outskirts of the city.

"I have three radios at home," said Señor Ramirez.

"Ah," said Inez. "One for the morning, one for the night and one for the afternoon." Julia listened to Inez with interest and wonder. They were on the edge of a deep ravine, going round a curve in the road. The mountainside across the ravine was in the shade, and some Indians were climbing toward the summit.

"Walk, walk, walk ..." said Julia mournfully. "Oh, how tired it makes me feel to watch them."

Inez pinched her friend's arm. "Listen," she whispered to her. "You are not in your room. You daren't say things like that. You must not speak of being tired. It's no fun for them. They wouldn't like it."

"We'll be coming to that picnic spot in a minute," said Señor Ramirez. "Nobody knows where it is but me. I like to have a spot, you know, where all my friends won't come and disturb me. Alfredo," he added, "are you hungry?"

"I don't think this Alfredo is very nice, do you?" Inez asked very softly of Julia.

"Oh, yes," said Julia, for she was not quick to detect a mean nature in anybody, being altogether kind and charitable herself. At last, after driving through a path wide enough for only one car, they arrived at the picnic spot. It was a fair-sized clearing in a little forest. Not far from it, at the bottom of a hill, was a little river and a waterfall. They got out and listened to the noise of the water. Both of the women were delighted with the sound.

"Since it is so sunny out, ladies," said Señor Ramirez, "I am going to walk around in my underpants. I hope that my friend will do the same if he wants to."

"What a lucky thing for us," said Inez in a strident voice. "The day begins right." Señor Ramirez undressed and slipped on a pair of tennis shoes. His legs were very white and freckled.

"Now I will give you some champagne right away," he said to them, a little out of breath because he had struggled so quickly out of his clothes. He went over to where he had laid the basket and took from it a champagne bottle. On his way back he stumbled over a rock; the bottle fell from his hand and was smashed in many pieces. For a moment his face clouded over and he looked as though he were about to lose his temper; instead, seizing another bottle from the basket, he flung it high into the air, almost over the tops of the trees. He returned elated to his friends.

"A gentleman," he said, "always knows how to make fun. I am one of the richest businessmen in this country. I am also the craziest. Like an American. When I am out I always have a wonderful time, and so does everyone who is with me, because they know that while I am around there is always plenty. Plenty to eat, plenty to drink, and plenty of beautiful women to make love to. Once you have been out with me," he pointed his finger at Julia and Inez, "any other man will seem to you like an old-lady schoolteacher."

He turned to Alfredo. "Tell me, my friend, have you not had the time of your life with me?"

"Yes, I have," said Alfredo. He was thinking very noticeably of other things.

"His mind is always on business," Señor Ramirez explained to Julia. "He is also very clever. I have gotten him this job with a German concern. They are manufacturing planes." Alfredo said something to Señor Ramirez in German, and they spoke no longer on the subject. They spread out their picnic lunch and sat down to eat.

Señor Ramirez insisted on feeding Julia with his own fingers. This rather vexed Inez, so she devoted herself to eating copiously. Señor Ramirez drank quantities of whiskey out of a tin folding cup. At the end of fifteen or twenty minutes he was already quite drunk.

"Now, isn't it wonderful to be all together like this, friends? Alfredo, aren't these two women the finest, sweetest women in the world? I do not understand why in the eyes of God they should be condemned to the fires of hell for what they are. Do you?"

Julia moaned and rose to her feet.

"No, no!" she said, looking up helplessly at the branches overhead.

"Come on," said Señor Ramirez. "We're not going to worry about this today, are we?" He took hold of her wrist and pulled her down to the ground beside him. Julia hid her face in her hands and leaned her head against his shoulder. Soon she was smiling up at him and stroking his face.

"You won't leave me alone?" she asked, laughing a little in an effort to bring him to terms with her. If anyone were to be pitted successfully against the Divine, she thought, it would certainly be someone like Señor Ramirez. The presence of such men is often enough to dispel fear from the hearts of certain people for whom God is more of an enemy than a friend. Señor Ramirez's principal struggle in life was one of pride rather than of conscience; and because his successes were numerous each day, replenishing his energy and his taste for life, his strength was easily felt by those around him. Now that he was near her,

Julia felt that she was safe from hell, and she was quite happy even though her side still hurt her very badly.

"Now," said Inez, "I think that we should all play a game, to chase gloomy thoughts out of this girl's head."

She rose to her feet and snatched Señor Ramirez's hat from where it lay beside him on the ground, placing it a few feet away upside down on the grass. Then she gathered some acorns in the picnic basket.

"Now," she said. "We will see who can throw these acorns into the hat. He will win."

"I think," said Señor Ramirez, "that the two women should be naked while we are playing this; otherwise it will be just a foolish children's game."

"And we are not children at all," said Inez, winking at him. The two women turned and looked at Alfredo questioningly.

"Oh, don't mind him," said Señor Ramirez. "He sees nothing but numbers in his head."

The two girls went behind some bushes and undressed. When they returned, Alfredo was bending over a ledger and trying to explain something to Señor Ramirez, who looked up, delighted that they had returned so quickly, so that he would not be obliged to listen.

"Ah," he said. "Now this looks much more like friends together, doesn't it, Alfredo?"

"Come on," said Inez. "We will all get into line here with this basket and each one will try to throw the acorn into the hat."

Señor Ramirez grew quite excited playing the game; then he began to get angry because he never managed to get the acorn into the hat. Inez screeched with laughter and threw her acorn wider and wider of the mark, each time purposely, in order to soothe, if possible, the hurt pride of Señor Ramirez. Alfredo refused to play at all.

"Games don't interest me," said Señor Ramirez suddenly. "I'd like to play longer with you, daughters, but I can't honestly keep my mind on the game."

"It is of no importance at all, really," said Inez, busily trying to think up something to do next.

"How are your wife and children?" Julia asked him. Inez bit her lip and shook her head.

"They are well taken care of. I have sent them to a little town where they are staying in a pension. Quiet women – all three of them – the little girls and the mother. I am going to sleep." He stretched out under a tree and put his hat over his face. Alfredo was absorbed in his ledger. Inez and Julia sat side by side and waited.

"You have the brain of a baby chicken," Inez said to Julia. "I must think for both of us. If I had not had a great deal of practice when I had to keep count of all the hundreds of tortillas that I sold for my mother, I don't know where we would be."

"Dead, probably," said Julia. They began to feel cold.

"Come," said Inez. "Sing with me." They sang a song about leaving and never returning, four or five times through. When Señor Ramirez awakened he suggested to Julia that they go for a walk. She accepted sweetly, and so they started off through the woods. Soon they reached a good-sized field where Señor Ramirez suggested that they sit for a while.

"The first time I went to bed with a woman," he said, "it was in the country like this. The land belonged to my father. Three or four times a day we would come out into the fields and make love. She loved it, and would have come more often if I had asked her to. Some years later I went to her wedding and I had a terrible fight there. I don't even remember who the man was, but in the end he was badly hurt. I can tell you that."

"If you put your arms around me," said Julia, "I will feel less cold. You don't mind my asking you to do this, but I love you very much and I feel very contented with you."

"That's good," said Señor Ramirez, looking off at the mountains and shielding his eyes from the sun. He was listening to the sound of the waterfall, which was louder here. Julia was laughing and touching various parts of his body.

"Ah," she said. "I don't mind my side hurting me so badly if I can only be happy the way I am now with you. You are so sweet and so wonderful."

He gave her a quick loud kiss on the mouth and rose to his feet.

"Listen," he said. "Wouldn't you like to come into the water with me?"

"I am too sick a woman to go into the water, and I am a little bit afraid."

"In my arms you don't have to be afraid. I will carry you. The current would be too strong for you to manage anyway." Señor Ramirez was now as gay as a lark, although he had been bored but a moment before. He liked nothing better than performing little feats that were assured of success from the beginning. He carried her down to the river, singing at the top of his voice.

The noise of the falls was very loud here, and Julia clung tightly to her escort.

"Don't let go, now," she said. But her voice seemed to fly away behind her like a ribbon caught in the wind. They were in the water and Señor Ramirez began to walk in the direction of the falls.

"I will hold tight, all right," he said. "Because the water runs pretty swiftly near the falls." He seemed to enjoy stepping precariously from one stone to another with Julia in his arms.

"This is not so easy, you know. This is damned hard. The stones are slippery." Julia tightened her grip around his neck and kissed him quickly all over his face.

"If I let you go," he said, "the current would carry you along like a leaf over the falls, and then one of those big rocks would make a hole in your head. That would be the end, of course." Julia's eyes widened with horror, and she yelled with the suddenness of an animal just wounded.

"But why do you scream like that, Julia? I love you, sweetheart." He had had enough of struggling through the water, and so he turned around and started back.

"Are we going away from the waterfall?"

"Yes. It was wonderful, wasn't it?"

"Very nice," she said.

He grew increasingly careless as the current slackened, with the result that he miscalculated and his foot slipped between two stones. This threw him off his balance and he fell. He was unhurt, but the back of Julia's head had hit a stone. It started to bleed profusely. He struggled to his feet and carried her to the riverbank. She was not sure that she was not dying, and hugged him all the more closely. Pulling her along, he walked quickly up the hill and back through the woods to where Inez and Alfredo were still sitting.

"It will be all right, won't it?" she asked him a bit weakly.

"Those damn rocks were slippery," he growled. He was sulky, and eager to be on his way home.

"Oh, God of mine!" lamented Inez, when she saw what had happened. "What a sad ending for a walk! Terrible things always happen to Julia. She is a daughter of misfortune. It's a lucky thing that I am just the contrary."

Señor Ramirez was in such a hurry to leave the picnic spot that he did not even want to bother to collect the various baskets and plates he had brought with him. They dressed, and he yelled for them all to get into the car. Julia wrapped a shawl around her bleeding head. Inez went around snatching up all the things, like an enraged person.

"Can I have these things?" she asked her host. He nodded his head impatiently. Julia was by now crying rhythmically like a baby that has almost fallen asleep.

The two women sat huddled together in the back of the car. Inez explained to Julia that she was going to make presents of the plates and baskets to her family. She shed a tear or two herself. When they arrived at the house, Señor Ramirez handed some banknotes to Inez from where he was sitting.

"*Adios*," he said. The two women got out of the car and stood in the street.

"Will you come back again?" Julia asked him tenderly, ceasing to cry for a moment.

"Yes, I'm coming back again," he said. "*Adios*." He pressed his foot on the accelerator and drove off.

The bar was packed with men. Inez led Julia around through the patio to their room. When she had shut the door, she slipped the banknotes into her pocket and put the baskets on the floor.

"Do you want any of these baskets?" she asked.

Julia was sitting on the edge of her bed, looking into space. "No, thank you," she said. Inez looked at her, and saw that she was far away.

"Señor Ramirez gave me four drinking cups made out of plastic," said Inez. "Do you want one of them for yourself?"

Julia did not answer right away. Then she said: "Will he come back?"

"I don't know," Inez said. "I'm going to the movies. I'll come and see you afterwards, before I go into the bar."

"All right," said Julia. But Inez knew that she did not care. She shrugged her shoulders and went out through the door, closing it behind her.

First published in *Cross Section 1945: A Collection of New American Writing*, edited by Edwin Seaver (1945).

Señorita Córdoba

ONE MORNING SEÑORITA CÓRDOBA received a letter from her mother. She sat beside the fountain reading it.

My Dear Violeta –

I do hope you are enjoying every minute of your stay in the city of Antigua. It is a great miracle to think that Antigua has been destroyed once by fire and once by water. My father pointed out the beauty of this city to me at an early age. He said to me, "When you go to Europe, you need not bow your head in shame that you have come from a country inhabited almost entirely by Indians, as many Europeans are wont to believe. But say to them proudly, "If Europe were a crown and in this crown one jewel were missing – the most beautiful jewel of all – you would find it in my country situated between two volcanoes and surrounded by hills. Its name is Antigua." At that age I loved to sit among the ruins, but Aunt Mercedes (who has come to agree with me),

Aunt Mercedes and I still think it a little unwise for you to have taken such a trip at this particular moment. I realize it is only a few hours away, of course. Did you say that your board was fifty cents a day? For that they should serve you all the chicken you wanted and if they don't I hope you will be sure to demand your just rights. The lady of the pension will understand. I think perhaps that I as your mother have been a little too spiritual all my life. I do not want you to be the same. Perhaps, though, spiritual would not be the correct term to apply to you. Aunt Mercedes and I have been contenting ourselves with eggs and beans. The meat has been unusually hard this week and so very dear. I don't want you to worry about this or let it spoil your lovely holiday. You might try to buy a picture of the All Saints' Day parade from someone who has a camera. Try not to buy it – ask for it, nicely. Señora Sanchez was in the other evening. She was riding by on a horse and she stopped in. She was complaining bitterly about prices, and insulted me grossly, I thought, by handing me half a chicken enveloped in some newspaper, which I handed over to the servants, of course. Aunt Mercedes didn't think that was quite wise. She is a great chicken eater, while I myself am more or less indifferent to all foods, as you know. Aunt Mercedes thought it dreadful that she should be riding on a horse, so soon after her husband's death. We send you our best wishes for an agreeable holiday. May the Lord bless you and keep you well.

Your mother

Señorita Córdoba frowned and looked into the fountain. "Such an old-fashioned letter," she thought to herself. "My mother and my aunt are living like cliff dwellers. Such people write a letter about a chicken." She took a pencil from her bag and made some figures on a piece of paper. She knew just about how much money she needed to get back to Paris and to live there for a little while, while she was starting her dress establishment. She was going to make dresses with a Latin spirit. There was only one way for her to get hold of this money, she was certain, and that was through a man. She had seen a lot of this going on in Paris, and she thought that she would know how to handle such a situation if she could possibly meet a man rich enough in Guatemala. "It would all be in a first-class way," she had assured herself.

On the following morning Señorita Córdoba overheard Señora Ramirez telling the children that their father would arrive that day. She was delighted to hear this, because she knew Señor Ramirez to be one of the richest men in the country ... and a great lady lover. It was on the chance that he would come to Antigua to visit his wife and children that she herself had decided to spend the Holy Week in Señora Espinoza's pension. She knew that Señora Ramirez had been spending the Semana Santa there now for many years, or so she had heard tell from her mother and her mother's friends, who had never understood why Señor Ramirez did not send his wife to a more expensive touristic hotel. He had never been seen at the pension with her until the previous year, when he had suddenly appeared in Antigua and stayed there for several days. However, most people said that he had come to spend his time with his friend Alfonso Gutierres, who had opened an unfrequented but very elegant hotel which was reputed to have the best wine cellar and hard liquor stock in the country. Señorita Córdoba, having heard of his former visit, had been very much in hopes that he would return again this season. She had thought the short journey well worth the risk, particularly as she was tired of helping her mother with the coffee finca and the house – two things which interested her less than anything in the world. She was delighted that he was arriving so promptly. She was never able to relax or enjoy anything that was not concerned directly with the making of her life. Now she was in a feverish state, pulling her dresses out of her trunk and examining them for holes. The figure that she had decided was the minimum sum which she would demand for her trip and to cover the initial investment in her dress shop, and of course her first six months living in Paris, she had marked down on a pad which lay on the bureau. She went over and looked at the pad now, and her cheeks were quite flushed with the intensity of her figuring. She stood there for a long time and then she changed the number on the pad. She made it a little lower.

She picked up a long silk ball dress that she had not worn for many years. It was pink, and to the bodice were pinned some shapeless silk flowers. She decided to wear this to dinner, as it was the fanciest thing she had and was certain to please a Spanish man. She lay down on the bed. Her face was strained and stiff. She shut her eyes for a moment and thought of the name of her shop. It was to be called "Casa Córdoba." "Now," she said to herself, "for what the French call beauty sleep. No thoughts – no thoughts – just rest." She could hear marimba music playing over the radio. She loved listening to music, and it made her think of all the things which she considered beautiful – Venice and the opera and the hall of mirrors in the palace at Versailles. To her, luxury and beauty (beauty there was none without at least the luxury of past splendor) were synonymous with morality, and when people lived well she considered them to be good people and when they lived really luxuriously she considered them to be saints. The marimba music and her memory of Venice and her walk through the hall of mirrors gave her such a feeling of the goodness of God that she crossed herself and decided to buy a candle in the church after her siesta.

The diners had all taken their places when Señorita Córdoba entered the room. The Ramirez daughters, Consuelo and Lilina, were seated on either side of their father, wearing their fiesta dresses. The servant stood in confusion before Señor Ramirez because he had ordered her not to bother with the soup but to bring him instead a large portion of meat and some beer right away.

"Wouldn't you like some soup first?" María asked him. Ramirez was beginning to lose his temper when he saw Señorita Córdoba enter the room. She had brightened her cheeks with some rouge, and on the whole she looked quite beautiful. Señor Ramirez's mouth hung open. He turned completely around in his chair and stared at Violeta. The traveler rose at the same time and rushed over to Señorita Córdoba as though he had never seen her before. She blushed a bright pink and her eyebrow twitched. To get away from all this attention she went over to the English lady in the corner and began to talk to her. The English lady was very much surprised because she had never received more than a curt nod from Miss Córdoba before this moment.

"Miss," said Violeta, "I wish you would take a walk with me some morning. I think it is a shame that we haven't become better acquainted with one another."

"Yes, it is, isn't it," answered the English lady. Miss Córdoba's armpits were wet with nervous sweat. She was terribly embarrassed since she had entered the room in her ball dress. She was bending over the English lady with one hand placed flat on the table, and she noticed that the English lady was looking into her bodice, a faint expression of disgust visible in her face, the disgust of an English person who does not like to be near to a foreigner.

"You Spanish girls all have such beautiful olive skin," she said. This was a completely hysterical thing for her to say because Violeta's skin was whiter than her own. She continued, "I would be very glad to take a walk with you but I am sure you will still be in the arms of Morpheus when I have already eaten my breakfast and written my letters for the day. I can't walk after ten because the sun tires me so. I have as a matter of fact covered the ground here thoroughly but I am looking forward to the processions. A friend described them to me so beautifully that I've been longing to see them ever since. A wonderful gift, to make other people see things. I am more or less mute myself. I have been impressed by the colors here. What a sense of color the Indians have. They are famous for it, aren't they?"

"Oh yes, very famous. I will see you then soon?"

"Perhaps."

"Señorita Córdoba had nothing to do but to go back to the table and submit to the stares of Señor Ramirez and the appraising glances of the traveler. Out of exuberance Señor

Ramirez decided to focus his attention on his older, eleven-year-old child, Consuelo.

"Now I think it would do you some good if you drank a big glass of beer," he said. "The Germans always give their children beer and look what a fine race of people they are."

"I don't want any beer, thank you, papa."

"You've never tried it so you don't know whether or not you like it." He poured her some beer and put it in front of her but she made no attempt to drink it. "You heard papa say that he wanted you to drink some beer."

"What kind of a crazy idea is this?" asked Señora Ramirez.

"What kind of a crazy girl is that that she won't drink beer?" answered Señor Ramirez.

"Yes, drink, Consuelo," said Señora Ramirez. "What is the matter with you?" She pushed the glass up to her daughter's lips but Consuelo refused to drink, although her mouth was covered with foam. The girl's eyes were beginning to shine. With a sudden jerking of her arm she knocked the glass out of her mother's hand, and the beer flowed over the table. Then she jumped up and down and screamed. Señorita Córdoba turned halfway around in her chair and looked at her bitterly. And partly for this reason, and partly because Consuelo was herself in love with the traveler and certain that the traveler in turn loved Señorita Córdoba, Consuelo lunged toward her and started to scratch Señorita Córdoba's face and to tear her coiffure apart. Violeta, with an icy smile on her face, stuck her leg out in order to trip Consuelo, but in so doing she miscalculated and slid off her chair onto the floor. Consuelo ran from the room, and both the traveler and Señor Ramirez helped Violeta up from the floor. She leaned her head on her hand

and cried a little because the incident had so unnerved her. Señor Ramirez ordered a glass of beer for Señorita Córdoba.

"You drink that, Señorita," he said, "and when I am finished eating I will beat my daughter. I promise you that."

"I hope that you will," said Señorita Córdoba.

"Never before," said the English lady, "have I met three such horrid people. The daughter is a real Fury, unable to control herself, the father a child-beater, and the young woman full of revenge, willing to have the child beaten. My digestion is spoiled." She threw her napkin onto the table and left the room.

"Who is that one?" Señor Ramirez asked his wife.

"A tourist who eats here every day."

"She takes everything hard," said the traveler, turning to Señorita Córdoba. "Single women of her age do, you know. In our country we call them old maids."

"What is the difference what she is," said Señorita Córdoba. "To me she is no more than a flea."

"That's right," said Señor Ramirez. "That's right. Most people are fleas – fleas with big stomachs but nothing in their heads."

"But those big stomachs have to be fed," said the traveler, thinking that this was going to be a political discussion. "Or do you believe in letting them eat cake?"

"Cake? I don't care what they eat." The traveler decided not to explain about Marie Antoinette. Señorita Córdoba had composed herself completely by now, and she turned to Señor Ramirez.

"I am Señorita Violeta Córdoba," she said to him, disregarding all traditions of ladylike behavior, for she had always been able to throw tradition to the four winds without being in the least revolutionary. "Thank you for having lifted me from the floor onto my seat."

"And what about me?" said the traveler. "Don't I count in this at all?" Señorita Córdoba nodded to him without smiling. Ramirez stood up and toasted Señorita Córdoba with his beer. "To a beautiful lady," he said, "as beautiful as a red rose." They were speaking together in English.

"A thousand thanks," said Señorita Córdoba quickly. "Let us hope that you mean what you say, and are not just a poet."

"I can be a poet when I want to be, but it is only one of twenty or thirty things that I can do."

◆ ◆ ◆

Señor Gutierres' hotel was austere but very elegant. The patio around which it was built was very small and almost always very dark. Looking down into it from the third floor, it was hard to distinguish the bushes and the few flower beds. Each bedroom was decorated in order to look as much like the bedroom of a Spanish king or nobleman as possible. The beds were on raised daises and the monogram of the hotel was on each pillow slip. The walls were rough and decorated with crossed sabers and blue or gold banners. The chairs were made of a very dark wood with carved narrow backs and little satin cushions tied to the seats by means of four tassels. Off the patio were two small dining rooms for those guests who preferred not to eat in the presence of strangers, and one large dining room that was public. In the public living room there was a veritable collection of sabers with fancy hilts, and chairs with backs that reached halfway up the wall. It was impossible to see in this room at all during thc day, and at night the weak electric lamps left the corners of the room in total darkness.

Señor Gutierres was a gloomy businessman born in Spain who claimed to have noble blood. He was out in the back court, a place to which the guests had no access, wrangling with the cook about a chicken which he was holding by its feet and pinching. He was very thin and had deep circles under his eyes. There were a great many badly made rabbit hutches around and a tremendous chicken coop. He was one of the few people in the country who kept his chickens in a coop. However, there were three large holes in the wiring and the chickens stepped in and out of the coop freely. The courtyard was a mess and it was just beginning to drizzle when Señor Ramirez came out and clapped his friend on the shoulder. "How about coming down to the bar and having a drink with me?" Señor Gutierres nodded and smiled for a second and together they went to the bar, which was underground and smelled very strongly of new wood. The bar stools were made of barrels. Señor Ramirez sat down on one of these and Señor Gutierres dropped the chicken, which he was still holding, onto the floor. The chicken began to strut around the shiny wooden floor, pecking at whatever it saw.

"How do you like my bar now that it is completed?"

"I will like your brandy even better when I have completed a bottle of that."

"Do you like my bar?" Señor Gutierres said again, determined to get an answer out of Señor Ramirez.

"Beautiful."

"I have designed the whole hotel for movie actresses and actors when they are on their vacations. They will be coming down over that highway like flies when it is finished." He looked at Señor Ramirez to see if he was of the same opinion, but his friend was staring hard at the labels on the bottles.

"A lot people on their honeymoons, too. Rich people who like to go far, far away when they get married." He took down a bottle of brandy from the shelf and served himself and Señor Ramirez.

"You don't think much about this new highway. I dream about it by day and by night. You will see a difference in the hotels in this country when it is built. You won't recognize the place you were born in inside of five years. No?"

Señor Gutierres could never get it through his head that Norberto Ramirez was not interested in anything but having a good time and wielding a certain amount of power. He had inherited most of his money and was successful because he had the character of a bully. Señor Gutierres could not imagine that anyone as important and as impressive as Señor Ramirez should not be interested in business. He believed that his friend's disinclination to talk on any subject of interest was merely a ruse, which he had long ago decided to ignore.

"I have built my hotel purposely so soon because later it will not be so cheap. I have already quite a few guests who come here because they know they get good quality. They are all quality people. Everything has to be right for them. It is just as cheap to be right as to be wrong, my friend, you know that, and with a war coming in Europe, all those with quality who used to go to Biarritz will come here. And I am not going to make cheap prices for them. They mustn't pay anything different from what they were paying in Biarritz, otherwise they will say to themselves, Look, what is this? There is something wrong – so cheap, and they will even get to worry that there might be lower-class people in the same hotel. No, they must be taken like sleeping babies from one bed to another, quietly, so they don't wake up. A little Spanish decoration for a change will be all right. But if you notice this hotel is made to remind you more or less of a palace."

One of the Indian servants appeared in the doorway. She looked to be about forty and she was nursing a baby at her breast and smiling. "What do you want, Luz?" asked Señor Gutierres.

"I have come for the chicken, Señor. He must feel very sad for he is estranged from the other chickens, his brothers and his sisters, and the poor little thing cannot find anything to eat here." She started to chase it. The chicken spread its wings and ran as fast as it could around and around the room. The baby started to howl.

"Stop it, stop it!" shouted Señor Gutierres. "You can come and get him later."

"No, wait a minute, man," said Señor Ramirez, climbing down from his stool. "I will get this chicken." He spread his arms out and chased it from corner to corner, making terrible scratches in the wooden floor with the heels of his shoes, to the horror of Señor Gutierres, who began to rub his nose nervously with the back of his hand. Señor Ramirez was quite red in the face by now and beginning to lose his balance. He made a lunge toward the chicken and managed to corner it, but in so doing he fell sideways onto the floor and managed to crush the chicken beneath him.

"Ay," said the servant. "Now it is dead we shall have to cook it for tomorrow night's supper."

"Take it away, for the love of God," said Señor Gutierres, lifting his friend to his feet and handing the bloody chicken to the servant.

"What a shame, what a shame." The servant shook her head and left the room. They had another brandy together and did not bother to clean up the blood and the feathers which stuck both to one side of Señor Ramirez's coat and to the floor.

◆ ◆ ◆

Señorita Córdoba meanwhile had had enough of waiting around the patio for the problematic return of Señor Ramirez. "My God," she said to herself, "I have no time to lose. I am behaving like a person with not a brain in her head." Besides, it had begun to rain and it was incredibly gloomy sitting there under the eaves, which projected a little bit from the house for the purpose of protecting one from the sun and from the rain. She went into her room, painted her face a bit more, and changed to a short dress. Then she decided to knock on Señor Ramirez's door and by some ruse try to find out where this lady's husband was likely to be. This she did and at first received no answer.

She knocked a little harder. "Gome in," said Señora Ramirez in a voice that was caught in her throat. Señorita Córdoba opened the door and saw that Señora Ramirez and the two girls were lying on their beds, in a row. Consuelo's dark eyes showed intense suffering as she rolled them slowly in the direction of the door. Lilina, seeing that it was Señorita Córdoba, pulled her pillow out from behind her head and buried her face beneath it. Señora Ramirez's eyes were swollen with sleep and she looked very much as though nothing would ever interest her again. Señorita Córdoba decided to ignore the mood that was in the room and she went hastily to the foot of Señora Ramirez's bed.

"I thought perhaps that you would be feeling rather badly as a result of this afternoon's events, and I came in to tell you more or less not to brood about it, and to ask you whether or not I could help you with anything."

Señora Ramirez nodded her head, and closed her eyes. Señorita Córdoba was growing impatient. She looked down at Consuelo. "You, young girl," she said, "You should apologize to me." Consuelo shook her head from side to side. "No," she said, "no, you are a very bad woman." She patted her heart.

"Well, Señora Ramirez, your daughter is a maniac. I am a religious woman and I am a very busy woman. That is all that anybody can say of me."

"Certainly," agreed Señora Ramirez, opening her eyes. "That is all anyone can say. And of me they can say that I am a mother of two children, and also a woman with a great many heartaches."

"I suppose you are wondering where your husband is at this very moment."

"No, no," said Señora Ramirez. "He is always outside somewhere."

Señorita Córdoba was exasperated. "But *where*? Where could he be?"

"With Gutierres, drinking."

"Who is Gutierres?"

"He is the owner of a hotel. It is called the Hotel Alhambra. My husband has never taken me to meet him and I shall probably never meet him before the day that I die."

Having gathered the information that she had been seeking, Señorita Córdoba hurriedly took her leave, warning Consuelo at the door that she had better repent shortly. And then she was on her way, with an even and decided gait, like someone who has been sent on an important mission by the head of an organization. She was not a person who envisioned failure often, but only the interminable steps towards success.

When she arrived at the hotel she found a servant in the patio and inquired of her where she could find Señor Gutierres. "He is in the bar," said the servant, leading the way slowly.

"Good evening,' said Señorita Córdoba, entering the room. "I hope that I have not interrupted a serious business conversation. Women have a very bad habit of doing this."

"Women have no bad habits," said Señor Ramirez, climbing down from his stool and taking her by the arm a little roughly.

"I got it into my head," said Señorita Córdoba, "that I would like to look at some rooms here."

"I am sure you will take great pleasure in seeing them." Señor Gutierres had bounded to the door in his eagerness, but Señor Ramirez held his hand up in the air.

"Before the rooms," he said, "we are all going to have a drink together to celebrate the arrival of a lady. Champagne for her, Gutierres. Sit down, Señorita."

Señorita Córdoba complied with this request only too willingly and took her seat at the bar.

"How delightful," she said. "I always like to drink champagne because it reminds me of Paris, where I belong."

"Paris is a very gay city. The night life there is very beautiful," said Señor Gutierres, believing that he was dealing with an elegant client. "Here in this hotel there is everything to remind you of Paris. I have letters from there asking for reservations. Your father no doubt owns a finca, and you no doubt have lived all your life in Paris and in Biarritz. And now you find this country strange, like the jungle – *bien?*"

"This lady," said Señor Ramirez, "lives in the pension, where I always put my wife and my two girls. That is how I know her."

Gutierres' face fell. He had hardly expected to draw his customers from Señora Espinoza's pension, which he considered a step below the large touristic hotels.

"I know the lady who owns the pension," he said sadly, "but very little, only to speak to. I know very few people in this town. My servants buy for me, so why should I speak to anyone?"

"You are better off keeping your life to yourself," said Señorita Córdoba, "than having companions that are doing nothing but just sitting and trying to find someone to laugh with."

A shadow seemed to pass across the face of Señor Ramirez. For a moment he thought of going back to the capital right away. "Here, here," he shouted. "What is all this about your life alone? Let's be together, friends – like baby chickens under the wings of the mother hen."

Señor Gutierres was now just a little bit drunk, and he was beginning to wander on to things that he scarcely knew he thought about. "No," he said, "no – no chickens under one wing. Each man alone, proud, acting as he has been taught to act by his family, never living in a house that is lower than the house in which he was born. Each man remembering his father and his mother and what he has been taught is sacred."

"The only thing that is sacred, my poor boy, is money," said the pleasure-seeking Norberto.

"No, it is one's class," insisted Señor Gutierres. "We must love our own class. I cannot talk and be friendly with people whose childhood I know has been different from mine, who did not have the same silver on the table when they sat down to eat."

"You would be glad to talk with me, Gutierres, even if I ate with pigs when I was a little boy."

"No, no, I would not. There is real friendship only between men who have always been used to the same things. Between two such men no words need be spoken, because each one knows that the other will do nothing to disgust him or upset him, and the pleasure of being with such a friend is quite enough. I have such a friend here, who knows the value of every piece of furniture in the Alhambra. And there is no wine that is familiar to me that is not familiar to him. We don't have to say anything to each other. Each of us remembers the same things. His family and my family come from the same part of Spain. I feel so close to him that I might say that I would even wear his underclothes. Forgive me, Señorita." He bowed his head.

"But *my* underwear you would not put on for five thousand *quetzales*, eh, Señor?" said Ramirez, throwing his chest out.

Señor Gutierres, having started off talking about his thin code which he considered to be a universal and important ideology, had necessarily to go on further. His astute business sense was completely obliterated by the fanaticism that all men feel about whatever it is they believe makes the world an orderly and respectable place in which to live. "No, Señor," he said, "I would not wear your underwear, for your education is far below mine and your family, as I know, were not much more than peasants before they came to this country."

"Oh, how rude you are," said Señorita Córdoba, taking hold of Señor Ramirez's hand. "And I am sure it is not true."

"Certainly it is true," said Señor Ramirez, "and this monkey will soon find out what else is true." Señorita Córdoba was surprised that Señor Ramirez had as yet not kicked the bar stools over, but apparently his family was not a sensitive point with him, and perhaps also he was having a very pleasurable reaction from the drinks and was not inclined to fight.

"Let him kiss his chairs," continued Señor Ramirez, "and see how many women he will get to kiss. He is probably a miserable eunuch anyway. Kiss me." He put his hand under Señorita Córdoba's chin and kissed her full on the mouth. Señorita Córdoba wondered whether or not she should resist this kiss, and decided very quickly that it was wiser to pretend to enjoy it. She passed a fluttering hand over his ear, which was one of the few love gestures she knew about.

"This woman is a trollop," said Señor Gutierres in a trembling voice. Señor Ramirez could not possibly let this remark pass so he stopped kissing Señorita Córdoba and gave Gutierres a sock on the jaw that knocked him off his stool and onto the floor, where he lay unconscious.

"Now," he said to Señorita Córdoba, lifting her down from her stool, "let us find an agreeable place in this beautiful Alhambra Hotel." He spat on the floor.

"Oh, well," said Señorita Córdoba, deciding that it was time for her to be a little bit shy. "Shall we stand in the patio a little bit and then go home?"

"No," he said. "I want to go where I can see your beautiful face." He led her upstairs, and with his foot he kicked open the door to one of the bedrooms, and turned on the light.

She went and sat down on one of the chairs which Señor Gutierres considered to be beautiful and folded her hands in her lap. "I have always been interested to know a man like you," she said, "with such a wonderful way of knowing how to live."

"There are no disappointments in my life," said Señor Ramirez, "and I love it. I can show you some wonderful things."

"My life is a terrible disappointment to me," said Señorita Córdoba, and her heart beat very quickly as she felt she was approaching her goal.

The room was badly lighted and she searched his eyes avidly to see what effect her words had made on him. It seemed to her that they had a slightly blank look, like the eyes of anyone who is gazing at a particular object without really seeing it.

"You have not had the right kind of love," he said.

"That is not the only reason," said Señorita Córdoba, shaking her head vigorously. Señor Ramirez was feeling suddenly very drunk and he threw himself down on the bed.

"You must not go to sleep," she said nervously, rising to her feet.

"Who in the devil is going to sleep?" Señor Ramirez leaned on his elbows and looked at her like an angry bull.

"Listen," she said, "I'm so miserable on that finca where I am living that I think that if it goes on any longer I will certainly drown myself in the river."

"Drowning is no good," said Ramirez. "That's only good for scared fools, like those little dogs that shiver all the time – they have them in Mexico. You are not on your finca now. Come here on the bed and stop talking so much." He put his arm out and caught at the air with his hand.

"I want to go away to Paris, where I have friends, and start a dress shop."

"Sure," said Señor Ramirez.

"But I have not got any money."

"I have so much money."

"I need five thousand dollars."

He started to unbutton his pants. Señorita Córdoba remembered that many men were not interested in ladies nearly as much after they had made love to them as they were beforehand, so she decided that she had better make sure that she received a check first. She did not know how to do this tactfully but her own greed and the fact that he was drunk, and that she thought him a coarse person anyway, made her believe that she would be successful. She walked quickly to the window and stood with her back to him.

"What are you looking at outside the window?" asked Señor Ramirez, in a thick voice, smelling trouble.

"I am not looking at anything. On the contrary, I am just thinking about you, and how little you are really interested in whether or not I will open a dress shop."

"You can open a thousand dress shops, my beautiful woman. What is the matter with you?"

"You lie. I cannot even open one dress shop." She turned around and faced him.

"Wildcat," he said to her. She tried to look more touching.

"You will not help me to open a dress shop. Must it be someone else that will help me?"

"I am going to help you open fifty dress shops – tomorrow."

"I would not ask you for fifty, only for one. Would you make me happy and give me a check tonight so that I know when I go to sleep I will have my dress shop? I would like to sleep in peace just for once and know that I am not going to have to go back to that terrible finca, and listen to the dogs howling and my mother praying out loud. This one check would banish all these horrible things from my mind right away and I would be eternally grateful to you. I would be so glad that it had been you who did it, too."

"Well, then, come here."

She sat down on the bed beside him and he kissed her, but while he was kissing her she pushed him away and said to him, "Give me the check now."

"What is this?" asked Señor Ramirez. "Are you still talking about this damn foolish check?"

"Yes," said Señorita Córdoba, seeing that it was no use any longer to employ tact. "I will not go to bed with you unless you first give me a check for five thousand *quetzales*, or a piece of paper saying that you owe this sum of money to me."

Certainly this remark was not having the right effect on Señor Ramirez, who struggled with difficulty down from the bed and buttoned his trousers. She watched him attentively and noticed that the glands in his neck were moving. "Angry again," she said to herself, but she could think of nothing to say that would calm him except "Where are you going?" which she asked in a rather ironical tone of voice, all her false ardor dampened now by her own conviction that she would fail to get her money. Señor Ramirez was trembling and very red in the face. She stood still and appeared to be very calm even when he finally stumbled out of the room, but when she heard him clambering down the stairs she walked out onto the balcony and looked down over the railing into the patio. One light was burning and in a moment Señor Ramirez came into the patio and picked up what she saw was a large urn with a tall plant growing out of it. This he threw to the ground not very far from his feet, because it was very heavy. It smashed in many pieces, but made less noise than she expected to hear because the dirt inside the urn muffled the sound that it would otherwise have made.

She could not understand his fury, knowing so little about deeply outraged feelings and the fact that so much of people's violence is spent in the elaborate and grim protection of a personality as underdeveloped as a fetus yet grown quickly to tremendous proportions, like a giant weed. Being stupid herself, she did not recognize the danger inherent in all those whose self-protective instincts are far greater than the personality they are protecting, because their armor can only be timeworn and made up of the most stagnating of human impulses. Señorita Córdoba was unwounded if unintelligent, and her rages were unimportant nervous discharges.

Señor Ramirez was struggling with the big wooden doors that led into the street and making a terrible racket shaking the heavy iron chains, but it was to no avail because the doors were locked from the inside. She could only hear him now without being able to see him, since the bulb threw no light into the front of the patio. Suddenly he stopped rattling the chains and she heard him walking back in the direction of the staircase.

"My God," she thought, "he has murder in his heart, certainly," and she sneaked around to another side of the balcony. Fortunately the servant who had before been looking for the chicken was awakened by the noise and she now came into the patio to find out what the trouble was. "The door is locked," Ramirez shouted at her.

"Yes," she whispered. "I'll fetch the key."

She returned with the key and let Señor Ramirez out of the patio into the street. Señorita Córdoba decided to wait a little while before returning to the pension herself. She was thinking very hard of a way to redeem herself on the following day. She was like certain mediocre politically minded persons upon whose minds failure leaves no deep impression, not because of any burning belief in the ideal for which they are fighting, but rather because they are accustomed to thinking only of what to do next. These people are often valuable but at the same time so removed from reality that they are ridiculous. After sitting a while in the gloomy Spanish bedroom Señorita Córdoba went downstairs and in turn awakened the Indian servant, who let her out.

First published in *The Threepenny Review 6:1* (Spring 1985).

Jane Bowles in Mexico, 1941, at the time of writing *Two Serious Ladies*

Out in the World

'Andrew', 'Emmy Moore's Journal' and 'Friday' are fragments of an unfinished novel which Jane intended to call 'Out in the World'. They were edited by Paul Bowles from five notebooks, written mostly during Jane's stay in Paris in the winter of 1949 and continued over the following two years in Tangier. Jane's biographer Millicent Dillon wrote that the novel 'is more directly autobiographical than anything else Jane ever wrote ... Jane is both Emmy Moore and Andrew [the two central characters] in a way she had neither been Mrs Copperfield or Miss Goering.' Emmy Moore is 'fat and in her mid-forties, and has come to the Hotel Henry in a little town in New England to be alone and to write. Andrew McLain is a soldier in his early twenties, who falls in love with another soldier [Tommy].' Later, Jane added a third main character, Agnes Leather, a young woman in love with Andrew, who is the subject of the final fragment, 'Friday'.

Andrew

ANDREW'S MOTHER LOOKED at her son's face. "He wants to get away from us," she thought, "and he will." She felt overcome by a mortal fatigue. "He simply wants to spring out of his box into the world." With a flippant and worldly gesture she described a flight through the air. Then abruptly she burst into tears and buried her face in her hands.

Andrew watched her thin shoulders shaking inside her woolen dress. When his mother cried he felt as though his face were made of marble. He could not accept the weeping as a part of her personality. It did not appear to be the natural climax of a mood. Instead it seemed to descend upon her from somewhere far away, as if she were giving voice to the crying of a child in some distant place. For it was the crying of a creature many years younger than she, a disgrace for which he felt responsible, since it was usually because of him that she cried.

There was nothing he could say to console her because she was right. He wanted to go away, and there was nothing else he wanted at all. "It's natural when you're young to want to go away," he would say to himself, but it did not help; he always felt that his own desire to escape was different from that of others. When he was in a good humor he would go about feeling that he and many others too were all going away. On such days his face was smooth and he enjoyed his life, although even then he was not communicative. More than anything he wanted all days to be like those rare free ones when he went about whistling and enjoying every simple thing he did. But he had to work hard to get such days, because of his inner conviction that his own going away was like no other going away in the world, a certainty he found it impossible to dislodge. He was right, of course, but from a very early age his life had been devoted to his struggle to rid himself of his feeling of uniqueness. With the years he was becoming more expert at travesty, so that now his mother's crying was more destructive. Watching her cry now, he was more convinced than ever that he was not like other boys who wanted to go away. The truth bit into him harder, for seeing her he could not believe even faintly that he shared his sin with other young men. He and his mother were isolated, sharing the same disgrace, and because of this sharing, separated from one another. His life was truly miserable compared to the lives of other boys, and he knew it.

When his mother's sobs had quieted down somewhat, his father called the waitress and asked for the check. "That's good tomato soup," he told her. "And ham with Hawaiian pineapple is one of my favorites, as you know." The waitress did not answer, and the engaging expression on his face slowly faded.

They pushed their chairs back and headed for the cloakroom. When they were outside Andrew's father suggested that they walk to the summit of the sloping lawn where some cannonballs were piled in the shape of a pyramid. "We'll go over to the cannonballs," he said. "Then we'll come back."

They struggled up the hill in the teeth of a bitterly cold wind, holding on to their hats. "This is the north, folks!" his father shouted into the gale. "It's hard going at times, but in a hot climate no one develops."

Andrew put his foot against one of the cannonballs. He could feel the cold iron through the sole of his shoe.

◆ ◆ ◆

He had applied for a job in a garage, but he was inducted into the Army before he knew whether or not they had accepted his application. He loved being in the Army, and even took pleasure in the nickname which his hutmates had given him the second day after his arrival. He was called Buttonlip; because of this name he talked even less than usual. In general he hated to talk and could not imagine talking as being a natural expression of a man's thoughts. This was not shyness, but secretiveness.

One day in the Fall he set out on a walk through the pine grove surrounding the camp. Soon he sniffed smoke and stopped walking. "Someone's making a fire," he said to himself. Then he continued on his way. It was dusk in the grove, but beyond, outside, the daylight was still bright. Very shortly he reached a clearing. A young soldier sat there, crouched over a fire which he was feeding with long twigs. Andrew thought he recognized him – he too was undoubtedly a recent arrival – and so his face was not altogether unfamiliar.

The boy greeted Andrew with a smile and pointed to a tree trunk that lay on the ground nearby. "Sit down," he said. "I'm going to cook dinner. The mess sergeant gives me my stuff uncooked when I want it that way so I can come out here and make a campfire."

Andrew had an urge to bolt from the clearing, but he seated himself stiffly on the end of the tree trunk. The boy was beautiful, with an Irish-American face and thick curly brown hair. His cheeks were blood red from the heat of the flames. Andrew looked at his face and fell in love with him. Then he could not look away.

A mess kit and a brown paper package lay on the ground. "My food is there in that brown bag," the boy said. "I'll give you a little piece of meat so you can see how good it tastes when it's cooked here, out in the air. Did you go in for bonfires when you were a kid?"

"No," said Andrew. "Too much wind," he added, some vague memory stirring in his mind.

"There's lots of wind," he agreed, and Andrew was unreasonably delighted that the boy considered his remark a sensible one. "Lots of wind, but that never need stop you." He looked up at Andrew with a bright smile. "Not if you like a fire and the outdoors. Where I worked they used to call me Outdoor Tommy. Nobody got sore."

Andrew was so disarmed by his charm that he did not find the boy's last statement odd until he had heard the sentence repeated several times inside his head.

"Sore?"

"Yes, sore." He untied the string that bound his food package and set the meat on a little wire grate. "They never got sore at me," he repeated, measuring his words. "They were a right nice bunch. Sometimes guys don't take to it if you like something real well. They get sore. These guys didn't get sore. Never. They saw me going off to the woods with my supper every evening, and sometimes even, one or two of them would come along. And sometimes twenty-five of us would go out with steaks. But mostly I just went by myself and they stayed back playing games in the cottages or going into town. If it had been winter I'd have stayed in the cottages more. I was never there in winter. If I had been, I might have gone out anyway. I like to make a fire in the snow."

"Where were you?" asked Andrew.

"In a factory by a stream." The meat was cooked, and he cut off a tiny piece for Andrew. "This is all you're going to get. Otherwise I won't have enough in me."

"I've eaten. With the others," said Andrew shortly.

"You've got to try this," the boy insisted. "And see if you like eating it this way, cooked on the coals outdoors. Then maybe you can get on the good side of the mess sergeant and bring your food out here, too. They're all right here. I could stay in this outfit. Just as good as I could stay back home in the hotel."

"You live in a hotel?"

"I lived in a hotel except the summer I was in the factory."

"Well, I'll see you," Andrew mumbled, walking away.

One night after he had eaten his supper he found himself wandering among the huts on the other side of the mess hall. It was Saturday night and most of the huts were dark. He was dejected, and thought of going into town and drinking beer by himself. Andrew drank only beer because he considered other forms of alcohol too expensive, although most of the other soldiers, who had less money than he, drank whiskey.

As he walked along thinking of the beer he heard a voice calling to him. He looked up and saw Tommy standing in the doorway of a hut only a few feet away. They greeted each other, and Tommy motioned to him to wait. Then he went inside to get something.

Andrew leaned against a tree with his hands in his pockets. When Tommy came out he held a flat box in his hand. "Sparklers," he said. "I bought them after the Fourth, cut-rate. It's the best time to buy them."

"That's good to know," said Andrew. He had never touched fireworks except on the day of the Fourth. He had a brief memory of alleys on summer nights, where boys were grinding red devils under their heels in the dark. Compared to him they were poor, and he was therefore, like all well-off children, both revolted by them and envious of them. The fact that they played with fireworks after the Fourth of July was disgusting in a way. It had a foreign flavor, and made him feel a little sick, just as the Irish did, and the Jews, and circus people. But he was also excited by them. The sick feeling was part of the excitement.

Andrew had never dressed as a ragamuffin on Thanksgiving, and he had once almost fainted when two boys disguised as hags had come begging at the door. His father's rage had contributed greatly to the nightmarish quality of the memory. It was usually his mother, and not his father, who was angry. But he remembered that his father had seemed to attach great importance to the custom of masquerading on Thanksgiving. "He should be dressed up himself and out there with the others!" he had cried. "He has no right to be lying there, white as a sheet. There's no earthly reason for it. This is a holiday. It's time for *fun*. My God, doesn't anyone in the house ever have any fun? I was a ragamuffin every year until I was grown. Why doesn't he tear up an old pair of pants and go out? I'll take the crown out of my straw hat if he wants to wear it. But he should go out!"

Quite naturally Andrew had thought of running away. This was one of his worst memories. He hated to hear his father speak about the poor. His own romantic conception of them made his father's democratic viewpoint unacceptable. It was as incongruous as if he had come into the parlor and found his father offering one of his cigarettes to a pirate or a gypsy. He preferred his mother's disdain for the poor. In fact, she liked nothing but the smell of her intimates. Of course, she made him feel sick, too, but sick in a different way.

"Come on. Take one," Tommy was saying, and he lighted a sparkler. Andrew stared at the needle-like sparks. The hissing sound of the sparkler awakened old sick feelings, and he longed to pull the little stick from between Tommy's fingers and bury the bright sparks in the earth. Instead, he looked gloomy and said nothing. He liked the fact that Tommy was poor, but he did not want him to be so poor that he seemed foreign. Then he realized that others might not see a connection between being a foreigner and playing with sparklers after the Fourth of July, and he was aware that there was really no logical connection. Yet he himself felt that there was one. Sometimes he wondered whether or not other people went about pretending to be logical while actually they felt as he did inside, but this was not very often, since he usually took it for granted that everyone was more honest than he. The fact that it was impossible to say anything of all this to Tommy both depressed and irritated him.

"I saved a whole box of sparklers for you," Tommy said. "I thought you'd be coming to the clearing."

Andrew could not believe he was hearing the words. At the same time his heart had begun to beat faster. He told himself that he must retain a natural expression.

"I don't know if you like to fool around with stuff they make for kids," Tommy went on. "Maybe you think it's not worth your while. But you don't have to pay much attention to these. You light 'em and they burn themselves out. You can swing 'em around and talk at the same time. Or you don't even have to swing 'em. You can stick 'em in the ground and they go on all by themselves, like little pinwheels. There's not much point to 'em, but I get 'em anyway, every summer after the Fourth of July is over with. This isn't the box I saved for you. That one I gave to someone else who had a nephew." He handed the box to Andrew.

Andrew's face was like stone and his mouth was drawn. "Here." Tommy tapped the back of Andrew's hand with the flat box. "Here are your sparklers."

"No," said Andrew. "I don't want any sparklers." He was not going to offer any explanation for refusing them. Tommy did not seem to want one in any case. He went on tracing designs in the night with his sparkler. "I'll just stash this box away if you don't want 'em. I can use 'em up. It's better to have one of these going than nothing, and sometimes there's no time for me to build a bonfire."

"You take things easy, don't you?" Andrew said.

First published in *Feminine Wiles* (Black Sparrow Press, 1976).

Emmy Moore's Journal

ON CERTAIN DAYS I forget why I'm here. Today once again I wrote my husband all my reasons for coming. He encouraged me to come each time I was in doubt. He said that the worst danger for me was a state of vagueness, so I wrote telling him why I had come to the Hotel Henry – my eighth letter on this subject – but with each new letter I strengthen my position. I am reproducing the letter here. Let there be no mistake. My journal is intended for publication. I want to publish for glory, but also in order to aid other women. This is the letter to my husband, Paul Moore, to whom I have been married sixteen years. (I am childless.) He is of North Irish descent, and a very serious lawyer. Also a solitary and lover of the country. He knows all mushrooms, bushes and trees, and he is interested in geology. But these interests do not exclude me. He is sympathetic towards me, and kindly. He wants very much for me to be happy, and worries because I am not. He knows everything about me, including how much I deplore being the feminine kind of woman that I am. In fact, I am unusually feminine for an American of Anglo stock. (Born in Boston.) I am almost a "Turkish" type. Not physically, at least not entirely, because though fat I have ruddy Scotch cheeks and my eyes are round and not slanted or almond-shaped. But sometimes I feel certain that I exude an atmosphere very similar to theirs (the Turkish women's) and then I despise myself. I find the women in my country so extraordinarily manly and independent, capable of leading regiments, or of fending for themselves on desert islands if necessary. (These are poor examples, but I am getting my point across.) For me it is an experience simply to have come here alone to the Hotel Henry and to eat my dinner and lunch by myself. If possible before I die, I should like to become a little more independent, and a little less Turkish than I am now. Before I go any further, I had better say immediately that I mean no offense to Turkish women. They are probably busy combating the very same Turkish quality in themselves that I am controlling in me. I understand, too (though this is irrelevant), that many Turkish women are beautiful, and I think that they have discarded their veils. Any other American woman would be sure of this. She would know one way or the other whether the veils had been discarded, whereas I am afraid to come out with a definite statement. I have a feeling that they really have got rid of their veils, but I won't swear to it. Also, if they have done so, I have no idea when they did. Was it many years ago or recently?

Here is my letter to Paul Moore, my husband, in which there is more about Turkish women. Since I am writing this journal with a view to publication, I do not want to ramble on as though I had all the space in the world. No publisher will attempt printing an *enormous* journal written by an unknown woman. It would be too much of a financial risk. Even I, with my ignorance of all matters pertaining to business, know this much. But they may print a small one.

My letter (written yesterday, the morrow of my drunken evening in the Blue Bonnet Room when I accosted the society salesman):

Dearest Paul:

I cannot simply live out my experiment here at the Hotel Henry without trying to justify or at least explain in letters my reasons for being here, and with fair regularity. You encouraged me to write whenever I felt I needed to clarify my thoughts. But you did tell me that I must not feel the need to *justify* my actions. However, I *do* feel the need to justify my actions, and I am certain that until the prayed-for metamorphosis has occurred I shall go on feeling just this need. Oh, how well I know that you would interrupt me at this point and warn me against expecting too much. So I shall say in lieu of metamorphosis, the prayed-for *improvement*. But until then I must justify myself every day. Perhaps you will get a letter every day. On some days the need to write lodges itself in my throat like a cry that must be uttered.

As for the Turkish problem, I am coming to it. You must understand that I am an admirer of Western civilization; that is, of the women who are members of this group. I feel myself that I fall short of being a member, that by some curious accident I was not born in Turkey but should have been. Because of my usual imprecision I cannot even tell how many countries belong to what we call Western Civilization, but I believe Turkey is the place where East meets West, isn't it? I can just about imagine the women there, from what I have heard about the country and the pictures I have seen of it. As for being troubled or obsessed by real Oriental women, I am not. (I refer to the Chinese, Japanese, Hindus, and so on.) Naturally I am less concerned with the Far Eastern women because there is no danger of my being like them. (The Turkish women are just near enough.) The Far Eastern ones are so very far away, at the opposite end of the earth, that they could easily be just as independent and masculine as the women of the Western world. The ones living in-between the two masculine areas would be soft and feminine. Naturally I don't believe this for a minute, but still, the real Orientals are so far away and such a mystery to me that it might as well be true. Whatever they are, it couldn't affect me. They look too different from the way I look. Whereas Turkish women don't. (Their figures are exactly like mine, alas!)

Now I shall come to the point. I know full well that you will consider the above discourse a kind of joke. Or if you don't, you will be irritated with me for making statements of such a sweeping and inaccurate nature. For surely you will consider the picture of the world that I present as inaccurate. I myself know that this concept of the women (all three sets – Western, Middle and Eastern) is a puerile one. It could even be called downright idiotic. Yet I assure you that I see things this way, if I relax even a little and look through my own eyes into what is really inside my head. (Though because of my talent for mimicry I am able to simulate looking through the eyes of an educated person when I wish to.) Since I am giving you such a frank picture of myself, I may as well go the whole hog and admit to you that my secret picture of the world is grossly inaccurate. I have completely forgotten to include in it any of the Latin countries. (France, Italy, Spain.) For instance, I have jumped from the Anglo world to the semi-Oriental as if there were no countries in between at all. I know that these exist. (I have even lived in two of them.) But they do not fit into my scheme. I just don't think about the Latins very much, and this is less understandable than my not thinking about the Chinese or Javanese or Japanese women. You can see why without my having to explain it to you. I do know that the French women are more interested in sports than they used to be, and for all I know they may be indistinguishable from Anglo women by now. I haven't been to France recently so I can't be sure. But in any case the women of those countries don't enter into my picture of the world. Or shall I say that the fact of having forgotten utterly to consider them has not altered the way I visualize the division of the world's women? Incredible though it may seem to you, it hasn't altered anything. (My having forgotten all Latin countries, South America included.) I want you to know the whole truth about me. But don't imagine that I wouldn't be capable of concealing my ignorance from you if I wanted to. I am so wily and feminine that I could live by your side for a lifetime and deceive you afresh each day. But I will have no truck with feminine wiles. I know how they can absorb the hours of the day. Many women are delighted to sit around spinning their webs. It is an absorbing occupation, and the women feel they are getting somewhere. And so they are, but only for as long as the man is there to be deceived. And a wily woman alone is a pitiful sight to behold. Naturally.

I shall try to be honest with you so that I can live with you and yet won't be pitiful. Even if tossing my feminine tricks out the window means being left no better than an illiterate backwoodsman, or the bottom fish scraping along the ocean bed, I prefer to have it this way. Now I am too tired to write more. Though I don't feel that I have clarified enough or justified enough.

I shall write you soon about the effect the war has had upon me. I have spoken to you about it, but you have never seemed to take it very seriously. Perhaps seeing in black and white what I feel will affect your opinion of me. Perhaps you will leave me. I accept the challenge. My Hotel Henry experience includes this risk. I got drunk two nights ago. It's hard to believe that I am forty-seven, isn't it?

My love,
Emmy

Now that I have copied this letter into my journal (I had forgotten to make a carbon), I shall take my walk. My scheme included a few weeks of solitude at the Hotel Henry before attempting anything. I did not even intend to write in my journal as soon as I started to, but simply to sit about collecting my thoughts, waiting for the knots of habit to undo themselves. But after only a week here – two nights ago – I felt amazingly alone and disconnected from my past life, so I began my journal.

My first interesting contact was the salesman in the Blue Bonnet Room. I had heard about this eccentric through my in-laws, the Moores, before I ever came up here. My husband's cousin Laurence Moore told me about him when he heard I was coming. He said: "Take a walk through Grey and Bottle's Department Store, and you'll see a man with a lean red face and reddish hair selling materials by the bolt. That man has an income and is related to Hewitt Molain. He doesn't need to work. He was in my fraternity. Then he disappeared. The next I heard of him he was working there at Grey and Bottle's. I stopped by and said hello to him. For a nut he seemed like a very decent chap. You might even have a drink with him. I think he's quite up to general conversation."

I did not mention Laurence Moore to the society salesman because I thought it might irritate him. I lied and pretended to have been here for months, when actually this is still only my second week at the Hotel Henry. I want everyone to think I have been here a long time. Surely it is not to impress them. Is there anything impressive about a lengthy stay at the Hotel Henry? Any sane person would be alarmed that I should even ask such a question. I ask it because deep in my heart I *do* think a lengthy stay at the Hotel Henry is impressive. Very easy to see that I would, and even sane of me to think it impressive, but not sane of me to expect anyone else to think so, particularly a stranger. Perhaps I simply like to hear myself telling it. I hope so. I shall write some more tomorrow, but now I must go out. I am going to buy a supply of cocoa. When I'm not drunk

I like to have a cup of cocoa before going to sleep. My husband likes it too.

◆ ◆ ◆

She could not stand the overheated room a second longer. With some difficulty she raised the window, and the cold wind blew in. Some loose sheets of paper went skimming off the top of the desk and flattened themselves against the bookcase. She shut the window and they fell to the floor. The cold air had changed her mood. She looked down at the sheets of paper. They were part of the letter she had just copied. She picked them up: "*I don't feel that I have clarified enough or justified enough*," she read. She closed her eyes and shook her head. She had been so happy copying this letter into her journal, but now her heart was faint as she scanned its scattered pages. "I have said nothing," she muttered to herself in alarm. "I have said nothing at all. I have not clarified my reasons for being at the Hotel Henry. I have not justified myself."

Automatically she looked around the room. A bottle of whiskey stood on the floor beside one of the legs of the bureau. She stepped forward, picked it up by the neck, and settled with it into her favorite wicker chair.

First published in *The Paris Review* 56 (Spring 1973).

Friday

He sat at a little table in the Green Mountain Luncheonette apathetically studying the menu. Faithful to the established tradition of his rich New England family, he habitually chose the cheapest dish listed on the menu whenever it was not something he definitely abhorred. Today was Friday, and there were two cheap dishes listed, both of which he hated. One was haddock and the other fried New England smelts. The cheaper meat dishes had been omitted. Finally, with compressed lips, he decided on a steak. The waitress was barely able to hear his order.

"Did you say steak?" she asked him.

"Yes. There isn't anything else. Who eats haddock?"

"Nine tenths of the population." She spoke without venom. "Look at Agnes." She pointed to the table next to his.

Andrew looked up. He had noticed the girl before. She had a long freckled face with large, rather roughly sketched features. Her hair, almost the color of her skin, hung down to her shoulders. It was evident that her mustard-colored wool dress was homemade. It was decorated at the throat with a number of dark brown woolen balls. Over the dress she wore a man's lumber jacket. She was a large-boned girl. The lower half of her face was long and solid and insensitive-looking, but her eyes, Andrew noted, were luminous and starry.

Although it was bitterly cold outside, the lunchroom was steaming hot and the front window had clouded over. "Don't you like fish?" the girl said.

He shook his head. Out of the corner of his eye he had noticed that she was not eating her haddock. However, he had quickly looked away, in order not to be drawn into a conversation. The arrival of his steak obliged him to look up, and their eyes met. She was gazing at him with a rapt expression. It made him feel uncomfortable.

"My name is Agnes Leather," she said in a hushed voice, as if she were sharing a delightful secret. "I've seen you eating in here before."

He realized that there was no polite way of remaining silent, and so he said in an expressionless voice, "I ate here yesterday and the day before yesterday."

"That's right." She nodded. "I saw you both times. At noon yesterday, and then the day before a little later than that. At night I don't come here. I have a family. I eat home with them like everybody else in a small town." Her smile was warm and intimate, as if she would like to include him in her good fortune.

He did not know what to say to this, and asked himself idly if she was going to eat her haddock.

"You're wondering why I don't touch my fish?" she said, catching his eye.

"You haven't eaten much of it, have you?" He coughed discreetly and cut into his little steak, hoping that she would soon occupy herself with her meal.

"I almost never feel like eating," she said. "Even though I do live in a small town."

"That's too bad."

"Do you think it's too bad?"

She fixed her luminous eyes upon him intently, as if his face held the true meaning of his words, which might only have seemed banal.

He looked at the long horselike lower half of her face, and decided that she was unsubtle and strong-minded despite her crazy eyes. It occurred to him that women were getting entirely too big and bony. "Do I think what's too bad?" he asked her.

"That I don't care about eating."

"Well, yes," he said with a certain irritation. "It's always better to have an appetite. At least, that's what I thought."

She did not answer this, but looked pensive, as if she were considering seriously whether or not to agree with him. Then she shook her head from side to side, indicating that the problem was insoluble.

"You'd understand if I could give you the whole picture," she said. "This is just a glimpse. But I can't give you the whole picture in a lunchroom. I know it's a good thing to eat. I know." And as if to prove this, she fell upon her haddock and finished it off with three stabs of her fork. It was a very small portion. But the serious look in her eye remained.

"I'm sorry if I startled you," she said gently, wetting her lips. "I try not to do that. You can blame it on my being from a small town if you want, but it has nothing to do with that. It really hasn't. But it's just impossible for me to explain it all to you, so I might as well say I'm from a small town as to say my name is Agnes Leather."

She began an odd nervous motion of pulling at her wrist, and to his surprise shouted for some hotcakes with maple syrup.

At that moment a waitress opened the door leading into the street, and put down a cast-iron cat to hold it back. The wind blew through the restaurant and the diners set up a clamor.

"Orders from the boss!" the waitress screamed. "Just hold your horses. We're clearing the air." This airing occurred every day, and the shrieks of the customers were only in jest. As soon as the clouded glass shone clear, so that the words GREEN MOUNTAIN LUNCHEONETTE in reverse were once again visible, the waitress removed the iron cat and shut the door.

First published, as one of 'Three Scenes', in *Antaeus* (Autumn 1977).

Going to Massachusetts

This fragment was also intended as part of a novel, to be called Going to Massachusetts. *Jane worked on it sporadically from the 1960s up until her early years in the clinic in Malaga. It was originally published in the Tangier-based journal* Antaeus *in 1972, a year before Jane's death, as 'The Courtship of Janet Murphy'.*

The Courtship of Janet Murphy

BOZOE RUBBED AWAY some tears with a closed fist.

"Come on, Bozoe," said Janet. "You're not going to the North Pole."

Bozoe tugged at the wooly fur, and pulled a little of it out.

"Leave your coat alone," said Janet.

"I don't remember why I'm going to Massachusetts," Bozoe moaned. "I knew it would be like this, once I got to the station."

"If you don't want to go to Massachusetts," said Janet, "then come on back to the apartment. We'll stop at Fanny's on the way. I want to buy those tumblers made out of knobby glass. I want brown ones."

Bozoe started to cry in earnest. This caused Janet considerable embarrassment. She was conscious of herself as a public figure because the fact that she owned and ran a garage had given her a good deal of publicity not only in East Clinton but in the neighboring counties. This scene, she said to herself, makes us look like two Italians saying goodbye. Everybody'll think we're

Italians. She did not feel true sympathy for Bozoe. Her sense of responsibility was overdeveloped, but she was totally lacking in real tenderness.

"There's no reason for you to cry over a set of whiskey tumblers," said Janet. "I told you ten days ago that I was going to buy them."

"Passengers boarding Bus Number Twenty-seven, northbound ..."

"I'm not crying about whiskey tumblers." Bozoe managed with difficulty to get the words out. "I'm crying about Massachusetts. I can't remember my reasons."

"Rockport, Rayville, Muriel ..."

"Why don't you listen to the loudspeaker, Bozoe? It's giving you information. If you paid attention to what's going on around you you'd be a lot better off. You concentrate too much on your own private affairs. Try more to be a part of the world."

◆ ◆ ◆

"*... The truth is that I am only twenty-five miles away from the apartment, as you have probably guessed. In fact, you could not help but guess it, since you are perfectly familiar with Larry's Bar and Grill. I could not go to Massachusetts. I cried the whole way up to Muriel and it was as if someone else were getting of the bus, not myself. But someone who was in a desperate hurry to reach the next stop. I was in mortal terror that the bus would not stop at Muriel but continue on to some further destination where I would not know any familiar face. My terror was so great that I actually stopped crying. I kept from crying all the way. That is a lie. Not an actual lie because I never lie as you know. Small solace to either* *one of us, isn't it? I am sure that you would prefer me to lie, rather than be so intent on explaining my dilemma to you night and day. I am convinced that you would prefer me to lie. It would give you more time for the garage.*"

"So?" queried Sis McEvoy, an unkind note in her voice. To Janet she did not sound noticeably unkind, since Sis McEvoy was habitually sharp-sounding, and like her had very little sympathy for other human beings. She was sure that Sis McEvoy was bad, and she was determined to save her. She was going to save her quietly without letting Sis suspect her determination. Janet did everything secretly; in fact, secrecy was the essence of her nature, and from it she derived her pleasure and her sense of being an important member of society.

"What's it all about?" Sis asked irritably. "Why doesn't she raise kids or else go to a psychologist or a psychoanalyst or whatever? My ovaries are crooked or I'd raise kids myself. That's what God's after, isn't it? Space ships or no space ships. What's the problem, anyway? How are her ovaries and the rest of the mess?"

Janet smiled mysteriously. "Bozoe has never wanted a child," she said. "She told me she was too scared."

"Don't you despise cowards?" said Sis. "Jesus Christ, they turn my stomach."

Janet frowned. "Bozoe says she despises cowards, too. She worries herself sick about it. She's got it all linked up together with Heaven and Hell. She thinks so much about Heaven and Hell that she's useless. I've told her for years to occupy herself. I've told her that God would like her better if she was occupied. But she says God isn't interested. That's a kind of slam at me, I suppose. At me and the garage. She's got it in for the garage. It doesn't bother me, but it makes me a little sore when she tries to convince me that I wouldn't be interested in the garage unless she talked to me day and night about her troubles. As if I was interested in the garage just out of spite. I'm a normal woman and I'm interested in my work, like all women are in modern times. I'm a little stockier than most, I guess, and not fussy or feminine. That's because my father was my ideal and my mother was an alcoholic. I'm stocky and I don't like pretty dresses and I'm interested in my work. My work is like God to me. I don't mean I put it above Him, but the next thing to Him. I have a feeling that he approves of my working. That he approves of my working in a garage. Maybe that's cheeky of me, but I can't help it. I've made a name for myself in the garage and I'm decent. I'm normal." She paused for a moment to fill the two whiskey tumblers.

"Do you like my whiskey tumblers?" She was being unusually spry and talkative. "I don't usually have much time to buy stuff. But I had to, of course. Bozoe never bought anything in her life. She's what you'd call a dead weight. She's getting fatter, too, all the time."

"They're good tumblers," said Sis McEvoy. "They hold a lot of whiskey."

Janet flushed slightly at the compliment. She attributed the unaccustomed excitement she felt to her freedom from the presence of Bozoe Flanner.

"Bozoe was very thin when I first knew her," she told Sis. "And she didn't show any signs that she was going to sit night and day making up problems and worrying about God and asking me questions. There wasn't any of that in the beginning. Mainly she was meek, I guess, and she had soft-looking eyes, like a doe or a calf. Maybe she had the problems the whole time and was just planning to spring them on me later. I don't know. I never thought she was going to get so tied up in knots, or so fat either. Naturally if she were heavy and happy too it would be better."

"I have no flesh on my bones at all," said Sis McEvoy, as if she had not even heard the rest of the conversation. "The whole family's thin, and every last one of us has a rotten lousy temper inherited from both sides. My father and my mother had rotten tempers."

"I don't mind if you have a temper display in my apartment," said Janet. "Go to it. I believe in people expressing themselves. If you've inherited a temper there isn't much you can do about it except express it. I think it's much better for you to break this crockery pumpkin, for instance, than to hold your temper in and become unnatural. For instance, I could buy another pumpkin and you'd feel relieved. I'd gather that, at any rate. I don't know much about people, really. I never dabbled in people. They were never my specialty. But surely if you've inherited a temper from both sides it would seem to me that you would have to express it. It isn't your fault, is it, after all?" Janet seemed determined to show admiration for Sis McEvoy.

"I'm having fun," she continued unexpectedly. "It's a long time since I've had any fun. I've been too busy getting the garage into shape. Then there's Bozoe trouble. I've kept to the routine. Late Sunday breakfast with popovers and home-made jam. She eats maybe six of them, but with the same solemn expression on her face. I'm husky but a small eater. We have record players and television. But nothing takes her mind off herself. There's no point in my getting any more machines. I've got the cash and the good will, but there's absolutely no point."

"You seem to be very well set up," said Sis McEvoy, narrowing her eyes. "Here's to you." She tipped her glass and drained it.

Janet filled Sister's glass at once. "I'm having a whale of a good time," she said. "I hope you are. Of course I don't want to butt into your business. Bozoe always thought I pored over my account books for such a long time on purpose. She thought I was purposely trying to get away from her. What do you think, Sis McEvoy?" She asked this almost in a playful tone that bordered on a yet unexpressed flirtatiousness.

"I'm not interested in women's arguments with each other," said Sis at once. "I'm interested in women's arguments with men. What else is there? The rest doesn't amount to a row of monkeys."

"Oh, I agree," Janet said, as if she were delighted by this statement which might supply her with the stimulus she was after. "I agree one thousand percent. Remember I spend more time in the garage with the men than I do with Bozoe Flanner."

"I'm not actually living with my husband because of my temper," said Sis. "I don't like long-standing relationships. They disagree with me. I get the blues. I don't want anyone staying in my life for a long time. It gives me the creeps. Men are crazy about me. I like the cocktails and the compliments. Then after a while they turn my stomach."

"You're a very interesting woman," Janet Murphy announced, throwing caution to the winds and finding it pleasant.

"I know I'm interesting, " said Sis. "But I'm not so sure life is interesting."

"Are you interested in money?" Janet asked her. "I don't mean money for the sake of money, but for buying things."

Sis did not answer, and Janet feared that she had been rude. "I didn't mean to hurt your feelings," she said. "After all, money comes up in everybody's life. Even duchesses have to talk about money. But I won't, any more. Come on. Let's shake." She held out her hand to Sis McEvoy, but Sis allowed it to stay there foolishly, without accepting the warm grip Janet had intended for her.

"I'm really sorry," she went on, "if you think I was trying to be insulting and personal. I honestly was not. The fact is that I have been so busy building up a reputation for the garage that I behave like a savage. I'll never mention money again." In her heart she felt that Sis was somehow pleased that the subject had been brought up, but was not yet ready to admit it. Sis's tedious work at the combination tearoom and soda fountain where they had met could scarcely make her feel secure.

Bozoe doesn't play one single feminine trick, she told herself, and after all, after struggling nearly ten years to build up a successful and unusual business I'm entitled to some returns. I'm in a rut with Bozoe and this Sis is going to get me out of it. (By now she was actually furious with Bozoe.) I'm entitled to some fun. The men working for me have more fun than I have.

"I feel grateful to you, Sis," she said without explaining her remark. "You've done me a service. May I tell you that I admire your frankness, without offending you?"

Sis McEvoy was beginning to wonder if Janet were another nut like Bozoe Flanner. This worried her a little, but she was too drunk by now for clear thinking. She was enjoying the compliments, although it was disturbing that they should be coming from a woman. She was very proud of never having been depraved or abnormal, and pleased to be merely mean and discontented to the extent of not having been able to stay with any man for longer than the three months she had spent with her husband.

"I'll read you more of Bozoe's letter," Janet suggested.

"I can't wait," said Sis. "I can't wait to hear a lunatic's mind at work first-hand. Her letter's so cheerful and elevating. And so constructive. Go to it. But fill my glass first so I can concentrate. I'd hate to miss a word. It would kill me."

Janet realized that it was unkind of her to be reading her friend's letter to someone who so obviously had only contempt for it. But she felt no loyalty – only eagerness to make Sis see how hard her life had been. She felt that in this way the bond between them might be strengthened.

"Well, here it comes," she said. "Stop me when you can't stand it any more. *I know that you expected me to come back. You did not feel I had the courage to carry out my scheme. I still expect to work it out. But not yet. I am more than ever convinced that my salvation lies in solitude, and coming back to the garage before I have even reached Massachusetts would be a major defeat for me, as I'm sure you must realize, even though you pretend not to know what I'm talking about most of the time. I am convinced that you do know what I'm talking about and if you pretend ignorance of my dilemma so you can increase efficiency at the garage you are going to defeat yourself. I can't actually save you, but I can point little things out to you constantly. I refer to your soul, naturally, and not to any success you've had or to your determination. In any case it came to me on the bus that it was not time for me to leave you, and that although going to Massachusetts required more courage and strength than I seemed able to muster, I was at the same time being very selfish in going. Selfish because I was thinking in terms of my salvation and not yours. I'm glad I thought of this. It is why I stopped crying and got off the bus. Naturally you would disapprove, because I had paid for my ticket which is now wasted, if for no other reason. That's the kind of thing you like me to think about, isn't it? It makes you feel that I'm more human. I have never admired being human, I must say. I want to be like God. But I haven't begun yet. First I have to go to Massachusetts and be alone. But I got off the bus. And I've wasted the fare. I can hear you stressing that above all else, as I say. But I want you to understand that it was not cowardice alone that stopped me from going to Massachusetts. I don't feel that I can allow you to sink into the mire of contentment and happy ambitious enterprise. It is my duty to prevent you from it as much as I do for myself. It is not fair of me to go away until you completely understand how I feel about God and my destiny. Surely we have been brought together for some purpose, even if that purpose ends by our being separate again. But not until the time is ripe. Naturally, the psychiatrists would at once declare that I was laboring under a compulsion. I am violently against psychiatry, and, in fact, against happiness. Though of course I love it. I love happiness, I mean. Of course you would not believe this. Naturally darling I love you, and I'm afraid that if you don't start suffering soon God will take some terrible vengeance. It is better for you to offer yourself. Don't accept social or financial security as your final aim. Or fame in the garage. Fame is unworthy of you; that is, the desire for it. Janet, my beloved, I do not expect you to be gloomy or fanatical as I am. I do not believe that God intended you for quite as harrowing a destiny as He did for me. I don't mean this as an insult. I believe you should actually thank your stars. I would really like to be fulfilling humble daily chores myself and listening to a concert at night or television or playing a card game. But I can find no rest, and I don't think you should either. At least not until you have fully understood my dilemma on earth. That means that you must no longer turn a deaf ear to me and pretend that your preoccupation with the garage is in a sense a holier absorption than trying to understand and fully realize the importance and meaning of my dilemma. I think that you hear more than you admit, too. There is a stubborn streak in your nature working against you, most likely unknown to yourself. An insistence on being shallow rather than profound. I repeat: I do not expect you to be as profound as I am. But to insist on exploiting the most shallow side of one's nature, out of stubbornness and merely because it is more pleasant to be shallow, is certainly a sin. Sis McEvoy will help you to express the shallow side of your nature, by the way. Like a toboggan slide.*"

Janet stopped abruptly, appalled at having read this last part aloud. She had not expected Bozoe to mention Sis at all. "Gee," she said. "Gosh! She's messing everything up together. I'm awfully sorry."

Sis McEvoy stood up and walked unsteadily to the television set. Some of her drink slopped onto the rug as she went. She faced Janet with fierce eyes. "There's nobody in the world who can talk to me like that, and there's not going to be. Never!" She was leaning on the set and steadying herself against it with both hands. "I'll keep on building double-decker sandwiches all my life first. It's five flights to the top of the building where I live. It's an insurance building, life insurance, and I'm the only woman who lives there. I have boy friends come when they want to. I don't have to worry, either. I'm crooked so I don't have to bother with abortions or any other kind of mess. The hell with television anyway."

She likes the set, Janet said to herself. She felt more secure. "Bozoe and I don't have the same opinions at all," she said. "We don't agree on anything."

"Who cares? You live in the same apartment, don't you? You've lived in the same apartment for ten years. Isn't that all anybody's got to know?" She rapped with her fist on the wood panelling of the television set. "Whose is it, anyhow?" She was growing increasingly aggressive.

"It's mine," Janet said. "It's my television set." She spoke loud so that Sis would be sure to catch her words.

"What the hell do I care?" cried Sis. "I live on top of a life-insurance building and I work in a combination soda-fountain lunch-room. Now read me the rest of the letter."

"I don't think you really want to hear any more of Bozoe's nonsense," Janet said smoothly. "She's spoiling our evening together. There's no reason for us to put up with it all. Why should we? Why don't I make something to eat? Not a sandwich. You must be sick of sandwiches."

"What I eat is my own business," Sis snapped.

"Naturally," said Janet. "I thought you might like something hot like bacon and eggs. Nice crisp bacon and eggs." She hoped to persuade her so that she might forget about the letter.

"I don't like food," said Sis. "I don't even like millionaires' food, so don't waste your time."

"I'm a small eater myself." She had to put off reading Bozoe's letter until Sis had forgotten about it. "My work at the garage requires some sustenance, of course. But it's brainwork now more than manual labor. Being a manager's hard on the brain."

Sis looked at Janet and said: "Your brain doesn't impress me. Or that garage. I like newspaper men. Men who are champions.

Like champion boxers. I've known lots of champions. They take to me. Champions all fall for me, but I'd never want any of them to find out that I knew someone like your Bozoe. They'd lose their respect."

"I wouldn't introduce Bozoe to a boxer either, or anybody else who was interested in sports. I know they'd be bored. I know." She waited. "You're very nice. Very intelligent. You *know* people. That's an asset."

"Stay with Bozoe and her television set," Sis growled.

"It's not her television set. It's mine, Sis. Why don't you sit down? Sit on the couch over there."

"The apartment belongs to both of you, and so does the set. I know what kind of a couple you are. The whole world knows it. I could put you in jail if I wanted to. I could put you and Bozoe both in jail."

In spite of these words she stumbled over to the couch and sat down. "Whiskey," she demanded. "The world loves drunks but it despises perverts. Athletes and boxers drink when they're not in training. All the time."

Janet went over to her and served her a glass of whiskey with very little ice. Let's hope she'll pass out, she said to herself. She couldn't see Sis managing the steps up to her room in the insurance building, and in any case she didn't want her to leave. She's such a relief after Bozoe, she thought. Alive and full of fighting spirit. She's much more my type, coming down to facts. She thought it unwise to go near Sis, and was careful to pour the fresh drink quickly and return to her own seat. She would have preferred to sit next to Sis, in spite of her mention of jail, but she did not relish being punched or smacked in the face. It's all Bozoe's fault, she said to herself. That's what she gets for thinking she's God. Her holy words can fill a happy peaceful room with poison from twenty-five miles away.

"I love my country," said Sis, for no apparent reason. "I love it to death!"

"Sure you do, Hon," said Janet. "I could murder Bozoe for upsetting you with her loony talk. You were so peaceful until she came in."

"Read that letter," said Sis. After a moment she repeated, as if from a distance: "Read the letter."

Janet was perplexed. Obviously food was not going to distract Sis, and she had nothing left to suggest, in any case, but some Gorton's Codfish made into cakes, and she did not dare to offer her these.

What a rumpus that would raise, she said to herself. And if I suggest turning on the television she'll raise the roof. Stay off television and codfish cakes until she's normal again. Working at a lunch counter is no joke.

There was nothing she could do but do as Sis told her and hope that she might fall asleep while she was reading her the letter. "Damn Bozoe anyway," she muttered audibly.

"Don't put on any acts," said Sis, clearly awake. "I hate liars and I always smell an act. Even though I didn't go to college. I have no respect for college."

"I didn't go to college," Janet began, hoping Sis might be led on to a new discussion. "I went to commercial school."

"Shut up, God damn you! Nobody ever tried to make a commercial school sound like an interesting topic except you. Nobody! You're out of your mind. Read the letter."

"Just a second," said Janet, knowing there was no hope for her. "Let me put my glasses on and find my place. Doing accounts at the garage year in and year out has ruined my eyes. My eyes used to be perfect." She added this last weakly, without hope of arousing either sympathy or interest.

Sis did not deign to answer.

"Well, here it is again," she began apologetically. "Here it is in all its glory." She poured a neat drink to give herself courage. "*As I believe I just wrote you, I have been down to the bar and brought a drink back with me. (One more defeat for me, a defeat which is of course a daily occurrence, and I daresay I should not bother to mention it in this letter.) In any case I could certainly not face being without one after the strain of actually boarding the bus, even if I did get off without having the courage to stick on it until I got where I was going. However, please keep in mind the second reason I had for stopping short of my destination. Please read it over carefully so that you will not have only contempt for me. The part about the responsibility I feel toward you. The room here over Larry's Bar and Grill is dismal. It is one of several rented out by Larry's sister whom we met a year ago when we stopped here for a meal. You remember. It was the day we took Stretch for a ride and let him out of the car to run in the woods, that scanty patch of woods you found just as the sun was setting, and you kept picking up branches that were stuck together with wet leaves and dirt …*"

First published in *Antaeus* (Spring 1972).

Sketches

Paul Bowles collected and edited these fragments from Jane's notebooks for the journals Threepenny Review *and* Antaeus, *and the books* Feminine Wiles *and Virago's* Everything Is Nice: The Collected Stories.

Looking for Lane

THE TOWN OF X— was built on six or seven different levels. Right behind it there rose a heavily wooded mountain range, while below it stretched a swampy valley divided in the middle by a dark green river. Big wooden steps with iron handrails served as short cuts between one level of the town and the next. On the bottom level were the main streets, the shops, and the largest houses. On the third level at the end of the street there was a swift little waterfall near which Miss Dora Sitwell lived in a log house with her sister Lane. Lane was the younger but both sisters were in their middle years. Dora was a tall bony woman with bold black hair which she wore straight and pointing in toward her cheeks on either side. Her eye was bright and her nose long. Her sister was the opposite type – rather chunky and a blonde.

One morning in the fall of the year Dora was mending a pair of antique bellows and her sister lay in bed with a light case of grippe. She called in to Dora:

"Winter is coming and the damp is starting to seep in here already from that mountain. It's too near the house. As a matter of fact the whole town should be leveled. What's the point of living built into the side of a mountain? Why don't we go to Florida?"

"I like the change of seasons," Dora said pleasantly. "I love to watch each season come in— "

"We're too old for that winter summer spring stuff," Lane objected. "We should go to Florida and rest."

"I have as much zip as ever," Dora answered, "and I love the different seasons. So do you."

"I don't at all," said Lane.

Dora hung the bellows on their hook and walked into a dark and crowded corner of the room where she picked up a yellow crock designed to imitate a squash. She uncorked it and poured herself some sherry.

She drank sherry very often during the day but never so much that she lost interest in sewing or household work. Actually, she was more industrious and swifter than Lane, who did not drink but sat still dreaming for long periods of time. Dora returned to the couch which she herself had upholstered with two Indian blankets of different designs. There were a number of Indian and Russian objects in the room.

Afer a long period of silence, Lane called again.

"You can't tell me you enjoy November."

"I have nothing against November," said Dora. "In fact it's likely to make me feel zippy." Lane's feet thrashed angrily under the covers.

"It's not even natural to be as good-tempered as you are," she complained. "Every woman's got to have her humors."

"But I have nothing that makes me sad."

"Your husband died, didn't he?"

"Yes," Dora answered. "But he's so fortunate to be where he is. It's lovely up there."

"Well," Lane continued crossly. "You won't ever get there from this cluttered-up stupid little log house, I can tell you that."

"You don't have any knack for religion, Lane," Dora said. "You don't get what it's about – you never have."

Lane's face darkened. In referring to her religious inclination her sister had touched on a very sore spot. Lane did not have the fear of God.

She felt ashamed of this, and pretended to fear Him and to think about Him. She was free as well from any fear of the night or of wandering among the hills alone, and from any fear of strangers. This lack too she guarded from her sister's knowledge. It is impossible to foretell what a person will be ashamed of when finally grown up. Lane had no admiration at all for the type of woman so often described as "a dauntless woman" or even sometimes as a "she-devil". It had not even occurred to her that such a woman could be attractive, since moral character rather than personality concerned her, even though at a very underdeveloped level.

She also lived in fear that her sister would discover one day that she had never really formed any attachments. She felt attachment neither for her house, for her sister, nor for the town where she had been born. This secret, bitter but small in the beginning when she had first become conscious of it, had slowly come to contain her whole life. Not an hour passed that found her oblivious of the falsity of her position in the world. As a child believes that in five minutes he will have wings and be able to fly, so Lane hoped that she would awaken one day with a feeling of attachment and love for her sister and for the house, and with the fear of God in her heart.

She picked on her sister night and day, but concerning this behaviour she felt no remorse.

Now Lane looked over her shoulder out of the window, and saw the wooded hill rising straight up behind the house. The trees were bare. A white dog ran along beneath the trees, with the dry deep autumn leaves almost covering his back each time his paws touched the ground.

"I wonder," Lane said, "if that dog's going to be out all night."

"What dog, dear?"

"There's a white dog running through the forest."

"I guess he's after chipmunks," said Dora, "or just taking the air. Dogs like air, you know."

"I don't believe they care about air," Lane frowned. "They like food and smells ..."

"... and their masters," Dora added. "Don't forget their loyalty – their admirable attachment to their masters. I wish we had a dog."

"He might be taking a short cut through the woods and striking out for the next town," Lane said, her heart sinking.

"With nothing but his tail as luggage, instead of a lot of satchels," Dora added. "Human beings don't know it all. Animals have things more conveniently. Think of the fuss a human being makes when he goes on a journey."

The word "journey" struck deep into Lane's heart, and she closed her eyes for a minute, overcome with shame and anxiety. "You are like that dog," a voice inside of her said. She turned away from the window so that the light would be in back of her and her face could not be seen.

Even though Dora had walked to the far corner of the room again and was lifting the yellow crock, she knew that her sister had "passed into darkness" – a phrase she used to describe certain of Lane's moods, but only to herself. A curious reticence had prevented her from ever wondering why her sister did "pass into darkness" – nor had she ever shown by word or expression that she knew anything was amiss with her sister at these moments.

Lane's moods lent a certain dignity to Dora which she would not otherwise have possessed. Dora loved the existence she led with Lane so passionately that she had actually to sit still on the sofa during certain moments of complete awareness of it, the impact of her joy acting upon her like a blow.

She had been pleased at the death of both her parents and her older sister because this left her free to sell the Sitwell homestead and to construct with the proceeds a log house, which she had been planning to do all her life. She had always longed as well to live in a house built on one floor only and to roll her meals into the parlor on a tea-table. This she did with Lane every day, and with unfailing delight. She lived for pleasure alone, which she thought was the way of an artist – it being natural for certain women to love even the word artist. And not all of them feel this way for snobbish motives. Sometimes when she was in particularly high spirits she referred to herself as an artist. At other times she merely mentioned that she lived like one. One afternoon when she was really tipsy in the hotel barroom she had referred to herself many times as "the artist in the little log house." Because of the wild and joyous look in her black eyes, her neighbors could not believe that her pleasures were simple ones.

Dora had started to love Lane one night when Lane was five years old and she herself was eleven. Her mother and father had told her to bathe Lane because they were going to a show. She prepared the tin tub with warm water and told Lane to wait in the kitchen while she went to fetch some soap. When she returned Lane was no longer in the kitchen. She searched throughout the house for nearly three hours, but she could not find Lane anywhere. Finally, bewildered and tired, she sat on the floor in the hall, planning to wait for her parents' return. While she sat there, it suddenly came to her that she loved Lane more than anything else in the world. "Lane," she said aloud. "You angel pie – you're better than Baby Jesus." She began feeling in her heart that Lane's flight from the kitchen was in the nature of a declaration of love and secret pact, and her own search through the dark cold rooms – some of them empty of everything but dust and unfamiliar to her – had caused her to feel that in Lane were centered the light and the warm colors of the universe. "Lane is a beautiful rose," she thought, thinking of Lane's curls on her short fat neck.

Later with the help of her parents she searched the barn and they found Lane curled up in the sleigh under some filthy horse blankets.

Dora leaned over and picked Lane up in her arms. Lane, groggy with sleep, bit Dora on the chin and made it bleed. Their mother started to scold, but Dora kissed Lane passionately for a long time, squeezing Lane's head against her own skinny chest. Mrs Sitwell wrenched them apart in a sudden fury and pulled Dora's hair.

"Why do you kiss her, you little maniac? She just bit you!" Dora smiled but she did not answer.

"Why do you kiss her when she just bit you?" Mrs Sitwell repeated. "Are you a maniac?"

Dora nodded.

"I won't have it," said Mrs Sitwell, now cold with fury. "You tell her you're mad she bit you." Dora refused. Mrs Sitwell twisted her arm. "Tell her you're mad she bit you."

"Lane and me are maniacs," said Dora, in a very quiet voice, still smiling. Mrs Sitwell slapped her hard on the face.

"No one is a maniac," she said, "and you can't speak to Lane for two days." Then she burst into tears. They all went across the grass to the house. Mrs Sitwell was sobbing freely. She was a very nervous woman and she had drunk a bit too much at the party. This had made her very gay at first, but later she had grown increasingly belligerent. They all went into the parlor, where Mrs Sitwell sank into a chair and began staring at Lane through her tear-dimmed eyes.

"They should go to bed," her husband said.

"Lane doesn't look like anybody in the family on either side," said Mrs Sitwell. "Why does she have such a short neck?"

"One of her antecedents most likely had a short neck," Mr Sitwell suggested. "An aunt or an uncle."

"I don't feel like going on," said Mrs Sitwell. "Everything is beyond me." She buried her face in her hands. Dora and Lane left the room.

After that Dora organized a game called "Looking for Lane" which she played with her sister. It was the usual hide-and-seek game that children play but it gave Dora a much keener pleasure than any ordinary game. Finally the search extended over the countryside and Dora allowed her imagination to run wild. For example, she imagined once that she would find Lane's body dismembered on the railroad tracks. Her feelings about this were mixed. The important thing was that the land became a magic one the moment the search began. Sometimes Lane didn't hide at all, and Dora would discover her in the nursery after searching for nearly a whole afternoon. On such occasions she would become so depressed that she wouldn't eat.

Lane never explained anything. She was a quiet child with round eyes and a fat face.

This game stopped abruptly when Dora was fourteen, and she never again thought about it.

Each time that Lane "passed into darkness" Dora had a curious reaction that was not unlike that of a person who remembers a sexual gratification when he does not expect to. She was never alarmed, nor did she feel lonely. To live with a person who is something of a lunatic is certainly a lonely experience even if it is not an alarming one, but Dora had never felt loneliness. Sometimes, although she knew Lane was having a spell, she continued talking.

"Suppose," she said on this particular day, "that we plan our itinerary for next spring. There are several mountains that I'd like to visit. As one grows older one has access to many more pleasures than one ever had as a young person. It's as if at a certain age a thick black curtain were wrenched aside, disclosing row upon row of goodies ready to be snatched. We're put on this earth for us to enjoy – although certain others get their thrill out of abstinence and devotion. That's just doing it the other way around. Not that I care at all what others do – too much contact spoils the essence of things. You'll agree to that, because you're a first-class hermit, anyway. Do you want to have dinner at the hotel?"

Lane did not answer, but looked again out of the window.

"If you're looking for that white dog, Lane, he's certainly deep into the woods by this time."

First published in *Everything Is Nice: The Collected Stories* (Virago, 1989).

Laura and Sally

LAURA SEABROOK WAS LYING in her bed at four in the afternoon. She lived with Sam Brewster, a mechanic trained as an engineer who helped in many different ways around Camp Cataract. He often drove the truck into town for provisions, or the bus that fetched those people who had no cars from the railroad station. He ran the wood-chopping machine and tended all the roofs and defective screens. He was very happy at his different tasks and did not seem to regret his engineering studies. He regretted having disappointed his mother, but he was usually satisfied with what he was doing, as long as his life was among friendly people and out of doors. He could not bear to live in cities but he did not out of this dislike make a cult of nature.

Laura's hair hung to her shoulders and fell over half of her brooding face. No sunlight penetrated through the thick black pine trees into her cabin, but a blue bulb simulating daylight hung over her head. She was a very great beauty.

Sally McBridge was standing on the door sill smiling at Laura. Hers was a delicate pink face with round but fanatical blue eyes. She came every summer to Camp Cataract and the staff considered her to be somewhat of a lunatic and a fool. She dressed in a provincial out-of-date manner and altogether seemed to belong to either another country or another time. At this moment she was wearing a black coat with an orange full collar and a bonnet-shaped hat. She could not have been much more than thirty-nine or forty.

"How are you?" she asked Laura. "I thought you'd be dressed and ready to have your dinner."

"I can't dress," said Laura without looking at her.

"Do you have your melancholia?" Sally questioned her with a smile. Laura refused to answer.

"I'll tell you one thing," Sally continued. "You have to live in peace whether you have it or not. You can beat life if you want to." Sally's expression at that moment was almost wicked and even calculating. Laura looked at her for the first time.

"And then what's left to you after you've beaten life?" she asked sullenly.

"Happiness is left," Sally said. "Life is chaos and happiness is system – as if in a very delicately wrought but strong cage, while the life chaos remains outside. But remember I said cage and not room. The distinction is tremendous."

"What distinction?"

"Between room and cage. Do you know what I'm implying?"

Laura shrugged her shoulders. "Don't tell me," she said. For she was very aware that Sally's explanation would be wordy and very boring to her. Sally continued, however, ignoring her remark.

"If your happiness system is like a very delicate cage, you can see out and others can see in, even though your protections are as strong as the silver wires of a cage," she said. "But in a room you're really shut off."

Laura covered her face with her hands. "I hate Camp Cataract," she said. "That's all I know."

"I love it," Sally replied in a simple tone. "Perhaps because an evergreen is my favorite tree. It's modest and always there, like a friend or a loyal dog, winter and summer alike. And when its branches are heavy with snow, there is no tree more beautiful in the universe. Do you like evergreens?"

Laura did not answer. Her eyes were brooding.

"I'm certain you would like some place like Hawaii," Sally said to her. "You're such an impatient restless type of person. A palm tree is more your emblem than a pine. Isn't that so?"

"I have never thought of it," Laura replied. "I don't think of any of the things you think of. I don't believe I've ever looked at a tree, much less thought of one. I don't have a light enough heart to sit and think about things like that."

"My heart is not light, Laura," Sally said. "I have to spend many hours in my cabin alone. I'm going there now – I had a fit of nervous irritability this afternoon, and I want to think about it."

"Anyone who can speak of a happiness system is lighthearted," Laura said flatly.

"Don't talk nonsense, Laura. The finest brains have been occupied with such systems since the beginning of time ... orientals and occidentals alike."

"That's religion you're speaking of," said Laura. "Not a happiness system."

Quite suddenly Sally's face fell apart. She backed away from the cabin door, and Laura could hear her feet moving through the leaves.

Laura cocked an ear, but it was impossible to tell by listening to the rustle of dead leaves whether Sally was advancing deeper into the pine grove toward her cabin or if she had turned back in the direction of the lodge.

"I've hurt Sally's feelings," Laura thought. The brooding expression left her face, and at once a look of gravity and even nobility took its place. She rose to her feet. "I must go and find her."

She pulled a black dress of very thin material over her head and brushed out her stiff hair. Then she set out through the pine grove in search of Sally.

Her gait was a slow rolling one like that of a sailor. Her lips she kept held parted, and to the gravity of her expression was added a look of wonder which deepened as she approached the lodge. There was no longer any trace of apathy in her countenance. When she reached the dining terrace she stood still and looked about for Sally. The wind was blowing hard, somewhat deadening the roar of the waterfalls. Laura saw Sally moving with difficulty between the last row of tables (the row nearest to the precipice) and the heavy chain which separated the dining terrace from its edge.

"Why does she choose to cross there?" Laura asked herself. "There's barely space to get through without brushing against the diners." She hastened across the terrace herself, but at a more convenient place near the lodge steps. Pine groves surrounded the terrace at the other side as well, but through these groves a path had been cut leading to the main road. Laura reached the path first and hid behind a tree until Sally walked past. Then she came out from her hiding place and followed her. Laura knew that Sally was going to Mr Cassalotti's restaurant in the village. During the last three weeks she had followed Sally several times to the village and joined her there.

◆ ◆ ◆

Sally's fits of temper and shame were becoming more and more necessary to Laura. They stirred her blood. And while she hated Sally to such an extent at these moments that she wanted to strike her face, her own dignity at once seemed to swoop down upon her like some great and unexpected bird. It was not to comfort Sally, therefore, that she followed her to the village, but to enjoy for a while this calm and noble self born each time out of the other woman's rage.

She kept at a sufficient distance from Sally so that the other did not hear her footsteps. Camp Cataract, although situated in authentically wild country, was not at a very great distance from a little center, which could hardly have been called a town, but which included several stores, a restaurant, and a railroad station.

It was at this restaurant that Sally now stopped and mounted the stairs. She went into the dining room, located at the back of the house and reached only through the store which opened on the front steps. It was a dark room, with only five or six tables. There was no one about, but she could hear the members of the family moving overhead in their apartment. She chose a table next to a glassed-in scene that Mr Cassalotti had inserted in a large wall niche. The painted drop was of a cottage with lawn and woods and a little stream running to one side of it. Mr Cassalotti had extended the real lawn by using stage grass, and there were even little trellises about, stuck with old paper roses, too many of them contrasting oddly with the pastel-shaded flowers painted on the drop. Crowding the lawn was an assortment of poorly selected men and women fashioned in different styles and out of different materials, some being brightly painted lead and others carved out of wood. There was also, to complete the pointless staging, a child's miniature orange automobile set down right in the very midst of the lawn gathering and driven by a tiny rubber baby doll. The scene was illuminated from the sides and at this moment supplied the only light in the dining room.

The immediate urge of any diner with even the slightest degree of sensibility, if not to the actual aesthetic offense, then at least to the offense against order and the fulfillment of intention, was to punch through the glass and remove the automobile, if not half the figures. Only to the Cassalotti family and to children there was no disturbing element in this glassed-in scene.

Sally stared for a bit at the familiar lawn group, and even though she was a fanatic with usually one obsession at a time she felt a strong desire to remove the orange truck, which for a second absorbed her completely. She looked around automatically, as everyone else did, for an opening in the glass, although she knew perfectly well that there was none. Then she turned her back upon it and closed her eyes. She was trembling, and the wings of her nostrils were drawn. However, far from taking fright at the hysteria Laura's words had unloosed, or even growing despondent over it, Sally merely underwent the experience very much the way she stood behind the waterfalls each day at Camp Cataract. Far behind her new fit she was smiling to herself unbeatable and optimistic.

She knew that Laura had intended to upset her by drawing a line between her happiness system and the religions of the world. But it was not the seriousness of this demarcation that Sally was upset about so much as the simple fact that Laura had attacked her at all. Any criticism or show of aggression on Laura's part was enough to set Sally spinning backwards like someone clubbed over the head. This did not alter the fact that Sally considered herself to be the eventual victor. She knew too, without ever having had to reflect upon it, that Laura's connection with the universe was of greater depth and perception than her own – even though Laura was lazy and frankly jeered at life as without purpose. She had merely to speak of a serious subject when immediately the accent of her voice, the expression in her eye, lent to her words the weight of true gold. If Sally had been sincerely interested in becoming a wonderful person, she would have certainly been alarmed at recognizing a deeper accent of truth in Laura's voice than in her own. She would then have known the despair which comes of recognizing that what another understood automatically she herself would have to strive ceaselessly to understand throughout her life, and this would have caused her either to give up her own struggle – even if only temporarily, in a fit of jealous impotence – or, had she the strength, to continue along her own path, but wiser and more humble for her acquaintance with Laura.

She did neither, but instead set herself the task of conquering Laura – although exactly in what sense she meant to conquer her friend she did not herself know. Hers was an instinctive chase with a concealed objective. It is a curious fact that Sally, whose life was a series of tests and rituals of purification imposed upon herself, should have reacted so unscrupulously to the superiority – whether genuine or imagined by herself – of another woman. It was probable that she related the best and most spiritual part of her mind and heart to her life's purpose and only coarser elements in her nature to her friends.

◆ ◆ ◆

The door opened and Laura entered the dining room. Her beauty was even darker and more mobile than usual, as she stood for a second in the light of the half-open doorway. Sally looked up and noted how the shadows gave to Laura's face its actual dimension, which ordinarily in a cruder light lay behind the features, only half guessed at by the beholder. Now her features and the beauty behind them were the same thing. Sally looked at her beauty but was neither covetous nor jealous. She was conscious only of the effort it cost her to control her own features and even her arms and legs.

"I hate my nervous system," she said to herself, "but I'll get the better of it someday." Laura was approaching slowly toward the table, a look of great sobriety and weariness upon her face. Sally saw this out of the corner of her eye. "That's the way the attack always begins," she commented to herself. "I mustn't let her get started. I'm the one who should attack anyway. But perhaps today is not a very appropriate day for a beginning. Why are the Cassalottis sitting around their rooms in the middle of the afternoon?" Laura was upon her. She could not conceal this from herself any longer.

"Hello, Sally," Laura said to her, and with no further remarks she seated herself at the table. Sally's eyes were stretched wide in their sockets with the strain of attempting to control her nerves while she waited for Laura's assault to begin. These attacks were never overt but on the contrary so disguised that any third person present would not suspect any aggression at all. Even Sally, by some mysterious but compelling rule of conduct, never raised her voice or in any way let it be too apparent in her answers to Laura that she was conscious of any hostility. And although Sally was quite aware that she was being attacked, her temper was held in abeyance by some mysterious rule of manners, and she spoke pleasantly as if she did not understand the hostility behind Laura's words.

Camp Cataract, for so many years a symbol of escape from the strife of difficult human relations, had become since Laura's arrival the very seat of this type of strain for Sally. But it was a strange fact that Sally did not realize this at all. Having divided her life into two parts, she was incapable of including a third, or at least of treating with it in a profound manner. With Laura, although she never let this be apparent, she was greedy, belligerent, and without scruple.

Neither one of them spoke for a little, and then Laura asked where the Cassalottis were.

"Hanging around their apartments, Italian style, I guess," said Sally.

"Well, I would like a beer," said Laura. "So I'm going to go and get them down in a minute. Would you like a beer?"

Sally looked straight with glistening round eyes and a little fixed smile on her lips. "You know I don't drink, Laura," she said.

"I forgot," Laura answered, "and anyway, you might change."

"I don't change."

"Really?" Laura pretended surprise. "Well, you should try to see what it's like to behave like somebody else for a change.

Why don't you get drunk?" Laura rested her chin in her hand and looked thoughtfully at Sally.

"You want nothing but havoc and destruction around you, isn't that so?" Sally asked.

"Do you think I do?"

"You're a wrecker – look at your cabin. I'm not criticizing, but please don't ask me to be like you." Sally's head began to jerk a little with excitement. "Please don't ask me to be like you," she repeated.

Laura was surprised – Sally had never been so openly antagonistic before.

"I would not want you to be like me, Sally," she said in her sincere voice, with even a note of tenderness in her tone. "I would not want anyone to be like me. I've got melancholia. You know that." Her beautiful eyes were now so warm and solicitous that Sally could not continue to snap at her without making a fool of herself, so she kept her mouth tightly shut.

After a bit Laura spoke again.

"You like to sit in your cabin alone, don't you?" she asked Sally.

"I love it," said Sally.

"Why don't you get a sterno cooker? Then you could heat cans and make little stews for your dinner in the cabin."

"I like to sit on the terrace and watch the waterfall while I eat," said Sally, immediately feeling on her guard.

"Beryl could choose things from the lodge kitchen and bring them to you. A sterno cooker doesn't cost very much."

"I'd just as soon sit on the dining terrace and watch the waterfall while I eat," Sally repeated. She was almost sure the attack was on again, but not positive.

"Those little cookers are not very smelly either," Laura continued. "And Beryl could easily bring you plates and cutlery from the main dining room. You could tip her and she would even wash the plates each day and return them to you."

"I don't want to eat in my cabin," Sally said. But the spirit which had moved her a while ago to reprimand Laura was gone, and instead the familiar sensation of heaviness and impotence invaded her limbs and her head.

"Well, I think you really do," said Laura casually, turning away and glancing about the room, as if to demonstrate that she was losing interest in the conversation, "I suppose you really do but you haven't got a sterno cooker."

Sally half shut her eyes. "This is the attack, all right," she said to herself. "But I'll sit through it this time and not defend myself. It's nearly over anyway, I think."

Sally was correct in her guess that Laura's attack was nearly over. In fact, no sooner had she voiced this opinion to herself than Laura was on her feet.

"I am going upstairs," she said, "to drag the Cassalottis down here. I want my beer. Come with me."

Sally rose a little uncertainly to her feet. It was difficult for her to get up quickly when she was in a nervous state, and for one awful moment she thought she was going to fall back in her chair once more but she managed to reach Laura's side looking fairly normal. They left the dining room and went into a small dark hallway. Laura, who was very familiar with the Cassalotti house, pulled on a door which opened onto a closed stairway. The walls of the stairway were papered in a small flower pattern and very dirty. They started to mount the stairs – slowly because of their steepness. Sally felt her head turning a little. The air in the stairway was stale. But her dizziness was more the result of Laura's proximity than of the bad air in the stairway. Since there was no banister, she let the flat of her palm travel along the cold, flower-papered wall. This comforted her to a certain extent until they reached the landing.

The terrible gloom and boredom that had descended upon Laura earlier in the day, back at Camp Cataract, had now completely vanished, not from her memory but from her feelings. At last the day was cluttered with possibilities and adventures. The ascension of the stairs aided her optimism, and by the time she reached the landing a happy excitement was fully upon her.

"Cassalottis!" she called in her husky voice, now ringing with gaiety.

"Hello, Laura Seabrook." Rita Cassalotti's voice was gentle but without warmth.

Laura fairly galloped down the length of the uncarpeted hallway, knocking into a wrought iron stand that supported a trough of ferns on the way. The stand teetered for a moment on its high legs, but it did not fall over.

"I want beer, you bums," Laura shouted as she flung open the Cassalottis' parlor door. Greetings were exchanged while Sally hung back in the hallway, not caring to move forward or backward. She knew that Laura wanted to be rid of her.

"She's moved on to the Cassalottis and everybody else might as well be dead," Sally reflected. "But I'll stay. Certainly I shan't come and go at her convenience." Her head was beginning to ache as a result of the afternoon's complications.

She promised herself that on the following day she would go down into the chasm a mile south of Camp Cataract, where descent was more gradual, and walk along the river bed. She reminded herself too that she had already gone three quarters of the way toward directing her life current, as she termed it, into a peace stream, in spite of her bad nervous system. "Camp Cataract," she said to herself, "is definitely carrying off the honors, and *not* my sister's apartment." This thought cheered her up and she started down the hall toward the parlor, where the girls were laughing and talking so loudly that they did not even notice her entering the room.

◆ ◆ ◆

Mr Cassalotti was there, Berenice and Rita – his oldest daughters – an aunt, and some of the younger children. Everyone was dressed, with the exception of Rita Cassalotti, who was wearing a pink wrapper made of an imitation thick velours. There were more ferns here in the upstairs parlor, just like the ones Laura had barely missed knocking over in the hallway. A linoleum stamped with a red and black design covered the floor. The chairs and the sofa were all occupied by the family, with the exception of one odd Victorian chair made of carved black wood in Chinese style, which stood near a window and was seldom used.

Sally seated herself in this chair and folded her hands in her lap. "Now we'll see how far she'll go," she thought, fixing her eyes on Laura, and she felt elated without noticing that she did.

Rita Cassalotti had a small head and eyes a little too close together but she was pretty. Her teeth were very even and the canines beautifully shaped. Men adored her but she was neither vain nor inclined towards flirtation or love-making. She loved the food she got at home, her bedroom furniture and her clothing. Her body was unexpectedly heavier than anyone would have guessed just from seeing her small head and slender neck, but she was not fat, merely soft and round, although only a sensitive man – even if a stranger – might have sensed coldness lurking in her soft frame.

"What brings you here this afternoon, Laura Seabrook?" Rita questioned her pleasantly.

"I was so bored at Camp Cataract," said Laura, "that I thought the world was coming to an end. Then I remembered that you always cheered me up." This statement was true, at least partially. The Cassalottis did cheer Laura up, but she had forgotten that her original intention had been to pursue Sally and not to visit the Cassalottis.

Rita let out a peal of merry laughter. She always reacted more strongly to what seemed to her the grotesque than to situations or states of feelings that might easily have been included in the content of her own life.

"Do you have a sewing machine, there at Camp Cataract?" Rita asked with a twinkle in her eye.

"No ... I'm not sure," Laura answered her.

Rita thought this was even more hysterically funny than Laura's first statement.

"Rita! Stop being foolish – you sound like a dope." Her younger sister Berenice silenced her with a look from her big flashing eyes. She was a swarthy, short-legged girl with dark bushy hair and a raucous low voice. Her chin was delicately cleft and her nose was Roman and very beautiful. She was enthusiastic and tempestuous, with a warmth not often encountered in a young girl.

"Why are you talking about machines?" she stormed at Rita.

"Well," said Rita, not in the least disturbed by her sister's outburst. "She said she thought the world was coming to an end, and I thought that if she had a sewing machine she could make some dresses when she didn't know what else to do."

"You're crazy," said Berenice.

"No, I'm not," Rita answered, laughing merrily again. "What's crazy about a sewing machine? You're the one who's on the crazy side, not me."

"Laura's got a lot of trouble," said Berenice. "She wouldn't get no relief from a sewing machine."

"No?" Rita raised her eyebrows and looked questioningly at Laura. "Maybe not," she said with half-hearted interest. The conversation seemed to be losing its grotesque quality and turning on the serious. The very prospect of hearing about anyone else's trouble tired Rita and she yawned.

Mr Cassalotti, who had not bothered to greet either Laura or Sally, was sitting on a small cane chair and staring ahead of him with hands thrust in his pockets. Without warning he got up from his chair and started toward the door.

"Poppa," said Berenice, "where are you going?"

"I'm going to let the beer out and make raviolis. Come on downstairs and we'll have a little party." He looked back over his shoulder at Laura and nodded to her without changing his expression.

"Just plain havoc, with no thought behind it," Sally was thinking. "That's what she likes, instead of the beautiful. She thinks it's exciting and adventurous to sit indoors in the afternoon with people eating raviolis and drinking beer. She doesn't know where real happiness lies. If she could only be persuaded to stay outdoors a little more. It would be at least a beginning."

Laura was hustling the Cassalottis through the parlor door as hastily as she could, in her eagerness to get at the beer. The children remained always silent and strange whenever Laura appeared. They leaned against the wall looking after her with sober brown eyes.

The Cassalotti sisters, followed by Laura and Sally, started down the steep stairway single file.

"Gee, it's nice you came," said Berenice affectionately to Laura, who was behind her. She turned around and squeezed Laura's leg to emphasize her pleasure. "It will only take Poppa a little while to get the raviolis going, and we can drink beer while we wait anyhow ..." She gave Rita a little shove and pulled her hair. "Why don't you get dressed, you?" she said.

At that moment Laura's joy at being among the Cassalottis reached its peak – and with it came a familiar chill at the bottom of her heart. "Oh, God," thought Laura. "I had almost forgotten for a moment. I wish I could be really here, having the kind of fun I think it is to be here."

She was quite accustomed to this cold fright that gripped her heart whenever her pleasure was acute, but it was not fright itself that interested her. She was quite sure that most sensitive people were familiar with this feeling. What disturbed her more than fright was the chain of questions about whatever she was doing, so that she could never wholeheartedly enter into anything for more than a few seconds at a time.

"How exhausting," she said to herself as she felt the chill settling like a thick fog around her heart. The tormenting question which followed in the wake of her anguish was this: should she consider the anguish to be the natural underlying side of life itself, that side which gives depth and gravity to the sense of living from hour to hour, and which is to be endured simply and accepted, or was it on the other hand a signal for departure – a signal for a decision? It was this last possibility that she found so upsetting, for she was actually, in her thinking at least, a very conscientious person.

They reached the landing and Laura stood for a second, uncertainly, with Sally waiting behind her on the bottom step.

She wished she had the courage to go out the door onto the wooden porch and thence down the road through the pine woods, instead of sitting down to eat ravioli and to drink beer. The very thought that such an action was incumbent upon her made her feel faint.

"A silly struggle over two silly alternatives – to eat ravioli or to walk in the woods," she whispered to herself, without believing it. She bit her lips hard and a happy thought struck her: "The Cassalottis would be very insulted if I left. How could I have overlooked it?" The relief she felt, having voiced this sentence to herself, was immediate. Her face lost its hunted animal look, and she took long strides in the direction of the dining room.

◆ ◆ ◆

The others had gone back into the kitchen behind the dining room and were watching Mr Cassalotti, who was using the ravioli machine. He was very neat and very systematic in his cooking, being a great admirer of both American factory technique and sanitation. He had already selected four cartons and labeled them neatly with the names of friends. "You can take these back to Camp Cataract with you when you go," he said to Laura. "Tell them a ravioli present from Gregorio Cassalotti – and remind them that Wednesday night is Chicken Cassalotti night. Chicken Gacciatore died when Chicken Cassalotti was born." He laughed to himself.

He did not in any way resemble Laura's conception of an Italian, except physically. He was industrious and really only happy when he worked. The girls took the beer into the dining room and they all seated themselves near the glassed-in scene, including Sally, who sat with her chair exaggeratedly far from the table and turned sideways.

"Pull yourself in," said Berenice.

"No, thank you," Sally answered her. "I'm not going to eat or drink. I'm all right here."

Berenice stared at Sally uncomprehendingly, but she felt herself so remote from the other woman that she could not, as she ordinarily would have done, urge her to join them in eating and drinking.

The Cassalotti sisters had brought to the table about fifteen bottles for beer. Laura, so recently released from her small but painful struggle, was giddy as a result of her escpe. There still lurked a doubt in her heart but it was a muffled doubt, reserved for a little later. She was determined now to get drunk, and to have the Cassalottis share her renewed gaiety, though of a completely different variety (with real joy as its source, rather than than pained joy), matched her own. So it was to Rita she addressed herself.

"Rita, do you like Sunday?" she asked her. Rita's face remained closed, and she appeared to have no intenton of answering Laura's question at all. Often she did not answer Laura's questions with even so much as a nod of her head. This made Laura all the more determined to find out how Rita felt about everything. She tried formulating her question to Rita differently.

"Do Sundays make you nervous?" she asked this time.

"I don't know," said Rita, without the faintest expression in her voice.

"I like 'em, good weather or bad," put in Berenice. "If it's bad weather, I go fishing or hunting for berries and mushrooms, and if it's bad weather I listen to the radio. In the winter, of course, I don't go after berries or mushrooms."

"Do you go after berries and mushrooms too, on Sundays?" Laura asked Rita, interrupting Berenice.

Sally was exasperated with Laura for showing such a keen interest in Rita Cassalotti's Sundays.

"Why doesn't she ask me what I do on Sunday, instead of asking that trollop? She certainly can't do much of any interest if she stays in her wrapper all day."

"If only Berenice would keep her mouth shut for a minute," Laura thought. "I might then be able to drag something out of Rita." She was a little put out with herself for not being able to imagine Rita's attitude toward Sunday. But all the while Berenice continued to fill the glasses with beer the moment they were emptied, so that Laura very soon cared less and less about finding out anything from Rita.

In fact, she was unpleasantly startled when Rita asked Berenice whether she remembered the Sundays at Felicia Kelly's.

"Not as good as you do," said Berenice. "Because I was a little tyke."

"That was ten years ago," Rita said. "I was twenty years old and you were ten. She had her bushes and trees growing so close to the walk there that we used to get soaking wet from the branches after the rain. I used to rub Berenice's hair with a Turkish towel when we got in the house – my own too. It's a mistake to plant them so close." Rita was actually addressing Berenice rather than Laura, for she was never certain that Laura could really understand much of what was said. Berenice, who was interested in almost any topic of conversation, listened attentively.

"She made tutti-frutti ice cream for her family on Sunday, so she always served us some. It was very good quality. You could see the Old Man and the Old Woman on clear days from her kitchen window, I think you could see the Old Man from the parlor window too, but not the Old Woman. I'm sure you couldn't see the Old Woman from the parlor – no, you couldn't have, it wasn't facing right. Berenice used to get a kick out of that. We can't see any mountain peaks from here, just the valley and the woods. But Berenice could see those two peaks very clear from the Kellys', so she was pleased about that, I guess. Do you remember the Old Man and the Old Woman, Berenice?"

Laura was thoroughly bored by the present turn in the conversation, but she felt compelled to question Rita further, since this account about Felicia Kelly's house was a roundabout answer to Laura's, original question "Do you like Sundays?", which proved that at least Rita had heard her question, and that the possibility of finding out more concerning Rita and her tastes was not entirely closed to her.

"Did you like going to see Felicia Kelly on Sunday?" Laura asked her, trying to conceal her weariness by tossing her head back and smiling.

Again Rita's face was closed, and instead of answering Laura's question she poured herself some beer very carefully so as to avoid its forming a head.

"Rita doesn't go to see Felicia Kelly any more," said Berenice, and there was such warmth and radiance shining in her eyes even as she made this announcement that Laura felt recompensed, in spite of Rita's queer stubbornness, and was not annoyed with Berenice for interrupting.

"Really?" she said.

"No. One Sunday she went all the way over there – it's about fifteen miles from here – and nobody was home, not even the dog. The cat was there but the dog wasn't. So she never spoke to Felica Kelly again."

"We drove all the way over there," said Rita, "and then we had to come all the way back without seeing anyone. Poppa was mad too. He used to drive us over there in the truck and call for us every Sunday. She didn't leave a note, either."

"What happened to her?" Laura asked with some degree of real interest.

"I don't know," said Rita. "I never talked to her again."

"She called up once or twice but Poppa just told her Rita wouldn't talk to her, and then he'd hook the receiver on the telephone," put in Berenice.

"Then you never knew why she wasn't home?" Laura asked Rita, looking at her with wonder.

"No," said Rita. "I never talked to her again." She seemed pleased with the end of her story.

At this point Laura gave up thinking about Rita because she was so much of a mystery to her that there seemed to be no hope of her ever understanding any more about how Rita felt than she did that afternoon, even had she persisted in questioning her for the next fifty years. In a sense it was satisfying to know that such mysteries existed and that she did not have to exert herself any further.

◆ ◆ ◆

Just then, Mr Cassalotti, came in with the raviolis. He had dished out the portions in the kitchen and now carried the full plates over to the table on a tray.

"I got everything ready so all you have to do now is eat. Move your chair in," he said to Sally, putting a plate of raviolis down on the table for her.

They had all forgotten Sally's presence, and looked toward her with surprise. She had moved her chair even further away from the table during the conversation about Felicia Kelly, although no one had noticed it.

"No, thank you," said Sally, her aloof expression changing quickly into one of vivid revulsion. "I'm going home in a minute."

"Not before you eat your ravioli," said Mr Cassalotti calmly, and going over to her chair he got behind it and lifted her over to the table, where he set her down, chair and all, in front of her raviolis.

Berenice had a hunted, frightened look in her eyes as she watched her father with amazement. Ordinarily she would have laughed heartily at such playfulness, but being extremely sensitive, she felt that Sally was not a person to be lifted through the air even in jest. Rita wasn't either worried or amused.

"Oh, Poppa," she said. "If she don't want to eat don't force her."

Mr Cassalotti returned to the kitchen and there was silence in the dining room. Even Rita noticed the queer strained look on Sally's face, and she stared at her shamelessly while Laura and Berenice averted their eyes.

Sally was so insulted by Mr Cassalotti's gesture that, although she wanted to flee from the room, she remained rooted to her chair by such shame and by an anger so burning that it temporarily blotted from her mind its source, so that only the present moment existed for her. Her eye fixed on a red-and-white checked curtain on the wall opposite, and immediately she felt that to draw this curtain was her only hope against suffocation. Then the fear that she would not reach the curtain gradually stole the place of both her shame and her anger, imparting a more pitiful and appealing expression to her eyes.

"It's so hot in here," said Berenice, whose sensitive nature was becoming more and more aroused.

Sally heard the remark and now her heart started to beat with panic lest Berenice reach the window before she did. She felt it was absolutely necessary that she herself draw the curtains and not Berenice.

With what seemed to her superhuman effort, she rose to her feet and then walked like a person lightheaded with fever over to the window. She drew the curtains aside with a shaky hand. Behind them was a black shade which Mr Cassalotti had hung there so that no daylight would ever penetrate the restaurant. He thought that to eat by electricity was more elegant, and that all restaurateurs should equip their restaurants so as to appear in a land of perpetual night.

Sally lifted the shade and there at last was the window. It had been pouring outside only a moment before, so that streams of rain were still sliding down the window pane. Through the pane the leaves of the elm, whose branches almost brushed against the side of the house, appeared larger and more glistening than they actually were. The grass, a brilliant green in the afterlight of the storm, seemed particularly so around the thick wet trunk of the tree.

Sally felt that she was losing ground faster and faster every minute, a condition which she qualified at calmer moments as "going too fast for myself." But it was not because she was so much of a lady or even particularly dignified that Mr Cassalotti's gesture had insulted her so deeply. The insult lay in the suddenness of the actual interruption, which had violated abruptly her precarious state of balance.

"I'll have to get out on the ground," she said to herself three or four times. Behind her she could hear the subdued voices of the two other women and Berenice. But they seemed far away, as if they were speaking in a separate room. She felt along the glass several times as if she would find a way of going through the window to get outside, but in a moment she sighed and turned around, scanning the room for the right door. In order to reach it she had to pass the table where the others were sitting. But she kept her head high and was in truth scarcely aware of their presence at all.

Unfortunately Laura was drinking her eighth beer, which suddenly changed her mood into one of lachrymose affection.

"Sally, sweetheart," she called as Sally stalked past the table. "Sally, darling, where are you going?" Sally already had her hand on the knob and was pulling on it, but Laura sprang to her feet and reach Sally's side before she was able to get through the door.

"You have to come and eat your ravioli, because it's delicious, but if you won't eat you can talk to Berenice and Rita and me," Laura said to her. Putting her arms around Sally she searched her face with tenderly swimming eyes.

Sally looked as though she were about to be sick, but with unexpected energy she wrenched herself loose from Laura's embrace and fairly flew out of the room.

The evening air was cold and still, now that the storm had passed, and the sky near the horizon was green, the color green that chills the heart of a person of melancholic or tempestuous nature. But Sally did not even notice it. No natural sight ever depressed her and she did not know what it was to be melancholic.

Pine cones, now soggy and darker-colored after the rain, were scattered about underneath the trees. Sally's sister Henrietta liked to paint pine cones different colors and then heap them into a bowl for decoration.

Sally felt infinitely weary as she looked at these cones, which seemed to be scattered about the grass as far as the eye could see. However (and in spite of the fact that pine cones were abundant in all the surrounding region and lay scattered about even at the very door of her own cabin at Camp Cataract), she flet challenged to gather some, soggy as they were, to take back to her sister. She had nothing but her hat to carry them in, which she determined to use. Squatting down on her heels, she was quickly absorbed in selecting the most perfect cones. In her thoughts there was not a shadow of concern about Laura or the Cassalotti sisters. As far as she was concerned, they did not exist.

◆ ◆ ◆

Laura had never seen Sally out of control before, and she returned to the table worried and yet excited. Although she was drunk enough to behave carelessly, her instincts forbade her to follow Sally out of doors.

"What do you suppose got into her?" Laura asked.

"A jackass," said Berenice.

Rita reprimanded her sister. "You don't have to use such talk," she said to her.

"She was quite beside herself when she left the room," Laura added, ignoring Berenice's language. Laura knew that she should not be discussing Sally with the Cassalottis, who were certain to interpret her more simply than her unbalanced nature merited.

"She's a stuck-up jackass," Berenice said again. "She doesn't want to associate with us or have you associating with us either. Don't you think I've known it all along? She didn't eat those raviolis just to insult Poppa. I'd like to see the rotten stinking food they got at her house."

"Fried skunk," said Rita placidly, without a smile.

"That's right." Berenice nodded her approval.

Laura had not expected the conversation about Sally to be on such a low level as this. She was particularly surprised to hear Berenice attack Sally so bitterly, since it had never occurred to her that Berenice could be anything but warmhearted and generous toward everyone.

"Poppa took a lot of trouble making that ravioli for her, and he's a very busy man. I didn't care how the crazy loon acted with us, but she's got to be decent with Poppa. She can't come in here anymore now, that's all ... Let her go to a stuck-up place."

"Sally isn't stuck-up," said Laura, who could never be

dishonest. "She is high-strung but not stuck-up. High and strict. She's got systems for living."

"So have Rita and me got systems, and one of them is not to look like a rat bit us if we are served food in somebody else's house. We say thank you and we eat our food. So do you, Laura. Don't make excuses for her. Anyway, she hates us."

Berenice was calming down. She scraped at her empty plate with her fork for a little while. Then soon the glow returned to her face, and her eyes were once again shining with warmth and enthusiasm.

"Life is too short ..." she said, smiling at Laura, and she poured some more beer. But Laura felt ashamed now to have referred to Sally's behavior at all, and she was determined to continue the conversation so as to vindicate in some way the cheapness of her original impulse to gossip.

"I don't think Sally hates you," she said to Berenice. "It's very possible that she loves you."

Berenice opened her eyes wide with incomprehension.

"It's not a bit unusual to love and to hate the same person," Laura continued. Her tone was didactic.

"Unusual," said Berenice. "It's impossible." But she spoke hesitatingly because she was really at sea thus far in the conversation.

"No, no," Laura insisted. "That's partly why living is such trouble. We are likely to love and to hate the very same person at the very same time, and yet neither emotion is more true than the other. You have to decide which you're going to cater to, that's all. Fortunately, if you are at all decent, you manage to keep pushing love a little bit ahead ... but it can be very, very difficult keeping it that way. I was that way about my mother, and I have been that way about one other person, but particularly my mother."

"Oh, no—" The words escaped Berenice involuntarily.

"Oh, yes!" Laura was vehement. "Sometimes I wanted to hit Mother so hard that it would knock her head right off her body. She's dead now but I think I would feel the same way if she were alive."

Berenice didn't say anything. She clasped both hands tightly around her glass of beer and stared ahead of her. Rita Cassalotti had long since been occupied with some private concern and remained mute.

After a moment Berenice broke the silence. "I've got to go out now," she announced. Cocking her head to one side, she smiled at Laura – a charming smile that showed the dimple in her cheek – and she looked for all the world like a young girl taking leave of her hostess at a tea party.

"But," said Laura, horrified at this unexpected announcement, "I thought we had hours ahead of us still. You didn't say anything ..."

Berenice stood up. "I've got to go into town," she said, and once more she tilted her head to one side and smiled enchantingly at Laura, but without meeting Laura's eye.

Berenice was leaving, and Laura knew somehow that she had no appointment, and knew too that no word she could utter would bring Berenice back into the room. Laura's cheeks were hot with shame. She could not bear to have Berenice turn away from her this way, although a moment before she had considered Berenice so shallow that she was ashamed to discuss Sally with her. She was in a panic lest Berenice should cast away their friendship, and her shame sprang from a suspicion that she had ruined something in Berenice's heart – not because of Berenice but because such a misdeed would reflect seriously on her own character.

"Oh, my God," Laura said to herself, "why did I bring up my theory about love and hate? She'll never, never forgive me." Laura had a wild respect for people who were capable of becoming so offended that they rose from their chairs and left the room where they were sitting, and sometimes even the house. And if it was for an ideal that they showed such offense and not for any egoistic personal reason, Laura regarded them as saints.

"She must forgive me," she repeated to herself, "she must, or it will be a real calamity."

◆ ◆ ◆

She recalled the moment on the bottom step, when she had not obeyed the seemingly mystical challenge to walk through the wet woods instead of sitting down to eat her raviolis. So now, by not having had the courage to heed this compulsion, she had lost the Cassalottis as well. In moments of stress she was very apt to see connections between her intimate world and the actions of other people, as if the adverse behavior of others was dependent at least indirectly upon an earlier wrong decision concerning a private matter of her own. She realized the idiocy of such reasoning but at the same time she thought that everyone else felt that way without noticing it. Certainly nothing was so personal to her as this way of being. In fact it was impossible for her to give it up.

Even so, to witness the shock Berenice had suffered as a result of her own careless remark was to Laura the worst possible punishment, because in the face of Berenice's distress, which overwhelmed this girl so naturally that any question or doubt as to whether she could choose or not choose to overlook her feelings was unthinkable, Laura's own feelings against herself assumed a grotesque and petty quality which made her blush. She continued, however, even though humiliated, to suspect that had she not eaten raviolis but really gone walking instead through the woods, she would not have found herself faced by the present quandary. How she was able to feel herself to be grotesque and comical, and at the same time so important that the outcome of her decisions controlled somehow the behavior of people not in the least connected to it, was a puzzle to Laura herself.

She saw all these things and even more, for she was educated enough in psychological matters to conceive that the source of Berenice's own violent reaction to her remarks about hating her mother lay not in what she, Laura, had decided earlier on the bottom step, or even in Berenice's genuine moral indignation, but in a hatred that Berenice might have felt and concealed from herself, at one time or another, toward her own mother. Laura knew about such things but they did not help her one bit when she was in the midst of a calamity.

With all these details very clear in her mind, still (like a person who jumps deliberately into a pit) she was falling deeper and deeper by the second into such an abject terror of Berenice's resentment that she longed for forgiveness more than for anything in the world. She appealed to Rita, hoping that after all she had imagined something amiss in Berenice's behavior while actually everything was really just as it had been a little while before. She had often enough imagined that she had horrified a friend when nothing of the kind had occurred.

"Rita, did Berenice have an appointment?" she asked.

"No, she didn't have no appointment," Rita said, shrugging her shoulders.

"Where did she go then, Rita?" Laura insisted, fixing her eyes on Rita's face.

"She went flying away with the birdies," said Rita Cassalotti, and with sudden animation she stretched out both her arms and moved them up and down in imitation of a bird's flight.

To see Rita thus unconcerned and jesting made Laura feel her plight ever more keenly, for she needed someone's sympathy badly right then. She plucked at Rita's pink sleeve, trying to halt the upward motion of her arm.

"Please stop flying, Rita, and talk to me."

She looked so peculiar that Rita burst out laughing.

"Rita," Laura pleaded, "why do you think she went away?"

Rita shrugged her shoulders. She never paid much attention to Berenice's comings and goings, and had actually scarcely taken notice when Berenice left the table. Rita yawned and got up. "I'm going to get dressed," she said. "I've got a real complete appointment tonight, including dinner, movies, drinks and dancing – with a married guy, too." She started to leave the room and Laura followed behind her. They mounted the stairs together in silence. Laura knew that Rita wanted to be left alone but she was far too nervous to remain by herself and her pride was nonexistent.

"I've got to get dressed," said Rita when she found Laura was behind her even in the bedroom.

"Oh, but please, Rita, let me stay here," Laura begged her, and she searched her mind rapidly for a topic of conversation that might interest Rita. "Rita," she said, her eyes full of concern, "I'm terribly worried about your going around with a married man."

"Why?" Rita asked with no interest. She took off her wrapper and stood before Laura in her bloomers. "I'm not afraid of his wife," she said, thrusting her chin out.

"But morally it's wrong." Laura searched her brain frantically, trying to remember at least one reasonable argument against adultery, but she couldn't think of any.

"If he don't go with me, he'll go with someone else," Rita said flatly. "Not that I give a hoot whether I go with him or anyone else. They're all alike, the men, and I never cared for their company much."

"Why not, Rita?" Laura asked her with great interest.

"I don't know," Rita said, "I just don't care for them. I wish you'd let me dress by myself," she said. "I can't keep my mind on it with you here."

There was nothing left for Laura to do but leave. She thought it was irritating that a dumbbell like Rita Cassalotti needed her privacy at all, and she went out angry as well as forlorn.

"I've ruined everything," she said to herself, descending the stairway slowly, one step at a time.

Not knowing whether it was useless or not to wait for Berenice's return, she wandered aimlessly about the dining room, straightening chairs and stopping now and then to gaze at the glassed-in scene, so provokingly flooded with light when the dining room itself lay in darkness. The orange truck driven by the celluloid baby held her eye. The doll, not designed to sit up, had been tilted against the back of the seat with its legs curled in the air almost over its head.

In spite of the incongruity apparent in this combination, she was overcome with boredom, looking at it as if she were seeing it not for the first but for the thousandth time. She turned herself away, almost in embarrassment, as though she herself were responsible for what she saw in the glass case. She would have liked to ponder on the mysterious effect these two objects had on her, but just then the full realization that Berenice Cassalotti would never have faith in her again seemed, like an ocean wave, to break over her head and wash all other thoughts away.

She hurried out of the dining room and into the store. It was empty. On all other occasions Berenice had taken her to the door flushed with beer and pleasure, and filled with the anticipation of Laura's next visit, for in Berenice's joyous heart even a departure took on the aspect of a return.

Laura closed the door behind her and started toward the road that led out of the village to Camp Cataract. It was a wide sandy road bordered by such tall pine trees that, with the exception of a few sunny hours at midday, the road lay constantly in the shadows. The sandy earth was cold and no grass grew anywhere.

Far ahead of her, out of hearing but not out of sight, Laura could see Sally walking along, her handbag swinging from her wrist. She was walking slowly, with small steps, her head bent, and at a pace suitable to a city street.

Laura had forgotten about her completely.

First published in *The Threepenny Review* (1987).

The Iron Table

THEY SAT IN THE SUN, looking out over a big new boulevard. The waiter had dragged an old iron table around from the other side of the hotel and set it down on the cement near a half-empty flower bed. A string stretched between stakes separated the hotel grounds from the sidewalk. Few of the guests staying at the hotel sat in the sun. The town was not a tourist center, and not many Anglo-Saxons came. Most of the guests were Spanish.

"The whole civilization is going to pieces," he said.

Her voice was sorrowful. "I know it." Her answers to his ceaseless complaining about the West's contamination of Moslem culture had become increasingly unpredictable. Today, because she felt that he was in a very irritable mood and in need of an argument, she automatically agreed with him. "It's going to pieces so quickly, too," she said, and her tone was sepulchral.

He looked at her without any light in his blue eyes. "There are places where the culture has remained untouched," he announced as if for the first time. "If we went into the desert you wouldn't have to face all this. Wouldn't you love that?" He was punishing her for her swift agreement with him a moment earlier. He knew she had no desire to go to the desert, and that she believed it was not possible to continue trying to escape from the Industrial Revolution. Without realizing he was doing it he had provoked the argument he wanted.

"Why do you ask me if I wouldn't love to go into the desert, when you know as well as I do I wouldn't. We've talked about it over and over. Every few days we talk about it." Although the sun was beating down on her chest, making it feel on fire, deep inside she could still feel the cold current that seemed to run near her heart.

"Well," he said. "You change. Sometimes you say you *would* like to go."

It was true. She did change. Sometimes she would run to him with bright eyes. "Let's go," she would say. "Let's go into the desert." But she never did this if she was sober.

There was something wistful in his voice, and she had to remind herself that she wanted to feel cranky rather than heartbroken. In order to go on talking she said: "Sometimes I feel like going, but it's always when I've had something to drink. When I've had nothing to drink I'm afraid." She turned to face him, and he saw that she was beginning to have her hunted expression.

"Do you think I *ought* to go?" she asked him.

"Go where?"

"To the desert. To live in an oasis." She was pronouncing her words slowly. "Maybe that's what I should do, since I'm your wife."

"You must do what you really want to do," he said. He had been trying to teach her this for twelve years.

"What I really want ... Well, if you'd be happy in an oasis, maybe I'd really want to do that." She spoke hesitantly, and there was a note of doubt in her voice.

"What?" He shook his head as if he had run into a spiderweb. "What is it?"

"I meant that maybe if you were happy in an oasis I would be, too. Wives get pleasure out of making their husbands happy. They really do, quite aside from its being moral."

He did not smile. He was in too bad a humor. "You'd go to an oasis because you wanted to escape from Western civilization."

"My friends and I don't feel there's any way of escaping it. It's not interesting to sit around talking about industrialization."

"What friends?" He liked her to feel isolated.

"Our friends." Most of them she had not seen in many years. She turned to him with a certain violence. "I think you come to these countries so you can complain. I'm tired of hearing the word *civilization*. It has no meaning. Or I've forgotten what it meant, anyway."

The moment when they might have felt tenderness had passed, and secretly they both rejoiced. Since he did not answer her, she went on. "I think it's uninteresting. To sit and watch costumes disappear, one by one. It's uninteresting even to mention it."

"They are not costumes," he said distinctly. "They're simply the clothes people wear."

She was as bitter as he about the changes, but she felt it would be indelicate for them both to reflect the same sorrow.

It would happen some day, surely. A serious grief would silence their argument. They would share it and not be able to look into each other's eyes. But as long as she could she would hold off that moment.

First published, as one of 'Three Scenes', in *Antaeus* (Autumn 1977).

Lila and Frank

FRANK PULLED HARD ON THE FRONT DOOR and opened it with a jerk, so that the pane of glass shook in its frame. It was his sister's custom never to go to the door and open it for him. She had an instinctive respect for his secretive nature.

He hung his coat on a hook in the hall and walked into the parlor, where he was certain he would find his sister. She was seated as usual in her armchair. Next to her was a heavy round table of an awkward height which made it useful for neither eating nor writing, although it was large enough for either purpose. Even in the morning Lila always wore a silk dress, stockings, and well-shined shoes. In fact, at all times of the day she was fully dressed to go into the town, although she seldom ventured from the house. Her hair was not very neat, but she took the trouble to rouge her lips.

"How were the men at the Coffee Pot tonight?" she asked when her brother entered the room. There was no variety in the inflection of her voice. It was apparent that, like him, she had never tried, either by emphasis or coloring of tone, to influence or charm a listener.

Frank sat down and rested for a while without speaking. "How were the men at the Coffee Pot?" she said again with no change of expression.

"The same as they always are."

"You mean by that, hungry and noisy." For an outsider it would have been hard to say whether she was being critical of the men at the Coffee Pot or sincerely asking for information. This was a question she had asked him many times, and he had various ways of answering, depending upon his mood. On this particular night he was uncommunicative. "They go to the Coffee Pot for a bite to eat," he said.

She looked at him. The depths of her dark eyes held neither warmth nor comfort. "Was it crowded?" she asked.

He considered this for a moment while she watched him attentively. He was near the lamp and his face was raspberry-colored, an even deeper red than it would have been otherwise.

"It was."

"Then it must have been noisy." The dropping of her voice at the end of a sentence gave her listener, if he was a stranger, the impression that she did not intend to continue with the conversation. Her brother of course knew this was not the case, and he was not surprised at all when a minute later she went on. "Did you speak with anyone?"

"No, I didn't." He jumped up from his chair and went over to a glass bookcase in the corner. "I don't usually, do I?"

"That doesn't mean that you won't, does it?" she said calmly.

"I wouldn't change my habits from one night to the next," he said. "Not sitting at the Coffee Pot."

"Why not?"

"It's not human nature to do that, is it?"

"I know nothing about human nature at all," she said. "Nor do you, for that matter. I don't know why you'd refer to it. I do suspect, though, that I at least might change very suddenly." Her voice remained indifferent, as though the subject were not one which was close to her. "It's a feeling that's always present with me ... here." She touched her breast.

Although he wandered around the room for a moment feigning to have lost interest in the conversation, she knew this was not so. Since they lied to each other in different ways, the excitement they felt in conversing together was very great.

"Tell me," she said. "If you don't expect to experience anything new at the Coffee Pot, why do you continue to go there?" This too she had often asked him in the past weeks, but the repetition of things added to rather than detracted from the excitement.

"I don't like to talk to anybody. But I like to go out," he said. "I may not like other men, but I like the world."

"I should think you'd go and hike in the woods, instead of sitting at the Coffee Pot. Men who don't like other men usually take to nature, I've heard."

"I'm not interested in nature, beyond the ordinary amount."

They settled into silence for a while. Then she began to question him again. "Don't you feel uneasy, knowing that most likely you're the only man at the Coffee Pot who feels so estranged from his fellows?"

He seated himself near the window and half smiled. "No," he said. "I think I like it."

"Why do you like it?"

"Because I'm aware of the estrangement, as you call it, and they aren't." This too he had answered many times before. But such was the faith they had in the depth of the mood they created between them that there were no dead sentences, no matter how often repeated.

"We don't feel the same about secrets," she told him. "I don't consider a secret such a great pleasure. In fact, I should hesitate to name what my pleasure is. I simply know that I don't feel the lack of it."

"Good night," said Frank. He wanted to be by himself. Since he very seldom talked for more than ten or fifteen minutes at a time, she was not at all surprised.

She herself was far too excited for sleep at that moment. The excitement that stirred in her breast was familiar, and could be likened to what a traveler feels on the eve of his departure. All her life she had enjoyed it or suffered from it, for it was a sensation that lay between suffering and enjoyment, and it had a direct connection with her brother's lies. For the past weeks they had concerned the Coffee Pot, but this was of little importance, since he lied to her consistently and had done so since early childhood. Her excitement had its roots in the simultaneous rejection and acceptance of these lies, a state which might be compared to that of the dreamer when he is near to waking, and who knows then that he is moving in a dream country which at any second will vanish forever, and yet is unable to recall the existence of his own room. So Lila moved about in the vivid world of her brother's lies, with the full awareness always that just beyond them lay the amorphous and hidden world of reality. These lies which thrilled her heart seemed to cull their exciting quality from her never-failing consciousness of the true events they concealed. She had not changed at all since childhood, when to expose a statement of her brother's as a lie was as unthinkable to her as the denial of God's existence is to most children. This treatment of her brother, unbalanced though it was, contained within it both dignity and merit, and these were reflected faithfully in her voice and manner.

First published, as one of 'Three Scenes', in *Antaeus* (Autumn 1977).

At The Jumping Bean

The interior of The Jumping Bean. Booths, colored paper lanterns. The bar will be supplied with bottles as well as with hamburgers and ketchup. Over the doorway there is a neon sign reading The Jumping Bean, *which the audience sees backward. Over the bar is a list written in huge letters:*

Bean Burgers … Our Jumping Specials. Unique.
Complete Chicken Dinners …. $1.33
Extra Cole Slaw Cup Free … "For them what likes it."
Free Jumpers with every order.
Beanaroo cocktail. "Swig it down. Then Jump."… 55 cents

BERYL JANE *and* GABRIEL *are seated at a table. She is dressed in a very feminine, pert manner.*

BERYL JANE They have such tiny little chickens here.

GABRIEL Yes, but they don't cost much.

BERYL JANE I know.

GABRIEL Maybe it's foolish to try and eat chicken at this price.

BERYL JANE The other kids do. They love them.

GABRIEL They're busy dancing and flirting. That's why they come here to The Jumping Bean. To dance and flirt.

I guess most of the guys buy these little chicken dinners more for show than they do for eating. If guys were alone they'd just stuff themselves on beanburgers and fill up. Some of them do anyhow. Even with a girl along, guys who are low on cash. And some guys who don't give a damn about showing off to a girl, don't care what impression they make on a girl. A lot of them don't even bother talking. Some of them don't even *like* girls.

GABRIEL They come in here, too.

BERYL JANE *[Thinking of the cabin she has rented]* What do they order?

GABRIEL *[Talking through his hat]* I guess they don't bother with much. They don't sit down to a table and order the dollar thirty-three, I don't guess. They have beers at the bar, and maybe beanburgers. They don't bother much. They're kind of without girls, and folks frown at them.

BERYL JANE There's everything in this world. Everything under the sun. But you can't spend your whole life worrying about other people.

GABRIEL Some people do. They worry about humanity.

BERYL JANE I worry about reality.

GABRIEL What do you mean?

BERYL JANE I mean everything that's close to me, that's real. Like my father and my projects, and ... and ... my front porch, the swing, and especially my own room, and science. Science is close to me. *[She hesitates.]* It really is. If I start thinking about far-off things, or things that are too different, then I get, like, paralized. I get off the track. Like kids thinking about eternity when they're little. We all hated it.

GABRIEL We hated eternity?

BERYL JANE But you have to think about those things more than I do, because you're a poet. *[The chicken dinners arrive and they stop talking while the waitress lays out the various plates.]* They really are small chickens, aren't they? They're smaller than they were last time.

WAITRESS But you've got five different items come with that chicken plate. You've got chips, greens, Juliennes, Parkers, and the slaw cup. *[She holds up the tiniest possible paper cup.* BERYL JANE *and* GABRIEL *look up at it.]* If you feel like you want your extra slaw cup right off I can bring it to you now. It's coming free with the dollar thirty three. *[Pointing to the list over the bar.]* "For them what likes it." *[She reads this in a dull routine voice. She has obviously no spirit of fun in her at all.]* And here's your jumpers. *[She tosses some jumping beans onto the table.]* They come free with all items, down to cokes.

GABRIEL We don't want any jumping beans. We want to talk and eat.

WAITRESS *[Ignoring his request]* We're open all night.

GABRIEL You can have another dollar thirty three if you want, Beryl Jane. If you're still hungry when you finish this one.

BERYL JANE You're not a millionaire, Gabriel.

GABRIEL If I was a millionaire I'd be traveling. I wouldn't be buying these little chicken dinners.

BERYL JANE If everything works out with the pigs the way it should, we'll have enough money to travel for two months out of the year. Switzerland or Paris. Or we could go and see the Northern Lights, or museums. Then, back home. *[She eats for a moment.]* You'd have your room upstairs for writing poetry. You'd come back from a trip full of inspiration. All those beautiful sights *[*GABRIEL *laughs.]* ... And you'd be real glad to be home in your own house ... in your own room. *[Her own deep unexpressed fear that none of this will come true communicates itself to the audience.]* We'll leave some of our land wild, with just natural pastures and woods. Your windows, Gabriel... *[She searches his face, but she is not sure he is listening.]* While you're writing your poetry you can look out the window at the wild beautiful land. The kind of land you always say you like. *[*GABRIEL *continues eating. He looks very sad.]* And the equipment and the buildings and the pigs. They'll all be on the other side of the house. You won't even know they're there. It will be just like you were off in a log cabin with nobody around. No pigs ...

GABRIEL I don't mind pigs. I like them.

BERYL JANE Well, maybe you don't like them around all the time. Anyway, not when you're writing poetry.

GABRIEL I don't care. They can all come into my room if they want to. Maybe I won't write poetry. *[He looks very defeated.]*

BERYL JANE The pigs aren't going to walk in and out of the house. It's going to be a very modern farm.

GABRIEL Can't we stop talking about the future? Why don't we dance? *[He gets up and goes over to the juke-box. It starts to play.]*

BERYL JANE I love the future. Except when it looks black. Pop says if the world blows up it won't be my fault. But he gets sore if he doesn't think I'm concentrating on my course. He says I should think about people all over the world and crises a normal amount, but he wants me to tend to my own business and follow my goal. He hates people who are wishy-washy, who don't know what they're doing. You know, like should I or shouldn't I.

GABRIEL He must be nuts about me.

BERYL JANE I told him you were interested and getting very excited about pig farming. I told him that you were a writer besides. He asked me if you wrote facts and I said you did. *[They dance for a moment.]* Gabriel ...

GABRIEL What?

BERYL JANE What time are we going to go back to the cabin? *[They stop dancing and stand still in the middle of the floor.]* It's because you've got so much on your mind all the time. You might forget ... about the cabin. I don't think we should go there so late that we're both so tired, you know. *[She stops and looks at him, a very peculiar expression on her face. She seems almost frozen, but she is compelled to go on. Then, in a strange childish voice:]* I get so tired at night. It's because I get up so early. I get so tired. *[He doesn't answer. His eyes are blank.]* Like a kid, isn't it? I'm like a little girl? *[There must be something terrifying about this scene. Her smile is crooked, as if she were being trampled inside.]* Don't you think so? *[An almost repulsive innocence.]* I still play marbles with my brother. And I climb apple trees.

GABRIEL Do you?

BERYL JANE Yes. Maybe you do, too.

GABRIEL No. I don't.

BERYL JANE Maybe I'll climb apple trees even after I have a baby. People don't get so old any more. My aunt's forty and she plays pool all the time. When it's summer she goes crabbing. *[He is silent.]* There's nothing much to having a baby any more, even. They get 'em walking right off, the mothers, I mean. I'll bet my aunt would get up and play pool the day after her baby was born, if she had a baby. But she's frigid. *[She sits down.]* Are we going?

GABRIEL I'm going to get a drink. Do you want one?

BERYL JANE Yes. I'll have a drink.

GABRIEL *[calling]* Waitress! Two drinks!

WAITRESS Two beanaroo cocktails?

GABRIEL Two whiskeys. And don't bring those jumping beans.

WAITRESS No jumpers? They come ...

GABRIEL I don't want any jumping beans with my drink. That's enough jumping beans.

BERYL JANE *[In panic embarrassment, but with a drive to get to the cabin no matter what, because she has planned it that way.]* Why are you so sore about the jumpers? You can just leave them alone. Just leave them alone on the table if you don't want to play with them.

GABRIEL Why do they treat us like kids on these routes? It's the same way at Larry's Devilburger.

BERYL JANE *[Pale, as if he were insulting her.]* They have no jumping beans.

GABRIEL They've got four cages with those little mice inside them, running up and down ladders like maniacs and swinging themselves.

BERYL JANE They're not mice. They're hamsters. Everybody loves them. Even people's grandparents.

GABRIEL And the Routeburger.

BERYL JANE They've got nothing. Nothing but the extra slaw cup free. That's the same as here, but no other attractions. An extra paper slaw cup and Juliennes and Parks and greens and dancing. They've got the dollar thirty three but no jumpers. *[She stops and looks at him.* GABRIEL *has drained his drink and wears a black look on his face.]* Gabriel?

GABRIEL What?

BERYL JANE If you don't like these joints we don't have to come to them. I don't care about them. *[He shrugs his shoulders.]* But I *am* beginning to feel tired, like I said. I'm more like a child than most girls. I like cocoa at night, and bread and jam. I like a child's dinner, not a grown-up dinner. If I'm alone ... Boy! I go straight for the cocoa and soft-boiled eggs and toast. I don't really give a damn about whiskey. [GABRIEL *takes her glass and finishes off her drink.]*

BERYL JANE Now? Gabriel, shall we pay our check and go now? I'll go stand in the doorway while you pay the check. [GABRIEL *goes to the bar.]*

GABRIEL *[to the Waitress]* Give me the check and I'll pay here.

WAITRESS I can bring the check to your table. There's no need for you to come here. You got table service.

GABRIEL I don't want to go back to my table. I want to pay here.

WAITRESS You' re kind of contrary, aren't you? [GABRIEL *shrugs.]* I've got a nephew who's contrary. Name is Norman. He came like that. Interferes with his making a living. He thinks nothing of sitting and letting the women work. Just so long as he can go on being his own contrary self. If he didn't come straight out of my only sister I'd boot him in the ass. He and I don't greet unless it's a calendar holiday. Then we greet because it looks too bad if we don't. But we make it short. He knows he's sitting on my sister while I'm bending my elbow at the Beanburger. [GABRIEL *leaves the bar angrily, and stands next to* BERYL JANE. *They are framed in the doorway.]*

GABRIEL There's no moon, Beryl. It's very dark out.

BERYL JANE I know. But there are lights all along the highway.

GABRIEL Don't you like the moon, though?

BERYL JANE I don't know. Not as much as some people. I never think about looking up unless someone says Beryl, look at the moon! When I'm by myself I never look at the moon. I don't know. I guess I'm not too keen on it.

GABRIEL Well, what do you like? *[There is a stillness to the scene. The restaurant lights darken, and they are illuminated only by the blue light of the upside down neon sign. Their faces look white.]*

BERYL JANE What do I like?

GABRIEL What beautiful sight? I mean, without traveling. What do you think is beautiful?

BERYL JANE I like ... I like tea-roses. And ... *[She falters.]* Do you mean anything that's beautiful?

GABRIEL Yes. You never mention much what you think is beautiful.

BERYL JANE *[very quickly, spontaneously, with sparkle and life]* I think snakes are beautiful. Those snakes with diamonds on their backs and very dark colored scales, deep green and purple and black.

GABRIEL *[uncomprehending]* Snakes.

BERYL JANE Yes, snakes. Some snakes anyway. *[She looks at him. He has moved away from her. Panic rising again.]* Maybe that's not the kind of beautiful thing you meant. Maybe you didn't want to hear about snakes. Maybe you meant more like what beautiful things do I love that the world loves. *[He does not answer.]* I told you, Gabriel. Tea-roses. And there are other things, but I don't want to talk about them now. Not in front of The Jumping Bean. I can't think here. And don't tell anybody I like snakes. I don't want people to think ...

[He has begun to walk. She stands still an instant, and then starts after him.]

First published in *Feminine Wiles* (Black Sparrow Press, 1976).

In the Summer House

Jane Bowles's play In the Summer House *was first performed in repertory at the Hedgerow Theater, Moylan, Pennsylvania, in 1951, before being staged at the Playhouse Theater on Broadway in 1953, with music by Paul Bowles. It has been revised sporadically since, notably in 1993 at the Lincoln Center, New York, with a new score by by Philip Glass.*

The play is set in the late 1940s on the border between Mexico and California, and its scenes, bordering on the surreal, have been compared to Pinter and Genet. Tennessee Williams wrote: 'it is not only the most original play I have ever read, I think it also the oddest and funniest and one of the most touching. Its human perceptions are both profound and delicate; its dramatic poetry is both illusive and gripping. It is one of those very rare plays which are not tested by the theater but by which the theater is tested.'

SCENES

ACT I

Scene i Gertrude Eastman Cuevas' garden on the coast, Southern California.

Scene ii The beach. One month later.

Scene iii The garden. One month later.

ACT II

Scene i The Lobster Bowl. Ten months later, before dawn.

Scene ii The same. Two months later, late afternoon.

Time: the present

Act One

Scene i

GERTRUDE EASTMAN CUEVAS' *garden somewhere on the coast of Southern California. The garden is a mess, with ragged cactus plants and broken ornaments scattered about. A low hedge at the back of the set separates the garden from a dirt lane which supposedly leads to the main road. Beyond the lane is the beach and the sea. The side of the house and the front door are visible. A low balcony hangs over the garden. In the garden itself there is a round summer house covered with vines.*

GERTRUDE *[A beautiful middle-aged woman with sharply defined features, a good carriage and bright red hair. She is dressed in a tacky provincial fashion. Her voice is tense but resonant. She is seated on the balcony]* Are you in the summer house?

*[*MOLLY*, a girl of eighteen with straight black hair cut in bangs and a somnolent impassive face, does not hear* GERTRUDE'S *question but remains in the summer house.* GERTRUDE, *repeating, goes to railing]*

Are you in the summer house?

MOLLY Yes, I am.

GERTRUDE If I believed in acts of violence, I would burn the summer house down. You love to get in there and loll about hour after hour. You can't even see out because those vines hide the view. Why don't you find a good flat rock overlooking the ocean and sit on it? *[Molly fingers the vine]* As long as you're so indifferent to the beauties of nature, I should think you would interest yourself in political affairs, or in music or painting or at least in the future. But I've said this to you at least a thousand times before. You admit you relax too much?

MOLLY I guess I do.

GERTRUDE We already have to take in occasional boarders to help make ends meet. As the years go by the boarders will increase, and I can barely put up with the few that come here now; I'm not temperamentally suited to boarders. Nor am I interested in whether this should be considered a character defect or not. I simply hate gossiping with strangers and I don't want to listen to their business. I never have and I never will. It disgusts me. Even my own flesh and blood saps my vitality – particularly you. You seem to have developed such a slow and gloomy way of walking lately ... not at all becoming to a girl. Don't you think you could correct your walk?

MOLLY I'm trying. I'm trying to correct it.

GERTRUDE I'm thinking seriously of marrying Mr Solares, after all. I would at least have a life free of financial worry if I did, and I'm sure I could gradually ease his sister, Mrs Lopez, out of the house because she certainly gets on my nerves. He's a manageable man and Spanish men aren't around the house much, which is a blessing. They're always out ... not getting intoxicated or having a wild time ... just out ... sitting around with bunches of other men ... Spanish men ... Cubans, Mexicans ... I don't know ... They're all alike, drinking little cups of coffee and jabbering away to each other for hours on end. That was your father's life anyway. I minded then. I minded terribly, not so much because he left me alone, but he wasn't in his office for more than a few hours a day ... and he wasn't rich enough, not like Mr Solares. I lectured him in the beginning. I lectured him on ambition, on making contacts, on developing his personality. Often at night I was quite hoarse. I worked on him steadily, trying to make him worry about sugar. I warned him he was letting his father's interests go to pot. Nothing helped. He refused to worry about sugar; he refused to worry about anything. *[She knits a moment in silence]* I lost interest finally. I lost interest in sugar ... in him. I lost interest in our life together. I wanted to give it all up ... start out fresh, but I couldn't. I was carrying you. I had no choice. All my hopes were wrapped up in you then, all of them. You were my reason for going on, my one and only hope ... my love. *[She knits furiously. Then, craning her neck to look in the summer house, she gets up and goes to the rail]* Are you asleep in there, or are you reading comic strips?

MOLLY I'm not asleep.

GERTRUDE Sometimes I have the strangest feeling about you. It frightens me ... I feel that you are plotting something. Especially when you get inside that summer house. I think your black hair helps me to feel that way. Whenever I think of a woman going wild, I always picture her with black hair, never blond or red. I know that what I'm saying has no connection with a scientific truth. It's very personal. They say red-haired women go wild a lot but I never picture it that way. Do you?

MOLLY I don't guess I've ever pictured women going wild.

GERTRUDE And why not? They do all the time. They break the bonds ... Sometimes I picture little scenes where they turn evil like wolves ... *[Shuddering]* I don't choose to, but I do all the same.

MOLLY I've never seen a wild woman.

GERTRUDE *[Music]* On the other hand, sometimes I wake up at night with a strange feeling of isolation ... as if I'd fallen off the cliffs and landed miles away from everything that was close to my heart ... Even my griefs and my sorrows don't seem to belong to me. Nothing does – as if a shadow had passed over my whole life and made it dark. I try saying my name aloud, over and over again, but it doesn't hook things together. Whenever I feel that way I put my wrapper on and I go down into the kitchen. I open the ice chest and take out some fizzy water. Then I sit at the table with the light switched on and by and by I feel all right again. *[The music fades. Then in a more matter-of-fact tone]* There is no doubt that each one of us has to put up with a shadow or two as he grows older. But if we occupy ourselves while the shadow passes, it passes swiftly enough and scarcely leaves a trace of our daily lives ... *[She knits for a moment. Then looks up the road]* The girl who is coming here this afternoon is about seventeen. She should be arriving pretty soon. I also think that Mr Solares will be arriving shortly and that he'll be bringing one of his hot picnic luncheons with him today. I can feel it in my bones. It's disgraceful of me, really, to allow him to feed us on our own lawn, but then, their mouths count up to six, while ours count up to only two. So actually it's only half a disgrace. I hope Mr Solares realizes that. Besides, I might be driven to accepting his marriage offer and then the chicken would be in the same pot anyway. Don't you agree?

MOLLY Yes.

GERTRUDE You don't seem very interested in what I'm saying.

MOLLY Well, I ...

GERTRUDE I think that you should be more of a conversationalist. You never express an opinion, nor do you seem to have an outlook. What on earth is your outlook?

MOLLY *[Uncertainly]* Democracy ...

GERTRUDE I don't think you feel very strongly about it. You don't listen to the various commentators, nor do you ever glance at the newspapers. It's very easy to say that one is democratic, but that doesn't prevent one from being a slob if one is a slob. I've never permitted myself to become a slob, even though I sit home all the time and avoid the outside world as much as possible. I've never liked going out any more than my father did. He always avoided the outside world. He hated a lot of idle gossip and had no use for people anyway. "Let the world do its dancing and its drinking and its interkilling without me," he always said. "They'll manage perfectly well; I'll stick to myself and my work." *[The music comes up again and she is lost in a dream]* When I was a little girl I made up my mind that I was going to be just like him. He was my model, my ideal. I admired him more than anyone on earth. And he admired me of course. I was so much like him – ambitious, defiant, a fighting cock always. I worshipped him. But I was never meek, not like Ellen my sister. She was very frail and delicate. My father used to put his arms around her, and play with her hair, long golden curls ... Ellen was the weak one. That's why he spoiled her. He pitied Ellen. *[With wonder, and very delicately, as if afraid to break a spell. The music expresses the sorrow she is hiding from herself]* Once he took her out of school, when she was ten years old. He bought her a little fur hat and they went away together for two whole weeks. I was left behind. I had no reason to leave school. I was healthy and strong. He took her to a big hotel on the edge of a lake. The lake was frozen, and they sat in the sunshine all day long, watching the people skate. When they came back he said, "Look at her, look at Ellen. She has roses in her cheeks." He pitied Ellen, but he was proud of me. I was his true love. He never showed it ... He was so frightened Ellen would guess. He didn't want her to be jealous, but I knew the truth ... He didn't have to show it. He didn't have to say anything. *[The music fades and she knits furiously, coming back to the present]* Why don't you go inside and clean up? It might sharpen your wits. Go and change that rumpled dress.

MOLLY *[*MOLLY *comes out of the summer house and sniffs a blossom]* The honeysuckle's beginning to smell real good. I can never remember when you planted this vine, but it's sure getting thick. It makes the summer house so nice and shady inside.

GERTRUDE *[Stiffening in anger]* I told you never to mention that vine again. You know it was there when we bought this house. You love to call my attention to that wretched vine because it's the only thing that grows well in the garden and you know it was planted by the people who came here before us and not by me at all. *[She rises and paces the balcony]* You're mocking me for being such a failure in the garden and not being able to make things grow. That's an underhanded Spanish trait of yours you inherit from your father. You love to mock me.

MOLLY *[Tenderly]* I would never mock you.

GERTRUDE *[Working herself up]* I thought I'd find peace here ... with these waving palms and the ocean stretching as far as the eye can see, but you don't like the ocean ... You won't even go in the water. You're afraid to swim ... I thought we'd found a paradise at last – the perfect place – but you don't want paradise ... You want hell. Well, go into your little house and rot if you like ... I don't care. Go on in while you still can. It won't be there much longer ... I'll marry Mr Solares and send you to business school. *[The voices of* MR SOLARES *and his family arriving with a picnic lunch stop her. She leans over the railing of the balcony and looks up the road]* Oh, here they come with their covered pots. I knew they'd appear with a picnic luncheon today. I could feel it in my bones. We'll put our own luncheon away for supper and have our supper tomorrow for lunch ... Go and change ... Quickly ... Watch that walk. *[*MOLLY *exits into the house.* GERTRUDE *settles down in her chair to prepare for* MR SOLARES' *arrival]* I wish they weren't coming.

I'd rather be here by myself really. *[Enter Spanish people]* Nature's the best company of all. *[She pats her bun and rearranges some hairpins. Then she stands up and waves to her guests, cupping her mouth and yelling at the same time]* Hello there!

[In another moment MR SOLARES, MRS LOPEZ *and her daughter,* FREDERICA, *and the three servants enter, walking in single file down the lane. Two of the servants are old hags and the third is a young half caste,* ESPERANZA, *in mulberry-colored satin. The servants all carry pots wrapped with bright bandanas.]*

MR SOLARES *[He wears a dark dusty suit. Pushing ahead of his sister,* MRS LOPEZ, *in his haste to greet* GERTRUDE *and thus squeezing his sister's arm rather painfully against the gate post]* Hello, Miss Eastman Cuevas! *[*MRS LOPEZ *squeals with pain and rubs her arm. She is fat and middle-aged. She wears a black picture hat and black city dress. Her hat is decorated with flowers,* Mr SOLARES *speaks with a trace of an accent, having lived for many years in this country. Grinning and bobbing around]* We brought you a picnic. For you and your daughter. Plenty of everything! You come down into the garden.

[The others crowd slowly through the gate and stand awkwardly in a bunch looking up at GERTRUDE.*]*

GERTRUDE *[Perfunctorily]* I think I'll stay here on the balcony, thank you. Just spread yourselves on the lawn and we'll talk back and forth this way. It's all the same. *[To the maids]* You can hand me up my food by stepping on that little stump and I'll lean over and get it.

MRS LOPEZ *[Her accent is much thicker than her brother's, smiling up at* GERTRUDE*]* You will come down into the garden, Miss Eastman Cuevas?

MR SOLARES *[Giving his sister a poke]* Acaba de decirte que se queda arriba. ¿Ya no oyes? *[The next few minutes on the stage have a considerable musical background. The hags and* ESPERANZA *start spreading bandanas on the lawn and emptying the baskets. The others settle on the lawn.* ESPERANZA *and the hags sing a raucous song as they work, the hags just joining in at the chorus and a bit off key.* ESPERANZA *brings over a pot wrapped in a Turkish towel and serves the family group. They all take enormous helpings of spaghetti,* MR SOLARES *serves himself]* Italian spaghetti with meat balls! Esperanza, serve a big plate to Miss Eastman Cuevas up on the porch. You climb on that.

[He points to a fake stump with a gnome carved on one side of it.]

ESPERANZA *[Disagreeably]* ¡Caramba!

[She climbs up on the stump after filling a plate with spaghetti and hands it to GERTRUDE, *releasing her hold on the plate before* GERTRUDE *has secured her own grip,* ESPERANZA *jumps out of the way immediately and the plate swings downward under the weight of the food, dumping the spaghetti on* MRS LOPEZ' *head.]*

GERTRUDE Oh! *[To* ESPERANZA*]* You didn't give me a chance to get a firm hold on it!

MR SOLARES ¡Silencio!

*[*ESPERANZA *rushes over to the hags and all three of them become hysterical with laughter. After their hysterics they pull themselves together and go over to clean up* MRS LOPEZ *and to restore* GERTRUDE'S *plate to her filled with fresh spaghetti. They return to their side of the garden in a far corner and everyone starts to eat.]*

MR SOLARES *[To* GERTRUDE*]* Miss Eastman Cuevas, you like chop suey?

GERTRUDE I have never eaten any.

MRS LOPEZ *[Eager to get into the conversation and expressing great wonder in her voice]* Chop suey? What is it?

MR SOLARES *[In a mean voice to* MRS LOPEZ*]* You know what it is. *[In Spanish]* Que me dejes hablar con la señora Eastman Cuevas por favor. *[To* GERTRUDE*]* I'll bring you some chop suey tomorrow in a box, or maybe we better go out to a restaurant, to a dining and dancing. Maybe you would go to try out some chop suey ... Would you?

GERTRUDE *[Coolly]* That's very nice of you but I've told you before that I don't care for the type of excitement you get when you go out ... You know what I mean – entertainment, dancing, etc. Why don't you describe chop suey to me and I'll try and imagine it? *[*MRS LOPEZ *roars with laughter for no apparent reason.* GERTRUDE *cranes her neck and looks down at her over the balcony with raised eyebrows]* I could die content without ever setting foot in another restaurant. Frankly, I would not care if every single one of them burned to the ground. I really love to sit on my porch and look out over the ocean.

MRS LOPEZ You like the ocean?

GERTRUDE I love it!

MRS LOPEZ *[Making a wild gesture with her arm]* I hate it!

GERTRUDE I love it. It's majestic ...

MRS LOPEZ I hate!

GERTRUDE *[Freezing up]* I see that we don't agree.

MR SOLARES *[Scowling at* MRS LOPEZ*]* Oh, she loves the ocean. I don't know what the hell is the matter with her today. *[*GERTRUDE *winces at his language]* Myself, I like ocean, land, mountain, all kinds of food, chop suey, chile, eel, turtle steak ... Everything. Solares like everything. *[In hideous French accent]* Joie de vivre! *[He snaps his fingers in the air.]*

GERTRUDE *[Sucking some long strands of spaghetti into her mouth]* What is your attitude toward your business?

MR SOLARES *[Happily]* My business is dandy.

GERTRUDE *[Irritably]* Yes, but what is your attitude toward it?

MR SOLARES *[With his mouth full]* O.K.

GERTRUDE Please try to concentrate on my question, Mr Solares. Do you like business or do you really prefer to stay home and lazy around?

MRS LOPEZ *[Effusively]* He don't like no business – he likes to stay home and sleep – and eat. *[Then in a mocking tone intended to impress* MR SOLARES *himself]* "Fula, I got headache ... I got bellyache ... I stay home, no?" *[She jabs her brother in the ribs with her elbow several times rolling her eyes in a teasing manner and repeats]* "Fula, I got headache ... I got bellyache ... I stay home, no?"

[She jabs him once again even harder and laughs way down in her throat.]

MR SOLARES ¡Fula! Esta es la última vez que sales conmigo. Ya, déjame hablar con la señora Eastman Cuevas!

MRS LOPEZ Look, Miss Eastman Cuevas?

GERTRUDE *[Looking disagreeably surprised]* Yes?

MRS LOPEZ You like to talk to me?

GERTRUDE *[As coolly as possible short of sounding rude]* Yes, I enjoy it.

MRS LOPEZ *[Triumphantly to* MR SOLARES*]* Miss Eastman Cuevas *like* talk to me, so you shut your mouth. He don't want no one to talk to you, Miss Eastman Cuevas because he think he gonna marry you.

*[*FREDERICA *doubles over and buries her face in her hands. Her skinny shoulders shake with laughter.]*

MR SOLARES *[Embarrassed and furious]* Bring the chicken and rice, Esperanza.

ESPERANZA You ain't finished what you got!

MR SOLARES Cállate, y tráigame el arroz con pollo.

*[*ESPERANZA *walks across the lawn with the second pot wrapped in a Turkish towel. She walks deliberately at a very slow pace, throwing a hip out at each step, and with a terrible sneer on her face. She serves them all chicken and rice, first removing the spaghetti plates and giving them clean ones. Everyone takes enormous helpings again, with the exception of* GERTRUDE *who refuses to have any.]*

GERTRUDE *[While* ESPERANZA *serves the others]* If Molly doesn't come out soon she will simply have to miss her lunch. It's very tiring to have to keep reminding her of the time and the other realities of life. Molly is a dreamer.

MRS LOPEZ *[Nodding]* That's right.

GERTRUDE *[Watching* FREDERICA *serve herself]* Do you people always eat such a big midday meal? Molly and I are in the habit of eating simple salads at noon.

MRS LOPEZ *[Wiping her mouth roughly with her napkin. Then without pausing and with gusto]* For breakfast: chocolate and sugar bread: for lunch: soup, beans, eggs, rice, roast pork with potatoes and guava paste ... *[She pulls on a different finger for each separate item]* Next day: soup, eggs, beans, rice, chicken with rice and guava paste – other day: soup, eggs, beans, rice, stew meat, roasted baby pig and guava paste. Other day: soup, rice, beans, grilled red snapper, roasted goat meat and guava paste.

FREDERICA *[Speaking for the first time, rapidly, in a scarcely audible voice]* Soup, rice, beans, eggs, ground-up meat and guava paste.

GERTRUDE *[Wearily]* We usually have a simple salad.

MR SOLARES She's talkin' about the old Spanish custom. She only come here ten years ago when her old man died. I don't like a big lunch neither. *[In a sudden burst of temerity]* Listen, what my sister said was true. I hope I am gonna marry you some day soon. I've told you so before. You remember?

MRS LOPEZ *[Laughing and whispering to* FREDERICA, *who goes off into hysterics, and then delving into a shopping bag which lies beside her on the grass. In a very gay voice]* This is what you gonna get if you make a wedding. *[She pulls out a paper bag and hurls it at* GERTRUDE*'s head with the gesture of a baseball pitcher. The bag splits and spills rice all over* GERTRUDE. *There is general hilarity and even a bit of singing on the part of* ESPERANZA *and the hags.* MR LOPEZ *yells above the noise]* Rice!

GERTRUDE *[Standing up and flicking rice from her shoulders]* Stop it! Please! Stop it! I can't stand this racket ... Really. *[She is genuinely upset. They subside gradually. Bewildered, she looks out over the land toward the road]* Something is coming down the road ... It must be my boarder ... No ... She would be coming in an automobile. *[Pause]* Gracious! It certainly is *no* boarder, but what is it?

MRS LOPEZ Friend come and see you?

GERTRUDE *[Bewildered, staring hard]* No, it's not a friend. It's ... *[She stares harder]* It's some sort of king – and others.

MRS LOPEZ *[To her brother]* ¿Que?

MR SOLARES *[Absently absorbed in his food]* King. Un rey y otros más ...

MRS LOPEZ *[Nodding]* Un rey y otros más.

[Enter LIONEL, *bearing a cardboard figure larger than himself, representing Neptune, with flowing beard, crown and sceptre, etc. He is followed by two or more other figure bearers, carrying representations of a channel swimmer and a mermaid.* LIONEL *stops at the gate and dangles into the garden a toy lobster which he has tied to the line of a real fishing rod. The music dies down.]*

LIONEL Advertisement.

[He bobs the lobster up and down.]

GERTRUDE For what?

LIONEL For the Lobster Bowl ... It's opening next week.

[Pointing] That figure there represents a mermaid and the other one is Neptune, the sea god. This is a lobster ... *[He shakes the rod]* Everything connected with the sea in some capacity. Can we have a glass of water?

GERTRUDE Yes. *[Calling]* Molly! Molly!

MOLLY *[From inside the house]* What is it?

GERTRUDE Come out here immediately. *[To* LIONEL*]* Excuse me but I think your figures are really awful. I don't like advertising schemes anyway.

LIONEL I have nothing to do with them. I just have to carry them around a few more days and then after that I'll be working at the Bowl. I'm sorry you don't like them.

GERTRUDE I've always hated everything that was larger than life size.

*[*LIONEL *opens the gate and enters the garden, followed by the other figure bearers. The garden by now has a very cluttered appearance. The servants,* MRS LOPEZ *and* FREDERICA *have been gaping at the figures in silence since their arrival.]*

MRS LOPEZ *[Finding her tongue]* ¡Una maravilla!

FREDERICA Ay, sí.

[She is nearly swooning with delight. Enter MOLLY. *She stops short when she sees the figures.]*

MOLLY Oh ... What are those?

LIONEL Advertisements. This is Neptune, the old god.

*[*MOLLY *approaches the figures slowly and touches Neptune.]*

MOLLY It's beautiful ...

LIONEL Here's a little lobster. *[He dangles it into* MOLLY'S *open palm.]*

MOLLY It looks like a real lobster. It even has those long threads sticking out over its eyes.

GERTRUDE Antennae.

MOLLY Antennae.

LIONEL *[Pulling another little lobster from his pocket and handing it to* MOLLY*]* Here. Take this one. I have a few to give away.

MOLLY Oh, thank you very much.

[There follows a heated argument between FREDERICA *and* MRS LOPEZ, *who is trying to force* FREDERICA *to ask for a lobster too. They almost come to blows and finally* MRS LOPEZ *gives* FREDERICA *a terrific shove which sends her stumbling over toward* LIONEL *and* MOLLY.*]*

MRS LOPEZ *[Calling out to* LIONEL*]* Give my girl a little fish please!

*[*LIONEL *digs reluctantly into his pocket and hands* FREDERICA *a little lobster. She takes it and returns to her mother, stubbing her toe in her confusion.]*

GERTRUDE *[Craning her neck and looking out over the lane toward the road]* There's a car stopping. This really must be my boarder. *[She looks down into the garden with an expression of consternation on her face]* The garden is a wreck. Mr Solares, can't your servants organize this mess? Quickly, for heaven's sake. *[She looks with disgust at* Mr SOLARES, *who is still eating, but holds her tongue. Enter* VIVIAN, *a young girl of fifteen with wild reddish gold hair. She is painfully thin and her eyes appear to pop out of her head with excitement. She is dressed in bright colors and wears high heels. She is followed by a chauffeur carrying luggage]* And get those figures out of sight!

VIVIAN *[Stopping in the road and staring at the house intently for a moment]* The house is heavenly!

*[*MOLLY *exits rapidly.]*

GERTRUDE Welcome, Vivian Constable. I'm Gertrude Eastman Cuevas. How was your trip?

VIVIAN Stinky. *[Gazing with admiration into the garden packed with people]* And your garden is heavenly too.

GERTRUDE The garden is a wreck at the moment.

VIVIAN Oh, no! It's fascinating.

GERTRUDE You can't possibly tell yet.

VIVIAN Oh, but I can. I decide everything the first minute. It's a fascinating garden.

[She smiles at everyone. MR SOLARES *spits chicken skin out of his mouth onto the grass.]*

MRS LOPEZ Do you want some spaghetti?

VIVIAN Not yet, thank you. I'm too excited.

GERTRUDE *[To* MR SOLARES*]* Will you show Miss Constable and the chauffeur into the house, Mr Solares? I'll meet you at the top of the stairs.

[She exits hurriedly into the house, but MR SOLARES *continues gnawing on his bone not having paid the slightest attention to Gertrude's request. Enter* MRS CONSTABLE, VIVIAN*'s mother. She is wearing a distinguished city print, gloves, hat and veil. She is frail like her daughter but her coloring is dull.]*

VIVIAN *[Spying her mother. Her expression immediately hardens]* Why did you get out of the taxi? You promised at the hotel that you wouldn't get out if I allowed you to ride over with me. You promised me once in the room and then again on the porch. Now you've gotten out. You're dying to spoil the magic. Go back ... Don't stand there looking at the house. *[*MRS CONSTABLE *puts her fingers to her lips entreating silence, shakes her head at* VIVIAN *and scurries off stage after nodding distractedly to the people on the lawn]* She can't keep a promise.

GERTRUDE *[Coming out onto the balcony again and spotting* MR SOLARES, *still eating on the grass]* What is the matter with you, Mr Solares? I asked you to show Miss Constable and the chauffeur into the house and you haven't budged an inch. I've been waiting at the top of the stairs like an idiot.

*[*MR SOLARES *scrambles to his feet and goes into the house followed by* VIVIAN *and the chauffeur. Enter* MRS CONSTABLE *again.]*

MRS CONSTABLE *[Coming up to the hedge and leaning over. To* MRS LOPEZ*]* Forgive me but I would like you to tell Mrs Eastman Cuevas that I am at the Herons Hotel. *[*MRS LOPEZ *nods absently.* MRS CONSTABLE *continues in a scarcely audible voice]* You see, Mrs Eastman Cuevas comes from the same town that I come from and through mutual friends I heard that she took in boarders these days, so I wrote her that Vivian my daughter was coming.

MRS LOPEZ Thank you very much.

MRS CONSTABLE My daughter likes her freedom, so we have a little system worked out when we go on vacations. I stay somewhere nearby but not in the same place. Even so, I am the nervous type and I would like Mrs Eastman Cuevas to know that I'm at the Herons ... You see my daughter is unusually high spirited. She feels everything so strongly that she's apt to tire herself out. I want to be available just in case she collapses.

MRS LOPEZ *[Ruffling* FREDERICA*'s hair]* Frederica get very tired too.

MRS CONSTABLE Yes, I know. I suppose all the young girls do. Will you tell Mrs Eastman Cuevas that I'm at the Herons?

MRS LOPEZ O.K.

MRS CONSTABLE Thank you a thousand times. I'll run along now or Vivian will see me and she'll think that I'm interfering with her freedom ... You'll notice right away what fun she gets out of life. Good-bye.

MRS LOPEZ Good-bye, Mrs. Vamos; despiértense. Esperanza. *[*MRS CONSTABLE *exits hurriedly. To* MR SOLARES*]* Now we go home.

MR SOLARES *[Sullenly]* All right. *[Spanish group leaves]* Esperanza! Esperanza! Frederica!

[Enter from the house VIVIAN, GERTRUDE *and the* CHAUFFEUR, *who leaves the garden and exits down the lane.]*

VIVIAN *[To* GERTRUDE, *continuing a conversation]* I'm going to be sky high by dinner time. Then I won't sleep all night. I know myself.

GERTRUDE Don't you use controls?

VIVIAN No, I never do. When I feel myself going up I just go on up until I hit the ceiling. I'm like that. The world is ten times more exciting for me than it is for others.

GERTRUDE Still I believe in using controls. It's a part of the law of civilization. Otherwise we would be like wild beasts. *[She sighs]* We're bad enough as it is, controls and all.

VIVIAN *[Hugging* GERTRUDE *impulsively]* You've got the prettiest hair I've ever seen, and I'm going to love it here. *[*GERTRUDE *backs away a little, embarrassed.* VIVIAN *spots the summer house]* What a darling little house! It's like the home of a bird or a poet. *[She approaches the summer house and enters it.* MRS LOPEZ *motions to the hags to start cleaning up. They hobble around one behind the other gathering things and scraping plates very ineffectually. More often than not the hag behind scrapes more garbage onto the plate just cleaned by the hag in front of her. They continue this until the curtain falls. Music begins. Calling to* GERTRUDE*]* I can imagine all sorts of things in here, Miss Eastman Cuevas. I could make plans for hours on end in here. It's so darling and little.

GERTRUDE *[Coldly]* Molly usually sits in there. But I can't say that she plans much. Just dozes or reads trash. Comic strips. It will do no harm if someone else sits in there for a change.

VIVIAN Who is Molly?

GERTRUDE Molly is my daughter.

VIVIAN How wonderful! I want to meet her right away ... Where is she?

[The boys start righting the cardboard figures.]

LIONEL Do you think we could have our water?

GERTRUDE I'm sorry. Yes, of course. *[Calling]* Molly! *[Silence]* Molly! *[More loudly]* Molly! *[Silence]*

LIONEL I think we'll go along to the next place. Don't bother your daughter. I'll come back if I may. I'd like to see you all again ... and your daughter. She disappeared so quickly.

GERTRUDE You stay right where you are. I'll get her out here in a minute. *[Screaming]* Molly! Come out here immediately! Molly!

VIVIAN *[In a trilling voice]* Molly! Come on out! ... I'm in your little house ... Molly!

GERTRUDE *[Furious]* Molly!

[All the players look expectantly at the doorway, MOLLY *does not appear and the curtain comes down in silence.]*

Scene ii

One month later.

A beach and a beautiful backdrop of the water. The SOLARES *family is again spread out among dirty plates as though the scenery had changed around them while they themselves had not stirred since the first scene.* GERTRUDE *is kneeling and rearranging her hair near the* SOLARES *family,* VIVIAN *at her feet,* MOLLY *and* LIONEL *a little apart from the other people,* MOLLY *watching* VIVIAN. *The two old hags are wearing white slips for swimming.*

The music is sad and disturbing, implying a more serious mood.

MRS LOPEZ *[Poking her daughter who is lying next to her]* A ver si tú y Esperanza nos cantan algo ...

FREDERICA *[From under handkerchief which covers her face]* Ay, mamá.

MRS LOPEZ *[Calling to* ESPERANZA*]* Esperanza, a ver si nos cantan algo, tú y Frederica.

[She gives her daughter a few pokes. They argue a bit and FREDERICA *gets up and drags herself wearily over to the hags. They consult and sing a little song. The hags join in at the chorus.]*

ESPERANZA Bueno sí ...

GERTRUDE *[When they have finished]* That was nice. I like sad songs.

VIVIAN *[Still at her feet and looking up at her with adoration]* So do I ... *[*MOLLY *is watching* VIVIAN*, a beam of hate in her eye.* VIVIAN *takes* GERTRUDE'S *wrist and plays with her hand just for a moment.* GERTRUDE *pulls it away, instinctively afraid of* MOLLY'S *reaction. To* GERTRUDE*]* I wish Molly would come swimming with me. I thought maybe she would. *[Then to* MOLLY, *for* GERTRUDE'*s benefit]* Molly, won't you come in, just this once. You'll love it once you do. Everyone loves the water, everyone in the world.

GERTRUDE *[Springing to her feet, and addressing the Spanish people]* I thought we were going for a stroll up the beach after lunch. *[There is apprehension behind her words]* You'll never digest lying on your backs, and besides you're sure to fall asleep if you don't get up right away.

[She regains her inner composure as she gives her commands.]

MRS LOPEZ *[Groaning]* ¡Ay! ¡Caray¡ Why don't you sleep, Miss Eastman Cuevas?

GERTRUDE It's very bad for you, really. Come on. Come on, everybody! Get up! You too, Alta Gracia and Quintina, get up! Come on, everybody up! *[There is a good deal of protesting while the servants and the* SOLARES *family struggle to their feet]* I promise you you'll feel much better later on if we take just a little walk along the beach.

VIVIAN *[Leaping to* GERTRUDE'S *side in one bound]* I *love* to walk on the beach!

*[*MOLLY *too has come forward to be with her mother.]*

GERTRUDE *[Pause. Again stifling her apprehension with a command]* You children stay here. Or take a walk along the cliffs if you'd like to. But be careful!

FREDERICA I want to be with my mother.

GERTRUDE Well, come along, but we're only going for a short stroll. What a baby you are, Frederica Lopez.

MR SOLARES I'll run the car up to my house and go and collect that horse I was telling you about. Then I'll catch up with you on the way back.

GERTRUDE You won't get much of a walk.

*[*FREDERICA *throws her arms around her mother and gives her a big smacking kiss on the cheek.* MRS LOPEZ *kisses* FREDERICA. *They all exit slowly, leaving* VIVIAN, LIONEL, MOLLY *and the dishes behind.* MOLLY, *sad that she can't walk with her mother, crosses wistfully back to her former place next to* LIONEL, *but* VIVIAN *– eager to cut her out whenever she can – rushes to* LIONEL'S *side, and crouches on her heels exactly where* MOLLY *was sitting before.* MOLLY *notices this, and settles in a brooding way a little apart from them, her back to the pair.]*

VIVIAN Lionel, what were you saying before about policies?

LIONEL When?

VIVIAN Today, before lunch. You said, "What are your policies" or something crazy like that?

LIONEL Oh, yes. It's just ... I'm mixed up about my own policies, so I like to know how other people's are getting along.

VIVIAN Well, I'm for freedom and a full exciting life! *[Pointedly to* MOLLY'S *back]* I'm a daredevil. It frightens my mother out of her wits, but I love excitement!

LIONEL Do you always do what gives you pleasure?

VIVIAN Whenever I can, I do.

LIONEL What about conflicts?

VIVIAN What do you mean?

LIONEL Being pulled different ways and not knowing which to choose.

VIVIAN I don't have those. I always know exactly what I want to do. When I have a plan in my head I get so excited I can't sleep.

LIONEL Maybe it would be a stroke of luck to be like you. I have nothing but conflicts. For instance, one day I think I ought to give up the world and be a religious leader, and the next day I'll turn right around and think I ought to throw myself deep into politics. *[*VIVIAN, *bored, starts untying her beach shoes]* There have been ecclesiastics in my family before. I come from a gloomy family. A lot of the men seem to have married crazy wives. Five brothers out of six and a first cousin did. My uncle's first wife boiled a cat alive in the upstairs kitchen.

VIVIAN What do you mean, the upstairs kitchen?

LIONEL We had the top floor fitted out as an apartment and the kitchen upstairs was called the upstairs kitchen.

VIVIAN *[Hopping to her feet]* Oh, well, let's stop talking dull heavy stuff. I'm going to swim.

LIONEL All right.

VIVIAN *[Archly]* Good-bye, Molly.

[She runs off stage in the direction of the cove. MOLLY *sits on rock.]*

LIONEL *[Goes over and sits next to her]* Doesn't the ocean make you feel gloomy when the sky is gray or when it starts getting dark out?

MOLLY I don't guess it does.

LIONEL Well, in the daytime, if it's sunny out and the ocean's blue it puts you in a lighter mood, doesn't it?

MOLLY When it's blue ...

LIONEL Yes, when it's blue and dazzling. Don't you feel happier when it's like that?

MOLLY I don't guess I emphasize that kind of thing.

LIONEL I see. *[Thoughtfully]* Well, how do you feel about the future? Are you afraid of the future in the back of your mind?

MOLLY I don't guess I emphasize that much either.

LIONEL Maybe you're one of the lucky ones who looks forward to the future. Have you got some kind of ambition?

MOLLY Not so far. Have you?

LIONEL I've got two things I think I should do, like I told Vivian. But they're not exactly ambitions. One's being a religious leader, the other's getting deep into politics. I don't look forward to either one of them.

MOLLY Then you'd better not do them.

LIONEL I wish it was that simple. I'm not an easygoing type. I come from a gloomy family ... I dread being a minister in a way because it brings you so close to death all the time. You would get too deep in to ever forget death and eternity again, as long as you lived – not even for an afternoon. I think that even when you were talking with your friends or eating or joking, it would be there in the back of your mind. Death, I mean ... and eternity. At the same time I think I might have a message for a parish if I had one.

MOLLY What would you tell them?

LIONEL Well, that would only come through divine inspiration, after I made the sacrifice and joined up.

MOLLY Oh.

LIONEL I get a feeling of dread in my stomach about being a political leader too ... That should cheer me up more, but it doesn't. You'd think I really liked working at the Lobster Bowl.

MOLLY Don't you?

LIONEL Yes, I do, but of course that isn't life. I have fun too, in between worrying ... fun, dancing, and eating, and swimming ... and being with you. I like to be with you because you seem to only half hear me. I think I could say just the opposite and it wouldn't sound any different to you. Now why do I like that? Because it makes me feel very peaceful. Usually if I tell my feelings to a person I don't want to see them any more. That's another peculiar quirk of mine. Also there's something very familiar about you, even though I never met you before two months ago. I don't know what it is quite ... your face ... your voice ... *[Taking her hand]* or maybe just your hand. *[Holds her hand for a moment, deep in thought]* I hope I'm not going to dread it all for too long. Because it doesn't feel right to me, just working at the Lobster Bowl. It's nice though really ... Inez is always around if you want company. She can set up oyster cocktails faster than anyone on the coast. That's what she claims, anyway. She has some way of checking. You'd like Inez.

MOLLY I don't like girls.

LIONEL Inez is a grown-up woman. A kind of sturdy rock-of-Gibraltar type but very high strung and nervous too. Every now and then she blows up. *[MOLLY rises suddenly and crosses to the rock]* Well, I guess it really isn't so interesting to be there, but it is outside of the world and gloomy ideas. Maybe it's the decorations. It doesn't always help though, things come creeping in anyway.

MOLLY *[Turning to* LIONEL*]* What?

LIONEL Well, like what ministers talk about ... the valley of the Shadow of Death and all that ... or the world comes creeping in. I feel like it's a warning that I shouldn't stay too long. That I should go back to St Louis. It would be tough though. Now I'm getting too deep in. I suppose you live mainly from day to day. That's the way girls live mainly, isn't it?

MOLLY *[Crossing back to* LIONEL*]* I don't know. I'm all right as long as I can keep from getting mad. It's hard to keep from getting mad when you see through people. Most people can't like I do. I'd emphasize that all right. The rest of the stuff doesn't bother me much. A lot of people want to yank you out and get in themselves. Girls do anyway. I haven't got anything against men. They don't scheme the way girls do. But I keep to myself as much as I can.

LIONEL Well, there's that angle too, but my point of view is different. Have you thought any more about marrying me if your mother marries Mr Solares? I know we're both young, but you don't want to go to business school and she's sure to send you there if she marries him. She's always talking about it. She'd be in Mexico most of the year and you'd be in business school. We could live over the Lobster Bowl and get all the food we wanted free, and it's good food. Mr Solares and Mrs Lopez liked it when they went to eat there.

MOLLY Yes, I know they did.

LIONEL Well?

MOLLY I won't think of it until it happens. I can't picture anything being any different than it is. I feel I might just plain die if everything changes, but I don't imagine it will.

LIONEL You should look forward to change.

MOLLY I don't want anything different.

LIONEL Then you *are* afraid of the future just like me.

MOLLY *[Stubbornly]* I don't think much about the future.

*[*VIVIAN *returns from her swim.]*

LIONEL *[To* MOLLY*]* Well, even if you don't think much about the future you have to admit that ...

[He is interrupted by VIVIAN *who rushes up to them, almost stumbling in her haste.]*

VIVIAN *[Plopping down next to* LIONEL *and shaking out her wet hair]* Wait 'til you hear this ... ! *[*LIONEL *is startled,* VIVIAN *is almost swooning with delight, to* LIONEL*]* It's so wonderful ... I can hardly talk about it ... I saw the whole thing in front of my eyes ... Just now while I was swimming ...

LIONEL What?

VIVIAN Our restaurant.

LIONEL What restaurant?

VIVIAN *Our restaurant.* The one we're going to open together, right now, as soon as we can. I'll tell you about it ... But only on one condition ... You have to promise you won't put a damper on it, and tell me it's not practical.

[Shaking him.]

LIONEL *[Bored]* All right.

VIVIAN Well, this is it. I'm going to sell all the jewelry my grandmother left me and we're going on a trip. We're going to some city I don't know which but some big city that will be as far from here as we can get. Then we'll take jobs and when we have enough money we'll start a restaurant. We could start it on credit with just the barest amount of cash. It's not going to be just an ordinary restaurant but an odd one where everyone sits on cushions instead of on chairs. We could dress the waiters up in those flowing Turkish bloomers and serve very expensive oriental foods, all night long. It will be called Restaurant Midnight. Can you picture it?

LIONEL *[Very bored]* Well, yes ... in a way ...

VIVIAN Well, I can see the whole thing ... very small lamps and perfume in the air, no menus, just silent waiters ... bringing in elaborate dishes one after the other ... and music. We could call it "Minuit" ... as it is in French ... But either way we must leave soon ... I can't go on this way with my mother snooping around ... I can't be tied down ... I've tried running off before, when I felt desperate ... But things didn't work out ... maybe because I never had a real friend before ... But *now* I have *you* – *[She stops, suddenly aware of* MOLLY *– then with a certain diffidence]* and Molly, of course, she must come too – we understand each other even if she is still waters run deep. She has to escape from her mother too ...

*[*MOLLY *starts at the word "mother." Her face blackens.]*

LIONEL Molly, you're shivering ... Why didn't you say something? *[Looking up]* The sun's gone behind a cloud, no wonder you're cold ... I can go back to the house and get you a jacket, unless you want to come along and go home now too. *[*MOLLY *does not move]* I'll go and get it. Sit nearer the rocks you'll be out of the wind. Vivian, do you want something heavier than that? *[Points to her robe.]*

VIVIAN No, thanks. I'm much too excited about Restaurant Midnight to notice anything. Besides I'm not very conscious of the physical, *[*LIONEL *exits.* MOLLY *gets up and walks to the rocks leading to the cliff]* Have you ever eaten Armenian vine leaves with little pine nuts inside of them?

*[*MOLLY *is climbing the rocks.]*

MOLLY Don't follow me ...

VIVIAN Oh their wonderful flaky desserts with golden honey poured ...

MOLLY Don't follow me!

VIVIAN *[Tapering off]* ... all over them ...

MOLLY The day you came I was standing on the porch watching you. I heard everything you said. You put your arm around my mother, and you told her she had beautiful hair, then you saw my summer house and you told her how much you loved it. You went and sat in it and you yelled, Come out, Molly. I'm in your little house. You've tried in every way since you came to push me out. She hates you.

VIVIAN What?

MOLLY My mother hates you! She hates you!

VIVIAN *[After recovering from her shock starts out after her in a rage]* That's a lie, a rotten lie ... She doesn't hate me ... She's ashamed of *you* ... ashamed of you. *[Exits, then repeating several times off stage]* She's ashamed of you ... ashamed of you ...

[Her voice is muffled by the entrance of the Mexicans and GERTRUDE. *The servants head the procession, chattering like magpies and singing.* MR SOLARES *and* FREDERICA *bring up the rear carrying a tremendous pink rubber horse with purple dots. The hindquarters are supported by* FREDERICA.*]*

MRS LOPEZ *[Signaling to one of the hags who puts a fancy cushion down on the bench, which she sits on, then yelling to* GERTRUDE*]* Well, how do you like our gorgeous horse? Pretty big, eh?

MR SOLARES It's worth thirty-two dollars.

[They all seat themselves.]

GERTRUDE Now that you've asked me I'll tell you quite frankly that I would never dream of spending my money on a thing like that.

MRS LOPEZ *[Popping a mint into her mouth]* Pretty big, eh?

GERTRUDE *[Irritably]* Yes, yes, it's big all right but I don't see what that has to do with anything.

MRS LOPEZ That right. Big, lots of money. Little not so much.

GERTRUDE *[Bitterly]* All the worse.

MRS LOPEZ *[Merrily]* Maybe next year, bigger. You got one? *[*GERTRUDE*, bored, does not answer]* You got one?

GERTRUDE What?

MRS LOPEZ A rubber horse?

GERTRUDE Oh, for heaven's sake! I told you I thought it was silly. I don't believe in toys for grownups. I think they should buy other things, if they have money to spare.

MRS LOPEZ *[Complacently folding her hands]* What?

GERTRUDE Well, I guess a dresser or a chair or clothing or curtains. I don't know but certainly not a rubber horse. Clothing, of course, one can always buy because the styles change so frequently.

MR SOLARES Miss Eastman Cuevas, how many dresses you got?

GERTRUDE *[Icily]* I have never counted them.

MRS LOPEZ *[To her brother]* Cincuenta y nueve, dile.

MR SOLARES She got fifty-nine back at the house.

GERTRUDE *[In spite of herself]* Fifty-nine!

MR SOLARES I bought them all for her, since her husband died. He was a no good fellow. No ambition, no brain, no pep.

MRS LOPEZ *[Smiling, and nodding her head to* GERTRUDE *sweetly]* Fifty-nine dresses. You like to have that many dresses?

[Enter MRS CONSTABLE *carrying a fishing pole and basket, although she is immaculately dressed in a white crocheted summer ensemble. She has on a large hat and black glasses.]*

MRS CONSTABLE *[Trying to smile and appear at ease]* I hope I'm not interrupting a private discussion.

MR SOLARES Happy to see you on this beautiful day. Sit down with us. We weren't having no discussion. Just counting up how many dresses the ladies got.

MRS CONSTABLE *[A little shocked]* Oh! I myself was hunting for a good spot to fish and I passed so near to your house that I dropped in to call, but you weren't there, of course. Then I remembered that you told me about a bathing spot, somewhere in this direction, so I struck out hoping to find you. Where are the children?

GERTRUDE They were here a little while ago ... They'll be back.

MRS CONSTABLE I think I might sit down for a few minutes and wait for my bird to come back. I call Vivian my bird. Don't you think it suits her, Mrs Eastman Cuevas?

GERTRUDE *[Bored]* Yes.

MRS CONSTABLE *[She sits down on a cushion]* I miss her very badly already. It's partly because she has so much life in her. She finds so many things of interest to do and think about. *[She speaks with wonder in her voice]* 1 myself can't work up very much interest. I guess that's normal at my age. I can't think of much to do really, not being either a moveiegoer, or a card player or a walker. Don't you think that makes me miss her more?

GERTRUDE *[Icily]* It might.

MRS CONSTABLE This morning after I was cleaned and dressed I sat on the porch, but I got so tired of sitting there that I went to the front desk and asked them to tell me how to fish. They did and I bought this pole. The clerk gave me a kit with some bait in it. I think it's a worm. I'm not looking forward to opening the kit. I don't like the old hook either. I'll wager I don't fish after all. *[She sighs]* So you see what my days are like.

GERTRUDE Don't you read?

MRS CONSTABLE I would love to read but I have trouble with concentration.

MR SOLARES *[Coming over and crouching next to* MRS CONSTABLE *on his heels]* How are you feeling today, Mrs Constable? What's new?

MRS CONSTABLE Not very well, thank you. I'm a little bit blue. That's why I thought I'd get a look at my bird.

MR SOLARES *[Still to* MRS CONSTABLE*]* You're looking real good. *[Studying her crocheted dress]* That's handwork, ain't it?

MRS CONSTABLE *[Startled]* Why, yes.

MR SOLARES You like turtle steak?

MRS CONSTABLE What?

MR SOLARES Turtle steak. You like it, Mrs Constable?

MRS CONSTABLE *[Stammering, bewildered]* Oh, yes ...

GERTRUDE Mr Solares!

MR SOLARES *[Looking up]* What is it?

GERTRUDE Perhaps I might try chop suey with you, after all. Did it originate in China or is it actually an American dish?

MR SOLARES I don't know, Miss Eastman Cuevas.

[Quickly turns again to MRS CONSTABLE.*]*

MRS LOPEZ *[Loudly to* GERTRUDE*]* Now you want to go eat chop suey because he's talkin' to the other lady. You be careful, Señora Eastman Cuevas or you gonna lose him.

[She chuckles.]

GERTRUDE *[Furious but ignoring* MRS LOPEZ*]* I thought we might try some tonight, Mr Solares – that is, if you'd like to ... *[Bitterly]* Or have you lost your taste for chop suey?

MR SOLARES No, it's good. *[Turning to* MRS CONSTABLE *again]* I'll call you up in your hotel and we'll go eat a real good turtle steak with fried potatoes one night. One steak would be too big for you, Mrs Constable. You look like a dainty eater. Am I right?

GERTRUDE *[Turns and sees* MOLLY *sitting on the rock]* Molly, we met Lionel. He's bringing the coats. *[She sees* MOLLY*'s stricken face and questions her]* Molly, what's happened? *[*MOLLY *doesn't answer]* What is it, Molly? What's happened to you ... Molly ... what happened? What is it, Molly? *[Looking around for* VIVIAN*]* Where's Vivian? *[*MOLLY *still does not answer]* Molly ... Where is she? Where's Vivian?

MOLLY *[In a quavering voice]* She's gathering shells ...

*[*MRS CONSTABLE *rises and starts looking vaguely for* VIVIAN*. Then she sits down again.* GERTRUDE *gathers her composure after a moment and speaks to* MR SOLARES*.]*

GERTRUDE *[Starts off and meets* LIONEL*]* Mr Solares, I'm going home. It's windy and cold ... The clouds are getting thicker every minute ... The sun's not coming out again. I'm going back to the house.

LIONEL *[Entering with the coats]* I brought these ... I brought one for Vivian too ... Where's Vivian?

GERTRUDE *[Takes sweater from* LIONEL*]* She's gathering shells. *[She puts sweater on* MOLLY*'s shoulders]* Molly, put this on, you'll freeze. *[She starts off and calls to* MR SOLARES*]* I'm going home.

*[*MOLLY *rises and starts to leave and comes face to face with* MRS CONSTABLE*. They look at each other a moment,* MOLLY *then rushes off, following her mother.* MRS CONSTABLE *goes back to the rock.* MR SOLARES *and the Spanish people start to gather up their stuff and prepare to leave.]*

MR SOLARES We're coming right away, Miss Eastman Cuevas. *[He gives the servants orders in Spanish. Then to* MRS CONSTABLE*]* Come on back to the house and I'll mix up some drinks.

MRS CONSTABLE No, thank you.

MRS LOPEZ *{Butting into the conversation]* You don't come?

MR SOLARES *[To* MRS LOPEZ*]* Acaba de decir, no thank you ... ¿No oyes nunca?

[The Spanish people all exit noisily.]

LIONEL *[As he leaves, sees* MRS CONSTABLE *alone]* Aren't you coming Mrs Constable?

MRS CONSTABLE I think I'll sit here and wait for my bird.

LIONEL But she might climb up the cliffs and go home around the other way. It's getting colder Mrs Constable ... I could wait with you ...

MRS CONSTABLE I don't want to talk. No, I'll just sit here and wait a little while.

LIONEL *[Going off]* Don't worry, Mrs Constable. She'll be all right.

MRS CONSTABLE *[Left alone on the stage]* I get so frightened, I never know where she's going to end up.

The curtain falls slowly.

Scene iii

Same as Scene i. There is an improvised stand in the upper right-hand corner of the garden (the corner from the house), festooned with crepe paper and laden with a number of hot dogs, as well as part of a wedding cake and other things. MOLLY *is leaning against the stand wearing a simple wedding dress with a round shirred neck. She has removed her veil and she looks more like a girl graduating from school than like a bride. She is eating a hot dog. The stage is flooded with sunlight.*

GERTRUDE *[Also in bridal costume. She is sitting on a straight-backed chair in the middle of the garden, with her own dress hiked above her ankles, revealing bedroom slippers with pompons. Eyeing* MOLLY*]* Molly! You don't have to stuff yourself just because the others stuffed so much that they had to go and lie down! After all, you and I are brides even if I did take off my shoes. But they pinched so, I couldn't bear it another minute. Don't get mustard spots all over your dress. You'll want to show it to your grandchildren some day.

*[*MOLLY'S *mouth is so full that she is unable to answer. The hags and* ESPERANZA *are lying with their heads under the stand, for shade, and their legs sticking way out into the garden.* MRS CONSTABLE *is wandering around in a widow's outfit, with hat and veil. She holds a champagne glass in her hand.]*

MRS CONSTABLE *[Stopping beside* GERTRUDE'*s chair]* I don't know where to go or what to do next. I can't seem to tear myself away from you or Mr Solares or Mrs Lopez or Molly. Isn't that a ridiculous reaction? *[She is obviously tight]* I feel linked to you. That's the only way I can explain it. I don't ever want to have any other friends. It's as if I had been born right here in this garden and had never lived anywhere before in my life. Isn't that funny? I don't want ever to have any other friends. Don't leave me please. *[She throws her arms around* GERTRUDE*]* I don't know where to go. Don't leave me.

[She squeezes GERTRUDE *for a moment in silence.]*

GERTRUDE Now you must stop brooding. Can't you occupy yourself with something?

MRS CONSTABLE *[Firmly]* I'm not brooding. I can think about it without feeling a thing, because if you must know it's just not real to me. I can't believe it. Now what does seem real is that you and Mr Solares are going away and deserting me and Mrs Lopez and Molly and Lionel too. And I don't want to be anywhere except in this garden with all of you. Isn't it funny? Not that I'm enjoying myself, but it's all that I want to do, just hang around in this garden. *[She goes over to the stand rather unsteadily and pours some champagne into her glass out of a bottle. She takes a few sips, then bitterly in a changed tone]* I want to stay right here, by this stand.

GERTRUDE *[Looking over her shoulder at* MRS CONSTABLE*]* Drinking's not the answer to anything.

MRS CONSTABLE Answer? Who said anything about answers? I don't want any answers. It's too late for answers. Not that I ever asked much anyway. *[Angrily]* I never cared for answers. You can take your answers and flush them down the toilet. I *want* to be able to stay here. Right here where I am, and never, never leave this garden. Why don't you have a drink, or one of these lousy hot dogs? *[She brushes a few hot dogs off the stand, onto the grass.* MOLLY *stoops down and picks them up]* Let's stay here, Gertrude Eastman Cuevas, please.

GERTRUDE You're being silly, Mrs Constable. I know you're upset, but still you realize that I've sold the house and that Molly and I are going on honeymoons.

MRS CONSTABLE *[Vaguely]* What about Mrs Lopez?

GERTRUDE Well, now, I guess she has her own affairs to attend to, and Frederica. Mrs Constable, I think a sanatorium would be the best solution for you until you are ready to face the world again.

MRS CONSTABLE *[Thickly]* What world?

GERTRUDE Come now, Mrs Constable, you know what I mean.

MRS CONSTABLE I know you're trying to be a bitch!

GERTRUDE Mrs Constable ... I ... *[She turns to* MOLLY *who has come to her side]* Molly, go inside. At once ... *[*MOLLY *runs into the house]* Mrs Constable, you ought to be ashamed. I won't tolerate such ...

MRS CONSTABLE YOU have no understanding or feeling. Mrs Lopez is much nicer than you are. You're very coarse. I know that even if I do hate to read. You're coarse, coarse and selfish. Two awful things to be. But I'm stuck here anyway so what difference does it make?

GERTRUDE *[Refusing to listen to any more of her rambling]* Mrs Constable, I'm surprised at you. I'm going in. I won't put up with this. What would Vivian think ...

MRS CONSTABLE Vivian was a bird. How do you know anything about birds? Vivian understood everything I did. Vivian loved me even if she did answer back and act snippy in company. She was much too delicate to show her true feelings all over the place like you do and like I do.

GERTRUDE *[Crossing to* MRS CONSTABLE*]* I've never in my life shown my feelings. I don't know what you're talking about!

MRS CONSTABLE *[Reeling about at the wedding table]* I don't know what I'm talking about ... *[She grabs a bottle of champagne and offers it to* GERTRUDE*]* Have another drink, Miss Eastman Cuevas.

GERTRUDE *[In disgust grabs the bottle from her and puts it on the table]* I don't like to drink!

MRS CONSTABLE Then have a hot dog. *[She drops it at* GERTRUDE'S *feet.* GERTRUDE *starts toward the house.* MRS CONSTABLE *stops her]* You and I grew up believing this kind of thing would never happen to us or to any of ours.

GERTRUDE What?

MRS CONSTABLE We were kept far away from tragedy, weren't we?

GERTRUDE No, Mrs Constable. None of us have been kept from it.

MRS CONSTABLE Yes, well, now it's close to me, because Vivian hopped off a cliff – just like a cricket.

GERTRUDE Life is tragic, Mrs Constable.

MRS CONSTABLE I don't want tragic.

GERTRUDE *[Can't put up with it any more]* Why don't you lie down on the grass and rest? It's dry. *[*GERTRUDE *starts toward the door of the house.* MRS CONSTABLE *takes the suggestion and falls in a heap behind the stump under the balcony of the house]* Take your veil off. You'll roast! *[*MRS CONSTABLE *complies and* GERTRUDE *goes into the house. The two old hags appear from behind the wedding table and start to take some hot dogs. They are stopped by* MOLLY *coming out of the house.* MOLLY *looks for a moment at the garden and then runs into her summer house. A moment later* GERTRUDE *calls to the garden from the balcony]* Molly? Molly, are you in the summer house?

MOLLY Yes, I am.

GERTRUDE They're getting ready. After we've left if Mrs Constable is still asleep, will you and Lionel carry her inside and put her to bed in my room? Tomorrow when you leave for the Lobster Bowl you can take her along and drop her off at her hotel. Poor thing. Be sure and clean up this mess in the morning. I have a list of things here I want you to attend to. I'll leave it on the table downstairs. Mr Solares and I will be leaving soon.

MOLLY No!

GERTRUDE Yes.

MOLLY Please don't go away.

GERTRUDE Now, Molly, what kind of nonsense is this? You know we're leaving, what's the matter with you?

MOLLY No, I won't let you go!

GERTRUDE Please, Molly, no mysteries. It's very hard getting everyone started and I'm worn out. And I can't find my pocketbook. I think I left it in the garden. I'm coming down to look, [GERTRUDE *leaves the balcony to come downstairs.* MOLLY *comes out of the summer house and stands waiting with a small bunch of honeysuckle in her hands.* GERTRUDE *comes out of the house and crosses to the wedding table. She looks at* MOLLY *and sees her crying and goes to her]* What on earth is wrong, Molly? Why are you crying? Are you nervous? You've been so contented all day, stuffing yourself right along with the others. What has happened now?

MOLLY I didn't picture it.

GERTRUDE Picture what?

MOLLY What it would be like when the time came. Your leaving ...

GERTRUDE Why not?

MOLLY I don't know. I don't know ... I couldn't picture it, I guess. I thought so long as we were here we'd go right on being here. So I just ate right along with the others like you say.

GERTRUDE Well, it sounds like nonsense to me. Don't be a cry-baby, and wipe your tears.

*[*GERTRUDE *starts toward the table when she is stopped by* MOLLY *who puts the flowers in her hands.]*

MOLLY Stay!

GERTRUDE Molly. Put them back. They belong on your wedding dress.

MOLLY No, they're from the vine. I picked them for you!

GERTRUDE They're for your wedding. They belong to your dress. Here, put them back ...

MOLLY No ... No ... They're for you ... They're flowers for you! *[*GERTRUDE *does not know what to make of this strange and sudden love and moves across the garden]* I love you. I love you. Don't leave me. I love you. Don't go away!

GERTRUDE *[Shocked and white]* Molly, stop. You can't go on like this!

MOLLY I love you. You can't go!

GERTRUDE I didn't think you cared this much. If you really feel this way, why have you tormented me so ...

MOLLY I never have. I never have.

GERTRUDE You have. You have in a thousand different ways. What about the summer house?

MOLLY Don't leave me!

GERTRUDE And the vine?

MOLLY I love you!

GERTRUDE What about the vine, and the ocean, what about that? If you care this much why have you tormented me so about the water ... when you knew how ashamed I was ... Crazy, unnatural fear ... Why didn't you try to overcome it, if you love me so much? Answer that!

[MOLLY, in a frenzy of despair, starts clawing at her dress, pulling it open.]

MOLLY I will. I will. I'll overcome it. I'm sorry. I'll go in the water right away. I'm going now. I'm going ...

[MOLLY rips off her veil and throws it on the wedding table and makes a break for the gate to the ocean. GERTRUDE in horror grabs MOLLY'S arm and drags her back into the garden.]

GERTRUDE Stop it! Come back here at once. Are you insane? Button your dress. They'll see you ... they'll find you this way and think you're insane ...

MOLLY I was going in the water ...

GERTRUDE Button your dress. Are you insane! This is what I meant. I've always known it was there, this violence. I've told you again and again that I was frightened. I wasn't sure what I meant ... I didn't want to be sure. But I was right, there's something heavy and dangerous inside you, like some terrible rock that's ready to explode ... And it's been getting worse all the time. I can't bear it any more. I've got to get away, out of this garden. That's why I married. That's why I'm going away. I'm frightened of staying here with you any more. I can't breathe. Even on bright days the garden seems like a dark place without any air. I'm stifling!

[GERTRUDE passes below the balcony on her way to the front door, MRS LOPEZ tilts a vessel containing rice and pours it on GERTRUDE's head.]

MRS LOPEZ That's for you, bride number one! Plenty more when you go in the car with Solares. Ha ha! Frederica, ándele, ¡tu también!

[FREDERICA, terribly embarrassed, tosses a little rice onto GERTRUDE and starts to giggle.]

GERTRUDE *[Very agitated, ill-humoredly flicking rice from her shoulders]* Oh, really! Where is Mr Solares? Is he ready?

MRS LOPEZ My brother is coming right away. Where is bride number two?

GERTRUDE *[Looking around for* MOLLY *who is back in the summer house]* She's gone back into the summer house.

[She goes out.]

MRS LOPEZ I got rice for her too! *[Calling down to the servants who are still lying with their heads under the food stand]* ¡Quinta! ¡Altagracia! ¡Esperanza! ¡Despiértense!

[The servants wake up and come crawling out from under the food stand.]

ESPERANZA *[Scowling]* ¡Caray!

[She takes an enormous comb out of her pocket and starts running it through her matted hair. There is a sound of a horn right after ESPERANZA *begins to comb her hair.]*

FREDERICA *[Beside herself with excitement]* It's Lionel back with the automobile, mamá! It must be time. Tell the musicians to start playing!

MRS LOPEZ Yes, querida. ¡Música! *[She kisses her daughter effusively and they both exit from the balcony into the house talking and laughing.* LIONEL *enters from the lane, hurries across the lawn and into the house, just as* FREDERICA *and* MRS LOPEZ *enter through the front door onto the lawn.* MRS LOPEZ *calling to the servants]* Cuando salga la señora Eastman Cuevas de la casa, empezarán a cantar. *[She sings a few bars herself counting the time with a swinging finger and facing the servants, who rise and line up in a row. Calling to* MOLLY*]* Bride number two! Bride number two! Molly!

[She takes a few steps toward the summer house and throws some rice at it. The rice gets stuck in the vines instead of reaching MOLLY *inside. After a few more failures, she goes around to the front of the summer house and, standing at the entrance, she hurls handful after handful at* MOLLY*. Enter from the house* LIONEL*, and* MR SOLARES*. The men are carrying grips.* MRS CONSTABLE *is*

still stretched out in a corner where she won't interfere with the procession. Some very naive music starts back stage (sounding, if possible, like a Taxco band), as they proceed across the lawn; then the maids begin to sing. While this happens MRS LOPEZ *gradually ceases to throw her rice and then disappears in the summer house where she takes the weeping* MOLLY *into her arms.]*

LIONEL Where's Molly?

MRS LOPEZ *[Over the music, from inside the summer house]* She don't feel good. She's crying in here. I cried too when I had my wedding. Many young girls do. I didn't want to leave my house neither.

[She steps out of the summer house.]

LIONEL *[Calling]* I'll be back, Molly, as soon as I load these bags.

[Enter GERTRUDE *as* MRS LOPEZ *comes out of the summer house. The music swells and the singing is louder.* GERTRUDE *walks rapidly through the garden in a shower of rice and rose petals.* MOLLY *comes out of the summer house and* GERTRUDE *stops. They confront each other for a second without speaking.* GERTRUDE *continues on her way.* MOLLY *goes back into the summer house.]*

GERTRUDE *[From the road, calling over the music]* Good-bye, Molly!

[The wedding party files out, singing, MRS LOPEZ *bringing up the rear. She throws a final handful of rice at the summer house, but it does not reach. They exit.* MOLLY *is left alone on the stage. The music gradually fades.]*

LIONEL *[Returning and coming into the garden]* Molly! *[There is no answer. He walks around to the front of the summer house and looks in]* Molly, I'm sorry you feel bad. *[Pause]* Why don't you come out? There's a very pretty sunset. *[He reaches in and pulls her out by the hands. He puts his arm around her shoulder and leads her toward the house]* We can go upstairs on the balcony and look at the sunset.

[They disappear into the house and reappear on the balcony, where they go to the balustrade and lean over it.]

MOLLY *[Staring down into the garden, in a very small voice]* It looks different.

LIONEL *[After gazing off into the distance very thoughtfully for a minute]* I've always liked it when something that I've looked at every day suddenly seems strange and unfamiliar. Maybe not always, but when I was home I used to like looking out my window after certain storms that left a special kind of light in the sky.

MOLLY *[In a whisper]* It looks different ...

LIONEL A very brilliant light that illuminated only the most distant places, the places nearest to the horizon. Then I could see little round hills, and clumps of trees, and pastures that I didn't remember ever seeing before, very, very close to the sky. It always gave me a lift, as if everything might change around me but in a wonderful way that I wouldn't have guessed was possible. Do you understand what I mean?

*[*MOLLY *shakes her head, negatively. He looks at her for a moment, a little sadly.]*

MOLLY *[Anguished, turning away from him]* I don't know. I don't know. It looks so different ...

Curtain

Act Two

Scene i

The Lobster Bowl, ten months later.

Just before dawn. The oyster-shell door is open and the sound of waves breaking will continue throughout this scene. MOLLY *and* LIONEL *are playing cards at one of the tables, Russian Bank or its equivalent. They are sitting in a circle of light. The rest of the stage is in darkness.* MRS CONSTABLE *is lying on a bench but can't be seen.*

MOLLY You just put a king on top of another king.

LIONEL I was looking for an ace.

MOLLY *[Smilingly]* It's right here, silly, under your nose.

LIONEL It's almost morning.

MOLLY *[Wistful]* Can't we play one more game after this?

LIONEL All right.

[They play for a while in silence, then LIONEL *stops again.]*

MOLLY What is it?

LIONEL Nothing.

MOLLY I don't think you want to play at all. You're thinking about something else.

LIONEL I had a letter from my brother ... again.

MOLLY *[Tense]* The one who's still in St Louis?

LIONEL That's right, the popular one, the one who'd like us to come back there.

MOLLY He's big and tall.

LIONEL Yes, he's big and tall, like most boys in this country. I've been thinking a lot about St Louis, Molly ...

MOLLY Inez says we've got bigger men here than they have in Europe.

LIONEL Well, Swedes are big and so are Yugoslavians ...

MOLLY But the French people are little.

LIONEL Well, yes, but they're not as little as all that. They're not midgets. And they're not the way people used to picture them years ago, silly and carefree and saying Oo ... la ... la ... all the time.

MOLLY They're not saying Oo ... la ... la?

LIONEL I don't know really, I've never been there. *[Dreaming, neglecting his cards]* Molly, when you close your eyes and picture the world do you see it dark? *[*MOLLY *doesn't answer right away]* Do you, Molly? Do you see the world dark behind your eyes?

MOLLY I ... I don't know ... I see parts of it dark.

LIONEL Like what?

MOLLY Like woods ... like pine-tree woods.

LIONEL I see it dark, but beautiful like the ocean is right now. And like I saw it once when I was a child ... just before a total eclipse. Did you ever see a total eclipse?

MOLLY I never saw any kind of eclipse.

LIONEL I saw one with my brother. There was a shadow over the whole earth. I was afraid then, but it stayed in my memory like something that was beautiful. It made me afraid but I knew it was beautiful.

MOLLY It's my game.

[They start shuffling.]

LIONEL *[Tentative]* Did you ever worry about running far away from sad things when you were young, and then later getting older and not being able to find your way back to them ever again, even when you wanted to?

MOLLY You would never want to find your way back to sad things.

LIONEL But you might have lost wonderful things too, mixed in with the sad ones. Suppose in a few years I wanted to remember the way the world looked that day, the day of the eclipse when I saw the shadow.

MOLLY *[Stops dealing her cards out very slowly, steeped in a dream]* She had a shadow.

LIONEL And suppose I couldn't remember it. What Molly?

MOLLY She had a shadow.

LIONEL Who?

MOLLY My mother.

LIONEL Oh ...

[He deals his cards out more rapidly, becoming deeply absorbed in his game.]

MOLLY It used to come and pass over her whole life and make it dark. It didn't come very often, but when it did she used to go downstairs and drink fizzy water. Once I went down I was twelve years old. I waited until she was asleep and I sneaked down into the kitchen very quietly. Then I switched the light on and I opened the ice chest and I took out a bottle of fizzy water just like she did. Then I went over to the table and I sat down.

LIONEL *[Without looking up from his cards]* And then ...

MOLLY I drank a little water, but I couldn't drink any more. The water was so icy cold. I was going to drink a whole bottleful like she did, but nothing ... really nothing turned out like I thought it would. *[*LIONEL *mixes all his cards up together in a sudden gesture,* MOLLY *comes out of her dream]* Why are you messing up the cards? We haven't begun our game ... *[*LIONEL *doesn't answer]* What's the matter?

LIONEL Nothing.

MOLLY But you've messed up the cards.

LIONEL I was trying to tell you something ... It meant a lot to me ... I wanted you to listen.

MOLLY I was listening.

LIONEL You told me about fizzy water ... and your mother. *[*MOLLY *automatically passing her hand over her own cards and messing them up]* I wanted you to listen. I don't want you to half hear me any more. I used to like it but ...

MOLLY *[Pathetic, bewildered]* I listen to you. We had a nice time yesterday ... when ... when we were digging for clams.

LIONEL *[Looking back at her unable to be angry, now with compassion]* Yes, Molly, we did. We had a very good time ... yesterday. I like digging for clams ... *[They hold, looking at each other for a moment]* I'm going upstairs. I'm tired. I'm going to bed.

*[*LIONEL *exits up stairs.* MRS CONSTABLE *comes out of the darkness, where she has been sleeping on her bench, into the circle of light.]*

MOLLY You woke up.

MRS CONSTABLE I've been awake ... for a while. I was waiting.

MOLLY I won the game, but it wasn't much fun. Lionel didn't pay attention to the cards.

MRS CONSTABLE I was waiting because I wanted to tell you something ... a secret ... I always tell you my secrets ... But there's one I haven't told you ... I've known it all along ... But I've never said anything to you ... never before ... But now I'm going to ... I must.

MOLLY *[Wide-eyed, thinking she is referring to* VIVIAN*]* It wasn't my fault! I didn't mean to ...

MRS CONSTABLE My husband never loved me ... Vivian?

MOLLY Vivian! It wasn't my fault ... I didn't ... She ... I didn't ...

*[*MOLLY *starts to sob.]*

MRS CONSTABLE *[Clapping her hand over* MOLLY'S *mouth]* Shhhhhh ... They belonged to each other, my husband and Vivian. They never belonged to me ... ever ... But I couldn't admit it ... I hung on hard to the bitter end. When they died ... nothing was left ... no memories ... Everything vanished ... all the panic ... and the strain ... I hardly remember my life. They never loved me ... I didn't really love them ... My heart had fake roots ... when the strain was over, they dried up ... they shriveled and snapped and my heart was left empty. There was no blood left in my heart at all ... They never loved me! Molly ... your mother ... It's not too late ... She doesn't ...

MOLLY *[Interrupting, sensing that* MRS CONSTABLE *will say something too awful to hear]* My mother wrote me. I got the letter today. She *hates* it down in Mexico. She hates it there.

MRS CONSTABLE Molly, if you went away from here, I'd miss you very much. If you went away there wouldn't be anyone here I loved ... Molly, go away ... go away with Lionel ... Don't stay here in the Lobster Bowl ...

MOLLY *[Commenting on her mother's letter and then reading from it]* She doesn't know how long she can stand it ... She says she doesn't feel very well ... "The climate doesn't suit me ...

I feel sick all the time and I find it almost impossible to sleep ... I can't read very much ... not at night ... because the light is too feeble here in the mountains. Mrs Lopez has two of her sisters here at the moment. Things are getting more and more unbearable. Mrs Lopez is the least raucous of the three. I hope that you are occupying yourself with something constructive. Be careful not to dream and be sure ..."

MRS CONSTABLE Why shouldn't you dream?

MOLLY I used to waste a lot of time day-dreaming. I guess I still do. She didn't want me to dream.

MRS CONSTABLE Why shouldn't you dream? Why didn't she want you to?

MOLLY Because she wanted me to grow up to be wonderful and strong like she is. Will she come back soon, Mrs Constable? Will she make them all leave there? Will she?

MRS CONSTABLE I don't know dear ... I don't know ... I suppose she will ... If she needs you, she'll come back. If she needs you, I'm sure she will.

MOLLY Are you going to walk home along the edge of the water?

MRS CONSTABLE I like wet sand ... and I like the spray.

MOLLY You'll get the bottom of your dress all soaking wet. You'll catch cold.

MRS CONSTABLE I love the waves breaking in this early light... I run after them. I run after the waves ... I scoop up the foam and I rub it on my face. All along the way I think it's beginning ...

MOLLY What?

MRS CONSTABLE My life. I think it's beginning, and then ...

MOLLY And then?

MRS CONSTABLE I see the hotel.

*[*MRS CONSTABLE *exits through oyster-shell door.]*

MOLLY *[She reads again part of her mother's letter]* "Two day ago, Fula Lopez went into the city and came back with a hideous white dog. She bought it in the street. The dog's bark is high and sharp. It hasn't stopped yapping since it came. I haven't slept at all for two nights. Now I'm beginning a cold ..."

[The lights fade as the curtain falls.]

Scene ii

The Lobster Bowl. Two months later.

INEZ *[She is middle-aged, full bosomed, spirited but a little coarse. She cannot see into* MOLLY's *booth from where she stands behind the bar]* I'd rather hit myself over the head with a club than drag around here the way you do, reading comic books all day long. It's so damp and empty and quiet in here.

[She shakes a whole tray of glasses in the sink, which make a terrific racket.]

MOLLY It's not a comic book. It's a letter from my mother.

INEZ What's new?

MOLLY It came last week.

INEZ What are you doing reading it now?

MOLLY She's coming back today. She's coming back from Mexico.

INEZ Maybe she'll pep things up a little. I hear she's got more personality than you. *[Shifts some oysters]* You didn't model yourself after her, did you?

MOLLY No.

INEZ Ever try modeling yourself after anyone?

MOLLY No.

INEZ Well, if you don't feel like you've got much personality yourself, it's an easy way to do. You just pick the right model and you watch how they act. I never modeled myself after anyone, but there were two or three who modeled after me. And they weren't even relatives – just ordinary girls. It's an easy way to do. *[Shifts some oysters]* Anyway, I don't see poring over comic books. I'd rather have someone tell me a good joke any day. What's really nice is to go out – eight or nine – to an Italian dinner, and sit around afterwards listening to the different jokes. You get a better selection that way! Ever try that?

MOLLY I don't like big bunches of people.

INEZ You could at least live in a regular home if you don't like crowds, and do cooking for your husband. You don't even have a hot plate in your room! *[Crash of stool to floor, followed by some high giggles]* There goes Mrs Constable again. You'd think she'd drink home, at her hotel, where no one could see her. She's got a whole suite to herself there. It's been over a year since her daughter's accident, so I could say her drinking permit had expired. I think she's just on a plain drunk now. Right? *[*MOLLY *nods]* You sure are a button lip. As long as you're sitting there you might as well talk. It don't cost extra. *[She frowns and looks rather mean for a moment. There is more offstage racket]* I think Mrs Constable is heading this way. I hope to God she don't get started on Death. Not that I blame her for thinking about it after what happened, but I don't like that topic.

[Enter MRS CONSTABLE.*]*

MRS CONSTABLE *[She has been drinking]* How is everyone, this afternoon?

MOLLY My mother's coming back today.

INEZ I'm kind of rushing, Mrs Constable. I've got to have three hundred oyster cocktails ready by tonight and I haven't even prepared the hot sauce yet.

MRS CONSTABLE Rushing? I didn't know that people still rushed ...

INEZ Here we go, boys!

MRS CONSTABLE Then you must be one of the fortunate ones who has not yet stood on the edge of the black pit. There is no rushing after that, only waiting. It seems hardly worthwhile even keeping oneself clean after one has stood on the edge of the black pit.

INEZ If you're clean by nature, you're clean.

MRS CONSTABLE Oh, really? How very interesting!

INEZ Some people would rather be clean than eat or sleep.

MRS CONSTABLE How very interesting! How nice that they are all so terribly interested in keeping clean! Cleanliness is so important really, such a *deep deep* thing. Those people who are so interested in keeping clean must have very deep souls. They must think a lot about life and death, that is when they're not too busy *washing*, but I guess washing takes up most of their time. How right they are! Hoorah for them!

[She flourishes her glass.]

INEZ *[With a set face determined to ignore her taunts]* The tide's pretty far out today. Did you take a look at the ...

MRS CONSTABLE They say that people can't live unless they can fill their lives with petty details. That's people's way of avoiding the black pit. I'm just a weak, ordinary, *very ordinary* woman in her middle years, but I've been able to wipe all the petty details from my life ... all of them. I never rush or get excited about anything. I've dumped my entire life out the window ... like that!

[She tips her whisky glass and pours a little on the floor.]

INEZ *[Flaring up]* Listen here, Mrs Constable, I haven't got time to go wiping up slops. I've got to prepare three hundred oyster cocktails. That means toothpicks and three hundred little hookers of hot sauce. I haven't got time to talk so I certainly haven't got time to wipe up slops.

MRS CONSTABLE I know ... toothpicks and hot sauce and hookers. Very interesting! How many oysters do you serve to a customer? Please tell me.

INEZ *[Only half listening to* MRS CONSTABLE, *automatically]* Five.

MRS CONSTABLE *[Smirking as much as she can]* Five! How fascinating! Really and truly, I can't believe it!

INEZ Balls! Now you get out and don't come back here until I finish my work. Not if you know what's good for you. I can feel myself getting ready to blow up! *[Shifts some more oysters]* I'm going upstairs now and I'm going to put a cold towel on my head. Then, I'm coming down to finish my oyster cocktails, and when I do I want peace and quiet. I've got to have peace and quiet when I'm doing my oyster cocktails. If I don't I just get too nervous. That's all.

MRS CONSTABLE I'm going ... whether you're getting ready to blow up or not. *[She walks unsteadily toward exit. Then from the doorway]* I happen to be a very independent woman ... But you are just plain bossy, Mrs Oyster Cocktail Sauce.

[Exit MRS CONSTABLE.*]*

INEZ Independent! I could make her into a slave if I cared to. I could walk all over her if I cared to, but I don't. I don't like to walk all over anyone. Most women do ... they love it. They like to take some other man or woman and make him or her into a slave, but I don't. I don't like slaves. I like everybody to be going his own independent way. Hello. Good-bye. You go your way and I'll go my way, but no slaves. I'll bet you wouldn't find ten men in this town as democratic as I am. *[Shifts some oysters]* Well, here I go. I guess I'll give myself a fresh apron while I'm up there. Then I'll be ready when they come for their oysters. *[Vaguely touching her head]* I don't like to eat oysters any more. I suppose I've seen too much of them, like everything else in life.

[She pulls the chain on the big light behind the bar so that the scene darkens. There is a little light playing on MOLLY's *booth and on the paper flowers and leaves,* MOLLY *puts her book of comics down, sits dreaming for a moment. There is summer house music to indicate a more lyrical mood. She pulls a letter out of her pocket and reads it. Enter* LIONEL.*]*

LIONEL Hey.

MOLLY Where were you?

LIONEL I was walking along the beach thinking about something. Molly, listen. I got a wire this morning!

MOLLY A wire?

LIONEL Yes, from my brother.

MOLLY The one in St Louis? The one who wants us to come ...

LIONEL Yes, Molly. He has a place for me in his business now. He sells barbecue equipment to people.

MOLLY To people?

LIONEL Yes, to people. For their back yards, and he wants my help.

MOLLY But ... but you're going to be a religious leader.

LIONEL I didn't say I wouldn't be, or I may end up religious without leading anybody at all. But wherever I end up, I'm getting out of here. I've made up my mind. This place is a fake.

MOLLY These oyster shells are real and so is the turtle. He just hasn't got his own head and feet. They're wooden.

LIONEL To me this place is a fake. I chose it for protection, and it doesn't work out.

MOLLY It doesn't work out?

LIONEL Molly, you know that. I've been saying it to you in a thousand different ways. You know it's not easy for me to leave. Places that don't work out are ten times tougher to leave than any other places in the world.

MRS CONSTABLE My sisters used to have cherry contests. They stuffed themselves with cherries all week long and counted up the pits on Saturday. It made them feel exuberant.

MOLLY I can't eat cherries.

MRS CONSTABLE I couldn't either. I'd eat a few and I'd feel sick. But that never stopped me. I never missed a single contest. I despised cherry contests, but I couldn't stand being left out. Never. Every week I'd sneak off to the woods with bags full of cherries. I'd sit on a log and pit each cherry with a knife. Then I'd bury the fruit in a deep hole and fill it up with dirt. I cheated so hard to be in them, and I didn't even like them. I was so scared to be left out.

LIONEL They are harder to leave, Molly, places that don't work out. I know it sounds crazy, but they are. Like it's three times harder for me to leave now than when I first came here, and in those days I liked the decorations. Molly, don't look so funny. I can explain it all some other way. *[Indicates oyster-shell door]* Suppose I kept on closing that door against the ocean every night because the ocean made me sad and then one night I went to open it and I couldn't even find the door. Suppose I couldn't tell it apart from the wall any more. Then it would be too late and we'd be shut in here forever once and for all. It's not going to happen, Molly. I won't let it happen. We're going away – you and me. We're getting out of here. We're not playing cards in this oyster cocktail bar until we're old.

MOLLY *[Turns and looks up the stairs and then back to* LIONEL*]* If we had a bigger light bulb we could play in the bedroom upstairs.

LIONEL *[Walking away]* You're right Molly, dead right. We could do just that. We could play cards up there in that God-forsaken bedroom upstairs. *[Exits.]*

MRS CONSTABLE *[Gets up and goes to* MOLLY*]* Molly, call him back.

MOLLY No, I'm going upstairs.

MRS CONSTABLE It's time ... Go ... go with Lionel.

MOLLY My mother's coming. I'm going to her birthday supper.

MRS CONSTABLE Don't go there ...

MOLLY I'm late. I must change my dress.

[She exits up the stairs.]

MRS CONSTABLE *[Stumbling about and crossing to the bar]* You're hanging on just like me. If she brought you her love you wouldn't know her. You wouldn't know who she was. *[*MRS CONSTABLE *sinks into a chair below the bar.* GERTRUDE *enters. She is pale, distraught. She does not see* MRS CONSTABLE*]* Hello, Gertrude Eastman Cuevas.

GERTRUDE *[Trying to conceal the strain she is under]* Hello, Mrs Constable. How are you?

MRS CONSTABLE How are you making out?

GERTRUDE Molly wrote me you were still here. Where is she?

MRS CONSTABLE You look tired.

GERTRUDE Where is Molly? *[*LIONEL *enters]* Lionel! How nice to see you! Where's Molly?

LIONEL I ... I didn't know you were coming.

GERTRUDE Didn't you?

LIONEL I didn't expect to see you. How are you, Mrs Eastman Cuevas? How was your trip? When did you arrive?

GERTRUDE Well, around two ... But I *had* to wait ... They were driving me here ... Didn't you *know* I was coming?

LIONEL No, I didn't.

GERTRUDE *[Uneasily]* But I wrote Molly. I told her I was coming. I wanted to get here for my birthday. I wrote Molly that. Didn't she tell you about it? I sent her a letter. The paper was very sweet. I was sure that she would show it to you. There's a picture of a little Spanish dancer on the paper with a real lace mantilla pasted round her head. Didn't she show it to you?

LIONEL *[Brooding]* No.

GERTRUDE That's strange. I thought she would. I have others for her too. A toreador with peach satin breeches and a macaw with real feathers.

LIONEL *[Unheeding]* She never said anything about it. She never showed me any letter.

GERTRUDE That's strange. I thought ... I thought ... *[She hesitates, feeling the barrier between them. Tentative]* Macaws are called guacamayos down there.

LIONEL Are they?

GERTRUDE Yes, they are. Guacamayos ...

LIONEL What's the difference between them and parrots?

GERTRUDE They're bigger! Much bigger.

LIONEL Do they talk?

GERTRUDE Yes, they do, but parrots have a better vocabulary. Lionel, my birthday supper's tonight. I suppose you can't come. You work late at night, don't you?

LIONEL I work at night, but not for long ...

GERTRUDE You'll work in the day then?

LIONEL No.

GERTRUDE Then when will you work?

LIONEL I'm quitting.

GERTRUDE What?

LIONEL I'm quitting this job. I'm getting out.

GERTRUDE Getting out. What will you do? Where will you work?

LIONEL I'm quitting. I'm going.

[He exits.]

GERTRUDE Lionel ... Wait ... Where are you going?

MRS CONSTABLE Come on over here and talk to me ... You need a drink.

GERTRUDE Where is she? Where's Molly?

MRS CONSTABLE She's gone down on the rocks, hunting for mussels.

GERTRUDE Hunting for mussels? But she knew I was coming. Why isn't she here? I don't understand. Didn't she get my letter?

MRS CONSTABLE *[Dragging* GERTRUDE *rather roughly to a table]* Sit down ... You look sick.

GERTRUDE I'm not sick ... I'm just tired, exhausted, that's all. They've worn me out in a thousand different ways. Even today ... I wanted to see Molly the second we arrived, but I had to wait. I tried to rest. I had a bad dream. It's hanging over me still. But I'll be all right in a little bit. I'll be fine as soon as I see Molly. I'm just tired, that's all.

MRS CONSTABLE I'm glad you're well. How is Mrs Lopez? If I were a man, I'd marry Mrs Lopez. She'd be my type. We should both have been men. Two Spanish men, married to Mrs Lopez.

GERTRUDE She was part of the whole thing! The confusion ... the racket ... the pandemonium.

MRS CONSTABLE I like Mrs Lopez, and I'm glad she's fat.

GERTRUDE There were twelve of us at table every meal.

MRS CONSTABLE When?

GERTRUDE All these months down in Mexico. Twelve of us at least. Old ladies, babies, men, little girls, everyone jabbering, the noise, the screeching never stopped ... The cooks, the maids, even the birds ...

MRS CONSTABLE Birds?

GERTRUDE Dirty noisy parrots, trailing around loose. There was a big one called Pepe, with a frightening beak.

MRS CONSTABLE *[Rather delighted]* Pepe?

GERTRUDE Their pet, their favorite ... Crazy undisciplined bird, always climbing up the table leg and plowing through the food.

MRS CONSTABLE *[Ingenuous]* Didn't you like Pepe?

GERTRUDE *[Dejected, as if in answer to a sad question, not irritated]* No, I didn't like Pepe. I didn't like anything.

Where's Molly?

[Going to oyster-shell door.]

MRS CONSTABLE When are you going back?

GERTRUDE Back? I'm never going back. I've made up my mind. From now on I'm staying in the house up here. It was a terrible mistake. I told him that. I told him that when he had to be there he could go by himself. We had a terrible fight ... It was disgusting. When he stood there saying that men should never have given us the vote, I slapped him.

MRS CONSTABLE I never voted. I would vote all right if I could only register.

GERTRUDE He's a barbarian. A subnormal human being. But it doesn't matter. He can stay down there as long as he likes. I'll be up here, where I belong, near Molly. *[Face clouding over]* What was he saying before? What did he mean?

MRS CONSTABLE Who?

GERTRUDE Lionel. He said he was quitting. He said he was leaving, getting out of here.

MRS CONSTABLE Lionel's sick of the Lobster Bowl. I'm not. Molly likes it too, more than Lionel.

GERTRUDE Molly. She couldn't like it here, not after our life in the ocean house.

MRS CONSTABLE Tell me more, Gertrude Eastman Cuevas. Did you enjoy the scenery?

GERTRUDE What?

MRS CONSTABLE Down in Mexico.

GERTRUDE I didn't enjoy anything. How could I, the way they lived? It wasn't even civilized.

MRS CONSTABLE *[Merrily]* Great big lunches every day.

GERTRUDE There were three or four beds in every single room.

MRS CONSTABLE Who was in them?

GERTRUDE Relatives, endless visiting relatives, snapping at each other, jabbering half the night. No wonder I look sick. *[Sadly to herself]* But I'll be fine soon. I know it. I will ... as soon as I see Molly. If only she'd come back ... *[To* MRS CONSTABLE*]* Which way did she go? Do you think I could find her?

MRS CONSTABLE She always goes a different way.

GERTRUDE She couldn't like it in this ugly place. It's not true!

MRS CONSTABLE They take long walks down the beach or go digging for clams. They're very polite. They invite me along. But I never accept. I know they'd rather go off together, all by themselves.

GERTRUDE *[Alarmed]* All by themselves!

MRS CONSTABLE When they play cards at night, I like to watch them. Sometimes I'm asleep on that bench, but either way I'm around. Inez doesn't know about it. She goes to bed early. She thinks I leave here at a reasonable hour. She's never found out. I take off my shoes and I wade home at dawn.

GERTRUDE I don't know what's happening to the people in this world.

[Leaves MRS CONSTABLE.*]*

MRS CONSTABLE Why don't you go back to Mexico, Gertrude Eastman Cuevas, go back to Pepe? *[*GERTRUDE *looks in disgust at* MRS CONSTABLE. *More gently]* Then have a drink.

GERTRUDE *[Fighting back a desire to cry]* I don't like to drink.

MRS CONSTABLE Then what do you like? What's your favorite pleasure?

GERTRUDE I don't know. I don't know. I don't like pleasures. I ... I like idealism and backbone and ambition. I take after my father. We were both very proud. We had the same standards, the same ideals. We both loved grit and fight.

MRS CONSTABLE You loved grit and fight.

GERTRUDE We were exactly alike. I was his favorite. He loved me more than anyone in the world!

MRS CONSTABLE *[Faintly echoing]* More than anyone in the world ...

GERTRUDE *[Picking up one of the two boxes she brought with her and brooding over it]* It was a senseless dream, a nightmare.

MRS CONSTABLE What's in the box?

GERTRUDE Little macaroons. I bought them for Molly on the way up. I thought she'd like them. Some of them are orange and some are bright pink. *[Shakes the box and broods again, troubled, haunted by the dream]* They were so pretty ...

MRS CONSTABLE Aren't they pretty any more?

GERTRUDE I had a dream about them just now, before I came. I was running very fast through the night trying to get to Molly, but I couldn't find the way. I kept losing all her presents. Everything I'd bought her I kept scattering on the ground. Then I was in a cold room with my father and she was there too. I asked him for a gift. I said, "I want something to give to my child," and he handed me this box ... *[Fingering the actual box]* I opened it up, and took out a macaroon and I gave it to Molly. *[Long pause. She looks haunted, deeply troubled]* When she began to eat it, I saw that it was hollow, just a shell filled with dust. Molly's lips were gray with dust. Then I heard him ... I heard my father. *[Excited]* He was laughing. He was laughing at me! *[She goes away from* MRS CONSTABLE *to collect herself]* I've loved him so. I don't know what's happening to me. I've never been this way. I've always thrown things off, but now even foolish dreams hang over me. I can't shake anything off. I'm not myself ... I ... *[Stiffening against the weakness]* When I was in the ocean house ... *[Covering her face with her hands and shaking her head, very softly, almost to herself]* Oh, I miss it so ... I miss it so.

MRS CONSTABLE Houses! I hate houses. I like public places. Houses break your heart. Come and be with me in the Lobster Bowl. They gyp you, but it's a great place. They gyp you, but I don't care.

GERTRUDE It was a beautiful house with a wall and a garden and a view of the sea.

MRS CONSTABLE Don't break your heart, Mrs Eastman dear, don't ...

GERTRUDE I was happy in my house. There was nothing wrong. I had a beautiful life. I had Molly. I was busy teaching her. I had a full daily life. Everything was fine. There was nothing wrong. I don't know why I got frightened, why I married again. It must have been ... it must have been because we had no money. That was it ... We had so little money, I got frightened for us both ... I should never have married. Now my life's lost its meaning ... I have nightmares all the time. I lie awake in the night trying to think of just one standard or one ideal but something foolish pops into my head like Fula Lopez wearing city shoes and stockings to the beach. I've lost my daily life, that's all. I've lost Molly. My life has no meaning now. It's their fault. It's because I'm living their way. But I'm back now with Molly. I'm going to be fine again ... She's coming with me tonight to my birthday supper ... It's getting dark out. Where is she? *[*LIONEL *enters at bar with basket of glasses]* Lionel. Wait ...

LIONEL What is it?

GERTRUDE What did you mean just now.

LIONEL When?

GERTRUDE Before ... when I came in. You said you were going, getting out.

LIONEL I am. I sent a wire just now.

GERTRUDE Wire?

LIONEL Yes, to my brother. I'm going to St Louis. He has a business there.

GERTRUDE But you can't do that! I've come back. You won't have to live in this stupid Lobster Bowl. You're going to be living in a house with *me*.

LIONEL We'll never make a life, sticking around here. I've made up my mind. We're going away ...

GERTRUDE You talk like a child.

LIONEL *[Interrupting]* I'm not staying here.

GERTRUDE You're running away ... You're running home to your family ... to your brother. Don't you have any backbone, any fight?

LIONEL I don't care what you think about me! It's Molly that ...

GERTRUDE What about Molly!

LIONEL I've got to get Molly out of here, far away from everything she's ever known. It's her only chance.

GERTRUDE You're taking her away from *me*. That's what you're doing.

LIONEL You're like a wall around Molly, some kind of shadow between us. She lives ...

GERTRUDE *[Interrupting, vehement]* I'm not a shadow any more. I've come back and I'm staying here, where I belong with Molly! *[*LIONEL *looks at her with an expression of bitterness and revulsion]* What is it? Why do you look at me that way?

LIONEL What way?

GERTRUDE As if I was some terrible witch ... That's it, some terrible witch!

LIONEL You're using her. You need Molly. You don't love her. You're using her ...

GERTRUDE You don't know what you're talking about. You don't know anything about me or Molly. You never could. You never will. When she married she was desperate. She cried like a baby and she begged me to stay. But you want to drag her away from me – from her mother. She loves me more than anyone on earth. She needs me. In her heart she's still a child.

LIONEL If you get what you want she'll stay that way. Let her go, if you love her at all, let her go away ... Don't stop her ...

GERTRUDE I can't stop her. How can I? She'll do what she likes, but I won't stand here watching while you drag her away. I'll talk to her myself. I'll ask her what she wants, what she'd really like to do. She has a right to choose.

LIONEL To choose?

GERTRUDE Between going with you and staying with me!

[LIONEL *is silent. After a moment he walks away from* GERTRUDE. *Then to himself as if she were no longer there.*]

LIONEL This morning she was holding her wedding dress up to the light.

GERTRUDE *[Proud]* She's going to wear it to my birthday supper. It's a party dress, after all.

LIONEL *[Not really answering]* She didn't say anything to me. She just held her dress up to the light.

GERTRUDE Go and find her. Get her now. Bring her back ... tell her I'm here.

LIONEL If you go half way up those stairs and holler ...

GERTRUDE No, Mrs Constable said she was hunting mussels on the beach.

LIONEL She's upstairs. *[*LIONEL *goes up to landing and calls]* Molly! Your mother's here. She wants you. Come on down. Your mother's back.

*[*MOLLY *enters down stairs.* LIONEL *backs away and lurks in the shadows near the bar.]*

GERTRUDE *[Tentative, starts forward to embrace her, but stops]* Molly, how pretty you look! How lovely ... and your wedding dress.

MOLLY *[Spellbound, as if looking at something very beautiful just behind* GERTRUDE*]* I took it out this morning for your birthday.

GERTRUDE I'm glad, darling. How are you? Are you well, Molly? Are you all right?

MOLLY Yes, I am.

GERTRUDE *[Going to table]* I have something for you. A bracelet! *[She hooks necklace around* MOLLY'S *neck]* And a necklace! They're made of real silver. Oh, how sweet you look! How pretty you look in silver! Just like a little girl, just as young as you looked when we were in the ocean house together. The ocean house, Molly! I miss it so. Don't you?

MOLLY I knew you'd come back.

[They sit down.]

GERTRUDE I knew it, too, from the beginning. They were strangers – all of them. I couldn't bear it. Nothing, really nothing meant anything to me down there, nothing at all. And you, darling, are you happy? What do you do in this terrible ugly place?

MOLLY In the afternoon we hunt for mussels, sometimes, and at night we play cards ... Lionel and me.

GERTRUDE *[Uneasily]* I spoke to Lionel just now.

MOLLY Did you?

GERTRUDE Yes, about St Louis.

MOLLY *[Darkening]* Oh!

LIONEL *[Coming over to them from the bar]* Yes, Molly. I'm arranging things now for the trip tomorrow. My mind's made up. If you're not coming with me, I'm going by myself. I'm coming down in a little while and you've got to tell me what you're going to do.

[LIONEL exits upstairs.]

GERTRUDE You see. With or without you he's determined to go. Don't look frightened, Molly. I won't allow you to go. You're coming with me, with your mother, where you belong. I never should have let you marry. I never should have left you. I'll never leave you again, darling. You're mine, the only one I have ... my own blood ... the only thing I'm sure of in the world. *[She clasps MOLLY greedily to her breast]* We're going soon, but we've got to wait for them, Mrs Lopez and Frederica. They're calling for us here. You're coming with me and you're never going back. Tonight, when you go to bed, you can wear my gown, the one you've always loved with the different colored tulips stitched around the neck. *[She notices MOLLY'S strange expression and the fact that she has recoiled just a little]* What is it, dear? Don't you like the gown with the tulips any more? You used to ...

MOLLY *[As if from far away]* I like it.

GERTRUDE Tomorrow, after Lionel has gone, I'll come back to pack you up. *[Fingering the necklace]* Did you like the paper with the dancing girl on it?

MOLLY I have your letter here.

GERTRUDE There are different ones at home – a toreador with peach satin breeches and a macaw with real feathers ...

[It is obvious to her that MOLLY *is not listening]* You've seen them, dear ... Those big parrots ... *[Anxiously]* Haven't you?

MOLLY What?

GERTRUDE *[Trying to ignore* MOLLY'S *coldly remote behavior]* How could you bear it here in this awful public place after our life together in the ocean house?

MOLLY I used to go back and look into the garden ... over the wall. Then the people moved in and I didn't go there any more. But, after a while ...

GERTRUDE *[Cutting in]* I'll make it all up to you, darling. You'll have everything you want.

MOLLY It was all right after a while. I didn't mind so much. It was like being there ...

GERTRUDE What, Molly? What was like being there?

MOLLY After a while I could sit in that booth, and if I wanted to I could imagine I was home in the garden ... inside the summer house.

GERTRUDE That's over, Molly. That's over now. All over. I have a wonderful surprise for you, darling. Can you guess?

MOLLY *[Bewildered]* I don't know. I don't know.

GERTRUDE I ordered the platform built, and the trellis, and I know where I can get the vines. Fully grown vines, heavy with leaves ... just like the ones ... *[She is stopped again by* MOLLY'S *expression. Then, touching her face apologetically]* I know, I know. I don't look well. I look sick. But I'm not ... I'm not sick.

MOLLY No, you don't look sick. You look ... different.

GERTRUDE It's their fault. It's because I'm living their way. But soon I'll be the same again, my old self.

[Enter MRS LOPEZ *and* FREDERICA *carrying paper bags.]*

MRS LOPEZ ¡Inez! ¡Inez! Ya llegamos ...

GERTRUDE Here they are.

INEZ *[Coming downstairs with a heavy tread]* Something tells me I hear Fula Lopez, the girl I love ...

MRS LOPEZ *[Grabbing* INEZ *and whirling her around]* Inez ... Guapa ... Inez. Aqui estamos ... que alegría ... We are coming back from Mexico, Frederica, Fula ... *[She spots* GERTRUDE*]* and Eastman Cuevas. *[Then to* MOLLY, *giving her a big smacking kiss]* Molly ... Hello, Molly! Inez, guapa, bring us three limonadas, please ... two for Fula and one for Frederica. Look, look, Eastman Cuevas. We got gorgeous stuff. *[She pulls a chicken out of a bag she is carrying and dangles it for* GERTRUDE*]* Look and see what a nice one we got ... Feel him!

GERTRUDE No, later at home.

MRS LOPEZ Pinch him, see how much fat he got on him.

GERTRUDE *[Automatically touching chicken for a second]* He's very nice ... *[Then swerving around abruptly and showing a stern fierce profile to the audience]* Why is he here?

MRS LOPEZ *[Looking stupid]* Who?

GERTRUDE The chicken. Why is he here?

MRS LOPEZ The chicken? He go home. We put him now with his rice and his peas.

GERTRUDE *[In a fury manifestly about the chicken. But her rage conceals panic about* MOLLY*]* But *what* rice and peas. You know what we're having ... I ordered it myself ... It was going to be a light meal ... something *I* liked ... for once ... we're having jellied consommé and little African lobster tails.

MRS LOPEZ *[Crossing back to center tables and stopping near* MRS CONSTABLE*]* That's right, jelly and Africa and this one too.

[She hoists chicken up in the air with a flourish. Enter MRS CONSTABLE.*]*

MRS CONSTABLE A chicken. I hate chickens. I'd rather have a dog.

*[*FREDERICA *pulls a thin striped horn out of one of the paper bags and blows on it.]*

GERTRUDE Frederica, stop that. Stop that at once! I told you I didn't want to hear a single horn on my birthday. This is a party for adults. Put that away. Come along, we're leaving. We'll leave here at once.

FREDERICA *[In her pallid voice]* And Umberto? My uncle ...

GERTRUDE What about him?

FREDERICA Uncle Umberto say he was calling for us to ride home all together.

GERTRUDE *[Automatically]* Where is he?

FREDERICA He is with Pepe Hernandez, Frederica Gómez, Pacito Sánchez, Pepito Pita Luga ...

GERTRUDE No more names, Frederica ... Tell him we're coming. We'll be right along ...

MRS LOPEZ And the limonadas ...

GERTRUDE Never mind the limonadas. We're leaving here at once ... Collect your bundles ... Go on, go along.

[The Mexicans start to collect everything, and there is the usual confusion and chatter. FREDERICA *spills some horns out of her bag.* MRS LOPEZ *screams at her, etc. They reach the exit just as* INEZ *arrives with the limonadas.]*

MRS LOPEZ *[Almost weeping, in a pleading voice to* GERTRUDE*]* Look, Eastman Cuevas, the limonadas!

FREDERICA *[Echoing]* The limonadas ... ¡Ay!

GERTRUDE No! There isn't time. I said we were leaving. We're leaving at once ...

INEZ *[To* MRS LOPEZ *as they exit, including* MRS CONSTABLE*]* Take them along ... Drink them in the car, for Christ's sake.

MRS LOPEZ *[Offstage]* But the glasses ...

INEZ *[Off stage]* To hell with the glasses. Toss them down the cliff.

GERTRUDE Molly, it's time to go. *[*MOLLY *starts for stairway]* Molly, come along. We're going. What is it, Molly? Why are you standing there? You have your silver bracelet on and the necklace to match. We're ready to leave. Why are you waiting? Tonight you'll wear my gown with the tulips on it. I told you that ... and tomorrow we'll go and I'll show you the vines. When you see how thick the leaves are and the blossoms, you'll know I'm not dreaming. Molly, why do you look at me like that? What is it? What did you forget?

*[*LIONEL *comes downstairs.* GERTRUDE *stiffens and pulls* MOLLY *to her side with a strong hand, holding her there as a guard holds his prisoner.]*

GERTRUDE Lionel, we're going. It's all settled. We're leaving at once. Molly's coming with me and she's not coming back.

MOLLY *[Her voice sticking in her throat]* I ...

LIONEL *[Seeing her stand there, overpowered by her mother, as if by a great tree, accepts the pattern as utterly hopeless once and for all. Then, after a moment]* Good-bye, Molly. Have a nice time at the birthday supper ... *[Bitterly]* You look very pretty in that dress.

[He exits through oyster-shell door.]

GERTRUDE *[After a moment. Calm and firm, certain of her triumph]* Molly, we're going now. You've said good-bye. There's no point in standing around here any longer.

MOLLY *[Retreating]* Leave me alone ...

GERTRUDE Molly, what is it? Why are you acting this way?

MOLLY I want to go out.

GERTRUDE Molly!

MOLLY I'm going ... I'm going out.

GERTRUDE *[Blocking her way]* I'll make it all up to you. I'll give you everything you wanted, everything you've dreamed about.

MOLLY You told me not to dream. You're all changed ... You're not like you used to be.

GERTRUDE I will be, darling. You'll see ... when we're together. It's going to be the same, just the way it was. Tomorrow we'll go back and look at the vines, thicker and more beautiful ...

MOLLY I'm going ... Lionel!

GERTRUDE *[Blocking her way, fiendish from now on]* He did it. He changed you. He turned you against me.

MOLLY Let me go ... You're all changed.

GERTRUDE You can't go. I won't let you. I can stop you. I can and I will.

[There is a physical struggle between them near the oyster-shell door.]

MOLLY *[Straining to get through the door and calling in a voice that seems to come up from the bottom of her heart]* Lionel!

GERTRUDE I know what you did ... I didn't want to ... I was frightened, but I knew ... You hated Vivian. I'm the only one in the world who knows you. *[*MOLLY *aghast ceases to struggle. They hold for a moment before* GERTRUDE *releases her grip on* MOLLY*. Confident now that she has broken her daughter's will forever]* Molly, we're going ... We're going home.

MOLLY *[Backing away in horror]* No!

GERTRUDE Molly, we're going! *[*MOLLY *continues to retreat]* If you don't *[*MOLLY, *shaking her head still retreats]* If you don't, I'll tell her! I'll call Mrs Constable.

MOLLY *[Still retreating]* No ...

GERTRUDE *[Wild, calling like an animal]* Mrs Constable! Mrs Constable! *[To* MOLLY, *shaking her]* Do you see what you're doing to me! Do you? *[*MRS CONSTABLE *appears in doorway.* GERTRUDE *drags* MOLLY *brutally out of her corner near the staircase and confronts her with* MRS CONSTABLE*]* I have something to tell you, Mrs Constable. It's about Molly. It's about my daughter ... She hated Vivian. My daughter hated yours and a terrible ugly thing happened ... an ugly thing happened on the cliffs ...

MRS CONSTABLE *[Defiantly]* Nothing happened ... Nothing!

GERTRUDE *[Hanging on to* MOLLY, *who is straining to go]* It *had* to happen. I know Molly ... I know her jealousy ... I was her whole world, the only one she loved ... She wanted me all to herself ... I know that kind of jealousy and what it can do to you ... I know what it feels like to wish someone dead. When I was a little girl ... I ... *[She stops dead as if a knife had been thrust in her heart now. The hand holding* MOLLY'*s in its hard iron grip slowly relaxes. There is a long pause. Then, under her breath]* Go ... *[*MOLLY'S *flight is sudden. She is visible in the blue light beyond the oyster-shell door only for a second. The Mexican band starts playing the wedding song from Act One.* GERTRUDE *stands as still as a statue.* MRS CONSTABLE *approaches, making a gesture of compassion]* The band is playing on the beach. They're playing their music. Go, Mrs Constable ... Please.

*[*MRS CONSTABLE *exits through oyster-shell door.]*

FREDERICA *[Entering from street, calling, exuberant]* Eastman Cuevas! Eastman Cuevas! Uncle Umberto is ready. We are waiting in the car ... Where's Molly? *[She falters at the sight of* GERTRUDE's *white face. Then, with awe]* Ay dios ... ¿Que pasa? ¿Que tiene? Miss Eastman Cuevas, you don't feel happy? *[She unpins a simple bouquet of red flowers and puts it into* GERTRUDE'S *hand]* For your birthday, Miss Eastman Cuevas ... your birthday ...

[She backs away into the shadows, not knowing what to do next, GERTRUDE *is standing rigid, the bouquet stuck in her hand.]*

GERTRUDE *[Almost in a whisper, as the curtain falls]* When I was a little girl ...

Jane Bowles (right) at a party in Tangier, 1949

Six Letters

Paul Bowles selected these six letters to include in the book Feminine Wiles* *(Black Sparrow Press, 1976), in which he also gathered the fragments from Jane's two unfinished novels and 'At the Jumping Bean'. The introduction to the book was by Tennessee Williams, who pronounced Jane 'the most important writer of prose fiction in modern American letters ... a totally original and delightful person ... darting between humor, anxiety, love and distraction. Her work, her life: deep truth, onserved without pretension, with humor and humanity.'*

**The title is taken from a line in 'Emmy Moore's Journal': 'But I will have no truck with feminine wiles.'*

Katharine Hamill and Natasha von Hoeschelmann were for many years on the staff of Fortune *magazine. 'Bupple' is Paul Bowles, as is 'Paul'. Libby Holman was a musical comedy star of the 1920s – the original 'torch singer' – and a lifelong friend of Jane and Paul Bowles. Cherifa (C) is the Tangier market trader who became Jane's lover and housekeeper through the 1950s and 60s.*

1

[Taghit, Algeria, Spring 1949]

Dearest Katharine and Natasha:

I can't tell you everything that's happened because if I tried to I wouldn't write at all. I *have* tried to before, and simply stopped writing because it was too exhausting. No one could have been happier than I was to receive your Xmas wire. It was wonderful to know you'd thought of me. (I sound like a real cripple or a public charge.) Certainly you were the only ones who did. Then I started many grateful letters and Jody was with me and it was all very complicated. Now I am in the Sahara desert. I got to Marseille in February, stayed four days and came back to Africa. Scared to go to Paris because there is a very long tunnel outside of Marseille. Lola can appreciate this. Of course I'm not neurotic any more, which is a good thing, but I do find it very hard to go *North*. This place we're in is an oasis – a very small one. We had to walk to it from the bus, with donkey carriers for our luggage. It is not a bus, but a very interesting and solidly built *truck* that goes to Timbuctoo. The dunes are extremely high, and I shall not attempt to climb them again. Well, maybe I will. Because it's so beautiful up there. Nothing but mountains and valleys of sand as far as the eye can see. And to know it stretches for literally hundreds of miles gives a very strange feeling. The sand is a wonderful beige colour. It turns bright pink in the evening light. I am impressed. It is not like anything else anywhere in the world, not the sand and the oasis, anyway. The rest is all rocks and rather terrifying. We saw a mirage called *Lake Michigan and the New Causeway* on our way here. I suppose there are mirages in New Mexico, but I can't remember. We are going on to Beni Abbes (Paul and I), next Friday. The hotel here is kept up for the army, since no tourists ever come. Occasionally army people stop by for lunch. There are just Paul and me, the Arab who runs the hotel, the three soldiers in the fort, and the natives. But *they* are just a little too native, and frightfully underfed. It is very very quiet. No electricity, no cars. Just *Paul* and *me*, and many empty rooms. The great sand desert begins just outside my window. I might almost stroke the dune with my hand. We are going further "in". (Oy!) But I am looking forward to the next place, though I doubt that it will be as beautiful as this oasis. Nothing could be. The little inn where we'll be going is run by a woman, a Mademoiselle Jury. Paul says she's a yenty old maid. I think there are eight or nine "whites" there – a real mob. Paul thinks there will be too much traffic because the truck goes through twice a week. There is no road leading *here* at all, so he's gotten used to that. We plan to be in the desert about a month, and then back to Fez. Then to Tangier, where I can resume my silly life with the grain market group: Tetum, Zodelia, Cherifa and Kinza. You remember them. I had Tetum x-rayed. She was determined to go to the doctor's because I'd taken Cherifa ten times about her foot. Tetum spent all morning in the doctor's waiting-room among the women wrapped in sheets. She was happy because she had caught up with Cherifa. She felt that the x-ray equaled the foot treatments Cherifa got out of me. It is all really about prestige, their life. But I cannot tell them even that I know they are making an ass out of me. I am always afraid they might find out I know. I'll tell you about it when I see you.

Forgive this disjointed letter, please. I have had a fly after me, and then in the middle of it the Arab who runs the hotel asked me to write a letter for him. (Naturally he can't write.) It was to a man living in a place called *Oil Tin Number Five*. It's a famous hellhole south of here. I hope we don't go there to live. Write me British Post Office, Tangier. If I'm still here they'll forward the mail.

Much love as ever,
Jane

2

17th Jan. [1950] Paris

Dearest Bupple,

I suppose I should single-space this, though I hate to. There is no room for corrections. I shall get all the disagreeable things off my mind first. My work went well last week. I had got into a routine, but this week it's all shot to hell again ... not because of my life really, but because I have come to the male character again. I must change all that I wrote about him in Tangier. Not all, but it must become real to me, otherwise I can't write it. I have decided not to become hysterical, however. If I cannot write my book, then I shall give up writing, that's all. Then either suicide or another life. It is rather frightening to think of. I don't believe I would commit suicide, though intellectually it seems the only way out. I would never be brave enough, and it would upset everybody. But where would I go? I daresay the most courageous thing to do would be nothing. I mean, to continue as I am, but not as a writer. As the wife of a writer? I don't think you'd like that, and could I do it well? I think I'd nag and be mean, and then I would be ashamed. Oh, what a black future it could be! That is why I have to use some control, otherwise I get in a panic. I am trying to write. Jody's being here is a hindrance and a help. A help because she gives a centre to my day, and a hindrance because if I read, and wrote the letters I should write, and simply wandered around chewing my cud as one does when one's writing, I would have very little time left for her. We have been seeing too many people ... not many different ones, but the same few over and over again. There have been very few dinners alone, and it has taken me some weeks to realize that Jody just doesn't want to have anyone much around. Though if they must be around, she prefers them to be men. Gordon she likes, and Frank Price. I have miraculously avoided a real bust-up drama, and have kept the most severe check on myself. I think now that things are well adjusted, and I am clear in my mind about how to conduct the rest of the winter until she leaves: in solitary confinement as much as possible. Strange that when she first arrived I thought we had a whole lifetime together; I guess that threw me into a panic. And now I feel I've done it all wrong. It would have been pleasanter and better for my work seeing no one else (the strain of wondering whether she was enjoying an evening or not gave me a headache), and instead getting into the habit of eating dinner in silence (unless I talk) which is, after all, not so bad. I don't know what I was afraid of. Despair, I guess, as usual. Now there seems to be not enough time left. I have grown used to her again, and fond of her, and we have moved into Frank Price's flat, which will be much better. I had taken my own room on the other floor because our room was not suitable for working; and because of a scene she made about my "walking out" on her, I felt guilty every time I was in my room and was not strictly working. She later explained how she felt, and tried to reassure me that she no longer felt that way about it, yet I could never be in my own room with any serenity. The fairies on the other side of the wall drove me crazy anyway, and turned out to be almost as bad as the children in the courtyard who had made work impossible for me in the room we had shared together (the same arrangement you and I had). It wasn't big enough anyway for actual living, though it was fine just for a week.

I want desperately to get another "clump" of work done in the next four or five weeks. There is simply no time for anything, ever. I know that I shall be terribly upset when she leaves. There will be a week of agony, I suppose. Changing from this charming flat into a cheap room, financial insecurity which I don't have now, and so on. I am sending you O's letter so that you know what's going on. If this option does get to me, instead of tearing up roots again, I may spend part of the spring in Paris ... how long I don't know. I may also go to Tangier, depending on whether you're there or not and a few other unpredictables. If however the play does go into rehearsal this summer, I *would* prefer, as Oliver suggests, to go back in July rather than in the spring. It would be better sailing, would give me longer to work on Yenti, if I'm still working by then, and I'd see you sooner, as I'd most likely get down to Africa eventually.

I see Alice Toklas now and then, but I'm afraid that each time I do I am stiffer and more afraid. She is charming, and will probably see me less and less as a result of my inability to converse. This is not a result of my shyness alone, but of a definite absence of intellect, or should I say of ideas that can be expressed, ideas that I am in any way certain about. I have no opinions really. This is not just neurotic. It is very true. And

Alice Toklas gives one plenty of opportunity to express an idea or an opinion. She is sitting there waiting to hear one. She admires your book tremendously. In fact, she talked of little else the last time I saw her. She won't serve me those little bread sandwiches in different colors any more because she says I like them more than the cake, and so eat them instead of the cake. I do like them better. And now I must go there and eat only sweets, which makes me even more nervous. Maybe she'll never speak to me again. Eudora Welty came over to dinner with Mary Lou Aswell and told me she was a great admirer of yours. She asked for *Camp Cataract* and took it home with her. After nearly a month she returned it with a note explaining that she failed on it, but would like to try something else of mine some day. I had met her on the street in the middle of the month, and she said then that she was having trouble with it, and so she never did finish it. I was disturbed by that as I have, since seeing you last, turned into an admirer of hers, and it would be nice for me to be admired by an established and talented American writer, instead of by my friends and no one else. That was upsetting, and also the fact that a friend in the hotel didn't like it really. (A very brilliant and charming girl called Natika Waterbury, who is now in Paris but whom I met long ago in New York.) This evening Sonia Sekula is giving a small party in her room. Mary Reynolds will come, and Lionel Abel and Pegeen. (Pegeen has two babies, apparently by her husband Hélion.) Jody will attend, perhaps, but I can't, because I am dining with, of all people, Sidéry, who was very excited when he heard I was your wife. I met him at one of the few cocktails I've been to, at Peggy's. He is quite charming, I think. I wrote you about Manchester, but you must simply have forgotten. I gave him to Truman, not because T wanted him (though if he did it was for my sake, not his) but because I didn't like his face or his nature when I returned. Though Donald was never a real Peke, he was cute from the very first minute, and this one was cute only because he was a little fluffy ball. His muzzle had gotten much whiter, and his face definitely more pointed, and his eyes closer together. I thought I had better give him away while I disliked his looks, as I'm sure he would have been a nuisance. I have a few clippings which I'll enclose, though I'm sure you have them already. The book, though second from the bottom, made the best-seller list, which I think is wonderful. Your literary success is a fact now, and it is not only distinguished but widespread. I think to have Connolly and Toklas and a host of other literary people, plus a public, is really remarkable and wonderful. You should soon write another book. I hope that you are pleased at last, and not simply because it is a way to make some money. You do deserve a success of this kind, and I think you are at the right age for it. I can get no news out of anyone in Tangier. Have written Ira and Jacqueline and the fact that I hear from no one confirms me in my belief that Esterhazy has gone. It is rather horrid not knowing what is going on. I am glad I have a little money down there because if anyone ever writes me I should like to send checks for Fathma. I have just about nothing left here, and I know this will horrify you, but it just happened, and without my going to nightclubs either. I am waiting from day to day for the option money to arrive from Audrey Wood via Oliver, rather than send for more from Tangier. Naturally I would have been more careful if I hadn't had a letter from Wood that sounded pretty definite about the option. *Blondes* is not only a hit but a smash hit. Laurence Olivier's head reader saw my play and wrote that it was morbid and depressing, and though not something to be dismissed, certainly nothing they could think of doing. Truman hates New York, and wrote: "Honey, even if your play is done I hope you won't have to come back for it." Alice T was delighted that you didn't really care for him very much. (I told her.) She said it was the one thing that really worried her. She could not understand how an intelligent person like you etc. She doesn't seem to worry in the least, however, about my liking him. So I'm insulted ... again.

Paris is so very beautiful, particularly in this dark winter light. I'm surprised you don't love it more. I still love Africa best I guess, but there one must shut one's eyes against a great many things too. Here there is the Right Bank, and there the Villes Nouvelles, the buses, and the European shoes. You know what I mean. To cross the river never ceases to excite me. I went to see Phèdre at the Comédie Française with Natika. I am wildly excited about it. The only thing I have enjoyed thoroughly in years. I have never heard French grand théâtre before. I don't know how good the players were, but one must be good to do Racine at all. I shall go there now as often as possible.

I have gotten rounder in the face from the nourishing food. I'm upset about it, but perhaps it is becoming. Poor Michael Duff's son was born dead. I don't hear from them. Just a funny postcard now and then. I am terribly sorry that I can't give you more information about your book. Certainly friends in New York can do better. I might as well be in Ceylon with you. I love the descriptions of it, by the way, though at the moment

I feel no need of adding any country to my list. I am puzzled enough with the Seine River and the Grand Socco. Oddly enough I still love Morocco best, though I do not admire it more. I think and think about what it means to me, and as usual have come to no conclusion. I dream about it too, in color, all the time.

Much much love, Bupple dear. I miss you very much. Write me your plans and don't stay away forever. I hope you'll return sometime this spring. Will you?

P.S. I had my tooth fixed. The dentist hurt like hell. Is Gore really joining you?

3

[1954]

Darling Natasha and Katharine:

I never stop thinking about you, but too much has happened. Please forgive me if this is not an amusing letter. I think I had better simply write you a gross factual résumé of what has happened. Then if I have any sense I shall keep notes. Because what is happening is interesting and funny in itself. I am a fool to have lost two whole months of it. I have no memory – only a subconscious memory which I am afraid translates everything into something else, and so I shall have to take notes. I have a very pretty leather book for that purpose.

The day you left I was terribly, terribly sad. ... I went down that long street, way down in, and landed in a room filled with eighteen women and a dozen or two little babies wearing knitted capes and hoods. One lady had on a peach satin evening dress and over it the jacket of a man's business suit. (A Spanish business suit.) I had been searching for Cherifa, and having been to three houses all belonging to her family, I finally landed there. I thought I was in a bordello. The room was very plush, filled with hideous blue and white chenille cushions made in Manchester, England. Cherifa wore a pale blue sateen skirt down to the ground, and a grayish Spanish sweater, a kind of school sweater, but not sporty. She seemed to be constantly flirting with a woman in a blue kaftan (our hostess). Finally she sat next to her and encircled her waist. Cherifa looked like a child. The woman weighed about 160 pounds and was loaded with rouge and eye makeup. Now I know her. An alcoholic named Fat Zohra, and one of two wives. She is married to a kind of criminal who I believe knifed his own brother over a card game and spent five years in jail. The other wife lives in a different house and does all the child-bearing. Fat Zohra is barren. There was one pale-looking girl (very light green), who I thought was surely the richest and the most distinguished of the lot. She wore a wonderful embroidered kaftan, a rich spinach green with a leaf design. Her face was rather sour: thin compressed lips and a long mean-looking nose. I was sad while they played drums and did their lewd belly dances, because I thought: My God, if you had only stayed a day longer. But of course if you had, perhaps they wouldn't have asked you in; they are so leery of strangers. In any case, at the end of the afternoon ... Cherifa took me to the doorway and into the blue courtyard where two boring pigeons were squatting, and asked me whether or not I was going to live in my house. The drums were still beating and I had sticky cakes in my hand ... those I couldn't eat. (I had stuffed down as many as I could; I loathe them) but I was really too sad because you had left to get down very many. I said I was (going to live in the house) but not before I found a maid. She told me to wait and a minute later came out with the distinguished pale-green one. "Here's your maid," she said. "A very poor girl."

Anyway, a month and a half later she became my maid. I call her Sour Pickle, and she has stolen roughly about one thousand four hundred pesetas from me. I told C about it. She advised me not to keep any money in the house. She is a wonderful maid, an excellent cook, and sleeps in.

Paul had typhoid in the hotel, and that was a frightening mess for two weeks. We were both about to move into our houses. He had found one on a street called Sidi Bouknadel (overlooking the sea) and I was coming here. Then he had typhoid, and then Tennessee came for two whole weeks. I moved in here while Paul was still in the hotel. For a while Ahmed and I were living together while Paul lingered on at the hotel in a weakish state. He is all right now. Ahmed stayed here during the month of Ramadan (the month when they eat at night) and I was with him during the last two weeks. Not very interesting, except that every night I woke up choking with charcoal smoke, and then he would insist that I eat with him, liver or steak or whatever the hell it was. At first I minded terribly. Then I began to expect it, and one night he didn't buy really enough for the two of us, and I was grieved. Meanwhile in the daytime I was in the hotel preparing special food for Paul, to bring his appetite back. There were always four or five of us cooking at once in the long narrow hotel kitchen, the only room that looked out on the sea. Meeting Tennessee and Frankie for dinner was complicated, too. (They were at the Rembrandt.) Synchronizing took up most of the time. We were all in different places.

One day before Ramadan and before Paul had paratyphoid, I went to the market and sat in a gloom about Indo-China and the Moroccan situation and every other thing in the world that was a situation outside my own. Soon I cheered up a little. I was in the part where Tetum sits in among the coal and the mules and the chickens. Two little boy musicians came by. I gave them money and Tetum ordered songs. Soon we had a big crowd around us, one of those Marrakech circles. Everybody stopped working (working?) and we had one half hour of music, myself and everybody else, in that part of the market. And people gathered from round about. Just like Tiflis. Tetum was in good spirits. She told me that Cherifa had a girl friend who was fat and white. I recognized Fat Zohra, though I shall never know whether I put the fat white picture in her mind or not. I might have said: "Is she fat and white?" I don't know. Then she asked me if I wouldn't drive her out to Sidi Menari, one of the sacred groves around here where Sidi Menari (a saint) is buried. They like to visit as many saints as possible, of course, because it gives them extra gold stars for heaven. I thought: "Natasha and Katharine will be angry. They told me to stick to Cherifa, but then, they didn't know about Fat Zohra." After saying this in my head I felt free to offer Tetum a trip to the grove without making you angry.

Of course it turned out that she wanted to take not only one, but two, neighbors and their children. We were to leave at eight thirty A.M., she insisted. The next day when I got to Tetum's house on the Marshan, with Temsamany (nearly an hour late) Tetum came to the door in a gray bathrobe. I was very surprised. Underneath she was dressed in a long zigdoun, and under that she wore other things. I can't describe a zigdoun, but it is quite enough to wear without adding a bathrobe. But when they wear our nightclothes they wear them over or under their own (which are simply the underpeelings or first three layers of their day clothes. Like in Tiflis.). She yanked me into her house, tickled my palm, shouted to her neighbor (asleep on the other side of a thin curtain) and in general pranced about the room. She dressed me up in a hideous half-Arab, half-Spanish cotton dress which came to my ankles and had no shape at all. Just a little round neck. She belted it, and said: "Now go back to the hotel and show your husband how pretty you look." I said I would some other day, and what about our trip to the saint's tomb? She said yes, yes, but she had to go and fetch the two other women who both lived in other parts of town. I said would they be ready, and she said something like: "bacai ... shouay." Which means just nothing. Finally I arranged to come back for her at three. Rather infuriated because I had gotten Temsamany up at the crack. But I was not surprised, nor was he. Tetum took me to her gate. "If you're not here at three," she said in sudden anger, "I shall walk to the grove myself on my own legs." (Five hours, roughly.) We went back at three, and the laundry bags were ready, and the children, and Tetum.

"We are going to two saints," Tetum said. "First Sidi Menari. And then we'll stop at the other saint's on the way back. He's buried on the edge of town and we've got to take the children to him and cut their throats because they've got whooping-cough." She poked one of the laundry bundles, who showed me a knife. I was getting rather nervous because Paul of course was expecting us back roughly around seven, and I know how long those things can take. We drove along the awful road (the one that frightened you) toward the grove, only we went on and on, much further out, and the road began to bother me a little after a while. You would have hated it. The knife of course served for the symbolic cutting of the children's throats, though at first I had thought they were going to draw some blood, if not a great deal. I didn't think they were actually going to kill the children or I wouldn't have taken them on the ride.

We reached the sacred grove, which is not far from the lighthouse one can see, coming into the harbor. Unfortunately they have built some ugly restaurants around and about the lighthouse and not far from the sacred grove, so that sedans are now constantly passing on the highway. The grove itself is very beautiful, and if one goes far enough inside it, far away from the road, one does not see the cars passing. We didn't penetrate very far into the grove because being a Christian (Oy!) I can't get to the vicinity of the saint's tomb. Temsamany spread the tarpaulin on the ground and the endless tea equipment they had brought with them, and they were off to the saint. He said: "I shall make a fire, and then when they come back the water will be boiling."

They came back. God knows when. The water was boiling. We had used up a lot of dead olive branches. They sat down and lowered their veils so that they hung under their chins like ugly bibs. They had brought an excellent sponge cake. As usual, something sweet. I thought: "Romance here is impossible." Tetum's neighbors were ugly. One in particular. "Like a turtle," Temsamany said. She kept looking down into her lap. Tetum, the captain of the group, said to the turtle: "Look at the world, look at the world." "I am looking at the world," the other woman said, but she kept looking down into her lap.

They cut up all the sponge cake. I said: "Stop! Leave it. We'll never eat it all." Temsamany said: "I'm going to roller-skate." He went off and we could see him through the trees. After a while the conversation stopped. Even Tetum was at a loss. There was a little excitement when they spotted the woman who takes care of the toilets under the grain market, seated not far off with a group somewhat larger than ours. But nothing else happened.

I went to look for Temsamany on the highway. He had roller-skated out of sight. 1 felt that all my pursuits here were hopeless. I looked back over my shoulder into the grove. Tetum was swinging upside-down from an olive tree, her knees hooked over a branch, and she is, after all, forty-five and veiled and a miser.

There is more to this day. But I see now that I have done exactly what I did not want to do. I have gone into great detail about one incident which is probably of no interest.

I always let Fatima (Sour Pickle) decide what we are to eat. It is all so terribly simple, all in one dish. Either lamb with olives or with raisins and onions, or chicken with the same, or ground meat on skewers, or beef or lamb. (You remember how wonderful they taste.) Or a fried potato omelette with onions, or boiled noodles with butter, and always lots of black bread and wine at five pesetas a quart. (Excellent.) I've had guests once ... Tennessee, in fact: white beans in oil and with salt pork, like the ones I cooked for you. Lots of salad, cucumber, tomato and onion all chopped up, almost daily. Fresh figs, bananas, cherries ... whatever is in season. Wonderful bowls of Turkish coffee in the morning, with piles of toast soaked in butter. At noon we eat very little. I go over to Paul's for lunch, except that he never eats until three thirty ... sometimes four. I get up at seven, and by then I am so hungry I don't even care, but I like seeing him. We eat soup and bread and butter and cheese and tuna fish. For me tuna fish is the main diet. I love this life and I'm terrified of the day when my money runs out. Please write. I shall worry now about this messy letter.

All my love, always, J. Bowles

4

[1955] Tangier

Dearest Bupple:

It has been very difficult for me to write you. I have covered sheet after sheet, but now I am less troubled in my head for some reason. Maybe because I hit bottom, I think. And now I feel that the weight is lifting. I am not going back in that wild despairing way over my departure from Ceylon, my missing the end of your novel, the temple of Madura, that terrible trip back alone (a nightmare to the end because it was the twin of the other trip I might have made with you). It was better toward the end, but I hit bottom again in Tangier. The house reeked of medicine and there was the smell of other people's stale soup in the velvet *haeti* and even in the blue wall. I put my nose on the wall. It was cold and I could smell soup. The first day I was in the house the whole Casbah reeked of some sweet and horrible chemical smell which doubled its intensity with each new gust of the east wind. The Arabs were holding their noses, but I didn't know that. On the first day I thought I alone could smell it, and it was like the madness I had been living in. A nightmare smell coming up from the port, and a special punishment for me, for my return. I really felt very bad. I can't even remember whether or not Cherifa came to me here that first night in the house. Truly, I can't. On the second day the barber came over to me in his white and black hood and asked me to go to the Administration about the smell. He was holding his nose. "There are microbes in the air. We will all perish," he said. As he spends his entire time in the mosque and is one of the few old-fashioned Arabs left in the quarter, I was amused. The smell is gone now. The sewer pipes had broken, and they were dumping some chemical into the sea while they were mending them. And from that day on I felt better. And the house smells better – at least, to me. Fathma said: "Naturally. Filthy Nazarene cooking. Everything made of pork. Pork soup, pork bread, pork coffee, an all-pork house." But now there is kaimon, and charcoal, in the air. I feel so much better. But I am terrified of beginning to work. I don't know what I'll do if that nightmare closes in on me again. I am sorry too that you have to live through it. I won't go near you if it happens again. Actually I cannot allow it to happen again. But I must work. I had some shattering news when I returned ... le coup de grace ... my taxes. Clean out of my mind from the first second that I banked the money. Somewhere way back, someone, either you or Audrey, warned me not to consider the money all mine, and I was a fool to forget. Having never paid taxes ... However, I suppose it is understandable. The slip of paper doesn't say much, not even what percent I am to be taxed. Perhaps all that has gone off to you. In view of the condition I was in this winter and on the boat, I should think this blow would have landed me in the hospital. In fact I went to bed and waited. But I got up again the next day alive and sane still, though my head was pounding with blood-pressure symptoms. I had to get out of that state, obviously, and I did. I tried writing you, but the letters were *magillahs*, and all about Madura and the tax and Mrs Trimmer and Cherifa in one *tajine*. Senseless and anguished, and they weighed a ton. Not the moment to start that, if I am to "resort to airmail."

Anyway, I think I have enough money in the bank to cover the tax, and if not, I have a Fabergé gold bracelet. And I have (if I must sell it, and if Oliver has made full payment on it) my beautiful Berman painting. Naturally, if I had known this was going to be waiting for me I would not have returned, because surely I should like to have discussed the thing with you. It's a terrible bore writing about it. There are so many angles to it: what exemptions I can get ... maybe a lot ... maybe none. Is it best to get off the double income-tax and pay direct to the government, or should I pay to you? Anyway, for God's sake don't do anything about it until you see me. I shall wait in Tangier and I shall lead my life as if it would go on. I cannot face the possibility of its not going on. Yet I would be unwilling to stay here if it meant your giving up Temsamany and the car. I consider them essentials, just as there seem to be essentials to my life here without which I might as well be somewhere else. Maybe I'll have to be, but it is best to face that when it comes, in two months or with luck, later, I have pulled every string possible in the sense of looking for a job. I can only do it through friends. There is a terrible depression in Tangier. Hotels empty, the Massilia closing, and ten people waiting for every job. Most people think I am mad, and that I should write or live on you, or both. It is not easy to make friends take my plight seriously. Not easy at all, unless I were to say that I was starving to death, which would be shameful and untrue. I spent just a little too much in every direction. The top floor expenses in New York which I took over for a few months, taxis, restaurants, coming over traveling with Natasha and Katharine, the Rembrandt, the Massilia, extravagances with C, I suppose more dinner parties than I need have given, doctors here for myself and Fathma. I don't know ... it went in every direction. But each thing separately is a drop in the bucket. It is just everything put together in the end. I suppose I've been bad, but not so bad. Please don't scold; I am miserable enough about the whole thing and would have pinched every penny as I am doing now, had I been less confident. Well, that is over the bridge and down the drain, like the money for Ceylon. But although Ceylon was wasted and I did not see the temples, or even Kandy, it has changed my life here to a degree that is scarcely believable. I very swiftly reduced expenses to a scale so much lower than anything C has ever expected of me when I was here that she is at the moment back in the grain market. I think it is a healthy thing for C to go to the market in any case, even if the funds were more adequate. Ramadan she will be going there a lot.

I am now exhausted. Ramadan would be an ideal time for me to escape to New York, I suppose, but I don't want to, until I know that I can come back here or that I can't, at least, not for a while – that is, if we are both too broke. I'll face that later too. If I go downhill again then I suppose I would go home. Finding it impossible to work again is the only thing I fear ... the hell with Ramadan. I am rather grateful that C does want to go to the market during that time. Because she can't come here in a straw hat, but must keep going back to the bottom of Emsallah to change into a veil and white gloves, it will be difficult for her to come regularly. And what with fasting, etc. She's been fasting now for two weeks. Hopscotch off and on, making up time. It's almost worse than real Ramadan. I am thinking of investing in a room I heard of, on the top floor of the Hotel Cuba. I will count it outside my budget, since it is not a permanent thing, but something I would like to try, just so I can get started working. Naturally when I first got back and realized about my taxes I was too accablé to do any work ... too harassed, and still in that funny state. I think the room is a good idea, if it is still there. I have not seen it yet. But I will look at it. I can ask Mother to give it to me as a special present, or if it works out I shall simply keep it on as an outlet for as long as it does work out. Because that would mean I was working. As for C and all that, I shouldn't even bother writing you about her since it is such a fluctuating uncertain quantity. At the same time I feel this terrible compulsion to write you about the geographical location of the grain market in relation to Emsallah and my house, and the awful amount of traveling she would have to do if she went often to the market during Ramadan, just to get in and out of her straw hat. I doubt that she will go often once the Aïd is over, but we'll see. I certainly do not wish to interfere with her work, ever (!). I have no right to, since my own position here is so precarious, and in any case I shouldn't. She has now expressed a desire to travel and to play tennis. Now I do have an upper hand that I never had when I spent more money. What is it? I suppose one must close one's fist, and allow them just the right amount of money to make it worthwhile and not shameful in the eyes of the neighbors. I understand many more of the family problems than I did. It was difficult before to find one's way in the maze. But for "the moment," I know that is over. Will explain when I see you, maybe, if I don't forget to. I'm sure you can't wait. I remember the glazed look you always got when I mentioned her before. I think however if that nonsense began again I would give up. If I could only work now I would feel quite peaceful.

Tangier looks worse. The Socco in the afternoon is mostly filled with old clothes. A veritable flea-market that I'm trying to preserve. I've been booming away at Phyllis about it, because she knows the new Administrator. I also asked her about my hair. She has me down on a list. It says: Janie, Grand Socco, hair. Which is just about it, isn't it? The same obsessions, over and over. When I am sure about my hair I will write. But I think the news is good. You will never know what that nightmare was like. I know you thought it was in my mind. I am going on with Bépanthène Roche. On the days I buy it I try to eat more cheaply, so that I can keep, as much as I can, within a budget. Phyllis gave me a blue bead for luck and to ward off the evil eye. Brion's restaurant is the only thing that does business in town. John Goodwin invited me to go to Spain any time during the Feria and Holy Week. He has an apartment for a month. But I'm not sure that the trip alone wouldn't come to a thousand pesetas or more. Also I never go anywhere, so why should I suddenly get to the Feria, since I didn't get to Madura. I would like to hear some Gypsies, but not with those tourists there. I do not think I will go. And certainly not if I'm working.

My terrace smells of male pipi. I suppose it will forever. Eric Gifford brought his male cat with him, Hassan, whom he never mentioned to me. Or else I wasn't paying attention. The worst of the bad weather is over, although the first two weeks at the Massilia were hell. Temsamany scared me so on the boat, about people being able to stay in one's house forever, that I offered them two weeks' grace in the house. I wrote you that I cheered up on the boat when I thought of George Jantos, and sure enough having him as a neighbor has made a lot of difference to me. I rather like their little group, and they are so near I can pop in there. He is bringing me some kif today. I had a cigarette of kif last night before supper and rather liked the effect. I had some drinks too, so I don't suppose I can judge, but it changed the effect of the drink noticeably.

I had dinner with Fathma, who is staying on for three hundred a month instead of five hundred, full-time as before. They have both been cooperative about buying cheap food, and C of course is in her element. But then, that was before she decided to go back to the market.

The baqals announced a three-day close-down in commemoration of the upset here two or three years ago, and they were closed one. *Plus ça change*. Now my left hand is tired. Please write, and especially about your book, and don't above all scold me or put me in a panic. We'll talk about it all when you come, if you ever do. I wonder if instead you'll go to England? Anyway, Bubble, I think the trip has done some good. Much love. I hope you are well and that it got really hot. Write everything.

Jane

5

February 1957 Tangier

Dear Paul:

I have just had my fortieth birthday the day before yesterday, and that is always, however long one has prepared for it, a shock. The day was not as bad as the day after it, or the following day, which was even worse. Something coming is not at all like something which has come. It makes trying to work that much more difficult (or could it possibly be more difficult?), because the full horror of having no serious work behind me at this age (or successful work, in any sense) is now like an official fact rather than something in my imagination, something to be feared, but not yet realized. Well, I don't suppose you can understand this, since when you reached forty you had already quite enough stacked up behind you.

I realized about your birthday, but I don't think I mentioned it in my letters, or thought of it at the time I wrote you. Anyway, it is over. I did not tell anyone about mine except Cherifa, and I celebrated with her on the night of the twenty-first because on the twenty-second an old man from Xauen, an uncle or grandfather, was expected at her house. However, Christopher heard about it from George and called me on the twenty-second to ask if it were true, and then I did have a busy day. I sound like your mother about to say that Ulla came over and that they took a drive and later popped corn in the grate. In spite of hating it to be forty (Anne Harbach toasted me and said: "Life begins ..." which was the last straw), I am still determined to write my play, and have no intention of going back to New York until my money runs out. I have somehow, thus far, staved off the terrible depression that was coming over me when I wrote you last – staved it off perhaps simply because I cannot ever again be the way I was in Ceylon. I mean that I will do everything in my power to pretend that I am not, even if I am. It was too horrible. And so I knocked off work entirely for a week and then went back to trying to write the play. My mind is not a total blank, which is more than I can say of the way it was before. Whether it will get beyond that, I don't know. I am sure you will come out all right because you always have.

Seth said his first word yesterday. "Dubz." He said it clearly three times, and again this morning. I daresay it is because Seth sits in the bathroom a lot and I am always lunging in after Dubz to stop him from using the tub, and of course calling out: "Dubz!" at the top of my lungs. I hope that he will keep saying it so you will hear him when you get back.

Mr Rothschild has been here for three days and I like him. He is giving me a subscription to the Sunday *Times* for a year, and it will be delivered to me from New York by boat of course, so it will always be two weeks late. It is for Berred and Dubz, for their pans.

Radiant sunshine, balmy weather and scarcely any rain. The beaches are crowded. I had lunch with Mr Mallan at the Catalana last week. The Mar Chica is booming again. Whether or not there are many Arabs in it I don't know. Apparently there is more drink than ever in their world, only not as openly. There seems to be not much fear about. Ramadan is in less than forty days, and I dread it as usual. Seth is so terribly noisy that I have to put him out on the terrace in order to do any work. I am furious that you are living in Colombo and have an oscillating standing fan. I would have loved that. If you like Weligama so much why don't you keep it ... or aren't you prepared to live alone there? Actually I don't think you would like that for long. But maybe you won't be able to sell it. Your life in Colombo doesn't sound too expensive thank God so I imagine you'll stay there until you sell the house. Seth is driving me mad.

Dubz just fell into the toilet up to his waist and I had to help him to dry off. Mr Mallan after beating around the bush for fifteen minutes finally asked me what color eyes Phyllis della Faille has. He is utterly ridiculous. Please write me about him. Cherifa bought Seth a length of strong wire which she has fastened around his cup and the bars of his cage so that he can no longer dump his seeds on the floor. It is to be a great saving in money and I am glad. He just said "Dubz" again. I try to say it over and over again to him so that he won't forget.

Much love, J.

6

[circa 1958]

Dearest Libby:

I am very sad not to have written you. It is too much of a task evaluating the whole situation and then writing what is important and what isn't. I can write down all my worries, and there are roughly about eleven major ones, including a very faint worry – not a worry actually, but an *awareness* that this is after all earthquake country, although we are not on the Agadir fault. That was such a nightmare. The reports on Agadir came here daily, and to top it off we had a tremor here. The people were so hysterical that they slept in the bullring all night. The Jews especially. I didn't know about it until the next morning. It is not fair to mention only the other worries since that one obsessed me for a good two months. Anyway, most of them will hold until I see you. But when will I see you? You write as if Paul and I were likely to go back to America together, or as if he would go back at all. He announced last night that he would have to see his parents eventually (I suppose within the next five years), which surprised me. So perhaps he will go back. I did not think that he would ever set foot in the United States unless it was to work. There don't seem to be any jobs for him any more now that he has so cut himself off from the market place in New York. He is more and more forgotten (even by Tennessee) unless it is simply that incidental music is too expensive and hardly worth importing someone to the States for, because of the fare. He would probably get more jobs if he lived in some accessible place, but naturally he wouldn't. And besides, his living expenses would be more, although they have trebled here in the last two and a half years. Many things are more expensive than they are in New York. Things have changed considerably, but I don't think there will be a revolution this year (according to my spies) and maybe not for many more years, depending on what happens in the rest of the world, naturally. I shall ask your permission not to mention politics. I don't like them any more.

The doctor does not want me to stay alone because of the danger that I might have a fit in the street or fall down and hit my head. I have a Spanish woman because she can keep accounts. My most solemn worry is about my work, and above all, do I really have any? Can I ever have any again? I will try to settle it this summer and next fall. (Within the next six or eight months.) For myself, anyway, because it has nothing to do with anyone else. Also there is nothing new except that I don't always know which is the stroke and which is the writer's block. I know some things have definitely to do with the stroke, and others I'm not sure of. The sheep festival is about to begin, in a month, and they are all buying their sheep now for the slaughter. I think that I will not be able to buy a sheep this year. They are too expensive for me, and Cherifa is having four teeth pulled, and later, a bridge made.

I have trouble with names, numbers, and above all the ability to add and subtract. I know perfectly well the general outlines. Two hundred dollars is less than three hundred dollars, and ten plus ten equals twenty, but the complicated divisions and subtractions and additions—! Adding more than two figures is impossible for me. That can be relearned, but I really need someone with me in this country, or they would all cheat me because I could not correct their own sums which are always wrong. So Angèle does that. I suppose that is the least of my worries, but I'm sure that none of this is psychosomatic, because I have no mental block about numbers, and they are worse than the rest. I don't think it would take more than six months to relearn the whole multiplication table. It is very funny but not bad, because I know what I need to know, and then can have someone else do the work. Some women are bad at computing even without strokes, and they are not as charming as I am. Don't ask Dr. Resnick anything. He might have discouraging news, and above all I must for once in my life keep my hopes up. Paul says that he spoke to the doctors and they said that nobody knew how much one could improve or how long it would take. The doctor in New York who sent me to that ghastly young man at Lenox Hill – I forget his name – said the hemianopsia was permanent, but not the aphasia, which has proved to be correct. I now know the meaning of all words. They register again on my brain, but I am slow because there is a tiny paralyzed spot in each eye which I apparently have to circumvent when I'm reading. One side is very bad, worse than the other, but on the whole I'm getting much more used to it. Don't say anything to Resnick because he can't possibly predict anything, and anyway he is apt to be frank, and maybe he would say something depressing. Undoubtedly. I have an awful feeling that I've written this whole thing before. I will send the blood pressure readings and ask if there are any new drugs besides serpasil. My own doctor is pleased with me.

Libby, there is so much talk about myself in this letter that I think I must stop. I have left half the things out that I wanted to tell you about. At least there are no politics in this one. I was fairly poetic in the old days.

Much love, J.

Jane Bowles, Tangier 1956

Jane Bowles Chronology

1917 Born Jane Sidney Auer, February 22, 1917, in New York City. Her parents, Sidney Auer and Claire Stajer Auer, are non-practicing Jews and comfortably off: Sidney works as an insurance agent, Claire had worked as a teacher prior to her marriage. Jane, their only child, is privately tutored by a French governess before going to Madame Tisnée's, a French school in Manhattan.

1927 Family moves to Woodmere, Long Island. In July 1930, aged 45, Sidney dies suddenly of 'hypertension'. Jane is left alone with her mother: 'the worst possible thing', she later told Paul Bowles. Shortly after the funeral, Jane and her mother move back to Manhattan.

1931 After a brief spell at a public school in New York, Jane is sent to Stoneleigh, an exclusive girls' school in Greenfield, Massachusetts. She falls from a horse, breaking her right leg, which had troubled her since childhood (and will give her pain throughout her life), and after a series of operations develops tuberculosis of the knee. Her mother takes Jane to Leysin, near Lake Geneva in Switzerland, to be treated at a sanatorium. Jane remains in treatment, much of the time in traction, until 1934 (from 15 to 17). She is tutored by a Frenchman and studies Gide, Proust, Céline and Greek mythology. She spends much of this period living in Paris.

1934 With the TB cured, Jane is brought back to New York by her mother, returning by liner, on which she meets the author Céline, whose work she is reading at the time. Back in New York, Jane and her mother move into the Hotel Meurice on West 58th Street. Jane tells her: 'I am a writer, and I want to write.'

1935–36 Jane completes her first novel, *Le Phaéton Hypocrite* (unpublished and now lost), a burlesque on the Greek myth of Phaeton, who drove the chariots of the sun. She spends much of her time in bars in Greenwich Village and begins her first lesbian relationships.

1937 In February Jane is introduced to Paul Bowles, then principally a composer, in New York. They meet again the following week at e.e. cummings' apartment. Bowles and his friend Kristians Tonny are planning a trip to Mexico, where Bowles plans to distribute anti-Trotsky stickers (he has 15,000 printed). Jane asks to come too, and they travel together by bus. Jane falls ill with dysentery a week after arriving in Mexico and returns home without telling her companions.

1938 Jane marries Paul Bowles on February 21. She comes into some money, and the couple honeymoon, carrying two trunks, 27 suitcases and a typewriter, in Panama and Guatemala – a trip which inspires *Two Serious Ladies* – then travel to Paris, where they meet Max Ernst and the painter and writer Brion

Gysin. The marriage becomes strained as Jane spends much of her time apart from Paul and they separate briefly when he goes to the south of France. Jane begins writing *Two Serious Ladies*. Returning to New York in the fall, when their money has run out, the Bowles move into the Chelsea Hotel, and then into a cheaper apartment. They join the Communist Party of America, in reaction to the rise of Hitler and the fall of Republican Spain.

1939 The Bowles rent a farmhouse on Staten Island (the model for Miss Goering's house in *Two Serious Ladies*), and Jane resumes writing her novel. In the summer they are joined by Mary Oliver (a flamboyant woman who practiced levitation and claimed to be an illegitimate daughter of Gurdjieff), who becomes Jane's friend and drinking companion, causing Paul to move out. Paul rents a room in Brooklyn and invites Jane to live with him. Jane refuses and moves with Oliver to a Greenwich Village apartment; the Bowles continue to go to parties and events together.

1940 Jane and Paul move to the Chelsea Hotel in March, but Jane ends their sexual relationship. Paul is commissioned to write music for a film about New Mexico, and Jane and Paul travel to Albuquerque, and later Mexico, with Jane's friend Bob Faulkner. They meet Tennessee Williams in Acapulco. Jane rents a house in Taxco, near Mexico City, without consulting Paul, who moves there reluctantly; Jane then begins a romantic relationship with Helvetia Perkins, an American woman, divorced, with a 21-year-old daughter, and an aspiring writer. Paul returns to New York alone to work on a theatre production. Jane follows and rents a room at the Chelsea Hotel, where Paul is staying, and is later joined by Perkins. She resumes work on *Two Serious Ladies*. The Bowles resign from the Communist Party.

1941 Jane and Paul move in to 7 Middagh Street in Brooklyn, an 'artist's house' whose other residents include W.H. Auden, Benjamin Britten, Virgil Thomson and Gypsie Rose Lee. Jane gets on well with Auden, in contrast to Paul. Paul receives a Guggenheim grant to compose an opera and travels to Taxco with Jane, where she resumes her relationship with Helvetia Perkins. Jane completes *Two Serious Ladies*, which Paul reads and edits, excising the 'Third Serious Lady'; these parts of the novel later form the stories *A Guatemalan Idyll, Out in the Open* and *Señorita Córdoba*.

1942 Jane returns to New York with Helvetia Perkins to look for a publisher for *Two Serious Ladies*. She attempts suicide by slashing her wrists but does not tell Paul about this for many years. Paul returns to New York with Mexican painter Antonio Álvarez. Jane moves in with Helvetia Perkins at her farmhouse in Vermont. Jane and Paul, however, continue to see much of each other.

1943 *Two Serious Ladies is* published on April 19 in the US by Knopf but receives largely negative reviews. However, Oliver Smith, a successful theatre producer and distant cousin of Paul's, gives Jane money to write a play and she begins *In the Summer House*. Paul is interviewed for army service and rejected. Jane and Paul travel in Canada.

1944 *A Guatemalan Idyll* (story) published. Paul is still working as a composer and writes incidental music for Tennessee Williams' *The Glass Menagerie*. Jane remains in Vermont with Helvetia and they are joined in the summers of 1944 and 1945 by the painter Maurice Grosser, who paints Jane's portrait.

1945 Jane and Paul, and Oliver Smith, rent three stories of a townhouse on West 10th Street, New York (where they live until 1947); Jane shares her floor with Helvetia Perkins and works on *In the Summer House*. *A Day in the Open* (story) published. *A Quarreling Pair* (puppet play), inspired by Jane's relationship with Helvetia, performed. Paul also begins writing fiction.

1946 *Plain Pleasures (story*) published in *Harper's Bazaar*, for whom Jane is photographed by Karl Bissinger (the famous shot in front of shutters). Jane begins work on a new novel, *Out in the World*.

1947 Jane publishes first act of *In the Summer House* in *Harper's Bazaar.* Paul publishes his first story, *A Distant Episode* and thereafter turns chiefly to writing. He sails from New York to Morocco, begins work on *The Sheltering Sky*, and, with Oliver Smith, buys a house in the medina (old quarter) of Tangier. Tangier will be Paul's home for the rest of his life. Paul meets Moroccan artist Ahmed Yacoubi, who will become his companion over the next decade.

1948 In January Jane joins Paul in Morocco, with her new lover, Cory, and they visit Fez along with Paul and Edwin Denby. There she has severe hallucinations and paranoia after taking *majoun* (cannabis jam). In Tangier, Jane meets and becomes obsessed by Cherifa, an illiterate Moroccan market trader; Cherifa will later become her lover and housekeeper. Paul and Jane live for a time in Fez, where Jane writes *Camp Cataract* (story). Paul finishes *The Sheltering Sky* and travels to New York to work on a score for a Tennessee Williams play, returning to Tangier at the end of the year, with Williams (who expresses admiration for her play).

1949 Jane and Paul travel to the Algerian Sahara for several months, where Jane writes *A Stick of Green Candy* – her last completed story. Later, in the year they travel to Paris, where Jane meets Alice B. Toklas, and to England with their Tangier friend, David Herbert (second son of the Earl of Pembroke). Paul sails to Ceylon and begins writing a new novel, *Let It Come Down*. Jane spends the winter in Paris with Cory; the relationship falls apart, but she works on a new novel to be called *Out in the World*. Jane's story *Camp Cataract* is published.

1950 Paul's novel *The Sheltering Sky* enters the New York Times bestseller list. Paul travels in Ceylon and South India, then joins Jane in Paris, where she is working on her play *In the Summer House*. Jane goes to New York, hoping to see the play staged, and Paul returns to Morocco. Jane writes a travel story, *East Side: North Africa* (published in *Mademoiselle* the following year), which will later re-emerge as the story *Everything is Nice*. She also writes the fragment, *An Iron Table*.

1951 *In the Summer House* is produced in repertory at the Hedgerow Theatre, Moylan, Pennsylvania. Jane travels to Paris, where she stays with Truman Capote. In the summer Paul drives to France with Ahmed Yacoubi and they return with Jane to Tangier. Jane spends most of her time with Cherifa and works distractedly on *Out in the World*. Paul travels to India with Yacoubi.

1952 Jane moves back to New York, where she remains for the next two years. Paul travels to Ceylon with Yacoubi where he makes an offer to buy the one-house island of Taprobane.

1953 Jane completes a final draft of *In the Summer House* which is produced in Ann Arbor. Paul agrees to write the music for its performance in New York, and sails to New York with Yacoubi, where he stays with Jane at Libby Holman's house in Connecticut. Holman (a singer and actress and longtime friend of the Bowles) begins an affair with Yacoubi, and Paul returns alone to Tangier. However, Yacoubi later returns to join Paul in Tangier. Paul completes the music (now lost) for *In the Summer House* in time for its December 14 performance in Washington D.C. and its six-week Broadway run. Tennessee Williams praises the play – as does the *New York Times* – but the short run is seen as a failure.

1954 Paul and then Jane return to Tangier, where Paul moves into a house with Yacoubi. Jane begins a relationship with Cherifa, who moves in with her at the Bowles's medina house. Jane tells Paul she has found packets of *tseubeur* (magic concoctions) under a mattress, which alarms him and Yacoubi; Cherifa denies knowledge. In December, hoping to ease tensions, Paul and Jane sail for Ceylon with Yacoubi and Paul's driver, Temsamany, where they stay on Taprobane. Paul works on *The Spider's House*, his third novel. Jane loathes the island house, which is full of bats at night, and is unable to write the play she has in mind. She also suffers severe depression, possibly the result of drugs for high blood pressure and excessive drinking. After two months, relieved only by a visit from Peggy Guggenheim, she returns to Tangier with Temsamany.

1955 Back in Tangier, Jane becomes increasingly dominated by Cherifa, who demands money if she is to stay. Jane offers her the medina house, which Paul agrees to transfer to her.

1956 Morocco gains independence on March 2, with Tangier remaining temporarily under international control, although the writing is on the wall. Jane leaves for New York and is given an advance to write a new play. Back in Tangier, Jane moves into an apartment adjacent to Paul in the Edificio San Francisco; Cherifa moves in with her, too. Jane writes the play scene, *At the Jumping Bean*, but finds concerted writing impossible. Paul and Yacoubi leave for Ceylon.

1957 Jane suffers a stroke in Tangier, where rumours circulate of poisoning by Cherifa. Paul, returning from Ceylon, takes her to England for treatment. Returning briefly to Morocco, Jane continues to have seizures, which impair her vision, and her psychological state deteriorates; she goes back to England for treatment and is diagnosed as having a brain lesion. Thereafter, writing and reading become challenging. Bowles and Yacoubi visit Jane and bring her back to Tangier in November. Jane's story, *A Stick of Green Candy* is published.

1958 Moroccan police, cracking down on sexual behavior amid the expat community, interrogate Bowles about Yacoubi and begin investigating Jane's relationship with Cherifa. The Bowles leave Tangier and travel to Madeira, where Jane's condition improves and she begins a new novel, *Going to Massachusetts*. However, Jane becomes depressed and leaves for New York in April, where she is looked after by friends. She develops aphasia and hemianopsia, an after-effect of the stroke, affecting her speech, vision and reading, and has problems walking. She is treated by a language therapist – for whom she manages to write compositions – but is later admitted to a psychiatric clinic in White Plains. In December Jane is released from the hospital and returns to Tangier with Paul.

1960 The Bowles move from their apartments in the Edificio San Francisco into a new building nearby – the Immeuble Itesa – taking separate apartments on the third and fourth floors. Jane and Cherifa share one apartment, with Cherifa having the larger bedroom, and a Spanish cook and a maid sleep in the living room; Cherifa runs the household, although her sexual relationship with Jane is at an end. The Bowles meet Mohammed Mrabet, who is working at the Immeuble Itesa.

1961 Jane is awarded a grant of $3,000 from the Ingram Merrill Foundation to write a play. She plans a drama based on her short story, *Camp Cataract*. She also inherits $35,000 from her Aunt Birdie, which makes her financially independent.

1962 In Tangier, Jane and Paul become close friends with the British novelist Alan Sillitoe and his wife, the poet Ruth Fainlight. In September, Jane and Paul travel to New York – Paul to write the music for a new Tennessee Williams play, Jane to visit her mother and to see a woman called Frances, with whom she has had an affair in Tangier.

1963 Paul rents a house in the medina at Asilah, a seaside town south of Tangier, and Jane spends several months there with him;

Larbi Layachi (whose stories Paul will translate) works for him at the house. Jane develops a close friendship with Alfred Chester, a young American writer. Jane's mother and stepfather visit her in Tangier. In November, Jane and Paul travel to Marrakesh and southern Morocco. Jane begins an affair with Martha Ruspoli, a wealthy writer, divorced from an Italian prince. *In the Summer House* has an off-Broadway revival but closes after a few weeks – a blow to Jane, who is still working on her new play.

1965 *Two Serious Ladies* is published for the first time in the UK, by Peter Owen, who also becomes Paul's publisher, and is favourably reviewed. Jane and Paul travel to the US and consider buying a house in Santa Fe before returning to Tangier. Paul begins to record and translate the spoken stories of Mohammed Mrabet, who becomes his closest companion.

1966 Paul compiles a collection of Jane's stories, which is published in the UK by Peter Owen as *Plain Pleasures*, and in the US – with *Two Serious Ladies* and *In the Summer House* – as *The Collected Works of Jane Bowles*. Paul's parents both die and he and Jane travel to New York. On their return to Tangier, Jane becomes ill and anxious, drinking heavily (which clashes with her medication), and increasingly obsessed by her relationships with Martha and Cherifa, who are hostile to each other. She is depressed by the deaths of her former lover Helvetia Perkins and her friend Jay Haselwood, co-owner of Tangier's Parade Bar.

1967 Jane and Paul sail to New York, with a view to Jane staying with her mother in Florida while Paul fulfills a writing assignment in Thailand. Jane then returns alone to Tangier, where she suffers from extreme anxiety and depression, taking her medications indiscriminately. Paul returns from Thailand and in April takes Jane to a clinic in Málaga, where she remains (undergoing shock treatment) until August. In July, Paul brings Jane back to Tangier, but she remains disturbed, unable to keep still. While Jane was in Málaga, Paul had discovered a 'magic' object in a plant pot in Jane's apartment and fired Cherifa, but Jane brings her back into the household. Jane then moves out of the apartment, with Cherifa, to stay at a small hotel, the Atlas, near the Parade Bar, where she drinks and gives away money to all-comers.

1968 Jane lapses into severe depression and can barely sleep or eat. Paul takes her back to the apartment but she continues drinking heavily. After a series of incidents, Jane is persuaded to return to Málaga to the Clínica de los Angeles. In June, Paul takes Jane to convalesce with friends in Granada but, needing full-time attention, she returns to the clinic, which is staffed by a small group of nuns and has a reputation for the humane treatment of its patients. In September, to earn money, Paul begins a job at San Fernando College in California, teaching a seminar on existentialism and the novel.

1969 Jane's condition improves and in February she returns with Paul to Tangier. But after four months her state has worsened. She lies on the floor of Paul's flat, refuses food and medication, and loses excessive weight. Paul takes Jane back to the Clínica de los Angeles, where she remains for the rest of her life.

1970 In May, Jane suffers another stroke and her condition deteriorates, causing her to lose her vision.

1971–2 Jane continues to deteriorate, eventually becoming blind and unable to move. Paul visits regularly, while working on his autobiography, *Without Stopping*, in Tangier. In the autumn of 1972, Jane undergoes conversion to Catholicism.

1973 Jane suffers a brain haemorrhage on April 30. Paul Bowles arrives at Malaga on May 4 and finds her unconscious. She dies later that evening. She is buried in the San Miguel cemetery in Málaga, in a numbered grave, with no cross.

In **1981** Millicent Dillon's biography – *A Little Original Sin: The Life and Work of Jane Bowles* – is published (Black Sparrow Press/ Virago Press), followed in **1986** by *Out in the World: Jane Bowles' Collected Letters* (Black Sparrow Press), edited by the same author. In October **1999**, a new grave site and monument for Jane Bowles is dedicated by Málaga council, with Paul Bowles's agreement. Paul Bowles dies on November 18, 1999.